OF GOOD

AND EVIL

a novel by

ERNEST K. GANN

New York

SIMON AND SCHUSTER

❖❖❖ ✦✦✦ *To Cahill and his men*

. . . in San Francisco

✧✧✧✦✦✦

A person may approach you and say, "What is written in that book is not entirely true." And you may agree with such a person —but remind him, if you will, how the only complete truth is in death. Everything else that happens among human beings is colored by our individual senses—the special condition of these senses at the very moment of occurrence, and the particular environment in which the events took place.

Truth is the most fragile and contrary of elements. It is often so volatile it will explode into a mass of untruths the moment we attempt to confine it in a convenient package.

As a consequence you will find in this book only the vaporous distillation of certain truths. Here are things which have happened to human beings and continue to happen even as you read. The reason these things happen is that a great many of us are not too far removed from savagery. This is a condition we are naturally reluctant to recognize. So we employ certain other human beings to attend to the matter and we call them policemen.

The cruel behavior of human beings toward each other is more a matter of official record than are their benefactions. Cynics claim the balance is unequal, but cynics are often drowned in prejudice. Optimists take the reverse view, but optimists are often buried in naïveté. We may accept certain truths more easily and still avoid hypocrisy if we remember that there is always a seasoning of evil in good people and an admixture of good in evil people.

We are always secretly at war with ourselves and with the society we have created. Only an artificial system of checks keeps our civilization from decay during times of peace, and from complete collapse during times of war. These checks are legal punishments which are often barbaric, and social penalties which are sometimes devastating.

There is no special town, city, or region, where alone the af-

fairs described in this book could have occurred. For that reason the locale is nameless and its description meager. This gesture toward anonymity is a deliberate attempt to establish the city as representative of all cities.

Yet here the city should be identified as San Francisco, because there are very few other cities in the world where the material for this book could have been so readily obtained. Thanks to an enlightened and nearly fearless police department, and a police commission of unusual dedication, the author was allowed not only to serve with the police, but to live as one of them.

—ERNEST K. GANN

✦✦✦

What is a good man?

Simply one whose life is useful to the world. And a bad man is simply one whose life is harmful to others.

✦✦✦

There are, however, those who are harmful and yet enjoy a good reputation, and who manage to profit by a show of unselfishness.

These are the worst of all.

—From a conversation between
Chang Chao and Hanchen
sometime in the fifteenth century

✦✦✦✦✦✦✦✦✦✦✦✦✦✦✦✦✦✦✦✦✦✦

IN THE MORNING...

✦✦✦✦✦✦✦✦✦✦✦✦✦✦✦✦✦✦✦✦✦✦✦✦✦✦✦✦

✦✦✦ 1 ✦✦✦

When he left the house before dawn he knew exactly what he was going to do.

He had slipped out of bed very quietly, found his trousers in the dark and, in his haste, pulled them on over his pajama pants. He was in such a hurry that he put on his shoes without bothering about his socks, although now he wished he had bothered because his ankles were cold.

He drove his car directly to the bridge and left it on a promontory facing east so that it would also greet the sun. As he walked away from the car, he laughed. Wouldn't it be something if someday the sun didn't rise in the east? Say, in the north, maybe? It would mean the world had skidded. Well it *was* skidding, wasn't it? No, this day the sun must stick to its business. Stay right on the good old track, sun! Together we'll show them togetherness.

He walked to the end of the great and graceful bridge, where he stood for a time feeling the chill wind on his ankles. He should have put on his red socks to match the sun, of course. Did Icarus wear red socks?

Finally he started to climb up the main support cable which curved toward a great tower. The hand guide wires which paralleled the cable were sticky with fresh paint in places. Very fine, he thought. What could be better than to have red paint all over everything?

As he climbed, he sang softly, marveling at how easily the tune came to him when in all his life he had never been able to carry a tune six inches. Now he could carry a fine tune up and up an iron highway—right to the sun. Of course if he were a black man he could have sung it better, but he was satisfied with the way he rolled one phrase.

Nobody knows de trouble I seen . . .

He continued to climb and sing, resting occasionally to catch his breath. He was certainly out of condition.

He climbed for a long time, very carefully, so that he would not slip.

He would give the sun a greeting such as it had not known since the Aztecs. He would crow like a rooster when it first appeared, long and loud, and it pleased him to think he knew exactly how a rooster sounded when the sun appeared. Everybody in the world would hear him and know he was mocking their stupid, bound-up, wretched, vile lives.

And then he would show them.

He breathed deeply as he climbed higher and higher. For as he progressed, he discovered there was nothing to smell except the sky.

✧✧✧ 2 ✦✦✦

There was a basic smell about the grime-encrusted, pseudo-Renaissance building that was far from the bridge and served the city as a hall of justice. On the first floor there were spasmodic penetrations of street air when the doors were opened and closed. And so on the first floor there was merely a faint aroma—a bouquet of crunched cigars, essence of public toilets, and time. Thus Tommie, the blind newsdealer, whose stand was beneath the marble stairway, was able to navigate unaided wherever he wished to go on the first floor.

The morgue was also at street level. Because it was in a far corner of the building and had its own entrance, and because those who worked in the area were extraordinarily alert to smells, the morgue's unique fragrance did not usually reinforce the basics. Yet there had been one occasion when a battered trunk was delivered to the coroner. The dismembered body within the trunk had been rotting for weeks and every inhabitant in the Hall of Justice complained. It was not of the basic.

The next two floors held courtrooms, and here the basic smell was still mild, although gaining authority through the introduction of perspiration and the nervous farting of troubled humanity. And time.

Above the courts was the Bureau of Identification, the photographic laboratory, and a loose complex of offices inhabited by various police details. Fraud had the most pleasant situation because they enjoyed two exposures, and consequently even the inspector whose desk was in the middle of the room could see what he was doing without the assistance of artificial light.

Narcotics was also fortunate. The quarters of the Narcotics detail were enhanced by a rather attractive arched window which reached from the floor to the ceiling. But the room was so small, the inspectors often gave up sitting on each other's desks and found it easier to take suspects into the hallway for questioning.

Vice, Armed Robbery, Auto, Missing Persons, Homicide, Safes, and Burglary, were all equally crowded for space, and in none of them was there sufficient light or air. Thus, the basic smell rising from the lower floors seemed to become compressed as it gained altitude, and it also took on a peculiar tartness.

The city prison was on the top floor, and here the smell achieved full resolution. Now it became a pungent blossoming of open latrines, aging paint, vomit, disinfectant, and effusions of steaming vats in the kitchen, all mixed with a master binding of continuous anxiety.

The prison was reached by a large elevator, which made a swift if somewhat unstable ascent to the top floor. It was the only normal means of access, and the turnkey on duty locked and unlocked the shaft door when the elevator arrived or departed. Occupants leaving the elevator could turn left, which brought them to the booking desk or to the pastel-green bars of the prison gates. A turn to the right led to the kitchen, then past the entrance of the women's prison, and finally into a long hallway decorated with crude murals of mountains, lakes and waterfalls, and here and there a sad-eyed deer. The now faded painting had been executed by some long-forgotten prisoner.

Though the entire Hall of Justice would soon be abandoned for a new and modern building, the murals were now being restored by one Appollo Petropoulos, a short, voluble trusty who had contrived to serve his latest six months' sentence in the city prison rather than the county jail. Appollo's trade as a sign painter had often been interrupted by confinements in various institutions, so his technique lacked polish; but now he worked with an almost frantic passion, racing against his own diminishing time and the rumor that the entire building would eventually be destroyed.

Appollo's voice would take on a wistful, pleading tone whenever he could find an audience sufficiently interested to pause and look at his work. He would not stop his daubing and smearing entirely, but would stand back a little and cock his head critically. He would encompass the entire wall with a flourish of his brush and say, "I hope they don't tear the joint down, I sure hope. Because these here murals are masterpieces. The guy who first painted them sort of stands for all guys who didn't get the breaks, you know what I mean? They never meant to bother nobody when they first started out, but they forgot to think. You know how I mean? Thinking is important. And the first thing they know is they're in a situation where a mountain to climb, or a lake to fish in, or a waterfall to listen to that ain't some toilet . . . sort of means a lot to them . . . even if they never give a good goddam about such things before in their whole lives. I say these here murals have gotta last forever because there will always be new guys to look at them."

Appollo ignored the fact that the chances of an ordinary prisoner's seeing his project were few. The hallway in which he painted led to the auditorium where lineups were held each morning and thus was rarely used by anyone except inspectors.

The basic odor was barely detectable in one part of the old building. This was the upwind side—when the wind prevailed. On the first floor, elevated just above the street, were the offices of the city's Police Chief.

His name was Hill, and at this early hour he found his office so quiet he could hear himself swallow. Every Friday he enjoyed such tranquility because his attendance at early Mass made it convenient to arrive at his office before the great old building truly roused itself. Hill's devotion to Mass was one of the few souvenirs he had kept of Ireland. It was still reassuring.

Hill had been immensely grateful to arrive in America. His initial gratitude had been expressed directly to God, followed at once by a special invocation for the immigration officers who were obviously God's disciples. He had sunk himself into America, lathering his strong, freckled body with it, sucking eagerly at its air as if the doing so might speed the entire process of adoption. Two weeks after his arrival he could recite the Bill of Rights and the Declaration of Independence by heart. In his youthful zest, he would sometimes astonish anyone who would listen by quoting long passages from the Constitution. Soon after his twenty-second birthday, he became a full citizen.

In spite of the squareness and solidity of Hill's body, it was his head which immediately captured attention. For it was the head of a mature lion. The uncanny resemblance began with the oblique slant of his eyes and became even more striking when, in irritation or enthusiasm, sprays of his tawny hair happened to fall across the permanent creases that lined his brow. And somehow, quite unconsciously, Hill had acquired certain leonine movements so that it was impossible for him to move his head in the most ordinary manner, or even rise from a chair, without fixing the impression that in some previous life he must have been a lion. When he walked he seemed to prowl, and even his most prosaic actions took on an air of natural majesty. As he grew older these effects had become more pronounced. Now when he merely placed his hands on a table or desk, they seemed to be paws. When he lowered his head and peered at a visitor from beneath the heavy oblique wrinkles that lined his brow, an impression of elemental sadness flowed from him if he was merely speculating. If he was suspicious or displeased, then it would have seemed perfectly natural for him to throw back his magnificent head and roar.

But Hill was a quiet lion and never roared. And what sadness he knew was caused by the existence of ungratefuls in his beloved land mass. He regarded ungratefuls as weeds in a nearly perfect garden. Now, because of their persistent survival, he knew these special moments of morning peace could not continue.

❖❖❖ ✦✦✦

He took up a sheet of paper in one powerful freckled paw and reviewed the list of his day's appointments. At eight-thirty the department secretary was listed for further discussion on how to use civilians instead of policemen for special duties. A citizens' committee had convinced themselves that this would help put the department on a businesslike basis. But how could you put any organization on a true business basis unless you could estimate its activity? One parade of protesters against something or supporters of something else could knock out the patrolman budget for a week. A minor riot, an unforeseen invasion of hoodlums, a series of rapes, the visit of a foreign dignitary who might be something less than popular with certain ethnic groups, could cause such dislocation and addition to patrol assignments or extra work by the Bureau of Inspectors, that no amount of juggling would restore the balance of budget.

At nine, a discussion of a new fingerprinting method with the head of Crime Lab. If only, Hill thought, we could untwist the sick minds as efficiently as we have developed means of revealing the twists—there indeed might be a hope of reducing the budget.

At nine-thirty, the manager of a local radio station. Something about a program praising the department, which was at least an unusual approach. The press delighted in doing the opposite, enlarging the smallest fault to scare headlines. In Hill's early days as a patrolman and then as an inspector, the seeming bias of the press had infuriated him. Now he recognized it as a sign of health in the land mass which he so revered. He knew of several countries where published criticism of the police was suppressed. In Hill's opinion they were not healthy countries. Even so, there were still occasions when he yearned to say, All right, we will all throw our stars in the ashcan and go fishing for forty-eight hours. Then see what happens to your city.

Flanner, the "sick" sergeant, would be in with his report on who had backaches or switchblade wounds, been kicked in the groin by some drunken whore or had his nose broken in a Donnybrook with some individual who simply had to show his resentment of authority.

At ten, Willets, the department legal counsel, about the rash of "model" studios. An amateur photographer could bring his equipment to such a place and photograph the models in various degrees of undress. It was art, claimed the proprietors. But the customers were forgetting to bring their cameras and the female models were getting younger. The Vice Squad said two sixteen-year-old girls were involved.

At eleven, Martin of the Intelligence detail, with the latest on an organization called the Muslims. Hill hoped he had somehow been misinformed about their creed and program. Some of their speech-makers advocated a direct line of action. They wanted, he had been told, to kill or enslave all whites. Fortunately, he thought, their membership was still small.

At eleven-fifteen, a small merchants' association, angry about an increase in shoplifting. Somehow they would have to be convinced shoplifting was the most special of misdemeanors because the true professionals were few. Shoplifting was human nature overwhelmed by the basic urge to get something for nothing. Little old ladies who were invariably somebody's doting mother were especially vulnerable. And too often they were ladies with a fat bank account and hard-working husbands. When they were apprehended, the answer was almost standard: "Why, I really didn't mean to take it. Somehow it just got mixed up with the other things I was carrying."

The press boys were certain to come in just before noon for more on the visiting African dance troupes. Was Hill going to demand that the female dancers cover their breasts, or just let them jounce in the stale air of the auditorium? The controversy gave the boys something to write about, but Hill wished it hadn't landed in the police lap. He would be damned whatever his decision. There would probably be another cartoon in one of the newspapers that always depicted Hill as a lion, and this time it might show him chewing morosely on a G-string or some other bit of theatrical costume. Editorially the papers would label him a lion without courage, or at least a blue nose ignoramus stifling great art, if he merely required a thread and a tassel—and the Mayor would be on the phone if he didn't. The Mayor was elected by the people, some of whom warned the performance was "lewd, lascivious, an insult to our city . . . et cetera . . . et cetera."

And Hill had been appointed by the Mayor. Working together,

they had made the city about as clean as any city could be. Hill was sorry for certain other chiefs he knew. By a sort of osmosis they had become as rotten as their mayors.

Before he went to lunch he would receive a delegation of the Civil Liberties Committee. They had a beef about one of their members, who had been arrested on a narcotics charge. The committee claimed the man was being persecuted because of his political beliefs, which were admittedly Communist. They claimed he knew nothing of narcotics. All right. Here was his record, ready for the delegation. It showed thirty arrests in eleven cities as a "hype." They could examine the scars on his arms, both old and new, if they liked.

Hill winced at the thought of lunch. He had vowed there would be no fat flatfoots on the force and at last there were relatively few, but policing a desk had brought him ten pounds of weight he didn't need. He reminded himself that if he was not more careful he would soon look the way an Irish police chief was supposed to look—and he preferred to look like a lion. The traditional image of a chief caused him to purse his lips in disgust. The days of the purple-nosed flatfoot with cap on the back of his head, paunch sagging over his belt, and a giant ham-fist in the cigar box were gone. Those Keystone cops with their shillelagh training were as obsolete as the horse-drawn paddy wagon. Hill wondered how their easygoing attitude would have handled the five wild animals who had recently attacked two families picnicking in a Midwestern park. The attackers were between fifteen and eighteen years old. After beating both husbands senseless with baseball bats, they turned on the wives. They tore their clothes off. They raped both women as their children watched and wept. This had happened in the America he loved, and Hill doubted if it would have happened in any other country in the world. And it didn't help to know that only twelve hours earlier, a judge who must have believed utterly in man's inherent goodness had released two of the attackers from custody. They had been arrested for auto-boosting. It didn't help to know that one of the ringleaders was on probation and another a parolee from the state reformatory. What would the Keystone cops have thought about that lovely Sunday afternoon? They certainly wouldn't understand a culture that could generate such action, or dignify it with the tolerant, almost romantic, label—juvenile delinquency.

Sometimes Hill found it difficult to avoid bitterness when he saw an ever growing number of individuals spitting in the face of his beloved country. And it was confusing because the majority could not be considered professionals. For the hardened criminal, the predictable antagonist in his personal war, Hill very occasionally admitted a grudging respect. But the conflict was changing and it seemed that a hideous pox had erupted across the face of America.

There was one interview for which Hill had not set a specific time. There had been too much dread of its very necessity. At Mass this morning he had watched while his old friend Inspector Timothy Hardy assisted the priest through his offices. Ordinarily, the spectacle of Hardy, who was built like a block of cement, lumbering about the altar with such fierce determination to be delicate offered moments of secret amusement to all who attended the special police Mass. It was the incongruity of Hardy's gladiatorial face set in worshipful concentration, his timid bows when his gun formed an obvious mound beneath his white robe, and his beefy hands arranging the wine and wafers with such unashamed humility that inspired the illusion that Timothy Hardy was personally accountable for the sins of everyone in the cathedral. On this morning Hill had found the illusion particularly convincing. But he had known no amusement. He could only think of what he must at last tell Hardy.

After the Mass Hill had met his friend on the steps of the cathedral and had simply said, "How about dropping by the office this morning?" And Hardy, lowering his head in the same humble manner he used at the altar, had merely replied, "Sure."

It was enough. Both men had been embarrassed because they knew the reason for the meeting and how it might destroy a friendship which had endured since they were working together. How, thought Hill, am I going to tell a man whom I have loved as my brother that he is through? How am I going to tell Tim Hardy who knows only too well that bullets do not always whine by harmlessly as in the movies, or conveniently nick a man in the shoulder so he can carry on as in television, that he is no longer to be in the Armed Robbery detail? I can suggest a "long rest." He'll see through that. I can shift things around so he's in a job where he cannot be harmed or, even more important, bring harm to others because his nerves have turned to jelly. And he'll see through that. And such a job will break my friend's heart as surely as if I stepped on it.

The hands of the electric clock on the wall stood at exactly eight o'clock. For a moment Hill ceased his brooding about Timothy Hardy and a thin smile creased his face as he watched the sweep second hand pass the vertical.

Some day there would be a major phenomenon—the emptying of the sea, or a visitor from Mars—and there just might not be a rap on his door at precisely eight o'clock. Which would signify that Deneen, his deputy, had been literally torn from the self-imposed rigidity of his schedule. And it would take some tearing, Hill thought, for Deneen was a dedicated machine. He was the antithesis of the old Keystone cop—educated, well-spoken, an alert, trained specialist. He knew the enemy and his ways.

The knock came and an instant later Deneen entered. The shining, metallic baldness of his head contributed to his perpetual air of concern, although his vigorous movements, which held all the grace of a fine athlete, the penetrating timbre of his voice, and the constant challenge in his intelligent eyes denied any suggestion that his worries might harass him.

"Good morning, Chief," he said.

Hill's smile became thinner because of Deneen's deliberate formality. He was not like Hardy, who just as deliberately kept their relationship on as jocular and friendly a basis as he possibly could. Long ago, when both Hill and Deneen were still patrolmen, they had served together in radio cars. But Deneen had not called him Colin since the day Hill had been appointed Chief. He had warmly congratulated Hill, smiled, and said, "Colin is dead. Long live the Chief." And now, no amount of persuasion could bring him to resume their original familiarity. Not even when Hill had shyly confessed that he was lonely.

"All chiefs are lonely," Deneen had answered. "You have my sympathy as well as my respect."

Now as he pulled a chair to the side of his desk, Hill wished Deneen would have started the morning with, "How the hell are you, Colin?" or perhaps as he would have only a few years back, "Colin, you're getting uglier every day. It's an insult to the map of Ireland." And then Hill could have said, "Your head is like the end of a watermelon."

Hill concentrated on the top of Deneen's bald head, placed his freckled paws defensively on the desk before him, and asked, as if he had no time for anything but official business, what was new.

Deneen held out a sheet of paper which listed the enemy's major activities during the past twenty-four hours.

. . . Aggravated assault by a white male American about 20 years of age, possibly driving a 1949 Hudson sedan, green color, license unknown. Victim also white male American in serious condition with head injuries. . . .

. . . Strong-arm robbery at 22 and Lake by one suspect. No physical description, but wearing tan car coat. Escaped south on 22 Avenue. Arrest made. Officers Drinkwater and Cassana. . . .

. . . Three purse snatchings, all committed by Negro male Americans. . . .

. . . Attempted murder on Freeway opposite 17 Street. Victim shot in head three times, but in satisfactory condition at General Hospital. . . .

"How could that be?" Hill asked.

"The bullets went through his mouth side to side. Tore up his face, broke his jaw, and he lost some teeth. Nothing more. Now please note the rape on Twenty-second Street," Deneen added. "The woman was sixty-six years old. She's also at General Hospital—in poor shape."

Hill shook his head and, despite all he had seen, wondered what kind of a wild animal would rape a woman *that* age.

Deneen spoke again in a voice that was almost totally without expression.

"For a dividend he beat her up. He left her lying in the street."

"Any luck?"

"Not yet. But when he dragged her from the car he left some

good palm prints on the door. Also a porkpie hat. The woman says
he knew her name, but mispronounced it."

"Is Moore on it?"

"Yessir."

"Don't 'sir' me, damn it." Hadn't Deneen any conception what
it was like to think and work alone all the time?

"Okay, Chief."

Was there at last a twinkle in Deneen's eyes?

Hill forced his mind back to the list.

> . . . Armed robbery . . . Federal Hotel, suspect white
> male American, 38 years, armed with .45-caliber automatic.
> Arrest made by Officer Robert McAdams, solo motor-
> cycle. . . .
> . . . Kidnap and rape at 1605 12 Street. Perpetrated by
> Julio Perez, Mexican male, 22 years, wearing brown wind-
> breaker. Also Antonio Perez, 20 years, 5′ 11″, 130 pounds.
> Suspects kidnaped 13-year-old Harriet Rankin, white female
> juvenile. Auto involved fits description of gas station holdup
> which occurred at 18 and Diamond at 9:15 P.M. . . .

"What about those individuals?" Hill had long employed the
term "individual" when referring to his ungratefuls. It was an
anonymous word which handily disregarded race, color, or
background. He never used the term for any other purpose, and
his lips puckered into a special signal of disgust when he pronounced it.

"They're upstairs. They'll be in the lineup this morning and
again for a showup with the victim this afternoon."

Glancing quickly at the balance of the list, Hill saw with
annoyance that two more elderly men had been attacked by
teenagers and robbed. In one case, not satisfied with the few
dollars meekly offered by the old man, the youths had shoved him
back and forth while they used him as a punching bag.

"How are we going to stop this sort of thing?" he asked.
"There's been about four or five this week."

"Get some new mothers and fathers," Deneen said flatly.

Hill grunted. "They all seem to happen in the Moravia district.

Put an extra radio car out there and tell the station to double the foot patrol for a week until we see what happens."

Deneen made a note, then stood up. The rest of the list was so routine it required no special review. Car thefts, tampering, traffic accidents, fires, activities of perverts, prostitutes and pimps, gambling, ordinary brawls, drunks, frauds, swindlers, indecent exposures, peepers, family fights, fits, strokes and vandalism were not even on the list. Such trifles were the constant undercurrent, the routine sewage flow, of any metropolis.

"There is one matter of interest not there, Chief," Deneen said, and now Hill hoped that the twinkle he saw in Deneen's eyes meant that even for a few minutes he might not be alone.

"A friend of yours is in town. He is staying in suite 12-A at the Brixham Hotel, the cost of which is forty-eight dollars per day. He has the suite reserved for a week, but told the clerk he may stay longer. The gentleman's name is Theo Lasher."

"Well . . . well . . ." Hill knew that his face had flushed, but he hoped not so conspicuously that Deneen would be aware of it.

Theo Lasher—also known as Ted Lasher, also known as Dimitris Laskil, Sal Lasso, Louis Breckman, Mori Breckman, and a score of other aliases, all of which were inscribed on his impressive record. In the days when Lasher was authentic heavy stuff, an intimate of the Mafia if not a full initiate, he had forged a national reputation as a muscle man. He was a graduate of Dannemora, Folsom, Michigan State, Sing Sing, and San Quentin. Hill knew him to be a rare creature. He was a waffle-ear with a brain.

Hill could visualize him instantly, although they had met but once. Of *course* he was in an expensive suite, and unless he had changed his ways, his baggage alone would be worth more than half a year's pay for any inspector.

The remarkable thing about Theo Lasher, considering his chosen career, was that he could actually think. He weighed risks, which was why he had long ago forsaken any personal reliance on weapons or his fists. He could now delegate such work to others because he had found an opening for his energies that was so exceedingly sweet he had once told a district attorney that he didn't believe it himself. For a long time he had been convinced there *must* be something wrong with such a situation. But there was nothing wrong, and from the day Lasher discovered the plight of the workingman and took his troubles to his iron heart, he had prospered. Wrapped in the holiness of a dedicated union leader, he had been able to engage in many things without the slightest fear of interference.

"So he's come at last," Hill said quietly. "I was wondering how soon it would be."

"Oh, one other matter," Deneen said as he turned back from the door. "There's an 800 on the bridge, not in the usual place, but on top of one of the towers. How he got up there is unknown, unless he sneaked by last night. Anyway, he's causing a real jam on the bridge. Cars are backed up all the way to the county line. We've got twenty men out there now trying to talk him out of jumping."

"Why don't they go up and get him?"

"They started to, but decided to wait. He's got a gun."

✦✦✦ 3 ✦✦✦

He looked down from his lofty perch and was satisfied. What a day for crowing! He looked down from the tower, now all so red in the sun, and saw a red fire engine among the hundreds of creeping cars, and the sight of its color especially intrigued him. Among the crowd of people who had gathered soon after his first experimental crowing, there was a separate rosette of white faces staring up at him. Most of them wore blue uniforms and caps and they had already tried to make him change his mind.

"Listen to me, you miserable creatures!" he yelled down at the faces. "Listen to me and you shall hear . . . ! You don't tell *me* what to do! I'll come down when I feel like it! Straight down! I'll splash red all over you if you don't get out of the way! My brains will look like oatmeal on your pretty uniforms! So just leave me alone, that's all! Just leave me alone! Go away! Far away! And stay away!"

He looked straight at the sun, which was blazing red, and when he looked away there were so many red dots swimming across his vision he spilled them on the faces below and made them much redder.

"Listen to me! You think I'm crazy! You have it backwards! *You're* crazy! Don't you feel the pressure, or are you all slugs? Go stone some whores! It suits you! If there's a man down there who is not a slug, come on up and join the sun! But don't try any tricks! I'll kill the first person who comes too close!"

He held out the gun and wiggled it at the faces below. Then he spit at the faces until his mouth was dry.

✧✧✧ 4 ✦✦✦

The watch in the city prison changed three times each twenty-four hours. Being a part of the watch was not considered a particularly enviable duty, if only because the one secret terror all policemen held in common was the perilous business of dealing with a drunken woman. Ordinary male drunks, even the more pugnacious, were never a match for a trained and sober officer. And usually they were mere boneless sacks, the pitiful slag of any city, who arrived so often the booking officer could sometimes type out their vag card from memory. Humble, locked in a near coma by wine or the residue of canned heat, they allowed themselves to be led slobbering through the pastel-green bars and into the large common cell known as the tank. The metallic *chink-chink* of the closing gates was seldom resented, for at last here was freedom from interference, cold, and the damnation of hard, reeling pavement. They stumbled into the tank, sighed, eased their aching bladders, and slept. Only a very few of the regulars ever shouted defiance, and these were considered by tank mates as not true drunkards, since even a swat with a bar rag would give them the d.t.s. They received little sympathy from their neighbors when given a dose of stinking paraldehyde to make them quiet down.

Female drunks were an entirely different problem. Judo, hammer locks, all the devices of sinew and brawn, could not contain a female drunk who had decided on a rampage. Instinct and tradition somehow combined to drain an officer's strength and absolutely forbade a straight blow, even in self-defense. A small woman screeching oaths, flailing and kicking in every direction, could make a shambles of the area in front of the booking desk. They bit as viciously as tormented panthers, they clawed at any available open flesh, and they kicked or kneed the nearest testicles with ferocious howls of triumph.

None of the duty men in the city prison wanted anything to do with female drunks. It was on a par with stopping a family fight. A policeman could not win.

In addition to the separate drunk tank, the city prison for men was divided into two sections, between which there was no communication. The misdemeanor block confined those charged with such petty violations as wife-beating, child-neglect, vandalism, ordinary assault, resisting, impersonating an officer, tampering, or fraud. Here the smell of anxiety was always the strongest because first offenders were comparatively numerous. They were sometimes referred to as cherries.

The felony block was exactly like the other except for the inhabitants. Here all suspects of crimes of violence were held, and any man with a previous record automatically became a resident. As in the misdemeanor block, the cells accommodated from six to eight men and faced on a narrow corridor known as the alley. The cell doors were left open during the day and the men gathered in the alley like neighbors in a common street. Here they smoked, paced, gossiped, strutted, or simply glowered, according to their status and fancy.

All men were strangers to each other in the city prison because their residence seldom exceeded a week and usually lasted only a few days. By that time, either a bail bondsman had arranged their liberation, or their hearing was set before a court and they were transferred to the county jail. If the offense was light, they might spend from thirty days to a year as guests of the county. Heavier sentences, usually pronounced after a trial before a jury, involved a further transfer to any one of the various state institutions—all of which were known as "the joint."

The city prison was far from an inactive place. The constant transfers, arrival of new prisoners, appearances at lineup, show-ups, call to court, call to the grand jury, conferences with bail bondsmen, releases, questioning by inspectors, and portrait sittings in the photo studio created a continuous flow of movement, and so the *chink-chink*ing of the pastel-green gates became a constant rhythmic accent to the constant shuffling of feet.

In the felony section, Harry Welsh thoughtfully fingered the collar of his still-clean white windbreaker while he listened to the older Perez brother. And since he was angry at the way things had gone the night before, and already feared constipation from the city prison food, and because both Perezes had given him cigarettes, he allowed the older brother to talk as much as he pleased.

"I can see," the older Perez began, "that you are a cherry."

He spoke with an air of superiority which annoyed Welsh, but the latter was out of cigarettes and there would not be a chance to buy any until the man came around with his cart later in the morning.

"You know what happens next?" Perez asked.

Welsh shrugged his powerful shoulders and wondered what the thin, shy-eyed little Perez boys could have done when it was obvious they lacked strength enough for anything except maybe making Mexican straw hats.

"You'll see," explained the older Perez. "The first thing on the program this morning will be the lineup. We all go down together and they got our names all listed in order so that's where they put you in line. Then we go in six or seven at a time and stand on the stage while some jerk reads off your record and asks a lot of dumb questions which you don't have to answer. All you do is stand there and look out at the rest of the fuzz who you can hardly see because they got no lights on them and you got plenty on you."

Perez paused and put his arm around his younger brother. With an air of a grand protector, he patted him gently.

"Yeah?" Welsh said.

"You don't have to answer the questions. You keep your mouth

shut if you want. After a few minutes the jerk tells you to face
left and off you go. That's all there is to it."

"Yeah?"

"Can you make bail?"

"Maybe," Welsh said.

"Well, if you need a bondsman I recommend Stanley Sussero.
Everybody knows Sussero. Stan is a real solid man."

"Yeah?"

"And then you need a lawyer if you have enough bread. If you
ain't got bread you get the Public Defender, who is supposed to be
on your side."

"Is he?"

"Of course not. Nobody is. If you were a black man they got
a national association helps you with everything, but you ain't
black. Have they talked to you yet?"

"Who's they?"

"The inspectors. Don't worry. They'll be along this afternoon.
Two of them—full of questions about everything from the last
time you got laid to whyn't you join the Boy Scouts. The less you
say the better because they twist it around and go tell the judge
or the grand jury or whoever handles your case and probably
they got a tape recorder going too, so the next thing you know
you're on your way to the joint."

"Yeah?"

"It's like that, see? But don't believe all that crap about the
inspectors knocking you around. That's only in the movies. They're
out to screw you, but they won't beat you up. Remember, if they
can't hang something on you in seventy-two hours they got to let
you go because you're a cherry."

"You know a lot," Welsh said, laughing inside. And he thought,
Wait until this greaseball of a Mexican punk hears them read out
my record.

◇◇◇ ✦✦✦

In the misdemeanor section, Lawrence Potter sat on the edge of
his bunk and worried about his canary. What would happen to
poor dear Lucille now that no one would be in the apartment to

change her water? This was simply dreadful, this whole messy thing. It was unearthly, a purgatory. The Mattachine Society should tell everyone how careful they must be because there was simply no understanding in the world—understanding of love, how beautiful and exciting it could be when two persons discovered each other and finally knew the true substance of devotion. Oh, why had one to be born now, to be treated as a witch! True enough, ten days in the county jail was not a burning at the stake . . . *actually* . . . but the pain was there, searing the heart if nothing else. And true enough, there would be a sensationally gay party when he came out and every single person there would be geared, but that simply wasn't a solution for the heart.

He would still be yearning a terrible yearning . . . until he could find someone to share love. Trying desperately only for a trifling of physical affection to soothe his starvation, trying in the darkened theater to merely touch a young and quite beautiful man, had brought him here. The young man had not understood because he had reached in his pocket and brought out a badge. He didn't *look* like a policeman, he was so fresh of face. But when they went outside Lawrence had seen that he just would not understand. It grieved him now to think that if he had been born in ancient Greece or Rome, everyone would have understood and even approved of his compulsion to love. Why, he thought . . . why . . . was it against the law to love?

❖❖❖ 5 ✦✦✦

Long after the others had left, Timothy Hardy lingered near the entrance to the cathedral. He wanted to be sure of absolute privacy before he tackled the problem which so distressed him, and his plans did not include the presence of even Father Curran whom he had assisted at Mass. But Curran would not go about his business. He wanted to talk baseball. As coaches of Little League teams they nursed a long-standing rivalry and usually both men found exhilaration in a tart exchange of insults.

"Why," Hardy said, hoping to prick a particularly embarrassing moment and so be rid of Curran, "it is a true shame, Father, that a man of your intelligence, on a day of national pride like the Fourth of July, should have called for a bunt when a line drive was the only possible chance to score. Let me see now. I believe it was already six-two in the fourth inning."

"I've known many police inspectors in my time, but never one who could bear such outrageous false witness. It was six-four in the seventh."

"I remember now. The Lord was pitching for you. He must have realized your kids were playing under a handicap. I can think of a hundred solid reasons why you should have lost—all coaching errors."

Curran smiled icily. "Thank you, Timothy. Apparently in your curiously twisted mind our four three-baggers in the eighth and two three-baggers in the ninth, which led to our overwhelming victory, were a miracle. There's an elementary book I recommend your reading and it's not the Bible. It's *How to Coach a Baseball Team . . . and Win.*"

They played two full games in detail before Father Curran abruptly terminated their meeting, remarking that even work on his Sunday sermon was more interesting than talking to frustrated Casey Stengels.

Glancing at his watch, Hardy saw that he still had over half an hour before he was due at the old building. He had mentally rehearsed what he was about to do several times, yet now new doubts assailed him. He had never been overly devout. Although he found it rewarding to assist his friend Curran with the Friday morning Mass, unscheduled prayer was better left to his sister with whom he lived. Her constant preoccupation with the church, he thought, was more than enough for the two surviving members of the Hardy tribe.

He removed his hat, and because it was the first time he had ever been alone in the cathedral, he paused uncertainly by the doorway. He was a huge and ugly man and he was all too aware that his appearance could become menacing if he neglected to shave twice a day. But there was nothing he could do about the permanent skin kink just below his left eye that so distorted its shape that the eye itself seemed artificial. There was nothing he could do about the liverish blotches on his nose, or the seemingly inexhaustible crop of small warts and larger wens which marred the back and sides of his neck.

Hoping to reassure strangers, Hardy had long made a habit of smiling on the slightest excuse, but he knew a period of time must pass before anyone could entirely forget his general appearance. For this he was profoundly sorry. The rebuffs of his youth had clearly demonstrated his lack of appeal to women, and even now he was deeply touched when one chose to return his smile. Soon after the war there had been an English girl who had taken a room in his sister's house. And she had once said to him, "Tim, you're so ugly you're beautiful." Her sincerity had established a very special relationship which became the nearest approach to romance Hardy had ever known. He grieved for weeks when she left to marry a druggist in Utah. He knew he could never forget her because she had said the same thing many times, and without laughing. There were occasions when he wondered if it was because of the English girl that his job as a policeman had become more than a career. It was his life.

Now he thoughtfully regarded the aisle separating the empty pews. It led straight to the altar where he had been completely at ease only a little while before. He had planned to go to the altar and in the solitude of the empty cathedral ask for help. He wanted to say, I know why Colin wants to see me and it is not just because we are old friends. He knows I have the willies bad. It began when that punk Landros shot at me in the Federal Market garage . . . it got worse going into the Rivoli bar after Henry Carpenter, which with all the other punks watching every move was like walking naked through a nest of snakes . . . and it finally reached a head the night the Water Street boys got drunk and hungry at the same time and jumped that United Express truck. The events happened too close together, within forty-eight hours to be exact, and a lot of ammunition was used. None of it connected with Your obedient servant, thanks to You, but it left me with the willies, which is almost as bad. Now how do I go about curing it?

He had thought it would be easy simply to walk down the aisle to the altar, or just kneel in a pew and quietly review his trouble, but now he found it impossible. He suddenly decided that he should not bother God with his professional problems. And most certainly he was not going to expose his new weakness to Curran. Let things be for a while. There were several handy excuses. For instance, any cop might catch at least a touch of the willies if he became involved in a series of bad capers. Why should you be an exception? Because you are Tim Hardy, which is reason enough. Some people around the old building might make their bum jokes, your friends in the department might even circulate their lousy poems about "our Handsome Hardy" on your birthdays, but no man on either side of the law ever questioned Tim Hardy's guts. Until now. It isn't easy being ugly and a has-been at the same time.

"I don't need a special bulletin to tell me what they're saying," he murmured. "But I do need help to prove them wrong."

He could not force himself to go down the aisle. Maybe another time if things get worse, he thought, but not now. A man troubled God when he had no friends. He had so many, especially Colin Hill. It would soon pass, this bugaboo of fear. It must. Save that altar for a final emergency.

He dipped his fingers into the holy water font, crossed himself, and hurriedly left the cathedral.

✧✧✧ 6 ✦✦✦

Normally, Communications was a quiet place in the morning. There were apt to be long intervals between the white lights which signaled incoming telephone calls. The city awakened and it was routine that certain people would convince themselves that a man was killing his wife over the breakfast table; a souse who was still drunk from the night before would find it imperative to express his opinions; or there would be a broken water main, a flooded sewer; children who had been packed off for school would fail to arrive; there would be a cat drowning, a dog fight, and the usual smashups of city people fighting their way to work.

After this initial surge there was invariably a lull, during which the four officers who handled the incoming traffic had time to read their newspapers and litter the long table before them with paper coffee cups. Or they might also have their shoes shined by a Chinese boy whose name was Marvin Fat. Though he could not have been more than ten years old, few people had ever bothered to wonder how Marvin Fat could be hustling about the old building making money while his duller contemporaries were in school.

Calls from the public were first filtered through the regular police department switchboard, then passed on to the long table. They were classified by a system of lights. A white light might be a woman complaining about her neighbors' trash or morals; a green light for a cry of loneliness or a squabble between mothers-in-law. Red lights were reserved for "hot" calls—holdups, gang fights, rapes—calls from people who very suddenly discovered the reason for police.

The officers who served in Communications were patient diplomats, but there were times when they could not resist speaking their thoughts and other times when they wanted to lower their heads and weep for all humanity. It was difficult to be patient with a mother who demanded the police find her missing boy . . . when the boy was twenty-seven years old and had missed coming home for tea.

An endless belt stretched the length of the long table and terminated before a double bank of radio equipment. As they received their telephone calls, the officers scribbled the facts on a slip of paper and placed it on the belt while the caller was still talking. The scribbles on the papers were immediately transmitted over the radio. Thus it was not uncommon for police to appear anywhere in the city less than two minutes after the original plea for help.

The tempo in Communications steadily increased during the day until by nightfall the flickering of lights was continuous. "There is a man prowling around my back yard. . . . They are shooting at my cat with a BB gun. . . . He's standing there right now in the window waving his penis at me. . . . Hurry, please hurry! She's screaming again. . . . He's on the sidewalk and I'm sure he's dead. . . . I'm afraid. . . . I am afraid. . . . I am in fear. I am terrified. . . . I am, I am, I am. . . . They are, they are. . . . He is, he is. . . . *Help* me!"

Communications was the mouth of a horn into which the troubled poured their woes.

No citizens had ever called the police to comment on the fullness of their lives. Even the gummy sentimentality of Christmas Eve failed to make a particle of difference. Somewhere in the city a husband was beating his wife, a man was pointing a loaded gun at someone who did not have a gun, and the men in Communications were impressed again and again with the impossibility that the meek would ever inherit the earth.

The men in Communications had no need to follow the phases of the moon, for whereas on ordinary nights the peak of activity was between eleven and midnight, when the moon was full, the lights along the table would flash continuously. The police made no attempt to analyze why this was so. They only sighed and said to each other that the natives were restless tonight.

Now on this morning there had been an unusual flurry of activity in Communications. Twenty-seven citizens had called to report the man on the bridge, even though it was incredible that if they could see the man they could not see the police waiting below. Thirty-one citizens had called to ask if he had jumped. One confided that she did not want to make the trip to the bridge if it was all over. Another citizen said the traffic jam created by the man had caused him to be late to work, and he just wanted to say that all cops, and especially those now on the bridge, were dumb, fatheaded Cossacks who persecuted the working peoples of the world, and that they would all sing a different tune when the glorious socialist movement triumphed. He was singing "Lenin Is My Leader" when the listening officer cut him off to take a call from a citizen who said the man on the bridge was a friend of his. The officer listened a moment, then, following orders, quickly transferred the call to Deneen.

"Deputy Chief speaking."

"I know the man on the bridge. Maybe what I tell you will help."

"I'm listening."

"He's a neighbor of mine by the name of Barbee. He has an attractive wife and a couple of kids. But even that is not the important thing. The world needs his kind. You have to get him down from there."

"You tell us how."

"It's no good yelling at him. You've got to understand why he's up there."

"Do you know, sir?"

"I think so. Barbee is an American."

"What's that got to do with threatening to jump off a bridge?"

"Plenty. He's been tricked."

"Who tricked him?"

"You and me. Because we won't face facts."

"I'm afraid I don't understand you, sir."

"Why should you? We're all so mixed up with the idea one man is as good as the next, we try to believe it. Don't get me wrong, mister. I honestly go along with the idea all men are created equal, but I don't think that after they've been around a while they stay equal. Barbee does, or rather his wife does. He's lost sight of what it's like to be humble. His wife won't let him be just plain John Barbee."

"This sounds pretty confusing."

"I realize that. But life in a matriarchy is full of confusion. The number one is prestige. I'm in the fur business and I know we sell more mink coats to women who can't afford them than to women who can."

"What's all this have to do with getting your friend off the bridge?"

"Plenty. He's been trying to live like a millionaire on a chemist's salary. He's the nicest little guy you'll ever meet, but I've heard he isn't even a very good chemist. He thinks too much and that's hard on anybody. But he has to think because his wife wears the pants in the family. She's got him living in a house he can't afford, belonging to clubs he can't afford, sending his kids to a school he can't afford, and driving cars he can't afford."

"That's an old story," Deneen said. "We can't tell people who should wear the pants in a family."

"Maybe you can. While she runs Barbee down all the time in front of everybody, she's also busy saving the world. It's all a part of the prestige angle. She's on every committee she can find. God knows what she says to Barbee in private, but it's obviously been too much for him. Somehow he temporarily escaped from the womb and I guess what he saw outside unbalanced him. He has to be put back. There's only one person can do that, so why not get his wife out to the bridge right away and make her tell him he's the greatest guy in the world?"

"Have you been to the bridge, sir?"

"Yes. I stopped for about ten minutes this morning on the way to my store, but I couldn't stand it any longer. He didn't seem to recognize me when I called to him."

"May I ask your name, sir?"

"I'd rather not say. I'm just a friend of Barbee's trying to help."

"But—"

The receiver clicked and Deneen wished he had put a tracer on the call from the start. The man had sounded intelligent and sincere. Yet he could have been just another crackpot, for Deneen remembered that fragile minds could not long observe another attracting attention. The ego demanded equal display; which was why if one nut put a bomb in an airplane or a theater, another nut would not be far behind.

Deneen made one turn around his desk while he thought about the man on the bridge. He disliked taking over from the sergeant in charge, but on the second turn around he decided he would go there himself. There was something about the way Barbee had done this thing that seemed to set him apart from the ordinary 800. If there was any truth in the call from his neighbor, maybe he was worth saving. There were a great many wonderful people, he thought, who were potential 800s.

❖❖❖ 7 ❖❖❖

No one knew if Barnegat's sourness was born with him or had simply been acquired during his long ascent from patrolman to Chief of Inspectors. Some said his acrimony was like a hat which he put on when he came to work and took off when he went home to his devoted family—but no one knew for sure. Possibly he considered sourness a requisite of his exalted station. It was certain that Barnegat seldom allowed himself to be caught with his lips in a position that might suggest a smile. His personal aloofness served as such a protective wall, few of his inspectors professed to know him well, many feared the venom of his tongue, and some secretly disliked the man. Yet, always, Barnegat was respected as a devoted policeman who knew his business thoroughly. His unforgiving discipline had somehow created a neuter image of himself, so that he became more symbol than man. There was no other accounting for the fact that his cutting sarcasms reinforced rather than destroyed the spirit of his inspectors.

Barnegat was not a large man and his need for glasses, his ultraconservative ties, and his fondness for tweed jackets contributed to the impression that he was a professor dangerously exasperated with his class.

Now, at precisely nine o'clock, he turned his back on the assembly of men seated in the auditorium and began to call the roll. There were more than fifty names. He pronounced each with such a corrosive rasp he seemed to detest the instant of recognition.

"Murray, Kelly, O'Bannon, Keim, Moore, Williams, Murphy, J., Murphy, L., Comber, Axelrod, Larkin, Phenis, Mahoney, Bradley, Hollihan, Stark, Fitzgerald, Boomer, Willkoff. . . ."

The staccato here's echoed through the auditorium without shading. There was no nonsense on the mornings Barnegat conducted the lineup.

When he had finished the list, he read off the announcements in a monotone. The wake and funeral of Officer Dennis Hancock to be held tomorrow afternoon. . . . A request from Father O'Neil of St. Thomas', volunteers wanted to help move furniture from the old to the new rectory. . . . Police Welfare Fund. . . . Change in shooting range hours due to winter. . . . Incorrect filing of overtime cards would result in cancellation of overtime. . . . Watch it. . . .

Barnegat's attitude toward prisoners was devoid of compassion or interest in their futures. It was for the courts to administer punishment. "I'm just a cop. I don't make the laws." His inspectors were asked to assemble enough legal facts to leave the courts no choice if the offender was guilty. And he insisted his inspectors must discover the truth by using their heads instead of their hands. He would not tolerate brutality no matter how hardened the suspect, or what the provocation. He considered it clumsy—an insult to his professional skill. But he also held in contempt the psychological nuances which might have compelled a man to violate the law. He had a standard answer for those idealists who would excuse a crime or indulge a prisoner because of some real or conveniently fancied mental blockade.

"If Freud were alive today, we'd vag the bastard."

Women prisoners and common drunks were not brought to morning lineup because their appearance would be time-wasting and meaningless to the intent of the ceremony. The large majority of women brought to the city prison were harlots, and if they were sober on arrival, they were always treated with courtesy and a sort of shamefaced regret at their temporary confinement. No one in the entire police department considered simple harlotry a true crime, but the law said otherwise. There were many police who thought the law was wrong. It should forgive the harlots and hang the pimps.

Major crimes committed by women were so rare and special, the matter of physical identification became automatic. Common drunks all looked exactly alike in time and certainly could not reclaim themselves long enough to pass for anything else. And so such prisoners were spared the morning lineup, which was held for inspectors as a part of their constant education. A year, two years, after a man appeared in lineup, he might be seen elsewhere. Perhaps he had changed his ways, but the chances were overwhelmingly against his even flirting with the notion. In any case, he should be remembered.

Barnegat signaled to the waiting turnkey, who turned out the lights in the auditorium. The stage was left fully illuminated.

"Bring them in," Barnegat said.

The turnkey opened a door at the side of the stage and the first group of six men shuffled up the steps and stood before the simple scenic background of a scale which showed their heights. Two of the men were Negro, four were white. They stood blinking at the light, trying to see into the auditorium, shifting their weight in embarrassment, and nervously scratching at their unshaven faces.

Barnegat told the two Negroes to take off their porkpie hats, then in a voice devoid of expression he read from the list before him.

"The first two men are Lovelace and Washington, suspects in a purse snatch which occurred at nine P.M., Eleventh and Baker Streets. Victim Irene Crew. Loss fifteen dollars. Arrest made by Officers Miller and Bogwarthy of Western Station."

Barnegat paused and looked at the men.

"Ever been arrested before, Lovelace?"

"No."

"How about you, Washington?"

"No."

Barnegat consulted a second list which he had placed on one side of his podium. He read quickly.

"William Lovelace. 1953 . . . suspect section one, gun law. Dismissed. 1954 Harrison Act. 1957 . . . possession narcotics. . . . 1958 in New Orleans, two charges possession and sale of narcotics, 1959 New York City aggravated assault, 1960 violation of parole two counts. 1961 Ft. Worth, Texas, purse snatching . . . ninety days. . . ."

Barnegat looked at the stage again.

"When did you come to this city, Lovelace?"

"Oh . . . last week, I guess it was . . . maybe a couple of weeks ago."

"Where do you live?"

"Oh . . . here and there."

"What do you do for a living?"

"Oh . . . mostly, ah . . . well ah . . . *promote*."

"It's looks like you tried to promote that lady's purse. The next man is Irving Washington . . . or Washington Irving. Which is it, man?"

"Irving Washington."

"You know the man standing beside you?"

"No, sir. I never seen him before."

"Not even last night when you two decided to snatch a few purses?"

Barnegat did not trouble to feign surprise. He was simply asking questions so their voices and manner could be observed.

"No, sir. This man, he don' know me and I don' know him."

"Then how come you were found in the alley together with the woman's purse and splitting the money?"

Washington hesitated and scratched at his head. "I dunno. We just happened to be in the same alley at like the same time, like that . . . I guess."

"All right."

Barnegat consulted his listings again and read aloud. "Irving Washington . . . 1958 Jackson, Mississippi . . . car boosting. . . . 1959 Boise, Idaho, drunk in and about a stolen car, 30 days. 1960, '61, '62 Woodland, Martinez, Spokane, and San Francisco . . . all petty thefts for which he served sentence."

Barnegat read on with only a brief glance at the stage. "The next man is Lawrence Potter of this city. He was arrested at four P.M. yesterday afternoon in the Fox Theater by Inspector Peterson of the fruit detail and is charged with attempting to commit an indecent act. Any truth to that, Potter?'

Lawrence Potter looked down from his station of agony and tried very hard to keep back his tears.

"I don't think . . . indecent . . . is the word."

"Did you make advances to the man sitting next to you?"

"Yes."

"Do you think they were proper?"

"What is *proper?*" Potter's voice became almost defiant.

"I'm asking the questions here," Barnegat said curtly. "Are you a user?"

"What do you mean?"

"Are you addicted to narcotics?"

"No."

"What do you do for a living?"

"I'm a window decorator."

"Have you ever been arrested before?"

"No."

Barnegat spoke out of the side of his mouth so that his words were directed more to the audience than the stage. He said simply, "This man has no record," and once more looked back to Lawrence Potter.

"Change your ways or leave town, Potter."

Without pausing, Barnegat went back to his list.

"The next two men, numbers four and five, are the Perez brothers. They both have long juvenile records. They are suspects in the kidnap and rape of thirteen-year-old Harriet Rankin yesterday evening. Julio, number four in line, was remanded to Youth Authority 1958. 1959 robbery, petty theft, asault and so forth . . . served six months county jail. 1960 violation probation, car theft, assault, carrying deadly weapon, dismissed. . . . 1961 Corpus Christi drunk . . . dismissed. Dallas drunk and disorderly, Ft. Worth . . . car boosting . . . ninety days, and so on. Antonio, number five in line, no record available except juvenile. . . . Vandalism Corpus Christi . . . dismissed . . . pandering, Dallas . . . dismissed. . . . Aggravated assault 1961 Brownsville. What are you trying to do, Antonio? Catch up with your big brother?"

Antonio looked at his older brother and smiled. But he remained silent as he had promised Julio.

"How old are you, Antonio?"

Antonio looked again at his brother who nodded permission. "Twenty."

"Why did you do it?"

"Do what?" The older Perez frowned, and seeing his displeasure, Antonio pressed his lips together primly. And he tried very hard to match the look of easy bravado Julio directed at the auditorium.

"You both must be conwise enough by now to know you're up on a serious charge."

The Perez brothers stared straight ahead and kept their silence.

"Whose car were you driving?"

"It belongs to a friend of mine," Julio said easily.

"What is your friend's name?"

Julio hesitated, then replied, "Manuel Olivera."

"Then how come the car was registered in the name of Peter J. Lynch of 1244 Oak Street, this city?"

Julio shrugged his shoulders and pretended to yawn.

"Why did you kidnap the little girl?"

"She weren't no little girl and she got in the car because she wanted to."

"You asked her?"

"No. She asked us."

"Why did you rape her?"

"We di'n't. We just played around a little."

"You play rough." Barnegat turned momentarily to the darkened auditorium. "Bruises about face and body voluntarily shown to duty doctor at General Hospital. Victim released without vaginal examination."

There was no detectable variation in Barnegat's voice when he turned back to the stage.

"The victim claims one of you held her while the other one raped her. Then you changed places. She also says you both knocked her around before and after. Any truth in that, Julio?"

"No. That's all a lie."

"Were you drunk at the time?"

"No. We had a few beers. That's all."

"The victim claims that afterward you took her within a block of her home and dumped her beside a trash can. Is that correct?"

"No. We took her home all right, but there wasn't nothin' wrong with her. What she done after we left her off, I dunno. Maybe somebody jumped her."

"What did you do after you left her?"

"Oh, we drove around a little."

"Where?"

"Here and there."

"How much gas was in the car?"

The Perez brothers looked quickly at each other, then shrugged their shoulders.

"Did you run short of gas about six-fifty P.M. at Eighteenth and Diamond Streets and fill up at the station on the northeast corner?"

The Perez brothers stared straight ahead.

"After you obtained the gas, did you ask for oil and, when the attendant was checking the level, hit him from behind with a blunt instrument and afterward take all the money in the cash box? About forty dollars?"

Barnegat waited. He seemed not to be interested in whether he would receive an answer or not.

Finally Julio said, "We dunno what you're talkin' about."

"Okay. . . ." Barnegat said, dismissing their existence. "The next man in line is Harry Welsh, who is not exactly a stranger to some of you in the audience. I will read only a part of his record since we haven't got all morning. 1942 vag and petty theft, San Francisco. . . . 1943 vag and 647 of the Penal Code, San Francisco. . . . Petty theft Santa Rosa 1943 . . . ninety days . . . again in '43, section 505 of the Civil Code and violation of probation. . . . 1945 another vag, Oakland. . . . Three charges robbery San Francisco, 1946 committed San Quentin . . . paroled 1947. . . . 1948 Oakland, car theft and parole violation for which he got one to five and served two years. . . . 1952 Las Vegas . . . vag. . . . Then numerous vags . . . Stockton . . . Beverly Hills . . . Ventura, Los Angeles . . . vag, vag, vag, 1953 through 1955. 1956 Fresno . . . burglary first degree and assault with deadly weapon . . . 1959 through 1961 numerous charges on burglary suspect . . . all dismissed, et cetera . . . et cetera."

Barnegat paused for breath, then looked at the stage.

"It looks like you'll be away for quite a while this time, Harry."

Harry Welsh turned his head slowly as if he had just discovered Barnegat. He looked down at him with casual indifference, then rocked slightly on the balls of his feet.

"Harry Welsh is suspect in the robbery of the National Store safe at Twentieth and Winston, eleven P.M. last night. When apprehended by Officers Dingle and McDonough, Welsh drew a .38-caliber gun and shot Officer Dingle through the left leg. Dingle is not in serious condition. Welsh was disarmed by Officer McDonough and brought to city prison. What have you got to say about all this, Welsh?"

"Balls."

"Were you doing a blow on the safe or a peel job or burning?"

"Nobody in their right mind does a blow these days."

Barnegat knew very well why. Peeling a safe or torching brought a sentence of merely one to fifteen years. The necessary use of explosives in blowing could send a man away for ten to forty years. At least, Barnegat thought, Welsh does have a touch of class.

"You always work alone, Harry?"

"You know it."

"The Safeway store on Franklin and Twelfth Street got hit last week. I don't suppose you had anything to do with it?"

"For sure not."

"Why not?"

"Because it's an E-type box."

Barnegat believed him. E-type safes were set in cement, close to a window, alarmed, and brilliantly lighted. A professional like Welsh left them alone. It was so much easier to work quietly on a safe that was concealed and locked in a back room by a merchant who was convinced he knew how to protect his money.

"Take them away," Barnegat said to the turnkey.

The next six men were all Negroes and Barnegat wished they were not, because he liked to keep his personal ideas as well as his department in strict order. Now, too often, he detected a bristling shock pass through his system and he hated the sensation. It was not professional. It swayed him when he should not have been swayed. For years he had been certain that he understood the Negroes' yearning for true equality, instead of the ration of pompous and hypocritical pap with which they had been bombarded for their votes. The present-day rebellion in itself did not shock him. He had long considered it inevitable. But the Negroes had been betrayed, he thought. They had been escorted by those who should know better, to a river of everlasting plenty, and advised they had only to swim across if they wished final triumph.

Barnegat could not think of a single guide who had bothered to teach them how to swim.

From Barnegat's vantage point on the shore of the river, the result was easily predictable. He had watched helplessly as the

Negroes' contribution to the crime rate increased. Now in his city it was 70 per cent. No one wanted to face such facts. It was much more comfortable to look the other way and suck on the thought that everything would work itself out eventually. The newspapers, terrified of the word *prejudice,* ignored the situation. The things he saw each day, which were not rumors or propaganda, but actualities, were fast persuading Barnegat things would *not* work themselves out.

And so the shivering in his system recurred more often each year. He could not seem to allay it. Hoping to reassure himself, he had discussed his uncertainties with the few Negro officers on the force. But their speculations had been more patronizing than helpful. Barnegat could only conclude they were also shocked. The idealists and theoretical do-gooders who knew where the river was, but forgot its deceptions, blamed bad housing, social confinement, and poverty. While Barnegat readily admitted these were contributing factors, he was far from satisfied they were the true reasons. The majority of Negroes living in the same conditions behaved themselves. And among the Orientals, also obliged to live as second-class citizens, the crime rate was almost nil. It was a rare day when an Oriental appeared in the morning lineup.

As for true grinding poverty, Barnegat had dismissed it from his meditations. His neo-welfare state had recognized a multitude of human needs and at the same time disregarded human nature. Now it was actually possible for a clever family to obtain more by not working than by working—more, Barnegat thought wryly, than some patrolmen took home. As a realist, Barnegat was not in the least surprised that so many people, both white and black, had decided the world owed them a living.

Barnegat's sourness was not mired in cynicism. He desperately wanted to know the real reasons why so many black men had refused the river and returned to the jungle.

The racial proportions in the next group of six were more encouraging: another Negro purse-snatcher, a shivering junkie already approaching his inevitable torment, and four white men, including a pickpocket of the Nogals school, a wife beater, and two large, puffy-faced men known as "fruit shakers." They wore ordinary business suits, and Barnegat reluctantly admitted that they might have passed for cops.

"The last two individuals are con men gone wrong. Both have long records—fraud, bunco, and check-passing. Which one of you geniuses thought up your new racket?"

Ignoring Barnegat, the puffy-faced men stared straight ahead.

"These men prey on perverts by representing themselves as police officers. After promising a fruit their lily-white bodies, they arrest him, then they get bighearted. They tell the victim they'll forget all about everything for a hundred dollars. Is that about the way it works?"

"About . . ." said the last man in line.

"Do you flash a badge or some kind of identity?"

"Badges."

"Is that before or after you take down your pants?"

Barnegat knew he would not receive an answer. "Take them away," he said, making no attempt to conceal his disgust.

The rest of the prisoners mounted the stage in groups of four and six. There were more than forty, which was about average for a Friday morning, and Barnegat noted they were all without class. There were home burglars, narcotics salesmen and users, a cheerful bigamist who said he had at least found peace, a pair of bookies familiar to everyone in the auditorium, a sad-eyed man accused of nonsupport, a pimp who said he was a wrestler by profession, a father-son team of car thieves, an abortionist who said he was *almost* a doctor, a holdup man who specialized in drugstores, and a fugitive from Oregon who insisted he was the wrong man in spite of his fingerprint identification and elaborate tattoos.

A large majority of the men had previous records. The group followed the same old pattern which made Barnegat brood upon the evils of parole as he had on a thousand other mornings. He could see no end to it or any possible hope of even minor change. The prisons were full and yet room must be made for the newly committed. So the parole board was more lenient than it might otherwise have been. It turned free men who had no intention of living peaceably, and men who intended well but had no basic resistance to the temptations they would surely meet.

Barnegat had no idea what it was that made criminals do the things they did. If there was any true path to the source of their desires and inspirations, then it was so devious only the psychologists were smug enough to claim they could follow it. There was no explaining criminals, Barnegat believed. Nor was it possible for a normal mind to comprehend their minds. Only on the rarest occasions did their actions make any sense. They consistently risked their freedom and often their lives for what might be bought for a few dollars. They lacked even the wisdom of making changes in their *modus operandi*. If a safe man was accustomed to making his original entry through a transom, he could be depended upon always to enter via a transom. If a rapist used a navy watchcap to conceal his eyes the first time, he would do so the next time and the next time, and again after he had been freed from prison to try again.

Barnegat was certain of two things. He was certain that all criminals were fundamentally stupid or they would not be criminals; and he was certain of what he called the cycle. A suspect would be caught and committed. As soon as possible he would be paroled, not only to relieve prison overcrowding, but because it was better to have a man working on the outside rather than living on the state. Once they were free, barely enough men succeeded to keep theory and hope alive. Yet Barnegat's daily reminder was always the same. With so many of the men in the morning lineup giving repeat performances, it was only a question of time before they would again be sent off to prison. Then the cycle would be once more complete and all the machinery would be exactly aligned for another rotation.

✧✧✧ 8 ✦✦✦

Hill was trying to decide whether to call Theo Lasher first and make an appointment, or just walk in on him. Then one of his three telephones buzzed and it was Deneen, who began by saying he had just heard from the bridge. The sergeant on the scene wanted advice.

"And I'm passing the buck to you, Chief, because the man is no ordinary 800 and it's a sticky situation. We can't blame the sergeant for marking time when he might lose one of his own men trying to save a nut."

"All right, all right," Hill said, without interest. He was still thinking of Lasher. No matter how he approached him, the meeting would not be construed as a reunion of dear friends. Lasher was not going to leave the city just because his presence displeased anyone.

"They found a car near the bridge which the sergeant thinks belongs to the 800, but the man denies it. He says he's always been a cipher and he's going to die that way. Auto detail has checked the car. It's a brand-new Chevrolet station wagon bought two days ago by a man named John Barbee, who is a chemist at Randall Products. I checked there and he hasn't shown up for work this morning."

"Sounds like he talks too much to be a real leaper."

"He won't admit his identity, but his physical matches. And that's not the problem or I wouldn't bother you."

"I'm here to be bothered."

"Not like this. About ten minutes ago I received an anonymous telephone call which gave a few leads, and I just finished confirming what the man told me and a few pieces more of background. It goes like this. Until he flipped, the man was a model husband and a father . . . three kids, two boys and a girl. He is an usher at the First Presbyterian church and plays the cello in some little string music society that meets every Thursday night. He was there last night. Apparently an all-around solid citizen. He has a nice house and all that goes with it.

"Now the sergeant feels he'll shoot sure as hell if they try to go up after him. So that's out for the moment. The sergeant wants to send a radio car for the wife, get the kids out of school, and bring them all down to the bridge. He figures that if the man sees his family he may change his mind."

"And what if he doesn't?"

"That's the problem. That's why I called you."

Hill thought about freckles and red hair. There was no other collective vision of his own three children.

"Keep the family away," he said firmly.

"He may jump any minute."

"Well, let's not help him give the performance in front of his family. They deserve better memories."

"Okay. . . ."

"Keep me posted."

Hill hung up the phone, and for a moment all he could see was three upturned freckled faces with their mouths open in horror. He wiped at his cheeks, pushed the end of his nose angrily from side to side like a boxer preparing for an attack, and forced himself to forget the faces and think about Theo Lasher. Now, should he go alone or take Deneen along?

A chief of police known to have been alone in the company of Lasher was asking for suspicion and trouble.

I must be very careful, Hill thought, not to put myself in the same position as that man on the bridge.

✧✧✧ 9 ✦✦✦

The first inspectors to leave the lineup auditorium were Moore and young Matthew Rafferty. Striding down the hallway past Appollo Petropoulos' murals, they paused while Moore gave the artist a cigar. Then they continued down the hallway toward the women's prison.

In spite of his height Moore moved gracefully, his long arms and legs swinging forward as if he carried flowing regimental colors. But the suggestion of military pride ended with his movements and physique, for there was a distinctly fatigued wisdom always humbling his eyes, and his smile was quick and disarming. At first glance nothing was extraordinary about Moore except his nose. It was a great carved monument, sculptured for another, much wider, face. Protruding from the oxhide texture of his skin, seeking sensation and meaning in every small thing, it became a lateen sail hard on the wind, an impassable divide between the continents of his cheeks.

It was a tribute to Moore's inner calm that he could smile at all. For his specialty was the class of suspect who had recently been governed entirely by lust. If their thundering urge had been to kill, then their doings would have fallen to Homicide. But any result of the second most powerful human compulsion became a matter for a department vaguely titled "General Works." Here, Moore and twelve other inspectors engaged themselves against their fellow man's tendency to seek the primitive. General Works was assigned all sex crimes, which were often a weird mixture of simplicity and the wildest complexity. The often harassed men in General Works complained they were also thrown every other felony or misdemeanor which, because of its nature, no one from Barnegat down knew exactly how to categorize. Thus General Works inspectors were unusually versatile and were as likely to find themselves involved in a bomb threat or newly angled extortion plot as in a prosaic rape.

Because of its diverse affairs, General Works had a larger staff than the other departments. Its inspectors had a predilection for cigars, possibly because the manipulations involved eased the constant air of tension in which they labored. Robbery detail rarely saw tears. Fraud as seldom. Narcotics dealt with an obvious and dangerous physical ailment, and Burglary with simple avarice. Hence it was easier for those departments to conduct their business in a detached manner. General Works was a storm center of screams, lamentations, accusations and counterthreats, hysteria and sensual astonishments. The ordinary crimes followed a pattern—hence something reasonable could be done about their prevention and detection. Nothing reasonable could be done about the prehistoric impulses which unpredictably exploded in the creature who stood erect.

General Works occupied a large gloomy room on the second floor of the old building. Dust, grime, and cigar smoke had drifted upward to the high ceiling for so long that it was now a deep sepia, although the original color had been white. There were three small, suffocating offices adjoining the main room. The General Works inspectors spent as little time as possible in these offices. If they were not actively engaged outside the building, they preferred the relaxation to be found in a large abandoned vault once used for the safekeeping of public records. It would accommodate from six to seven men depending on their sizes. Isolated in the vault, nearly invisible through cigar smoke, they would take special delight in a new coffee percolator which had been installed in defiance of Barnegat's order that none of his men were going to be wasting their time drinking coffee on the job. And they would speak of everything on earth except the animal ferocities which so constantly surrounded them.

As in Homicide and Armed Robbery, the inspectors assigned to General Works operated in pairs. Recently Moore had drawn young Rafferty, who had been relieved of duty as an undercover man in Narcotics because his fresh and innocent face had become familiar to hypes and pushers alike. The principal people involved in narcotics were never amateurs. They were ruthless businessmen, and anyone who might interfere with their business was treated without mercy. Word had come through informers that young Rafferty had been recognized. He was recalled immediately. To replace him with a man like Moore would have been ridiculous. The hypes and the pushers would have laughed their swirling heads off. They would laugh and say, There is one of "the fuzz." So a new man fresh out of the police academy and carefully selected for his lack of resemblance to "the fuzz" had taken Rafferty's place. His only contact with the police department was an occasional telephone call. Forbidden to carry a star or gun, he was now about his lonely and perilous work. If he were extraordinarily clever and fortunate, he might, like Rafferty, escape the routine patrol assignments in uniform and graduate directly to the Bureau of Inspectors. If his fortune held, he might even find himself with the veteran Moore as his mentor.

"This will only take a few minutes," Moore said when the matron admitted them to the women's prison. "It's a fluke, but maybe this girl can help us. Sometimes one little fluke can do more for you than a week's work."

He told the matron he wanted to talk with Celia Krank.

"This kid made a mistake in the company she keeps," Moore said. "Last night S-Squad picked her up in a car with a five-time loser. She had a .38 in her purse which, of course, he claimed was hers."

They waited in the largest cell, which served as the dining area. It was the first time Rafferty had ever been in the women's prison and he saw that some attempt had been made to soften the atmosphere. A series of rubber plants was entwined through the overhead bars, and their broad green leaves eased the harsh illumination from the skylight. The plants apparently absorbed the smells so pungent in the men's prison, and the floors were composition instead of cement. The bars were painted a light cream color. Rafferty heard a woman laugh at the far end of the prison; then another voice giggled. Otherwise the silence was broken only by the solid clack of the matron's heels as she went to bring Celia Krank. It was not at all like the men's prison, Rafferty thought. There was none of the constant murmuring undertone or shuffling of feet from nowhere to nowhere.

Rafferty wondered why they had come to the women's prison. He had thought they would begin the day with the Perez brothers. The name Celia Krank was not even on their work list.

They sat down at the wooden dining table and Rafferty watched Moore as he clipped the end of a cigar, lit it, and so officially started his day. Even in their short acquaintanceship Rafferty had discovered his guide to be a man of firm manual habits. He would light this first cigar, take one puff, and then allow it to go out. After several minutes he would rattle his match box and relight it. Another puff, perhaps two, and once more it would go out. The sequence of movement would be repeated over and over until the cigar was reduced to a dangerously short stub. The ultimate flares from Moore's matches would singe his eyelashes and he would tilt his head back to avoid setting fire to his great nose. Only when the stub threatened to burn his lips would he throw the cigar away—and take out a new one. And the ritual would be repeated until Moore's match supply was exhausted. To maintain the rhythm, Rafferty had already learned to carry a spare box.

Moore took a small paper pad and a ball-point pen from his pocket. He set both objects carefully on the table before him.

Then he asked Rafferty if he had read this morning's copy of the mimeographed "Matters of Importance to Bureau of Inspectors." Rafferty said quickly that he had.

"Carefully?"

"Yes."

"Notice anything special . . . a small item?"

Rafferty could think of nothing which might be considered special—it was the same old list of purse-snatching assaults, robberies. He had paid special attention only to the rape committed by the Perez brothers because he knew it must fall to General Works.

"Remember the little things," Moore said as he lit his cigar for the second time. "They are more likely to give you breaks than the big things. And don't confine your mind to just your own department. Did you notice the address of little Harriet Rankin?"

Rafferty was relieved. He answered quickly. "Twelfth Street. Sixteen . . . hundred block." He was disappointed not to see any signal of approval in Moore's eyes.

"Sixteen-oh-five, to be exact. Which is interesting because this Celia Krank girl gave her address as Sixteen-oh-nine Twelfth Street. That's only four numbers away . . . if she was telling the truth. Now just maybe . . . Celia Krank knows Harriet Rankin."

Rafferty wondered what difference it would make. A helpless thirteen-year-old girl had been brutally assaulted, and in his opinion the Perez brothers should be sent to the gas chamber.

The matron brought Celia Krank to the gate and Rafferty instantly forgot about the Perez brothers. For the girl who walked slowly toward them certainly did not belong in a steel cage. She was wearing a plain white dress with flecks of gold dotted through the fabric, and a gold braid belt encircled her waist. Rafferty saw that the dress was wrinkled and soiled in places, but as if to compensate, her face and hair gave no hint of her night in prison. Somehow she managed to appear freshly scrubbed. Her cheeks shone with health and her hair was swept back in an almost prudish style. She wore no jewelry except her eyes, which were tired; the deep alarm Rafferty now saw in them begged him to look away.

"Sit down, Celia," Moore said.

She slipped onto the bench opposite them gracefully, catching at her skirt in what Rafferty thought was just the right way. Then she placed her hands on the table and they trembled ever so little. At last, she glanced at Moore, then looked directly at Rafferty. And suddenly he was surprised to find himself hoping some idiot with a badge and too much authority had made a rotten mistake.

"I'm sorry you're in trouble, Celia," Moore began. "Is this the first time you've been arrested?"

"Yes!" There was a plaintive softness in her voice which had no business echoing against steel bars, Rafferty decided.

"Why were you carrying the man's gun, Celia?"

"It wasn't his gun."

"Whose was it then?"

She looked down at her hands. "Mine."

"Do you have a license to carry a gun?"

"No."

"What does a girl like you use a thirty-eight for? Target practice?"

She made no answer. Rafferty wished she would raise her head so he could look into her eyes again.

"How long have you known this man, Celia?"

"A few weeks."

"Did you know he was a felon, a five-time loser?"

"Maurice told me everything."

"Did he tell you that because he was an ex-con, carrying a gun would put him away again . . . even if he didn't use it? And that you would also be violating the penal code, even if neither one of you did anything? Did he tell you you could be sent to prison for conspiracy to violate, or aiding and abetting?"

She was silent and absolutely motionless. She seemed not to have heard the questions.

"He told you to say the gun was yours. He was using you, Celia. He doesn't care what happens to you."

"Maurice will have me out of here this morning," she said firmly. Then she raised her head and looked at them almost defiantly. "He promised."

"Just how was he going to manage that?"

"He promised he would arrange bail. Isn't that why you came? It's all arranged, isn't it?"

"It's all arranged for Maurice. He made bail early this morning and skipped town."

"That's not true. . . ."

Moore took a paper from his pocket, unfolded it carefully, then placed it before the girl. "That's a carbon of his release. Note the time and the bail bondsman's signature. I don't think you'll see your Maurice again."

"I . . ."

"You're in trouble, Celia. Consorting with a known felon is not a crime, but carrying his gun is conspiracy, and you—"

"It wasn't his gun!" She brought her clenched fists down on the table defiantly. Rafferty was astounded. He thought— She is afraid of us and yet she is not. She really believes in that bum.

Then suddenly she bent her head and buried her face in her hands. "Oh, get me out of this! Get me out. . . . *Please.* . . . Please. . . ."

Moore lit his cigar again and fondled his great nose while he studied his watch.

"You'll be called down to court pretty soon," he said quietly. "Just tell the truth and the judge will probably be easy on you if this really is your first arrest."

"I can't spend another night here. . . . Those women, those . . . prostitutes, they said they were going to do things to me . . . awful things. They said they wanted variety and here it was. They laughed about it all night. Please get me out!"

"If you don't pick better boy friends from now on, you'll wind up just like them. You're a poor liar, Celia. You haven't had enough practice. You're trying to protect Maurice even after he's run out on you."

Moore caught her eyes for only an instant, then deliberately became preoccupied with his cigar. He spoke to it instead of to Celia Krank, saying with an air of finality, "If you help us, maybe we can help you. Let's begin by your practicing true answers." He paused while he rolled the cigar back and forth in his fingers.

And his nose rose in the air like the end of an iceberg suddenly emerged from the sea. "Now, do you know a little girl named Harriet Rankin? She is a neighbor of yours."

After a moment she answered.

"Yes. Why? What's that got to do with me?"

"Nothing . . . we're practicing the truth, remember? Now, what do you know about her?"

"Well . . . she lives with her aunt and uncle."

"What kind of a little girl is she?"

"Well . . ."

"Remember. The truth, Celia."

"Well . . . she's not exactly a *little* girl."

"What do you mean by that? She's only thirteen years old."

"Well . . ."

Rafferty wondered at the way she constantly repeated "Well . . ."

"Well, I suppose she is then. But—"

"But what?"

"Well . . . I always thought she was older."

"Why?"

"I don't know." She shook her head. "What has this to do with me . . . and, and Maurice?"

"Let's forget about Maurice for the moment. Would you say little Harriet Rankin is precocious?"

"She wears lipstick, if that's what you mean."

"Does she behave like other little girls her age?"

"Well, she doesn't play with dolls exactly."

"Who does she play with? Don't tell me she has a boy friend."

"She does have dates. They go to the movies and things like that. It's sort of cute."

"Cute? All right. How old would you think Harriet Rankin is?"

"I never gave it a thought . . . maybe sixteen, seventeen. She's very well developed."

"Does she smoke?"

"I suppose she's tried."

"Drink?"

"I don't think so. But of course there are bottles around the house. Her uncle likes his little nip."

"You mean he's a drunkard?"

"I wouldn't say that, but he gets rambunctious sometimes. Sometimes we can hear him in our apartment."

"Hear him do what?"

"Well, he gets excited and throws things, but he doesn't mean any real harm. He's really a nice person except when he gets excited."

"Would you say it's a happy family?"

"Well, living with your aunt and uncle isn't quite the same as with your own parents."

"What happened to the parents?"

"They were killed in a bus accident about five years ago."

"Have you ever heard of two brothers named Perez?"

"No."

"Have you ever seen Harriet with boys who might be Mexican or Mexican descent?"

"No. . . ."

Moore stood up. He re-examined his cigar thoughtfully as if estimating its endurance. Finally he said, "Thanks, Celia. I'll speak to the matron. If you have to spend another night here she'll see that you aren't bothered."

He strolled to the cell gate and Rafferty followed him, although he wanted to stay. Moore turned around at the gate and looked back at the girl. She had not moved, nor did she look after them. Moore said, "Remember, the truth, Celia. It's the quickest way out of here."

❖❖❖ 10 ❖❖❖

Two men frequently chose to sleep through the night in the old building. The older of the pair was said to have once been a prosperous merchant, although another history placed him as a former bail bondsman with a heart, which inevitably caused him to lose his fortune. Whatever his previous life, it was now long extinguished and the transmigration of his soul had brought him absolute anonymity. So thorough had been the erasure of his personality that no one in the entire building knew the man's name, either the first or last. He was simply known as the man. He had become a part of the woodwork, and of the spit-stained marble floor upon which he so often elected to slumber. His favorite refuge was between a dusty gumball machine and a recess underneath the stairs which led upward to the courtrooms. Here, he was almost never disturbed since the same gumballs had been in the machine for years and the entire fixture was a relic of the twenties. Apparently its original proprietor had either forgotton it or simply recognized that in the present world of packaged confections it failed to attract customers and so was not worth the trouble of moving—which exactly suited the man who slept beside it. He considered the gumball machine a brother. Together they had achieved invisibility and were passed hundreds of times each year by men who looked right through them.

The man was not a drunkard, although it was thought that he must have served a long and dedicated apprenticeship. Certainly he had graduated from ordinary alcoholic stupefaction. He had managed to become a thing, an object capable of movement on two legs, yet apparently unaffected by cold, heat, the normal need for nourishment or the slightest concern for other objects moving on two legs. He had retained only his need for sleep, which he fulfilled in the old building he loved. Otherwise no one knew what he did with his time. He simply disappeared and then eventually reappeared. Uniformed patrolmen on duty rarely passed through this area of the old building, and so the man was left undisturbed. The inspectors, Barnegat, Deneen, even Chief Hill, were so accustomed to seeing his feet projecting from beneath the stairs, they had joined with the judges, thieves, attorneys, clerks, harlots, reporters, janitors, and all the other habitués of the old building, in seeing without thinking that the feet were just there.

Only Tommie, the blind newsdealer, troubled himself about the man. He knew it was going to be a terrible thing for the man when the building was torn down because he understood what it was like to love a familiar place.

The other man who often used the old building as a dormitory was Spearing, whose haven was a worn leather couch in the news-room. Spearing liked to claim that he was the world's oldest police reporter, which was a technical exaggeration because he was barely fifty. Yet in other ways he had some right to the title, for his withered outlook on all things except horse-racing gave him a demeanor which made Barnegat seem like Pollyanna. But Spearing reveled in his cynicism and never thought to question its value or origins. He deliberately forced himself to hope, so that he could be disappointed. Then he would take his disappointment and nurse it carefully until it grew and at length blossomed into a monumental disillusionment. Every conceivable action on the part of all human beings was not only suspect but automatically condemned. There was not an honest man in the city or anywhere else in the world, and this, Spearing would proclaim without hesitation, included Hill and all of his flatfooted, flatheaded cops. They were rivaled in chicanery and general cupidity only by the scoundrels who owned and edited Spearing's newspaper and tolerantly paid him scale and not a dime more each bitter week.

Spearing's face was a sallow assemblage of ill-matched features. His eyes were so deep-set as to seem buried in fleshy caverns, and the lids, which drooped until they half concealed his rheumy eyes, were like the sliding hoods of an owl. His sagging cheeks terminated in dewlaps which encased a bundle of flesh and formed his mouth. His teeth protruded from the bundle, making a petulant blossom of dull red and yellow which often exuded foul gases. He slept in the old building on every occasion when a fight with his wife was imminent, which was often.

On this morning Spearing leaned heavily against the long counter which served as a barricade in the Chief's outer office and surveyed even the furniture with the utmost suspicion. He had already fired his morning greeting by telling Captain Todd, the department secretary, that he should be put out to pasture since he was over retirement age. "You blew the pea out of the whistle fifty years ago," he had said. "Why don't you give the taxpayers a break and die?"

It infuriated Spearing to have his opening challenge turned

aside with a smile and the advice that this was the Chief's outer reception office, open to the public from eight to six, and that its principal purpose was to welcome all comers and to handle their complaints as swiftly and courteously as possible. "Even the likes of you," Todd had countered.

Handling those citizens who for various reasons thought it necessary to present their problems directly to the Chief of Police was a delicate affair. Since Hill himself could not possibly see all those people whose troubles had overwhelmed them, or who simply would not believe that a parking ticket could not be fixed, or who wanted to personally state their opinions on anything from police persecution of a darling juvenile son to the certain fact that their neighbor was a Russian spy—all of these things plus occasional praise were filtered through the Chief's outer office and required exact mixtures of firmness, patience, and diplomacy. Even sympathy was frequently demanded and given, which was why the officers assigned to the outer office were selected with special care.

While Spearing watched disapprovingly, Sergeant Boyd completed a morning ritual which had been necessary every day for more than a year. This involved the soothing of a woman whose nights were made sleepless by the visitations of Martians. They knocked on her windows, banged the doors, and generally made life unbearable. Sergeant Boyd's recommendations were invariably the same, and so far had always left his caller remarkably content. In his carefully modulated voice he told her to take a glass of warm milk and a bath neither too hot nor too cold.

"Why," asked Spearing when Sergeant Boyd finally wished the woman pleasant dreams and hung up the phone, "why don't you tell that crazy broad to find a viper and swallow it?"

"Because she's discouraged enough as it is," Boyd answered simply.

"Everybody's discouraged. No person has any right to be anything else."

"I'm not. For one thing I have friends to talk to. I don't think she does."

"You should have been a priest," Spearing said with such emphatic disgust his jowls waggled.

"Sometimes I wish I had been."

"Don't give me that Catholic holier-than-thou malarkey. This police department is so loaded with mackerel snappers it's worse than the Vatican guard." Spearing yawned until his buck teeth chewed at the air and he said in a voice that was almost a snarl, "What about this leaper?"

"What leaper?"

"Don't give me that. The 800 on the bridge. Who is he?"

"I don't know."

Spearing knew that Boyd either told the truth, kept his silence, or cleverly changed the subject. So he believed that Boyd actually did not know the man's name. Yet it so irked him to believe any man, let alone a cop, that he said, "What the hell is that star on your manly chest for if you don't at least know his name? All you dumb Irishmen are alike. Get on the public payroll, be sure you go to Mass, and stop thinking. It's the straight road to heaven."

"No one knows his name."

"Has he jumped yet?"

"We haven't heard anything new."

The loudspeaker on the outer office wall which normally repeated an almost continuous series of police radio calls was silent. Spearing stared at it accusingly. There was a similar speaker in the pressroom which offered identical information, but most of the time when he was alone or chose to spend his night on the beat-up couch, Spearing turned it off. He was being paid scale to work so many hours a week, not to have his dreams rattled by blatting police calls.

"How about you give me a call when he jumps? It's sure not worth my going all the way out to the bridge just for a leaper."

"Will do."

Spearing yawned again and turned away. He would go see Moore in General Works. Something about a new rape. Well, rapes were always good for a day's work. They came to you and you didn't have to go to them.

On his way to General Works, Spearing passed within a few feet of the gumball machine. But he did not see it, nor the marble stairs leading up to the courts, nor the feet projecting from beneath the stairs. He *did* see Tommie the blind newsdealer and waved to him.

✧✧✧ 11 ✦✦✦

In Fraud, Inspector Lowry loaded his miniature camera and then examined the morning newspapers. He slipped past the news section and went directly to the advertisements of department store sales. These he read with the interest a hunter might give to a passage of game birds. Lowry knew that his favorite enemies, who were the elite of thieves, would be reading the same advertisements and also the weather forecast as a basis for their day's strategy. Sales meant crowds, particularly if the weather held fine, and closely packed masses of people were fields to be harvested if a pickpocket had any enterprise at all. And they always did have, if only to satisfy their pride.

All of Lowry's clientele had class and considered ordinary thieves as vulgar and clumsy fools. Any idiot could snatch a purse, but it took a carefully trained expert to extract the valuables from a purse without disturbing its owner, or successfully remove a wallet from a man's rear pants pocket. Lowry knew people who could accomplish such things with ease. He thought of them more as artists than as technicians, because they had traditions as well as pride. If they found an address inside a wallet, the better pickpockets often mailed it back to its owner. The money would be gone, but as a sort of grand gesture, all identification cards, licenses, anything which might further inconvenience the owner, would be left intact.

Many of Lowry's clients were professional graduates of the school for pickpockets in Nogales, Mexico. Although they had paid as much as five hundred dollars to a masked professor who instructed them in useful legerdemain, a diligent student operating in fruitful areas could and did retrieve the cost of his schooling in one day.

Pickpockets were not dangerous. They relied on their wits instead of weapons, but their relative intelligence made them all the more difficult to catch. Lowry knew the stars of the profession by name and reputation. There was Escobar Portiro, who looked like an elderly pensioner. His sensitive fingers could open even a buttoned pocket without detection. And then there was Savanir Microvich, the almost legendary gypsy, whose hands were so deft he could lift a wallet, remove the contents, and then refine his performance by returning the wallet to its original position. Microvich had been caught only once in his long career and was said to be a rich man. Lowry longed to have Microvich visit his city again. Under the glass on his desk he kept a photo of him which he had taken with his miniature camera two years previously. It showed Microvich surveying a Christmas crowd. But Lowry had only the photo, for Microvich was also a "swivel-head." An instant after the camera had clicked he looked around, spotted Lowry as certain fuzz—and ceased all activity for the day. Lowry had never seen him again, but he waited, knowing the day must come.

When he had finished with the advertisements, Lowry further stimulated his mind by flipping through his personal gallery of photos. They were not the usual dull-eyed police mug portraits, but candid studies of his own which showed his specialists preparing for action. He constantly refreshed his memory because these faces must be instantly recognized in a sea of other faces. They passed through a crowd in seconds. They were never still.

All around him now, the other inspectors in Fraud prepared themselves for their opponents. They would not be dealing with violence either past or potential, but frequently with imagination— and that was always difficult. There were the usual check passers, some of whom maintained expensive equipment to forge payroll checks. There were bunco artists of every cunning, including the hoary Jamaica switch, and gypsy healers. Imagination had fathered newer methods, so designed that conviction became nearly impossible.

Every day brought new and inventive deceptions to the men in Fraud. And it was wondrous how imaginations could foresee and devise so that some schemes left the Fraud inspectors and the District Attorney's office thoroughly confused as to what was legal and what was not. What, if anything, could be done about the gentleman who posed as a field manager for a magazine subscription service? He paid his employees and was even careful to withhold their taxes. And after paying, his customers actually received their magazines. But his "sales meetings" consisted of more than the conventional pep talks. They were held in a cheap hotel in which the salesmen and saleswomen were kept and fed virtually as captives. And the sales meetings were actually rehearsals during which they were carefully taught their roles. Some learned to be epileptics advised by their doctors to call on the public and thus relieve their pitiful tensions. Others became crippled war veterans bravely carrying on in spite of their infirmities. Others were coached in accents so that they might be more convincing as the last survivors of concentration camps or Communist tyranny.

It was a business, claimed the field manager; it was a crime, thought the men in Fraud. But there was nothing clear-cut in the book of crimes to support them.

Lowry was grateful that his pickpockets and shoplifters took all of his time. They also had imagination, but at least they were handicapped by mechanical barriers. When he put on his hat and went into the streets, his frustrations were his own failures.

In Burglary, Inspector Mattemore, whose body suggested a beer keg, and Stoltz, who was a genial mountain of a man, had already studied the reports which would direct their day's activities. The reports had been prepared by various uniformed patrolmen who had been called to the scene of a burglary sometime during the night. If an arrest had been made, then a key statement from the suspect was quoted; if not, and too often it was not, statements of any witnesses in the area were included. These sometimes offered such useful clues as ". . . he had a round neck and ran that way."

The information offered in the reports was merely an introduction. Mattemore and Stoltz must now call upon the victims and, depending on the circumstances, sometimes spend hours examining whatever fragments of evidence the burglars had been so careless as to leave behind. And there was *always* something, though it might be as inconsequential as a bit of chipped metal one-eighth of an inch long.

Both Mattemore and Stoltz despised the ordinary burglar, holding him a dull and talentless thief who not only left an abundance of identifying spoors, but often was so witless as to take trinkets and miss the truly valuable. It was not unusual for an ordinary burglar to lug a heavy typewriter from an office and fail to find the cash box, or take a fur coat and a television set from a house and miss the jewels. And a burglar was always faced with the problem of disposal. Reliable fences were few and extremely avaricious. Knowing they had the burglar at their mercy, they never paid more than a small fraction of any item's actual worth.

Thus, the conviction record in Burglary was very high, but neither Mattemore nor Stoltz was particularly proud of it. A criminal who was a burglar was lacking in class. Catching one was like shooting at chickens when wild geese flew overhead.

On this morning, Mattemore and Stoltz put on their hats and prepared to call upon the Capital Casket Company, the Meadowland Dairy Company, the State Wreckers Company, the American Chicks Company, and the Thrifty Cleaners. All of these establishments, plus two residences in the Heights, had been burglarized during the night. As always, the number of nocturnal invasions had risen during the pre-Christmas weeks. But the burglars, Mattemore and Stoltz knew, would, as always, have a very thin Christmas.

In Missing Persons, Inspector Dinwiddie suffered such a cold, his nose had become a red pompon projecting from his ever-melancholy face. Between sneezes he resolutely attempted to complete the reading of his morning's mail, although he could predict the essence of each letter with absolute accuracy. The fundamental urge behind the writing of each letter was always the same, and the daily realization of what lay between the lines had made Dinwiddie a wistful man. It seemed as if he still hoped for humanity but was continually smitten by his daily mail. Dinwiddie carried a gun, handcuffs, and a shield because he was a policeman and followed regulations. But he had had need of none. When he opened for business, there would be only the mail, and afterward the usual frustrating search for people who could not be found or were furious if they were.

Dinwiddie fell into his most wistful mood when he reflected that the whole world failed to understand either him or his work. The outside world simply refused to believe that those human beings who would eventually be listed as a Missing Person had exercised an inherent human right. Dinwiddie knew that the overwhelming majority of people reported as missing persons *wanted* to be missing persons.

It was only their self-styled loved ones who wanted missing persons restored to handier locations. And almost without exception the reasons were based on a sound desire—money. It rose like the smoke of incense from every letter in the morning's mail, and Dinwiddie could smell it whether he had a cold or not.

> . . . he was last seen in your city driving a new Oldsmobile . . .
>
> . . . if the above mentioned person can be proved deceased, then the estate can be settled, and the heirs . . .
>
> . . . when she left my bed and board, she took certain papers which are necessary to . . .
>
> . . . now I want to marry this other gentleman who is willing to support me good and who won't wait forever . . .
>
> . . . he always wanted to be a merchant seaman so maybe you'll find him on some ship . . .
>
> . . . it's awfully hard to make ends meet without Maria bringing home her share. When you find her . . .
>
> . . . we will appreciate your immediate attention to this matter—Ritze Collection Service . . .

Only on rare occasions was Dinwiddie asked to find a missing person simply because the missing person was loved.

❖❖❖ 12 ✦✦✦

She was watching a square of sunlight creep across the floor of her precious little apartment and she was thinking about Thelma. She had been thinking about Thelma for weeks, until now it was all she thought about. Each morning she had risen achingly from the studio couch which served as her bed, and the vision of

Thelma would come to her even before she went into the bathroom. And each morning it had been more powerful. All through her morning toilet and the making of her tea and toast, which was all she had been able to eat for days, she thought about Thelma, and she saw her as clearly as if she really were there, sighing in the embrace of Otto. And sometimes the vision became so clear and her reaction so powerful she would return to the bathroom and lose the tea and toast. It was not the idea of Otto's physical contact with Thelma that created such nausea; a man of Otto's remarkable vigor could not be expected to be entirely chaste. She was willing to accept it as long as things did not go any further. After all, what was a harmless adventure to a man of sixty if he didn't start taking himself and the adventure seriously? But that was exactly what had happened. Thelma was stealing Otto—day by day a little more of him—until there was almost nothing of the old Otto left. He had merely telephoned with one excuse or another and hadn't come to the apartment for a long time.

It was the old, old story, she told herself. Thelma and Otto had set up this here business together, and every day they were mixed up in some deal which was supposed to involve their real estate partnership. And there, right before her eyes, was Otto, who was old enough to know better, drooling all around Thelma like a lost spaniel, when he had a perfectly good woman he had been keeping for years. Thelma was smart all right. She would hold out just enough to drive Otto crazy. And she would be closing in any day now for the kill.

She thought of Thelma closing in for the kill, using the word itself in combination with the thought several times, at first just using the phrase as another way of saying Thelma was going to get Otto to marry her—then after several thousand mental repetitions of the phrase the word *kill* stood out all by itself while the rest of the phrase melted away. At first the very taste of the word taken straight had shocked her, but now she had brooded so long and savored the word so endlessly, and missed Otto so much, and hated Thelma so much, she knew there was only one thing to do— and that was to kill Thelma.

It would take a little time for Otto to get over Thelma maybe, but after he did everything would be as before.

When the realization that something must be done about Thelma took hold, she only thought of hiring a professional to do it, no matter what it cost. They had experts in everything these days, didn't they? But she had no idea how to make contact with such people. It wasn't the sort of question a woman just asked around. So finally she could see that she would have to do it herself, and the more she thought about it, the easier the idea became to accept. If everything was going to be back like it was with Otto, then she must be very careful just how she did it.

Several ideas had occurred to her. She could invite Thelma up to her apartment for a heart-to-heart and poison her tea or maybe push her down the stairs, which were certainly long enough when you had to climb them. But maybe Thelma would only be injured and then she would be in the hospital with Otto *really* drooling over his poor dear.

Besides, in both schemes Thelma's body would be in a very embarrassing location, and there would be all kinds of explanations to make.

No. It must be done away from this place, away from anything which might seem to be a part of Otto's proper woman. And that eliminated just waiting outside the house where Thelma lived and accidentally running her down with the car. And again you'd have to be going awful fast to make sure she didn't end up all surrounded by flowers and gifts, lying all romantic in some nice private hospital room in some expensive negligee, while Otto sat beside the bed holding her hand, which would probably have a ring on it just to make her feel better, and he would be drooling like he was just back from World War I or something.

All kinds of ideas had occurred to her during the past weeks and none of them had really been any good. Until this morning.

Now, sipping thoughtfully at her breakfast tea, she believed she had found a way to do it so that no one, especially Otto, would have any questions. And if he was sad about Thelma for a while, then for comfort he would just naturally gravitate back to where he belonged.

❖❖❖ 13 ❖❖❖

As always, the day in Narcotics had begun with a flurry of activity. Although the sun shafted through the arch-shaped window, all the electric lights were still burning, and unless it proved to be an unusually quiet day no one would think to turn them off. The men in Narcotics were always pressed for time, and occasionally likened themselves to dogs chasing their tails. Their trouble was mainly economic, because the sale of narcotics was the crime that did pay—handsomely. Eager customers were always guaranteed and the only problem was supply. This was arranged by clever and enterprising men who remained far from the scene of distribution and hence rarely exposed themselves to ordinary city police. The logistics of supply extended from Thailand to Turkey to Bolivia, to Indian ports, French ports, Italian ports, Hong Kong and Macao. The chain of distribution was so complex and ever-changing, the street peddlers who were the normal visitors to the Narcotics detail knew nothing beyond the man above them. The organizational chart placed the users at the very bottom. They did not care who was on the board of directors. They did not care for anything so long as their needs were fulfilled.

Unlike Burglary, Armed Robbery, or even Homicide, the men in Narcotics dealt with an action that was actually happening, or soon would happen. They were not engaged after the fact. Thus, suspicion and conviction were almost simultaneous, which at least simplified the charges. A man was a dealer or a junkhead, a seller or a buyer; in either case he was guilty of a felony. A dealer was caught with a balloon of heroin, a piece of morphine, a bundle of cocaine, a lid of marijuana, or even singles, and his ever-thriving business was immediately terminated. But since the nature of the business obliged the customers to seek out the seller, and the supply was never sufficient to meet the demand, there were always new dealers ready to replace those temporarily bankrupt.

A buyer was a junkie or a hype and was easily identified by the needle marks on his arms if he was enslaved to any type of injected drug, or was fragrant with the musky smell of marijuana if that innocent-appearing plant was his favorite escape from reality. If the suspects had managed to dispose of their precious comfort before an arrest and still retained enough sense to fake awareness, then the Nalline test proved them users. A person once hooked paid astronomical prices for the periodic passage toward his misty land. A hype must somehow find at least thirty or forty dollars every day to maintain a satisfying supply of heroin. It was said that no one, except possibly multimillionaires, could afford to be a hype.

So all the constant activity in Narcotics was based on a single truism. No human being once given in bondage to any drug had ever found his own release except in death. They *must* have it. Men would bludgeon their mothers, girls fornicate with a hundred strangers, perverts scream beneath incredible sexual torture—and all would kill if killing was necessary to obtain their special anesthesia. This the suppliers and the peddlers knew for a certainty.

There were jokes and laughter to be heard in every other detail, even Homicide. But in Narcotics the atmosphere was heavy and cynical. For here was a plague which in one form or another had prevailed for centuries, and no one had yet discovered a way to stop either the roots or the creeping vines.

Stone was the chief of the Narcotics detail. He was a handsome man who combed his thick white hair straight back in a pompadour. From his desk of command nearest the arched window, he blinked thoughtfully through the single ray of sunlight. He listened in sadness while the frail girl who stood beside his desk lied to him. Her name was Sally Chew and Stone knew her to be one of the very few Chinese prostitutes in his city.

A splotch of tiny smallpox craters marred one cheek; otherwise her beauty was marvelously without blemish. And the delicate coloring which touched her olive skin seemed to absorb and welcome each change of light when she moved her head—so that her ebony hair and lemon flesh, combined with the boldly artificial claret of her lips, became a constantly harmonious reflection.

Standing in a shaft of sunlight now, she swayed like a reed subservient to a gentle wind. Stone saw that her eyes were already

cloudy and she was beginning to shiver. Soon, he knew, she would
be in agony, and he wished that he could have seen her before
she had been hooked.

"Where did you make the connection, Sally?"

"Upstairs."

"Where's upstairs?"

"Upstairs over my room."

"Is that a shooting gallery?"

"No."

"A party pad then?"

"No. Just a friend."

"Is he on the junk too?"

"No."

Of course not, Stone reflected. The bastards never were. It was
almost a certainty that her friend upstairs traded her heroin for
what she received from other men.

"How long since you've had a fix, Sally?"

For a moment her eyes brightened. And she said, "Yesterday."
Then she swayed forward and beseeched him with her fragile
hands. She did not actually go down on her knees, but Stone had
the uncomfortable impression that she did.

"Please, Mr. Stone. I gotta have a fix right now. You do it for
me, and Sally Chew never forget you." She began to pant like a
small animal that had run a long way and her face became damp
with anxiety. "Please . . ." she repeated again and again until
Stone's voice halted her.

"You're going away for a while, Sally. You'll get rid of the
monkey."

She shook her head and a wisp of ebony hair fell across her eyes.
She brushed it away with a sleepy gesture and Stone saw that now
her eyes were wretched with fear. Someone—another hype, or
more likely her pimp—had told her of the cruelty to come, and
even in the ruins of her fantasy she sensed how terrible it would
be. For now Sally Chew would be taken to the women's prison
and there become a "cold turkey." Every abused nerve in her
fragile body would come back to life, whimpering a little at first,
and then roaring in protest as each limb became like a thousand

limbs. They would come tingling back toward warmth as if from a long freeze, and the compensating jerkings and convulsions would be repeated over and over again until her exhausted body collapsed in a final spasm. The mental explosion was near madness and the goblins would dance long after her body fell still.

"Have you any money, or friends who would help you?" he asked, although he was certain of her answer. There were institutions which eased the torment. Stone wished they were not so expensive.

"No," she said.

"I'm sorry," Stone said, not liking the helplessness in his voice. "You'll just have to sweat it."

Sally Chew trembled in her jade-green dress, and he saw that already she could not control herself. So he telephoned the matron in city prison and told her she would soon have a problem on her hands, and he thought what a hell of a way it was to begin a sunny day.

✧✧✧ 14 ✦✦✦

Slowly the building came to life, and the multitudes of pigeons promenading the cornices, arches and windowsills, moved sedately through their deposits of guano to take better advantage of the sun. A few fluttered down to pluck some invisible tidbit from the pavements below, then ascended once more to their important duties.

On this morning, things were easy in Homicide. There had not been a murder in two weeks, the identity of a bloated corpse found in the bay the day before had been definitely established, and the only firm business at hand for the inspector was his everlasting skirmishes with abortionists. It was difficult and often frustrating work. While the inspector in Homicide knew all about caustics, catheters, curettements and tenaculums, the "doctors" they sought were elusive and unaccountably protected by their patients. For some mysterious feminine reason, a woman might freely admit intercourse, yet she would be damned and nearly die before she would concede the act had made her pregnant.

The morning began slowly and quietly in Prostitution because absolutely nothing of any special interest had been brought in during the night. And the older inspectors lamented the vanished streetwalker and the wide-open brothel. They were all gone now, probably forever, because they had been offensive to puritanical eyes. The older hands laughed. See no evil—is no evil. Streetwalkers and brothels were convenient to regulate and often, for selfish reasons, cooperated with the police. But now the same business, which had flourished since the beginning of time and which certainly would continue until the end of time, had become secretive, complex, and ever more artful, until it was difficult to be sure who was who and where the line between private enterprise and organized harlotry should be drawn. Call girls conducted their affairs in almost complete immunity. They could move from city to city as they pleased and, being rootless, were seldom useful sources of information. All police constantly needed information that they knew could not be obtained in sewing circles. Now an important link with the enemy had been severed and the loss was felt in every department from Fraud to Missing Persons.

On this morning the men in Prostitution were trying to devise some way to stop business in a massage parlor. They faced the problem with little confidence. A licensed business should be protected, not harassed, by the law. Yet in this place the masseuses all had records as long as their caressing arms. And their considerable experience had given them a special and marvelously acute sense of perception. If the most innocent-faced cop called for an appointment, his true identity was known the instant he entered the door. And the usual citizen clients who could afford twenty dollars for a massage were not inclined to admit certain dividends. The blockade was frustrating and the men in Prostitution longed for the older established ways when they could simply go to their reference library and choose an informant according to the immediate need. Their portraits still graced the long line of canvas-covered classbooks which were stacked along the wall according to year. Girls like Sally Chew had often been sources of information, and a multitude of her sisters could all be found in the books. One of them would know a man who knew a girl who knew a man who just might know exactly who it was who held up the bank the day before, or who was suddenly rich because a certain seaman on a certain ship had arrived with a kilo of heroin.

While the tempo limped in Prostitution, the day had begun more vigorously in the Intelligence detail. For Hill had telephoned and said he wanted two men assigned as tails on Theo Lasher and they had better not lose him. Then there were the Muslims with a new meeting scheduled, and a new pad of beatniks which was of interest only because the poetic recitations were now being addressed to audiences of still indeterminate sexual tendencies. All the men in Intelligence understood and held little resentment against the girls who joined the Daughters of Lebidus, or men who found solace in the Mattachine Society. They wished all sexual deviates would go to some other planet, but as long as they stayed with their own kind their activities simply made the average policeman vaguely uncomfortable. His personal anger rose only when they toyed with the very young.

The beatnik pads were enticing juveniles with a premature call to adventure. Vacavick, a young inspector who had reluctantly agreed to let his hair grow long and spend a month living with the beatniks, announced very firmly on this morning that he could stand the smells, the terrible wine, and even the public copulating, but he absolutely could not endure another line of their poetry.

In his chambers, Judge Thomas Brownell sipped thoughtfully at a paper coffee cup. He was a slight, gray-haired man with such incongruously large ears they seemed like a pair of wings designed to support his head in the air. The illusion was particularly strong whenever he moved from place to place in his judicial robe. For Brownell was an energetic man, and whether he was en route from his desk to his bookcase, or from his chambers to his bench, or even when bound for his private toilet, he traveled at a half-run. Then, with his robes flapping around his ankles and his great ears apparently negating gravity, he swooped about like an inquisitive crow.

Judge Brownell's hands were also incongruously large for the rest of his body. While he was somewhat self-conscious about his ears, he was proud of his hands because they were so forthrightly a legacy of his farming boyhood.

On this morning his thoughts followed their usual involuntary pattern that always began with his initial entrance into the old building. There was first the decision to give up smoking, which he knew would be reversed by a higher court the moment he had his first cup of coffee, and then the decision that on this day he was not going to allow his personal convictions to influence his verdicts. It was then convenient to remind himself that he was a human being disguised as something else by a black robe. Obviously no human being could keep his judgments entirely neutral, he thought, because a mere glance, an intonation of voice, even a wrong movement, could arouse suspicions and sympathies, and at once the delicate balance scale of justice was thrown completely out of kilter.

Brownell knew that his daily vow to use the exact provisions of the law as asylum would suffer dilution the moment he left his chambers and entered the court. The failures were waiting for him. The more conspicuous would be seated in the front row, scratching at their beards and coughing through the sudden silence which followed the bailiff's gaveling. "This court is now in session, Judge Thomas W. Brownell presiding."

The monotone announcement often caused Brownell to wonder exactly what it was over which he was supposed to be presiding. All too frequently it became a repetitious masquerade with miserable and inept guests moving dreamlike through cobwebs of lies and the mud of legal phraseology. Protocol and complication so drained the vital essence from truth that there were times when Brownell became quite lost in the maze of details and found his mind stumbling over the most elementary principles of right and wrong. It was always then, in the midst of his perplexities, that he tugged fiercely first at one ear and then the other.

There were no juries in Municipal Court to act either as a buffer or as a handy receptacle of responsibility. Major felons went before a formally selected jury, but in Brownell's court there was an everyday conflict between the police who were carrying out orders of the citizens, and various citizens who rarely admitted the police were in the right.

Brownell had no need to review his calendar. He knew what the morning would bring. Like acrobats in the old vaudeville shows, the 152s, otherwise known as common drunks, would open the show. There would be at least thirty, and they would all freely admit their violation of Section 152 of the Municipal Police Code. All, at the routine recommendation of the public defender, would waive time for sentence. He would dismiss most of the bedraggled unfortunates with a warning that would fail utterly to penetrate their exhausted brains. He would give a few of the more frequent offenders ten days in the county jail, which was a more comfortable place than most of them lived in. At least they would dry out. But any person who thought they would do so permanently knew nothing about dedicated drunkards. And, Brownell often asked himself as he stared down upon their pathetic heads, what had they really done that was wrong? They had offended the public eye, which was otherwise so insensitive that screaming billboards were left to deface a grove of trees.

After the 152s there would be a few auto-boosters, who would try to explain away the miracle of their acquisitions, and perhaps a burglar or two. During this performance the determination of right from wrong became very easy. Next the lewd acts for which he normally set suspended sentences plus an admonition to leave the city.

There would be at least one family fight affair. Solomon, Moses, Confucius, and perhaps even God would be at a loss to determine who was right and who was wrong.

A few prostitutes. He would send them on their way with a fifty-dollar fine and a warning. Both penalties were always accepted with the downcast eyes of a woman ashamed. But he knew those eyes would rise again—and soon, to stimulate a sluggish desire or increase the tribute through their dreary gates. But if buyer as well as seller was content, then where was the wrong? It was particularly ridiculous, Brownell thought, when the buyer was never required to stand judgment. *In flagrante delicto.* Presumably the buyer had merely sinned, which apparently was not the same as wronged.

Brownell knew that the whole of this sunlit morning would not pass without wrath. It would rise in him when the first child-beater was called, and even a case of nonsupport might cause him to clench his big hands and instinctively reach for the neck of the accused. His loathing for both types of offender was so powerful that he often called a recess—to smoke and tug at his ears in the hope of restoring reason and mercy. But his verdict was invariably the same, which was the maximum under the law. Though he knew very well the cases were not always clear-cut, he saw them so, and sometimes he found himself reflecting on the judgments handed down by the magistrates of ancient Heliopolis, Thebes, and Memphis. There was the rod, mutilation, exile to the mines, impaling, and a particularly stern sentence which caused the guilty to be embalmed alive and then slowly eaten by a coating of corrosive natron. Before he calmed down, Brownell envisioned a modern revival of such practices specifically for child-beaters. Even when his powers of reason returned, he thought that at least once in a while he knew what was truly wrong.

He dropped his cigarette in the paper cup, squashed the cup in his farmer's hand, and tossed it into the wastebasket. Then he rose and smoothed his black robe. It was time. He strode toward the heavy door that led to the courtroom, and his black robe swung in cadence with his quick steps. Now came the time during which he always recognized himself as a mediocre judge of a very minor court. Even so, the swinging of his robe never failed to generate a pleasant instant of pride. He heard the flute players announcing the magistrates of four thousand years before. So he moved in dignity. What was yesterday's truth was also today's. The penal code of the sixteenth century was more severe than it had been in the Middle Ages because it reflected the greater moral disorder of its time. Here little farm boy Tom Brownell, neither sage nor saint, was judging a nation in trouble. It was a minuscule division of the people, to be sure, but there it was all the same.

✧✧✧ 15 ✦✦✦

As soon as the delegation from the Civil Liberties Committee was convinced that their most recent martyr was somewhat tarnished and hence unlikely to prove a convenient display piece,

Hill escorted them to the door of his office. They shook hands all around but there were no smiles, and Hill knew their suspicions of him and all he represented would not diminish when they left the old building. Which was good, he thought. It was a nuisance and often discouraging to be badgered by various committees and associations that were fundamentally antagonistic to all policemen, but without such opposition the possibility of a police state was ever present. And Hill knew that his love affair with his adopted land would soon wither if the police ever started creating the law instead of merely enforcing what the citizens themselves had dictated. I would switch sides in a hurry, he thought. And then he chuckled, because the vision of himself throwing rocks at a policeman had not come to him in a long time. He could think of at least two cities larger than his own where some well-aimed rocks were in order. The police in those cities disgusted him. For one thing, they secretly welcomed men like Theo Lasher.

Only three persons were permitted to enter Hill's office without being asked or clearing through Sergeant Boyd. Barnegat could do so, simply because he was Barnegat. As Chief of Inspectors he considered himself entitled to certain privileges and he took them.

Deneen, as deputy, could also enter as he pleased, but he insisted on protocol and always knocked.

The third privileged person was Marvin Fat, who entered so silently it seemed he came through the mahogany-paneled wall. He would simply appear and, regardless of what Hill was doing or to whom he might be talking, he would seize one foot, place it on his box stand, and start shining. If the lion moved from one part of his den to another, Marvin Fat would wait until he had settled and then continue his work. They almost never spoke audibly on these occasions since their great difference in age and station made them slightly afraid of each other. But with the unavoidable fear there had developed an admiration and affection which had distilled into love, and they both avowed it again and again without need of sound. It was a matter of eyes. The lion would look down into Marvin Fat's black eyes and Marvin Fat would stare into the lion's eyes, and somehow a remarkable liaison was instantly established.

So they understood each other perfectly. Hill was Marvin Fat's god. Hill could only see the Chinese boy as a hungry Irish lad named Colin, though everything about him from his skin to his straight ebony hair was as far from Ireland as anything could be. Even though Hill knew very well he should do something about Marvin Fat's obvious truancy, he had never yet found the courage to begin. Each day he postponed asking the first questions—where Marvin Fat lived and why he wasn't in school. And so he said nothing at all. And Marvin Fat knew that if he spoke, then Hill would begin to ask such questions, and so he also was silent. Neither of them wanted to end such a very special thing. Both of them knew it must soon end.

Hill always gave Marvin Fat a dollar when the shine was done. Then Marvin would smile, pick up his box, and slip away as silently as he had come. But his smile was not for the dollar. He would happily have shined Hill's shoes a thousand times for just that final wink of one gray eye. And both of them knew this also.

Now Hill went to the telephone stand beside his desk. As he picked up the phone he suddenly became aware that he was not alone. He looked down and saw Marvin Fat reaching for his right shoe. And they smiled.

Hill placed a call to Henry Stanton, one of the three police commissioners. They were important men to Hill because so far they had trusted him implicitly. He wanted to keep things that way. The three commissioners were not politicians, but leading citizens who served without pay. They could break Hill if they pleased and they could rescue him if serious attacks were made. There was no conceivable reason for anyone to question their integrity and Hill constantly blessed the situation. He had often wondered how long he could stomach his job if he had to consult with professional politicians before he moved.

He told Stanton of Theo Lasher's arrival. He would call upon Lasher this afternoon . . . alone. He explained that he wanted all three commissioners to understand why it was dangerous for their Chief to be alone in a hotel room with a man like Lasher. It was almost asking for the first police scandal the city had known in years. Hill was fairly certain Lasher had been at least indirectly responsible for the sorry decay of the police chiefs in two other large cities. He was as persistent as he was clever and always began his campaigns very quietly.

"He finally woke up to the fact that this city is virgin territory," Hill explained. "He can't resist an opportunity. It could be that after he feeds his persecution story to the press it will be me you'll want to get rid of instead of him. I may need you. . . ."

"I'm surprised," Stanton said. "It sounds like you're afraid of him."

Hill smiled at the telephone. "I am," he said. "Alone."

After he had finished with Stanton, Hill picked up a sheaf of papers and went to the window. Marvin Fat followed him and started on his left shoe. The papers were Theo Lasher's record. He peered over the papers at Marvin Fat, but for once their eyes passed no message. Hill was entirely preoccupied with the twenty-three counts of assault and battery, vagrancy, peace disturbance, larceny, robbery, and one for embezzlement of union funds which Lasher had somehow squirmed away from. Hill noted that not a single charge in any of the cities mentioned drunkenness or narcotics. Not for Theo Lasher. He had no follies.

The next page led Hill back to more familiar ground. Spokane —a murder charge. First degree. Lasher had beat that one with a dubious alibi, but he had a fine lawyer. New Orleans—murder again. The record only showed "dismissed."

Hill wondered why it had been dismissed and then he remembered it was about the time Lasher became cozy with the Mafia. Which would explain the next assault-with-intent-to-kill charge in Memphis. Lasher did only a year in the workhouse before a considerate and sympathetic state government granted him parole. But afterward something must have gone wrong in Buffalo. Murder second degree, reduced to manslaughter because Lasher had arranged for his victim to have an accident instead of just shooting him. He *proved* it was an accident, but he had still whiled away four precious years in Dannemora.

After that, Lasher must have become more cautious or even smarter—or perhaps stayed away from the Mafia. From 1955 through 1960 there was only one arrest—for statutory rape. Hill remembered reading about the affair. For once the extortion wheel had turned the other way and an eighteen-year-old girl had cost Lasher several thousand dollars plus an unproductive year in Minnesota State Prison.

Hill smiled. The joke had been on Theo Lasher. He had been so beautifully conned. After lavishing presents on her and acting like a lovesick juvenile, Lasher had managed to seduce a girl who had been practicing since her early teens. As a final touching memento, she had left him with gonorrhea.

There was nothing after 1960. Lasher was clean, or at least had kept off the books. Maybe his union satisfied him? Hill smiled again at the naïveté of his own thoughts, and for an instant Marvin Fat hoped he was smiling at him. But Hill's eyes were far away and Marvin Fat knew instinctively that his god was puzzled.

❖❖❖ 16 ✛✛✛

A fitful wind had come in from the sea, so that what the man on the bridge called to those below was now sometimes difficult to hear.

The sergeant in charge at the bridge was vastly relieved when Deneen arrived. He massaged the back of his neck and said that he could not look up any longer because the last hour of watching the man had created a terrible crick in his neck.

There was a lull in the wind and Deneen heard clearly the voice which came from so high.

"You down there . . . with the hat! So they called out the boss? *You're* a boss . . . I can tell by the way you stand. You're a big-shot know-it-all. Well, you better know this. Don't try to come up here or I'll kill you just as dead as anybody. I'll go in my own time. When it pleases me. It's one thing I'm going to do exactly when it pleases me."

The man waggled the gun and then put it back in his pocket. He was silent for a while and turned his attention toward the sea. He seemed to have forgotten the crowd which had gathered at both ends of the bridge. Deneen saw that many of them, already weary of standing, had found boxes to sit on. A few had miraculously produced camp chairs, perhaps from their cars. They didn't want to be uncomfortable while they watched a man destroy himself, Deneen thought angrily. Bless their fat asses. And a cluster of mothers, fearful of missing something, had brought those of their children who were too young for school.

Deneen estimated the crowd on the nearer end of the bridge at two thousand. At the far end, where the view was not so advantageous, there was perhaps another thousand.

"Give this thing another hour," the sergeant grumbled, "and we're going to need more troops. I'm just waiting for the lieutenant to arrive and see what kind of a mess we got."

"How many men do you have now?" Deneen asked.

"Twenty-five counting the solo bike men. And the state boys are keeping traffic moving at the far end. But we need more men over there on the cliff. They're climbing through people's back yards, marching over their flowers, any goddamned thing to get a better look. I've seen leapers before, but never one who gave such a show for the price." The sergeant paused and rubbed the back of his neck again. Then he cocked his head carefully and glanced at the tower.

"Can't we bring his family out here? Before it's too late?"

"The Chief says no."

"But they're going to hear about him sooner or later."

"They don't have to see it." Deneen was silent for a moment while he studied the diminutive figure clinging to the cable. There was an elevator in the tower, but as long as Barbee stayed where he was the elevator offered no advantage. Barbee was almost exactly halfway between the tower itself and the point where the cable joined its concrete foundations. So both approaches to him were completely exposed. It was a long climb up the great round supporting cable—at least four hundred feet, Deneen thought. If it were only night it might be possible to use the elevator and approach Barbee from above and below simultaneously. But now Barbee commanded every view.

"I'm going to see if I can get a little closer," Deneen said quietly. "Tell those firemen to take their red wagon almost to the end of the bridge and set up a hell of a commotion. Ring the bell, run the ladders up and down, run around in circles with the siren if they have to. But tell them to try holding his attention while I'm on the way up."

The sergeant looked at Deneen unhappily. He winced and shook his head.

"Don't do it. What's one 800 worth against a good cop?"

"I'm not in uniform so he might listen to me. I won't provoke him if I can help it—and I won't go very far the first try. If it looks like he means what he says, I'll be right back down."

"But what the hell for?" the sergeant said very slowly.

Deneen shrugged his shoulders. "Somebody has to at least try."

Deneen strolled casually toward the base of the support cable. He did not look up again, even when he heard the distant voice begin a new oration. He stopped, jammed his hands in his pockets, and waited a moment. He watched the fire engine as it snorted past and continued toward the far end of the bridge. Good. They were ringing the bell as well as blowing the siren. They were making a fine racket.

He turned and resumed his stroll toward the huge cement block which held the bottom end of the supporting cable. He could barely distinguish the words from aloft over the sound of the siren and bells.

". . . and I say to every one of you idiots— *We* made this world! . . . We made our own God . . . and put words in his mouth . . . if you will be good you will go to heaven! Where is heaven? Down *there* with you? . . . It looks more like hell from up here! You smell! Any animal knows that. . . . You sanctimonious bastards . . . trying to pretend you aren't animals! The mouths you kiss with chew on pieces of dead animals. A few years ago all of you were nothing but a drop of slippery liquid! I'm a chemist so I'll give you the formula . . . one part hatred, one part coward, and one part grime, all held in a solution of filth!"

Deneen noticed the man's voice was getting hoarse. Good, he thought, as he hoisted himself to the top of the concrete block. Maybe he would soon lose his voice entirely.

He took a firm grip on the hard wire and slowly began the long climb up the support cable.

✧✧✧ 17 ✦✦✦

"You have some company," the matron said. She opened the gate of Celia Krank's cell and gave Sally Chew a gentle push. Then she closed the gate and went away.

Celia was uncertain how she should greet the Chinese girl. Did you say "welcome"? Or "sorry"? Did you ask why another girl had come, or talk about the weather? At least the Chinese girl didn't look like one of those other women. Celia shivered again when she thought of their threats. She could never have fought off all three of them.

"What's your name?" Sally asked listlessly. She leaned back against the gate and looked up at the overhead bars. She fumbled at the high collar of her Chinese dress and finally pulled it open. She is so thin, Celia thought. She cannot weigh more than ninety pounds. And she seems a little drunk.

"My name is Celia Krank."

"I'm Sally."

Rather than actually walking, she appeared to float across the cell until she stopped beside the empty cot. Then she melted upon it, collapsing a little at a time until her frailness was stretched out, face down.

"Don't bother me," she murmured, and Celia was astonished to see her teeth sink into the flesh of her arm.

"What are you doing?"

Sally turned her head and stared at Celia. "Go away from me."

"I . . . I can't."

"Get the hell away from me! Keep your hands off me!"

"I'm not touching you." Celia pressed herself against the cement wall. The Chinese girl was insane. This was what it was like in hell. Oh, Maurice! Come for me!

Sally's body became rigid for a time, then she began to sob. The cot shook beneath her. Suddenly she rolled off the cot and sprawled on the cement floor. She writhed and twisted her hips until the tight skirt split and exposed her upper legs.

Celia watched in horror and could only think that she looked like a little green bug that had been squashed not quite enough to die.

"Can I help you?" she finally managed to say.

Her answer was a long piercing wail, a cry of abysmal agony that terrified Celia. From down the cell block she heard a woman's raucous voice, all too familiar from the night before.

"Somebody shut that twist up!"

Celia turned to the gate. A wild sensation passed through her own body. She was surprised to find herself shaking the gate.

"Matron! Something is wrong!"

She was still tugging at the gate when the matron came. Celia pointed to Sally Chew on the floor.

"Oh, sure," the matron said, looking at Sally. "She'll get over it."

"Get over what? Can't you help her?"

"No, Celia. Nobody can help her. Let that be a lesson to you."

"I don't need a lesson! Get me out of here! Put me any place else!"

"You want to go back with the tramps down the line?"

"*No!* I wanta be—"

"Sure you do. But this is city prison. What kind of girls did you expect to meet here?"

"I didn't expect anything! I didn't expect to *be* here . . . ever! I'm not one of them—"

"You are for the time being. Now just settle down. You'll probably be called to court pretty soon. Meanwhile, we don't have private rooms for the ladies." She started away, then turned to look down at Sally Chew.

"Sally! You be a good girl and shut up. Maybe I'll give you a pop."

"You're lyin'!" Sally screeched.

"Sure I am. But you can pretend it's coming, can't you? Now be quiet, Sally."

The matron disappeared almost instantly beyond Celia's limit of vision. She pressed herself against the gate until the bars hurt her breasts. She yearned for physical pain—any hurt to keep her from thinking.

✦✦✦ 18 ✦✦✦

Deneen still had more than halfway to go up the supporting cable when he realized the man was watching him. He stopped instinctively, and his grip on the handrail became even tighter than it had been. The wind riffled his tie and sighed through the long support wires that stretched vertically to the bridge itself. Far out at sea he saw two ships, and a white spray of seagulls wheeled and whimpered against the cliffs behind him.

He took a few more steps upward. He again looked at the man, who was still so far away Deneen could not make out the expression on his face. Until he could see him better he could think of him only as the man, not a person with a name like John Barbee. The man seemed to be the only motionless thing on the bridge. Deneen was certain everything about him was swaying in the wind.

He looked up at the man and tried to smile. He considered waving and then decided against it. Any movement of his arms might be misinterpreted.

"Get off my bridge!" the man yelled.

"I only want to talk to you," Deneen answered, but he knew there was so little strength in his voice the man could never have heard him.

"Turn around and go down where you belong! With the other idiots!"

There was a crazy falsetto in the man's voice now. It was almost a screech. Deneen considered the distance between them. There was still a long way to go. He took one more step upward. He saw the man tug at his waist, then he heard the unmistakable high hissing of a bullet.

Deneen hesitated only a moment. He turned very deliberately and started down the supporting cable, hoping that his slow retreat would be taken for casualness. The sergeant had been right. It wouldn't help this miserable 800 if he was tempted to become a murderer.

They were waiting in a small barren room just off the booking desk in the city prison. The single window was so dirty that the bars beyond it lost definition and appeared only as vertical shadows. The view through the window would have been restricted even if better housekeepers cared for the room, since it faced upon the back side of the county jail, which was some ten feet distant; and between the two buildings true daylight was visible only at the sun's highest summer declination. But visitors to the room were rarely interested in what could be seen beyond the window. The inspectors were concerned with the phrasing of questions, and the prisoners with fabricating replies in such a way they might at least sound vaguely like the truth.

Moore brushed his thumb back and forth beneath his great nose, tipped back in the rickety wooden chair until it squealed under his weight, and when he had puffed twice on his cigar, looked thoughtfully at Rafferty.

"This morning you are the good guy," he said. His hand passed downward from the summit of his head, across his eyes, and followed the deep crevasses which fenced his mouth. "With a face like mine, the good guy department has always been unconvincing. And every year it gets worse. People just won't believe I am a real softy."

"Are you?" asked Rafferty.

It pleased Moore to realize suddenly that so far he had managed to deceive Rafferty. When he discovers what a real marshmallow I am, he thought, it may be a long time before I can regain his respect.

"Everybody gets spongy now and then." Moore sighed. He was thinking of Timothy Hardy and how the older and wiser inspectors had sensed and understood his present suffering. They knew the ravages of an occupational disease sometimes called "the willies"—which was a polite way of saying a man had lost his nerve through too frequent exposure to nerve-wracking situations.

And he wondered if Hill knew how desperately Timothy Hardy was trying to conceal his affliction. Moore was very glad he had never been honored with an invitation to work in Armed Robbery. When their telephone rang it was to announce that somewhere in the city a customer waited with a gun. Whether the customer was crazed with narcotics, or just naturally antisocial, or a really frightened wild animal, the lethal effect of his bullets could be all the same.

Moore stared thoughtfully at the grimy window and said to Rafferty, "Just remember, a good cop never gets wet and he tries not to be shot. It takes some doing in this business. Now, as for our own morning's business. . . . We have some scared characters coming in here. The chip the Perez boys have been carrying on their shoulders long enough to make them do whatever they did is going to be thrown right in our faces. As far as they're concerned you and I are personally responsible for the trouble they're in, and never forget it. Naturally, they hate us. You'll find it isn't very pleasant to be hated, even by punks."

"If these guys raped a thirteen-year-old girl, I don't care what they think. I think they should be hung."

"Would that give the girl back her virginity?"

"I don't give a damn," Rafferty said, his face reddening. "Just leave me alone with them—one at a time. I'll beat—"

"Sure you would. But who gave you the right to decide they deserve a beating?" When Rafferty was obviously not going to answer, Moore methodically relit his cigar. And through the cloud of smoke he said, "Number one lesson for today. Your badge doesn't give you any special right except to carry a gun. The difference it makes between you and most other citizens is that you get to ride free on a streetcar. It does not give you either the right or the ability to judge. So don't make up your mind until you know *all* the facts. Number two lesson. When you have turned in all the facts, forget the whole business or you'll go nuts. No matter what you think, the courts will think differently. You believe a man should do five years, they'll give him twenty. You believe the bastard should get life, they'll give him five. Don't brood on it. Your business is just listening to scared lies. There is no way I know of to make any scared person tell the truth. You have to help them out of their fright and you can't be too subtle about it. Which is why today you're the good guy."

Moore had never ceased to wonder at the way suspects would invent a story and grimly stay with it, when the legal consequences of their fantasy were often more serious than those called for by the simple truth. The legend of rubber hoses, presumably employed to beat confessions from suspects, still lingered, although neither Moore nor his fellow inspectors knew exactly why. Even the threat of brutality had been long abandoned. Moore remembered he had once splattered a baseball bat with red ink and placed it conspicuously near the door in an attempt to impress a particularly stubborn suspect. The device was a failure. The prisoner stared at it contemptuously all through his interview and deliberately kicked it out of position when he left. After considerable reflection, Moore had finally decided that one reason for the bat's failure was its mere presence. It was something to look at. You could talk all day to a suspect and discover nothing at all—*if* he had something to look at. A calendar on a wall, a photo of the Mayor, the Chief of Police, a movie star, or Churchill; it made no difference so long as it could become a point of visual focus. Once a prisoner could fix his attention on a physical object, his resolve was likewise frozen. You could not, during that session at least, catch his eyes and see into them again. Which was why the so-called "interviewing" room was now quite bare.

Moore had little use for lie detectors. There were too many variables, and prisoners willing to take the test were inclined to tell the truth anyway.

By far the most reliable avenue to the truth was the "good-guy-bad-guy" playlet. Young Rafferty, with his quiet manner and rather delicate features, should make an ideal counterfoil, Moore thought. And on this morning he had decided the performance would be traditional—in two acts.

"Always remember," Moore said, staring at the grimy window again as if he could actually see something beyond it, "no matter how tough they claim to be, every man in there behind those bars is deep down scared."

A turnkey opened the door and asked Moore which of the Perez brothers he wanted to see first.

"The younger one. He's not so smart." Then to Rafferty he said, "When it's your turn, don't hurry things. It takes time to make a pal."

Moore again relit his cigar and assumed his most forbidding manner before the door opened and Antonio Perez entered the room. Moore ignored him for a moment, then snarled, "Sit down!"

Antonio slipped into the chair by the window. Because he was heavier and stronger featured than most young men of Mexican descent, Moore decided there must be more Indian than Spanish in his blood. If so, Antonio Perez was not going to be so easy as he had hoped.

Moore waited to see how long it would be before he began to squirm in his chair, or pick at his face, or display his nervousness through any physical motion. He was soon disappointed. Antonio simply stared at the ceiling. Even his eyelids remained motionless.

"You're a punk," Moore rasped. "A no-good punk! A wise guy . . . you *think!* And your brother is also a punk, only he's dumber than you are. It's no surprise to me you have to go around raping little girls." Moore wrinkled his nose. "You stink. No real woman would let you near her."

There was absolutely no change of expression in Antonio's eyes.

"This trip, you're going to spend a long time in the joint," Moore said. "I'll see that you do."

Antonio turned his head slowly. He looked at Moore, then he looked back at the ceiling. Moore moved in front of his chair, doubled his fists, and looked down at him.

"How many other jobs have you two cheap punks pulled?" Moore did not expect an answer. He thought, I just want those eyes to move. Then he said very quietly, "When you come out of the joint you'll be too old to screw anybody."

Deep in Antonio's black eyes Moore saw the first flash of hatred and he was satisfied.

"What did you do? Get in the girl *after* your big brother? Always second, Antonio. Right? All your life the second fiddle, and for that you're going to spend the rest of your life in the joint. Who taught you all this? Your mother?"

"Cut it out," Rafferty said on cue. "That isn't necessary."

"I'll talk to this punk any way I want."

"Well, lay off his mother."

"Why should I be any different? His mother was a whore for sure. A greasy *puta!*"

Moore could feel Antonio grow rigid with suppressed rage. But the rigidity was inside, deep, where Moore could not get at it, and a touch of doubt crossed his mind.

"How old are you?"

"Twenty."

"How come you carry an I.D. card that says you're twenty-one?"

Antonio did not answer. He seemed intent on placing his tongue below the saliva in his mouth and raising it to blow a bubble.

"You raped the girl, beat her up, dumped her, and then took on the gas station attendant. You know what's going to happen to you if he dies?"

"Yeah," Antonio said, trying to blow another bubble.

"Who hit him? You or your brother?"

"My brother."

Antonio's answer astounded Moore. What was this? Who was calling the plays here? A brother combination invariably stuck together.

"You're a *real* punk! Selling out your brother! I suppose he was the only one who raped the girl!"

"No, he di'n't."

"Oh. You'll take the credit for that."

"No. Neither one of us laid her. We just played around a little, like we said."

"Then you beat her up! Is that the way you get your jollies?"

"No. We di'n't."

"Who the hell *did* then?"

Antonio shrugged his shoulders and looked up. And at last Moore saw the proper amount of hatred, defiance, and fear all mixed in the black eyes. It was there as surely as if he had injected it with a poisoned needle. But there was something else, an element foreign to the playlet, in Antonio's eyes, and it troubled him.

He took the cigar from his mouth and spat deliberately on Antonio's pants. Then, turning to Rafferty, he said, "I'm not going to listen to this punk any longer. I'm going to change their booking from rape and assault to kidnaping and attempted murder. Think about *that*, Perez!"

Moore strode to the door, yanked it open, and went out. He was careful to slam the door hard behind him. Then he walked slowly to the booking desk, where he picked up a newspaper. He turned at once to the sporting page and read eagerly about the run of striped bass in the bay. If there was ever time he would certainly love to do something about those bass. If only people would stop trying to prove they weren't marshmallows. . . .

But even as he read and dreamed, Moore knew the time would never be.

Rafferty held out a cigarette for Antonio Perez. He lit it for him, then allowed him to smoke in silence. Moore had said Antonio must be given time to think—but not too much time. He watched while Antonio took out a surprisingly clean handkerchief and carefully wiped at the spit on his pants. Rafferty could almost feel the heat from the fire in him.

"Antonio. How many people in your family?"

There was no reply. Rafferty wondered if he had even heard him.

"I come from a fair-sized family," Rafferty went on quietly. "I have three brothers . . . and two kid sisters."

"So who gives a shit?"

"I do." Rafferty smiled. "I have to. All my brothers were older than me. When I was a kid they really knocked me around."

"Bueno."

"Are you the youngest?"

"No."

"Where did you go to school?"

Antonio ignored him. He was staring at his pants.

"I never did very well in school. Too dumb, I guess."

Another silence, then Antonio's mouth seemed to explode. He spoke so quickly the words sounded like one.

"The dumb one is that copper pal of yours! I'll slice him!"

"He's no pal of mine. Or anybody else's."

"He got no right!"

"I agree with you. They ought to take his badge away. But meanwhile we're both stuck with him."

Rafferty began to pace the room. He walked casually, but he avoided passing behind Antonio's chair. He wanted Antonio to watch him and perhaps finally realize there was no hurry about anything. When that notion penetrated, then he might begin to lose hope. And hope in some unforeseen miracle was the only thing that kept the guilty fighting. When they lost it, there was little need for clever questions. The truth poured from them. And vengeance also died with hope.

No word passed between them for ten minutes. Rafferty was sure it was a much longer ten minutes for Antonio than for himself. "How about another cigarette?"

Antonio nodded and Rafferty handed him his entire pack. When it was offered in return Rafferty told him to keep it.

"You know there isn't so much difference in our ages . . . and my so-called pal has called me a punk too. I never knew a man who thought he knew so much about everything."

Rafferty hoisted himself to the table. While he waited for the flames in Antonio to diminish, he told him about his own family, how he had wanted to raise cattle instead of being a cop, and how he might have succeeded if only everybody wasn't against a young man trying to get anywhere . . . especially if he came from a poor family.

And after Antonio had smoked yet another cigarette, Rafferty drew him into a discussion of cars. He asked Antonio's advice. If he were about to buy, wouldn't it be a sports car? Then what did Antonio think was the best, considering a cop couldn't really afford to have one in the first place, but was going to make the down payment anyway?

Finally, Rafferty looked at his watch and said he didn't realize how much time had passed, and he had better take Antonio back to his cell block at once. He said that Moore would accuse him of goofing off. He wouldn't understand how they could find anything interesting to talk about.

"Ain't you gonna ask me no more questions?" There was almost a touch of disappointment in Antonio's voice.

"About what?"

"About my . . . trouble."

"No. You've been bothered enough for one day. Besides it wouldn't do any good. I'm just a punk and nobody would believe you would talk to me." Then Rafferty appeared to be suddenly concerned. "How you fixed for bread, Antonio?"

Antonio held out his hands.

"They'll set your bail sky-high, that's for sure. So forget about going anywhere. But I was thinking if you could afford a lawyer . . . boosting the car isn't such a tough rap, but the other stuff is grand jury. . . ." Rafferty shook his head unhappily. "Of course, the Public Defender will do the best he can for you . . . by the way, how'd you get the car started? Jumper wire?"

"Yeah."

"I hate to see you going for the full jolt on all this stuff. If you'd sort of level with me, I'll talk to the Public Defender and ask him to make some special effort." He paused and looked at his watch with concern. "After you boosted the car, how did you get the girl into it?"

"We was just drivin' along."

"Well, she sure didn't just jump in the car."

"Damn near. We wasn't even thinkin' about girls. She's standin' on the corner. We pass her. She waves and smiles. So down the street we stop and wait. In a minute she comes to the window and starts givin' us the business."

"What business?"

"You know, wettin' her lips all the time and twistin' around and bendin' into the car so we can see her tits and talkin' about how she'd sure like to go for a little ride and get some fresh air."

"Aw, come on, Antonio. I may be a dumb cop, but don't expect me to swallow that."

"It's so! I'm tellin' ya. She was real fly."

"Who was drivin' the car?"

"Julio. I tol' him she was a rabbit."

"If Julio was driving, you must have been the one who pulled her in."

"I di'n't pull her in. She got in."

"Where? In the back seat or the front seat?"

Rafferty appeared indifferent to Antonio's answer. He nervously looked at his watch again. He must reverse the sense of time now. Antonio must feel that he was about to miss an opportunity.

"She got in between us."

"Then you had to get out of the car. Or did she climb over you?"

"I got out."

"Anybody see that happen?"

"I don't guess so."

"Was she in the car when you knocked over the filling station?"

"No. That was after."

"After you raped her?"

"We di'n't rape her!"

"After you beat her up then."

"We di'n't beat her up! All we done was love her up a little and kiss her. We was laughing all the time."

"Did you ask her how old she was?"

"No."

"How old did you think she was?"

"Maybe seventeen or eighteen."

"You need glasses?"

"No."

"Did you give her anything to drink?"

"Yeah. One can of beer. We di'n't have no money so we took her home and said we'd be back when we got some more beer."

"What time was that?"

"About seven o'clock. It was almost dark."

"You knocked over the station at seven o'clock. How could you be two places at the same time?"

"Well, maybe I was wrong about the time."

"I guess I was wrong to think you'd level with me." Rafferty sighed. "Okay, Antonio, now take your clothes off. We'll send them up to the lab for a check. Your socks and shoes too. I'll bring you a shirt and some pants."

Rafferty went out the door without looking back. But he closed the door gently.

Later, when Antonio had been returned to his cell block, they brought Julio Perez to the room. Moore first examined his arms for needle marks and, finding none, asked if he smoked marijuana.

"Sure," Julio said.

"Did you give any to the girl?"

"What girl?"

"The girl you raped. Harriet Rankin."

"Oh. Is that supposed to be her name?"

Moore knew it would be a waste of time to enact the playlet for Julio. He was no longer a young man in spite of his youth. He was an old and poisoned man with a record which he wore like campaign ribbons. And Moore wished some of the reformists who believed so thoroughly in their rehabilitation theories could look into Julio's black eyes now. For only the color was like his brother's. They were black steel balls, utterly devoid of warmth or emotion. They were the eyes of a predatory animal drained of every illumination except savage survival. Moore did not pretend to know the original forces which had caused Julio's eyes to become as they were. But he firmly believed it was too late to change them. And he was also convinced the color of Julio's eyes had no more to do with his behavior than his olive skin. Moore had seen the same fanatic defiance in blue eyes, gray eyes, brown eyes, and hazel. It was mankind turning back half a million years. It was man speaking from long before such fancy veneers as humility or regret began to trouble him.

"Your brother told us the whole story," Moore said flatly.

"He did like hell."

"He told us how the girl got in the car and sat between you," Rafferty said.

"That's against the law?"

"It is when it's kidnaping. You can go away for a long time on that."

"Nobody kidnaped nobody."

"You don't look much like Antonio," Moore said. "Is he really your kid brother?"

"Sure."

"Then you aren't doing Antonio any favor by taking him away with you for so long."

"Don't snow me. We borrowed a car, okay. That's all. We'll be on parole in a year."

"How about the filling station?"

"I don't know anything about it."

"Antonio does. He admitted you knocked it over."

"Prove it."

"We will. This afternoon in a showup. The girl and the filling station attendant will both identify you. Making it rough for us is just making it tough for you. Why don't you tell us the whole story and get it over with?"

"Whyn't you go take a flyin' jump for yourself?"

"Okay, Julio. Take off your clothes. By the time the lab is through and the showup is over you won't be so cocky."

✧✧✧ 20 ✦✦✦

Theo Lasher was often an unhappy spectator at the contest between his body and his special desires. In some instances the fetish of his health won out, and it pleased him to announce that it had been ten years since he had smoked, and eight years since alcohol had passed down his size twenty neck. But other appetites frequently overwhelmed Lasher. He was incapable of passing a candy store without buying at least one box of chocolate caramels or, if they had them, Turkish Delights, which were his favorite sweet of all. And he demanded ice cream with every meal, including breakfast.

Theo Lasher's maverick sweet tooth worried him into spells of deep brooding wherein he occasionally recognized the distinction between right and wrong. The moods caused an even greater yearning within him. At such times his associates, both male and female, had learned to keep away from Lasher. There was still frightening power in his maullike hands, and he was inclined to swing them swiftly if too sharply irritated. When in such tempers he could sometimes be appeased and even reduced to semitranquility if a young girl could be persuaded to act as a sacrifice. In moments of distress his associates often tried to arrange such liaisons, but it was always a gamble and very expensive. Years of full living had transformed Lasher's once magnificent body into a great vase-shaped caricature of a fat man. His breasts were drooping sacks and they quivered whenever he made the slightest movement. Even the finest tailors had failed to minimize the bursting effect of his belly or the great flabby arcs of his buttocks. Only about his face was there still visible evidence of Theo Lasher's hardier past. Even his hippo jowls could not soften the deeply clefted chin, and when in moments of special displeasure he forced his jaw forward, it was as if a separate unit of his face was moved by some powerful machinery. His nose had been broken so many times it was almost shapeless, but its very eccentricity of line gave it a certain barbaric beauty. It was a perfect mate for his grotesquely distorted ears. His eyes alone remained as they had always been—large, innocent, blue, and extraordinarily clear. Though he was fifty years old, Lasher had never even thought about the need for glasses. His eyes were the one division of his health with which he was content.

As if he had swallowed a marvelous potion, all of Lasher's gross ugliness vanished the instant he began to speak. Where and how he had acquired such a vocabulary to complement his voice was unknown, but it had been a mighty factor in bringing a third-rate pugilist successfully through a multitude of jungles. He once stood before his union followers and said, "I have come to you from the ooze of poverty. If you give me the chance, I will lead you all out of the slime." It was impossible not to hear every word Lasher uttered, for his voice was a deep and melodious bellow. Its resounding volume was produced without apparent effort, and the tonality was constantly enriched with so many nuances of color that it seemed as if his throat was equipped with several sets of vocal cords, each capable of responding separately or together. Lasher could lie outrageously and be believed, command and be instantly obeyed, persuade and make conquest. Women who were at first revolted at the thought of physical contact with Lasher forgot their distaste once he began to speak.

Lasher knew the limitless wealth of his voice. He spent it

constantly, irrigating the halls of its passage with great sluicings of milk and honey, refertilizing the exotic character of his vocabulary with gleanings from his fantastic memory. His ears both resembled and acted as sponges. A word he had never heard before was stored away for later use, an idea, a phrasing, a technical term or a statistic all slid down a well-greased chute between his ears. So strangers believed that Lasher was an educated man.

When the telephone rang at eleven o'clock he had just finished a leisurely breakfast and was reading the *Wall Street Journal,* which always intrigued him. He particularly liked the quotations from various vice-presidents commenting on the state of their businesses. He liked them because he knew he could have phrased the same inane ambiguities in a far more interesting way. He would often quote a vice-president when he sensed that a meeting needed laughs. "Listen to what this jerk has to say . . ."

Then with his voluptuous voice cascading facts and statistics, clothing the dullest in unexpected adjectives, he would indeed make the man look like a simpleton.

He allowed the phone to ring several times before he hefted his bulk from the chair and ambled across the room. These days, all his movements had the tempo of serene confidence. He was Theo Lasher. He flew his banners even when he was alone.

"Yeah?"

"I have a call for you, Mr. Lasher, from a Sergeant Boyd in the Police Department."

Lasher blinked his blue eyes thoughtfully. The hairs on the back of his neck, which had developed an almost extrasensory perception, now tingled ever so slightly. He wrinkled his nose as if the telephone exuded a foul odor.

"All right. Put him on."

While he waited, he skewered at his free ear with his little fingernail. Lasher was inordinately fond of manicurists and each one was warned to leave the nail on his right little finger longer than the others so that he could conveniently prod at his ears. He wondered if he was going to be hit for benefit tickets. Every city was the same.

"This is Sergeant Boyd in Chief Hill's office, Mr. Lasher. The

Chief would like to see you this afternoon. What time would be convenient?"

"I'm not sure it would be convenient at all. I'm a busy man."

Lasher's memory instantly disgorged the pertinent facts. He had met Hill once . . . when? Eleven years ago. Where? Kansas City. Why? He was on a special assignment to a federal committee which was supposed to be investigating the Mafia. He should have been in the Boy Scouts. Some fluke had made him a chief. That, of course, could be changed, but meanwhile what was the little ex-door-rattler doing having a sergeant call? Who the hell did he think—wait a minute. Know thy enemy. Even the clowns.

"I'll rearrange my schedule. Tell Hill I'll see him at three o'clock. Here."

He put down the phone and at once began a thorough search of the bedroom; then he went into the living room of the suite and methodically examined every possible object that might conceal a microphone.

When he was satisfied with the rooms, he opened each window and leaned as far out as his belly would allow. He carefully examined the projecting masonry. There were no wires and he was content until he remembered the bathroom. There was a ventilator grill in the ceiling. He stood on top of the toilet and looked into it closely, even though he knew it was too far away from any useful location. But one of the reasons for Theo Lasher's success was his attention to detail. He firmly believed that careless people led themselves to trouble.

He returned to the living room and regarded it with new interest. Because it was on a corner, there were windows on two sides, which, he thought, was excellent. One wall separated the living room from the bedroom, which was also satisfactory, but the other wall was only partly taken up by the entryway and door. The rest of the wall?

He went outside and looked down the hall, which terminated at a place corresponding to the end of his living room. There was a firebox halfway down the hall. He examined it minutely and then separated each loop of the hose which hung beside it. And again he was satisfied.

Finally he turned and walked ponderously down the hallway. He took the elevator to the lobby and squeezed himself into a telephone booth. He dialed a number and used his beautiful voice for only one sentence.

"Don't call my room again until you hear from me."

He hung up at once and thought again how pleasant it was to have a well-oiled annuity like his union. But there were other enterprises which held even more promise. Until they were well launched, they deserved his full care and attention.

✦✦✦ 21 ✦✦✦

Peering down from the altitude of his elevated bench, Judge Thomas Brownell sometimes entertained the illusion that he was marooned on an island against which long rolling ocean swells hissed and slobbered and then subsided to come in again. The continuous flow of people below him—the bailiffs, clerks, policemen, lawyers, inspectors, witnesses, accusers and accused—surged against the surrounding physical outposts of his island in alternating waves and tumbled all concentration between cases. He visualized Miss Throckmorton, the court stenographer, as an outpost rock. She sat serenely, and touched at the small yet marvelous machine before her that exactly recorded the complaints, alarms, and woes of so many.

The court clerk was also a rock, although he often was awash and sometimes disappeared from view. When his cue came he would rise sufficiently to be seen. But he would keep his knees slightly bent as if on the alert to descend. He would begin his litany, "Do you solemnly swear to tell the truth, the whole truth . . ."

And when this was done and the witness murmured the standard affirmative, then the clerk would sink down, become engulfed in wavelets of papers for perhaps ten seconds, and thereafter manage to achieve near-invisibility. Brownell often wondered what the clerk's reaction would be if a witness simply stated that he would *not* tell the whole truth or anything like it, but would lie to the best of his ability, to protect himself, which is what most witnesses did anyway. But in all his years on the bench, Thomas Brownell had never heard "No" to the oath. Once he had descended behind his desk, the clerk seemed determined to preserve his isolation by ignoring whatever anyone said. Brownell was certain that if he recommended a suspect should be hung up by the thumbs, the clerk would pretend not to have heard the sentence.

A bulldozer and a pile driver snarled and hammered at an excavation across the street from the old building. The machines made so much noise, Brownell had reluctantly ordered the windows closed. Thus the air in the courtroom became heavier than ever and the morning sunlight stabbed through the dusty venetian blinds in thin shafts which appeared almost solid. Brownell now wished he had not ordered the windows to be shut, because he was having trouble staying awake. Yet he disliked reversing his order. If a man could not achieve a firm decision on the opening and closing of windows, then how could he presume to judge who was lying and who was telling the truth? The business of the windows was important, he believed, because vacillation was the first visible pox of dishonesty, and it could spread and become rampant so very easily. Cambyses, he remembered, was the only man who had ever known how to deal with a dishonest judge. He skinned the man alive, upholstered a chair with the resulting epidermis, and appointed his son to sit in it. The constant reminder made the son a constantly honest judge.

It has not been a bad morning anyway. He had dismissed all but one of the thirty common drunks presented, and then had enjoyed a secret chuckle as he heard the bewildering case of two elderly ladies, one of whom could have sat for the portrait of Whistler's mother. The other woman, Brownell decided, looked exactly like his own Aunt Hattie. The pair had gone to a local night club and there consumed considerable quantities of bourbon whiskey. When the bill came, they protested and attacked the waiter with great determination. When the police arrived they were not impressed. They attacked the officers so fiercely they had to be handcuffed.

Brownell regarded their now frosted faces and could not detect the slightest indication of remorse. He decided he would begin pompously so that what he had to say later might have a more stunning effect.

"You are both intelligent, and I should be very surprised if you did not pay a fair amount of taxes—a fact which does not automatically give you certain privileges. I do not consider it your privilege, or chic, or humorous, or in any other way justified, that you kick, bite, and strike out at those you hire to protect your . . ."

They were not listening, he knew, but perhaps they would listen now.

"You ladies have been very naughty. Your fine will be one hundred dollars each, and in addition . . . ten days in the county jail. There I trust you will have opportunity to remember your manners."

After the combative pair, there was a Lawrence Potter, whom the Assistant District Attorney announced as line five on the calendar. Line five. What a way, Brownell thought, to herald what the law described as a lewd act.

The Public Defender stood up and said, "We are ready to proceed, Your Honor. We will waive the reading of the complaint and the instructions, and our plea to the charge is guilty."

Brownell glanced through the police report which described how one Lawrence Potter, aged twenty-seven, had caressed Officer Peterson in a movie theater. Then he looked down at the young man who stood so irresolutely before him. His feet were held close together, as a girl might stand, and occasionally his delicate fingers fluttered to his face. He seemed to sway, even though Brownell knew he was standing quite still. There was simply no rigidity in his body, which Brownell considered a shame because he was otherwise rather handsome.

"Are you a registered sex deviate, Mr. Potter?"

"No, sir."

"Is this the first time you've been arrested on such a charge?"

"Oh, yes, sir."

Brownell tugged at his ear. What was to be done with these

people? During the past few years it seemed that more and more stood before him. The law said that their ways were wrong and society said they were evil. It was not evil for a man and woman to cohabit, provided they had paid a trifling license fee and stood momentarily before a minor official while he muttered a few words at them. It made not a particle of difference if the minor official was a total stranger and would never be seen again by either of the two principals. They could cohabit all they wanted, for a single night, a weekend, or the rest of their lives. Decent society was satisfied, though they might abuse each other cruelly and in time destroy whatever caused them to unite in the first place. Or even each other.

Brownell wondered, as he had so many times before, if this pitiful young man was a true enemy of society. And again he made a secret confession. He did not know. But the law said this young man was an enemy and should be locked up with thieves, murderers, rapists, and various other harmful enemies. The only possible deduction seemed to be that it was against the law for such people to be.

"Do you waive a jury trial, Mr. Potter?"

"Yes, sir."

"We are willing that it be submitted according to the police report," the Public Defender said.

Brownell tugged once more at his ear. What use to send this young person to further torture?

"Do you use narcotics?"

"Oh, no, sir."

"Are you a member of the Mattachine Society?"

"Yes, sir."

"Can't you people help each other?" Brownell asked. He was surprised to hear a note of despair in his voice. Lawrence Potter made no reply. He simply sighed.

"Are you employed, Mr. Potter?"

"Yes, sir."

"Where?"

"At Seaton's Department Store. I'm a window dresser."

"Very well. I find you guilty of violating Section 215 of the Municipal Police Code and 647.5 of the Penal Code. It will be the judgment of this court, Mr. Potter, that you pay a fine of one hundred and fifty dollars or fifteen days in the county jail. Additionally, you will be sentenced to thirty days in the county jail and that will be suspended and you will be placed on one year's probation to the Probation Department of this city. If you are picked up again, you will be in violation of probation and you will serve the full time. I am not going to be so naïve as to suggest you find a nice girl, but unless you think you can behave yourself, you had better leave this city."

Brownell saw the young man's eyes fill with tears and heard his whispered "thank you." Thanks for what? For a few more months of twilight before his hunger compelled him again? And next time he might appear before another judge who might see him only as an enemy. The other judge would possibly miss the difference between Lawrence Potter and others of his kind. There were the molesters of children. There were those disguised as prostitutes whose practice it was to lure some hapless idiot into a dark alley and give him a beating. The notion that sexual deviates were physically fragile Brownell knew to be entirely wrong. The effeminate manner, the recognizable swish, could be turned off and on at will. Many policemen had discovered to their sorrow that a fruit was more than a match for them. The "muscle men" whose highly developed bodies often decorated beaches and the pages of physical culture magazines were surprisingly prone to worship not only their own bodies but those of other men. And through some mysterious chemistry, their dedication led to the same passions and violent jealousies which were understood between man and woman. Occasionally the result was murder, and Brownell had seen police photographs of once superb torsos beaten and gutted in such a manner that he had moaned involuntarily.

He did not think Lawrence Potter was so far along the way—or ever would be.

"Lines six and seven are continued until tomorrow," the District Attorney read from his long list. "If Your Honor will now go to line eight . . . Oscar Stowe."

Oscar Stowe was a thief. He specialized in construction projects.

He called at night with his small truck and took away as much new material as it could carry. By morning he had sold the material for a fraction of its cost. This time he had been caught in actual operation by two policemen in a squad car.

Brownell gave him a year in the county jail and thought wryly that everyone was a loser. The contractor would have to waste at least a morning recovering his material from the police storeroom, where it had been placed for evidence; the taxpayers would now entirely support a fellow citizen for a year; Oscar Stowe's three children would be furnished with the necessities of life by the Aid for Needy Children; and his wife would unquestionably draw a relief check for as many months as she wished. All because of some piping and cement which Oscar himself estimated would not have brought him more than thirty dollars.

Line nine was a family fight which Brownell resolved by giving both husband and wife ten days and then suspending the sentence. As they left the courtroom, Brownell noticed the pair were about to go at it again, and he wondered why it was that people who hated each other so seldom actually parted.

"Line ten, Your Honor . . . Celia Krank."

Brownell looked up from his list and saw the blond young girl moving toward his island. For a moment he thought there must be some mistake. The girl could hardly be nineteen and so belonged in Juvenile Hall. But then he found the charge against her name and confirmed her age at once. He sensed a little shock pass through everyone in the courtroom when the oath was administered—everyone except the clerk, who, immediately after Celia had said yes, slipped down beneath his foam of papers.

"Your Honor, Celia Krank is charged with violation of Section 182 of the Penal Code and also violation of Section 12025 of the Penal Code," the District Attorney announced.

She moved into the witness chair and seemed to clutch at its mahogany arms for protection. Brownell looked at her a long time before he broke the unusual silence in his court. All of the sea surrounding him was suddenly calmed. If this girl were to address a kindergarten as teacher, then Brownell could easily believe it, but her carrying a gun and conspiring with a known criminal was not so easily envisioned.

"Miss Krank has asked me to handle the matter," the Public Defender said.

Brownell glanced through the police report, but he had great difficulty concentrating on it because of Celia Krank's face. The witness chair was placed at a lower level than his own, according to tradition. Instead of looking out at the courtroom so that he could see only a quarter view of her head, she had turned in her chair to gaze directly up at him. The windows were behind Celia Krank at some distance, and a bright line of sunlight, cut sharp and straight by the venetian blinds, passed horizontally behind her neck. The end of his desk was in shadow so that her head appeared to have been severed and placed on a mahogany block. It was a trick of light and angle, yet the apparition was so real, Brownell was startled. He leaned forward to change his angle of view only to find that the light behind Celia redoubled in intensity so that a halo was added to the specter. Brownell took off his glasses and found the overall effect even more disturbing. He put his glasses on again and thought that of all the countless eyes which had looked up at him for mercy, those of Celia Krank's were the most impressive. She could have been a blond Joan staring at the churchmen, a Saxon maid who had disgraced the tribe, or a slave girl waiting for the hot iron.

I am bewitched, Brownell thought. She is looking at me as if I were a god, and worse, suddenly creating in me the sense that I am one. Doesn't she know that I am a politician elected to this job, and that if I lose the next election I will be right back scratching for clients in the dismal law office whence I came? Doesn't she realize that when I take off this black robe I will look like her dentist, her Uncle Lester, her school principal, or perhaps the man who runs the drugstore on her corner?

I am not God, he wanted to explain aloud to her. So please have the consideration to look at me, if you must look at all, and see that I am a rather small and perpetually frightened man with comical ears. My wife knew the truth. When she was alive she ruled me with such tyranny I have never found the courage to try marriage again. She sat in her marital security as if it was an armed washtub and I was a mere slave at the oars. And my children, who are as old as you are, beheaded one, still refuse

to believe I know the true values of anything, let alone the difference between right and wrong. I hide behind these robes, my poor
girl, haunted by inadequacy. You are looking with hope at a
spiritual dwarf who yearns for your compassion—not the other
way around.

He ignored the District Attorney, who was about to start his
routine questioning of where and when.

"Why were you carrying this Maurice Stiller's gun?" Brownell
asked in the desperate hope her eyes might leave him.

"Because I love him," she said simply.

And alas, Brownell thought, why should we go any further? In
one sentence she had explained all there was to explain, except
why she had given her heart to a felon.

"What was he going to do with the gun?"

"I don't know."

"Do you believe that an ordinary man needs a gun?"

For the first time she lowered her eyes and Brownell was
vastly relieved. "No," she said softly.

The spell was broken and he was able to look down at the
surrounding sea and find the District Attorney. "You may proceed," he said. He tipped far back in his chair, pretending to
listen. But of all the questions asked by the District Attorney and
then the Public Defender, he heard very little.

In contrast Celia Krank's answers, though given so softly, were
easily absorbed. It obviously made no difference whether she believed a man needed a gun or not. If Maurice Stiller asked, she
would do. Willingly, because she loved. Yet there was no pro-
vision in the laws of man for the basic elements of either love or
hatred. The law was totally preoccupied with the consequences.

In this case I will twist some juice from the law, Brownell decided. Her friend Maurice never had a chance to complete whatever it was that he intended, and so his accomplice is here on a
mere technicality. As he is *not* here on a convenient technicality,
so I will hash all the technicalities. I will become the God she sees,
if only momentarily, and rule by my own instinct and desires. I will
not even give her a suspended sentence, or oblige her to listen to
my pomposities. I will defy what the law specifies should be done
and allow a moment of wisdom to relieve its hypocrisy.

✦✦✦✦✦✦✦✦✦✦✦✦✦✦✦✦✦✦✦✦✦✦✦

ALMOST EXACTLY AT NOON

✦✦✦✦✦✦✦✦✦✦✦✦✦✦✦✦✦✦✦✦✦✦✦✦✦✦✦✦✦✦✦✦

✧✧✧ 22 ✦✦✦

Exactly at noon, Communications sent out a time tick which was noted by all police radios. The signal was received by the men on three-wheeler motorcycle traffic duty, who moved constantly through chaos and filled out parking tags because no method has so far been devised to stretch a concrete street. The men on the three-wheelers were despised and reviled by all whose importance was so great they felt entitled to a free municipal garage. The traffic men estimated this group as 97 per cent of the driving population. No matter what remarks about their personalities, their doubtful lineage, intelligence quotients, resemblance to Cossacks, storm troopers or Communists fell upon their ears; no matter how many emergency stories or variations on the faulty parking meter theme they heard; the men on the three-wheelers remained aloof until some obviously insane citizen said, "I'm sorry. It was stupid of me to think I could park here all day."

Such an attitude shook the traffic men to their very souls.

The noon signal was also heard by the solo bikemen who roamed throughout the city. It was heard in the cars waiting on the bridge, the nine district police stations, and even by Spearing, who was hard at work in the newsroom studying his scratch sheet. Spearing did not trouble to compare his watch with the signal. He liked to think that his watch was always wrong, and if by chance it should happen to show the correct time, he would have been bitterly disappointed. For he would have lost a fuse which blew conveniently any time he chose to express his opinion of manufacturers. All, including those who advertised in his newspaper, as well as the makers of his watch, were dedicated to the production of inferior products. These were, in his considered opinion, the ultimate slaves of Mammon.

Moore and Rafferty did not hear the signal because they were already on their way to the North Star restaurant, where many of the inhabitants of the old building gathered for lunch because the food was excellent, the price reasonable, the atmosphere dependably masculine. Very few women had ever ventured into the North Star, and those who had been so bold created great embarrassment and confusion. The proprietors, Walter and Ernie Lagomosino, catered to police inspectors, judges, lawyers, a few newspapermen, and an occasional sprinkling of minor politicians who were not warmly welcomed because they had a tendency to take themselves seriously. Bail bondsmen were discouraged by common agreement. Their perpetual gloom and concern with finance spoiled the group appetite. Ordinary patrolmen were welcome, but they were either on duty or at home at noon, and it was unlikely they could afford proper participation in the raucous dice-throwing for drinks which preceded the serving of the meal. Thus the North Star had in time become a club with a single curious taboo. Discussion of the law in any form or of those who would violate it in any form was greeted with deliberately insulting yawns. Only one sign of the many pasted on the bar gave any hint of the customers' image:

> IT IS OFTEN EXCEEDINGLY DIFFICULT
> TO UNDO THE GOOD
> THE DO-GOODERS DO.

The habitués of the North Star found it a place of retreat from all that smelled of anything but whiskey and good food—and they intended to keep it that way. For in an hour, more or less, they knew they must return to the old building and rediscover the appalling follies of their fellow men.

The patrolmen of the mounted detail did not hear the noon signal because their anachronistic horses were not equipped with radios. They rode in the sunlit park trying to keep their fellow men from despoiling it by open fornication on the greens, defecating in the goldfish ponds, strewing garbage through the flowers, or seducing children bound for the zoo. The men on the mounted detail were deeply attached to their horses and held them in great respect because their equine dignity contrasted so favorably with what the men had seen in the park.

Other mounted men waited at certain street corners each weekday noon for the exodus from school. They did little except sit casually on their horses and greet those small students they knew. But their presence caused the demented to keep away and the idiot driver to slow down.

The tourists in Chinatown became less ubiquitous at noon, and certain more genuine activities slowly began. On the street where Sally Chew systematically abused her frail body, three laundries became abnormally active, although a customer so naïve as to bring in a dirty shirt would find a stony welcome. For the activity was in the back room of the laundry . . . to which the more sophisticated customers had a key. Here the games of fan-tan, pie-kew, and sometimes mah-jongg commenced for the day. Further along the street, other establishments, which had previously appeared to be deserted store fronts, hung red paper inscribed with certain characters in the dusty windows. The artistic characters simply announced that the place was open for business. Here a lottery enthusiast could test his luck with a stake in Doo Far or Bok Op Bui.

Later in the afternoon, certain other discreet advertisements would be displayed along the street, and to the untutored eye they would be meaningless. But to others, the characters which spelled out "White Sparrow" or "Young Willow" meant a prostitute waited upstairs. In recent years these signs had become very rare.

All of these things were understood and appreciated by the men of the Chinatown detail, but they might as well not have understood. Certainly they could break into a game, and if they were very quick indeed, they might find cards on the table. But usually every bit of evidence had magically disappeared and a hundred Oriental eyes would silently ask what monumental foolishness this could be. It was much less frustrating to stroll in the noonday sun, stopping occasionally to greet a Chinese friend and inquiring what was new—with the certain knowledge that whatever was really new would not be revealed to an Occidental policeman until it was very old.

Gambling was against the law, a fact which left the old-school Chinese incredulous, until some countryman with a fuller understanding of the Occidental's mysterious ways tried to explain; after

which both old- and new-school Chinese were equally dismayed.
How could any race, however barbarian, prohibit the flow of blood
through an artery? At least the men of the Chinatown detail, who
were students of such affairs, knew that gambling would always
flourish wherever more than two Chinese gathered. Therefore they
were tolerant and, except for an occasional raid to save face, they
had developed a special blindness.

It was better anyway to let the Chinese police themselves, which
they did so efficiently that the crime rate of the area was the lowest
in the city. Yet there was still the Chinese temperament, which
those who did not know Orientals thought to be calm and in-
scrutable. The men of the Chinatown detail knew it to be volcanic
and were never surprised when in a fit of displeasure one of their
charges chased another down the street with a meat ax.

Although violence was now banned by mutual agreement, the
On Leong Tong and the Hip Sing Tong still exerted a powerful
influence on Chinatown affairs, and what they did not administer
directly was handled by the Six Companies, a benevolent association known to the men of the Chinatown detail as "Look Dai
Gung See."

At noon, Inspector Crane of the detail walked casually past
the souvenir shops which were so familiar to him. The smoke from
his cigar mixed with the smell of incense designed to lure prospec-
tive customers out of the midday air. He was a very heavy and
solid man with strangely merry eyes and a deep, infectious laugh.
These attributes were of particular value when he set aside his
gun and cuffs each year and squeezed his bulk into a Santa Claus
costume. He was so convincing in the role, the Chinese children at
the Catholic school accepted his gifts of candy and worn-out jokes
just as solemnly as if they did not know he was Inspector Crane.

His passage along the street was as unhurried and amiable
as a successful alderman's strolling through his own small town.
He greeted by name John Joe who was a cook, Marvin Kee who
was a merchant, Leslie Choy who giggled and said if Crane
would come to his restaurant he would urinate in his soup, and
Fong Sam Lee who stuffed a cigar into Crane's pocket in honor of
his new son. All of these persons laughed easily in the noon light

when Crane repeated a joke they had heard at least twice. They neither feared nor resented his hearty pats on their shoulders, which because of the difference in their sizes almost sent them spinning. He was a part of the area—like the stylized lampposts, the overhanging balconies, and the tinkle of glass wind bells along the street. He could be seen coming the length of Chinatown—which was often convenient. And so there could be no harm in greeting Inspector Crane with enthusiasm. Two of the men he greeted had entered the country illegally and were still paying protection to their tongs lest their fortune be soured by an ill word to the immigration authorities. The others, by heritage alone, had seen all the trouble they ever wanted to see.

Far from Chinatown there was a section of the city where the mounted police could not chaperon the noon exit from school because it was conceivable that the students would have found some means to throw pepper in the horses' eyes or even to geld them. There was a high school from which every student emerged lighting a cigarette. There were no exceptions. They were students only because the law said they must be until they were eighteen. To be seen carrying a book was regarded as being a gopher and therefore inviting a beating. The girl students did the carrying of shivs, dusters, zips, and rolls of nickels tightly bound, which made a mallet of their true loves' fists. The girls had relatively unimpressive juvenile records, so if they were caught with such weapons it was better for all concerned. So many of their loves had already wasted valuable loving and fighting time when detained by the juvenile authorities. Both sexes found the experience boring.

As armor against their gnawing insecurities, the male loves wore the uniform of their units, which consisted of fabric windbreakers or leather jackets with the exact designation emblazoned across the back. The DRAGONS, BARBARIANS, SINNERS, MOONLIGHTERS, BOLT AND NUT were all represented by young men with long sideburns and a complete absence of joy. They walked into the noonday sun, squinted at it with the same feigned hatred they squinted at everything, put their arms about the waists of their sallow females, and sauntered defiantly away. Their exit from the school was like a tribal dance, slow-moving at the beginning, then gathering pace through the performance which took place five noons a week and was repeated at three-thirty in the afternoon. The antagonists passed each other with formalized gestures, walking as if the pavement was searing hot, taking care to look directly and unflinchingly at the two policemen who sat in the patrol car on the corner. Sometimes when they passed the car, the boldest loves would spit, or simply stop for a moment, stare fixedly at the policemen, and then continue on their way. They were annoyed when the officers failed to show the slightest reaction and became even more irritated when they saw the officers were not lobster-faced old men with vast bellies. There was about them an air of privilege and acceptance which so disturbed the loves, they were compelled to take a special hitch at their pants, and only those with wisps of mustaches managed to maintain a proper state of defiance.

Officer Rosenburg sat behind the wheel with a paperback edition of *The Decline and Fall of the Roman Empire* on his lap. He had read it once in college and now he intended to absorb it in a more leisurely fashion. He was a very serious young man with a special fondness for brooding on civilizations long gone.

"We are running out of time," he said to Dillon, his partner, who had long since stopped listening to him. "Somewhere the decay begins and there is no real way to stop it. In another three or four hundred years—"

"Who cares?" said Dillon, who heard the last part in his subconscious because he had heard it so many times before. Sitting for eight hours a day in the same car with Rosenburg, week after week, had convinced him the time would have passed more quickly if only Rosenburg knew something about baseball.

"Like I told you four hundred times, I don't give a damn what happens four hundred years from now," Dillon said. He pushed his cap forward until he could just see the faces of the passing loves beneath the edge of the visor. "They ought to put us out here in plain clothes. Nothing is going to happen with us hanging around in uniform."

"I guess that was the idea," Rosenburg said. He stopped reading and watched the parade of youths. He concentrated on their hostile faces and thought that he understood their need to move in packs and the constant urge to assert themselves against each other. As they boldly met his stare, he saw the declaration of war in their eyes and he wondered which of the loves had conceived their newest form of after-school play. It was a cruel refinement of the understandable conflicts among themselves. Now it was the fashion to prowl the whole area searching for elderly men who might be out for a stroll. The Veterans' Hospital was a rich provider for their needs. They would challenge their victim with a "Hi, daddy, what's doin'?" Then they would casually encircle their prey, even offering to help him across the street if he appeared infirm. When the man was sufficiently bewildered, one of them would reach for his pants and yank at his fly. And another would say, "Hey, daddy, you forgot to button your pants." And when the old man looked down, the first love would strike and then another and another and another, until the old man vanished in their midst. When he was beaten insensible, the sport was gone and so they left him lying in his own blood. Those loves who were chicken were not allowed to play.

"I think I've made one of our friends," Dillon said, using the standard police term of recognition. "The big fellow, two couples back. The one with the redheaded girl. He's been picked up by Juvenile until they're sick of him. His real name is Chelsy, but none of the kids dare call him that. They call him the Hammer."

"The Hammer?"

Then Rosenburg saw a youth who stood out from the others only because of his bulk. His size was grotesque for a boy who had to be less than eighteen. He still carried enough baby fat to give him an incongruous belly, and his shuffling walk seemed contrived to move him along with a minimum expenditure of energy. A scattered bouquet of pimples surrounded his slack mouth, and his eyes were sleepy and dull.

As he passed, Rosenburg leaned slightly forward for a better look at the fat boy who was called the Hammer. And for an instant he wondered if he was looking into the face of the day after tomorrow. . . . The day could easily come when one of his beatings would kill, and there was nothing to do but wait until it happened.

He was about to ask Dillon who he thought should be held responsible for such a face when the radio clicked and they both listened to the familiar voice from Communications: "A holdup in progress at 15th and Cypress. . . ."

That would be only ten blocks from where they sat.

Even as they made a U-turn and reversed direction, neither Rosenburg nor Dillon held any hope of being the first to arrive. It usually took a minute or a minute and a half for a call to be processed through Communications. Their progress for the ten blocks would be only a little faster than the normal traffic because to use red flasher and siren would merely frighten away the man who might still be in the vicinity. So it would take another three minutes, perhaps four, to reach the small grocery store on the corner. By that time a solo bikeman might be on the scene, or possibly another car from their own station.

It made no sense, Rosenburg thought as he took a careful look at the intersection ahead and then continued through a stop light. For six hundred dollars a month why should any man be in such a hurry to get himself shot at? All policemen would firmly deny the existence of any such desire, but their actions often seemed to contradict them. On a holdup the primary danger was a collision with another patrol car en route to a place where there was an excellent possibility of being shot at. It's a twist in our brains, Rosenburg had finally decided. The same twist which causes a man to become a cop in the first place. We're little boys who have never stopped playing cops and robbers, and the bullets are television bullets until they hit. We are trying to live up to an image, some of which is national heritage and the rest is something we created artificially. We are to-the-rescue a hundred times a day, sniffing the sweet odor of superiority. Never mind the public. We're playing hero to ourselves.

Rosenburg had tried to explain this urge to his wife when she would speculate on how much better they might be doing financially if he would just try another career. But his explanations had always failed because he could not find rational answers. His ineptness depressed him until he finally knew that there was no clear or even sensible reason why one sort of man should *choose* to police others. It was the same with the habitual outlaws. Both categories were compelled by some basic force in which money became only a symbol. It was conflict, something a man apparently needed as much as food.

There was a crowd around the store. A police car had already been angled into the curb. Rosenburg came to a stop alongside it. He saw that it was an Accident Investigation car and thought unhappily that he might as well have taken his time. Two men who were normally supposed to be measuring the distance between skid mark A and skid mark B and decorating the pavement with their chalk were savoring a little hero tonic.

They pushed through the crowd. Inside the store they found Bailey and Teller of Accident Investigation listening to a perspiring, balloonlike woman who alternately screamed and broke into incoherent moaning.

"What took you so long?" Bailey asked. Rosenburg understood his satisfied grin and tried not to resent it.

"All right," he sighed. "Go back to sweeping up your broken glass. We'll take it from here."

"If it will make you feel any better, we happened to be around the corner," Bailey said easily. "From what I can find out from this lady, he was a round man with a flat head and he ran backwards."

All very funny, Rosenburg thought as he watched Bailey and Teller leave the store. No one was being shot at this noon, but supposing it had been like so many other times when the man with the gun was still open for business? The crowd outside the scene of any holdup, which some mysterious human telegraph system brought together more efficiently than any police radio, always revealed the situation. If there was a crowd, you could be sure everything was over. If there was not, watch out. Which proved, Rosenburg thought, that the average citizen was smarter than a cop. The ordinary holdup man couldn't hit a sleeping buffalo at ten yards, but there was always the one who was not average. Or he might be just plain lucky. And for being shot at and not running away, which was unthinkable, Bailey and Teller, and possibly Dillon and himself, if things were still hairy enough, *might* have been eligible for a "meritorious"—which was a nice item to have on record when promotion time came along. And according to the amount of shooting involved, and whether a successful capture had been made, there would be a bonus of fifty or a hundred dollars for violating common sense and giving in to a basic urge.

Rosenburg, who had been shot at twice in the past year without qualifying for more than a commendation, had sometimes wondered if a cop had to be dead before he was a true hero.

A solo bikeman came through the door. He was all creaking leather and white crash helmet and had that special swagger which Rosenburg always found annoying. Solo bikemen were paid sixty-six dollars a month extra for stomping around in their boots and snarling up traffic and making like Marlon Brando, but as far as Rosenburg was concerned, they could have their gaudy costume and extra pay. Only a crazy man would risk his neck cowboying a motorcycle through wet streets, and the rest of the population outweighing him by tons. Their casualty list was frightful, and there was not a single solo bikeman on the force who had escaped at least one spell in the hospital. In his more tolerant moments Rosenburg admitted they had a certain esprit and drank of the hero tonic whenever they could.

"Let's see now," Rosenburg said casually to the bikeman. "What was it you wanted?" It was a rare opportunity. Because they could slip through traffic, solo bikemen were all too often first on the scene.

"Overtime," the bikeman said. "I was on my way in to the station."

"Next time get faster transportation," Rosenburg replied. "So long."

Now the holdup and all concerned with it belonged to Rosenburg and Dillon. It had happened on their beat. When their duty time was over, they could spend an hour or so composing a report and typing it on the ancient typewriter. Eventually it would be sent to the old building, where it would be studied by the inspectors in Armed Robbery. They might try to find the man if there was any hope, but there would be at least ten other similar reports from outlying stations, plus an accumulation of previous incidents. Holdups were good business if a man picked his locations with care and was quick to leave the vicinity. It was almost the only way hypes could continue to satisfy their needs.

"What time were you held up, ma'am?" Rosenburg took out his notebook, pressed the end of his ball-point pen, and waited patiently for the woman to answer. She had stopped moaning, but she puffed so hard between words Rosenburg had great difficulty in following her.

"I dunno! I dunno . . . it was just before noon!"

"And what did the man look like?"

"Well, he was tall . . . no, he wasn't very tall, and he had a hat on."

"What kind of a hat?"

"A *hat!* A hat's a hat! Oh, he took all my money and helped himself to the cigarettes." She drew a handkerchief from between her huge breasts and puffed violently while she mopped at her face.

"How much money?"

"About twenty dollars."

"What race was he?"

"Whaddya mean?"

"Was he a white man, black, or yellow?"

"White."

"How much would you say he weighed?"

"Well, he was sort of thin . . . you know like—"

"A hundred and fifty pounds . . . hundred and forty?"

"Who knows? He was not so thin really."

"What was he wearing?"

"A hat. I told you."

"Is that all?"

"No. He had pants on and a shirt."

"What did he say to you?"

" 'Give me your money.' Just like that he said, 'Give me your money.' "

"Is that all he said?"

"Yeah. He said, 'Don't call the police or I'll come back and kill you.' "

"Is that *exactly* what he said?" At least this much could be useful, Rosenburg knew. If and when the inspectors found any suspects, they could order them to repeat the same words and hope the woman could identify the voice.

"Exactly."

"What kind of a gun did he show?"

"I dunno. I don't know anything about guns except they scare me."

"Was it black, silver, big or little?"

"Well, it looked big to me. Especially the end of it."

"Was he driving a car?"

"I dunno. All of a sudden he was standing right there."

"Did you see him leave?"

"No. I ducked down behind the counter." Demonstrating, she disappeared behind the counter for a moment. The people who had crowded into the store laughed.

"Did you hear a motor going?"

"I wasn't listening to nothin' except my heart."

The people who had crowded into the store laughed again, and Rosenburg saw that the woman was beginning to enjoy herself. It is not every day, he thought, when she can attract and hold so much attention.

"There may be a couple of inspectors in to see you this afternoon or tomorrow morning." Rosenburg handed his notebook to Dillon and told him to radio the information into Communications.

"What are you going to do about it?" the proprietor demanded. "You should catch that man."

"This is a big city. We'll do the best we can."

"Well, I declare! What are we payin' taxes for? He's a million miles away by now."

"You're probably right, ma'am. Next time take a better look."

Rosenburg gave her a little salute and walked out the street door. He stood for a moment in the sun and studied the crowd.

"Did any of you see a car leave here?"

His only answer was silence. After a moment he moved through the crowd to join Dillon. Behind him he heard a man say, "Those dumb cops can't catch a cold."

True, Rosenburg thought unhappily. Where was the taste of hero tonic now?

✧✧✧ 23 ✦✦✦

Not all juvenile affairs were resolved in Juvenile Hall, which had been specifically designed for them. Citizens of self-importance often convinced themselves it was better to take their problems directly to the highest authority. So it was, as the noonday sun exposed the stark ugliness of the old building, that Sergeant Boyd took a telephone call from a man who insisted on talking to the Chief of Police. His seventeen-year-old daughter had been arrested the night before.

"Now my daughter might have been involved in a little harmless mischief, but we should recognize young people will be young people and an ice-cream soda never hurt anybody. The man who runs that drugstore is a sorehead, but that is not the important thing."

Boyd heard the man's voice rising in sudden fury.

"Now," the man yelled, "I don't like this highhanded business of carting my daughter off to Juvenile Hall. And furthermore, the cop who arrested my daughter took his own sweet time getting there. He went way out toward the beach, where he stopped the car and made indecent advances to my daughter. If the Chief doesn't fire that cop immediately I'll call the Mayor! And if the Mayor doesn't fire him I'll get up a citizens' committee and we'll tar and feather him!"

Boyd knew all about the fracas in the drugstore although such minor affairs were not included in the daily crime report. A small group of teenagers had spiked their Cokes with straight alcohol and soon afterward decided to "remodel" the place. "Remodeling" in teen language was, as any policeman knew, translated as "wrecking." "Destruction projects" were "stimulating," and could rescue those involved from utter "melancholia." All the participants in this affair had been very sad listening to "fat backs" on the jukebox, and until some one of them had the idea of "remodeling" the place, the evening was all pretty much "hockey do." They had "played the dozens," which was to speak ill of one's parents, until they were sick of the subject, and they had exchanged all the tales of persecution by parents and teachers they could imagine. So when the suggestion to remodel was made, it was instantly recognized as a necessary lift for their "psyches." They were all "toastys," which identified them as residents of a nice neighborhood, and it was agreed that some release was "important." A person could become psychologically stunted just living in a nice neighborhood.

The proprietor of the drugstore had been inconveniently alert, and when the first patrol car arrived, the remodeling had barely begun. Only one shelf of cosmetics had been dumped on the floor.

Boyd sighed and wondered if everything would not have stopped right there—if Officer Hubbel had been anywhere else. Boyd knew him as a bully with a star, and he had long hoped that some day Hubbel would get himself in a big enough mess for Hill to make a case against him. It was never an easy thing to do. Firing a civil service employee, cop or not, took a vast amount of doing. Unless the case was airtight, the offending cop too often wound up with a month's vacation while his hearing was in progress. He often came off laughing at the efforts of his superiors and collected retroactive pay.

One of the teenagers had said Hubbel looked like a baboon, which Boyd considered a perfect description. Instead of being patient and using his head, Hubbel used his fist. By that time some twenty other teenagers had gathered to watch the fun. The resulting rhubarb took four patrol cars and three solo bikemen to keep it from becoming a full-scale riot. Finally the most belligerent teenagers, including one girl who had kicked Hubbel in the groin, were packed off to Juvenile Hall. Hubbel deserved it, but . . .

"Do you know the name of the officer who escorted your daughter to Juvenile Hall?" Boyd asked.

"No. But his badge number is 7081. If you don't let me talk

to the Chief, I'm coming down there and break down his door!"

"May I call you back in five minutes, sir?"

"It better be no more than five minutes and it better be with an appointment to see the Chief."

Boyd wrote down the man's telephone number and hung up. He checked the map of the city which he kept beneath the glass on his desk. Then he checked his list of badge numbers and found the name Malone opposite 7081. He knew Malone only casually, but remembered him as a rather shy man who had been twice wounded in Korea. He called Malone's station and asked for the number of the car he had been driving the night before. Finally he telephoned Communications and asked for a quick rundown on car times.

Boyd called the man back in less than five minutes.

"Sir, I suggest you have another talk with your daughter. She was taken into car 21 at 11:17 last night. The speedometer reading was 9,202. She was delivered to the juvenile authorities six minutes later and signed over by Officer Malone to Matron Wilson. The speedometer reading was exactly 9,205. It is three miles from the drugstore to Juvenile Hall."

There was a long silence on the other end of the line.

"Every time a girl juvenile enters and leaves a patrol car the mileage and times are radioed into headquarters."

"Yeah?" The man grumbled something unintelligible, then he said, "Well . . . we'll see what's at the bottom of this."

Boyd heard the receiver click. The bottom, he thought, was an attempt at vengeance by a little girl who must now be convinced all cops were baboons, like Hubbel.

✧✧✧ 24 ✦✦✦

In an apartment on Twelfth Street, Harriet Rankin sat at the kitchen table in her bathrobe. She smeared an extra blob of peanut butter on her fourth piece of bread. She licked the knife clean and then sank her perfect white teeth into the bread until her upper lip was buried in the peanut butter. She didn't care if peanut butter *was* fattening like her aunt always kept saying. It was good and it soothed her nerves on this very exciting day.

Harriet looked at the electric clock on the kitchen wall for the fifth time in as many minutes and saw it was still running. It was almost twelve-thirty, which it had certainly taken forever to be. Now all she had to do was wait until two o'clock when the police said they would come for her. In a car of her own, if you please. La-dee-da. Like a queen. All she would have to do, they had explained on the phone, was sit in some kind of a theater and look at some men and say they did it.

It was about as exciting a thing as anybody could ask for. But what in the world was she going to do until two o'clock? There was Caesar, the cat, to talk to, and nobody else. She could feel him brushing along her bare legs beneath the table. He was smart enough to be human, that cat. Maybe he was. Maybe he was a reincarnation or something like that. Sometimes he looked at her just like Uncle Carl looked at her. Holy cats! That crazy man! He sure didn't feel like going off to work this morning and he never would have made it if Aunt Helga didn't have to go too.

It was most interesting being alone like this instead of having lunch with a bunch of dull poops at school. A regular *public* school. Ugh! Well, that would change now.

But what in the world to do with all this time? You could eat just so much peanut butter. You could have a beer—the icebox was mostly filled with beer. No, because the police would smell it and think probably you're a drunkard and they would tell Miss Baker at school and she would never give you a recco to the new private school, and holy cats, things would be worse than ever.

She wiped the mixture of peanut butter and lipstick from her lips with a paper napkin. Then she pushed away the table, revealing Caesar, and she said to him, "I suppose you're going to come and ogle while I get dressed. Well, ogle away all you want, you nasty old man."

She walked stiffly to her little room, which was just off the kitchen. She hurt in a lot of places, kind of all over, but at least the swelling around her right eye had gone down. And it didn't make any difference how much she hurt if people would just keep their promises.

She opened the cardboard box which served as her hanging closet and poked without interest at the clothes inside. Finally she looked down at Caesar and said, "I think I'll wear a sweater and skirt. And I'll swipe Helga's stone necklace. It's real square."

She took her green sweater and gray skirt into the big bedroom where Helga slept with Uncle Carl. There was a full-length mirror on Helga's closet door and sometimes Harriet would come home early from school just to stand in front of it and look at herself. Being alone and looking at yourself was interesting. Especially when you could act out things.

Now she stood before the mirror where occasionally she had carefully studied her entire body without any clothes on, and even touched herself sort of experimentally. She pulled back the bathrobe so she could see if the bruises were still on her shoulder. She let the robe fall away until she could examine the ugly discoloration on one side of her right breast.

She looked at her face. Her eye really was much better and her mouth didn't have that puffy look she had noticed in her small mirror when she had first awakened. There was still a little peanut butter left in the corner of her mouth so she wiped it away with her forearm. And she said to Caesar, "By two o'clock maybe my eye will be even better if I use a lot of Helga's eye shadow. If the cops bring me back right away like they promised I'll still have plenty of time to take it off before anybody gets home from work."

She let her bathrobe slip to the floor and stood gazing at her nakedness for several minutes. She stood on tiptoe, raised her arms above her head, and made a series of undulating movements with her hips. Finally she sighed audibly. She was vaguely annoyed when Caesar seemed to lose interest.

✦✦✦ 25 ✦✦✦

If he was going to meet Theo Lasher at three, there was no time for a leisurely lunch. Now all of Lasher's record was piled beside Hill's glass of milk and ham sandwich. There was probably more to Lasher's history in other cities, but even this amount was imposing. It was a true phenomenon, Hill thought, that such a list of misdeeds could be achieved by a man who was still as free as he pleased. In addition to the record, Hill had sent for Barnegat, whose brain seemed to hold some special acid which etched criminal histories forever on his memory.

Hill had forgotten that some of the record went back as far as the thirties, when Lasher was still an uncomplicated torpedo. Those exploits, mostly assaults, were not of much use now except as background. But Hill found the more recent record unsatisfying because of a curious omission. In 1958 Theo Lasher had been arrested on suspicion of murder. Hill had been in Wisconsin on an extradition matter, and since he was still an inspector then, all he knew of Lasher's activities came from police gossip and the newspapers. Now he remembered how the body of one Harry Bandaneria had been found stuffed in the trunk of his car, bound with wire, and his pants pulled down to his ankles. The newspapers had refrained from describing how Bandaneria's right arm had been lashed back underneath the wire and the third finger of his right hand inserted in his rectum. It was a typical Mafia stunt, in fact a deliberate identification, intended to keep all others who dealt with the organization in line.

The last man known to have been seen with Bandaneria was Theo Lasher. And Lasher would know how the Mafia liked things done. But apparently nothing had come of it. According to the record Lasher had been released on five thousand dollars bail two days after the arrest. Hill searched carefully, but he could not find any final disposition of the charge, or even whether the bail had been forfeited. So Lasher must have had an airtight alibi. Or did he? Ask Barnegat when he arrived. Barnegat would know. Barnegat knew everything.

There was a new file Hill had just received from the District Attorney's office that might be of more practical use. The offense involved was so minor it seemed a ludicrous charge to hang around Theo Lasher's fat neck, yet it just might be enough to drive him out of town. Two tapes had been sent along with the written material. Hill had played them through before his lunch. Now as he sipped at his glass of milk, he turned on the recording machine and listened again to one of several telephone conversations between a man and a woman. The man's voice was hoarse and Hill recognized a trace of Southern accent. The girl sounded young and well educated. And genuinely frightened, he decided. She should have been an actress.

After the phone rang, Hill heard her answer and the man said, "Listen, honey, you ain't got a thing to worry about."

"Well, I'm scared."

"Don't be. Everything is under control."

"But I think they're watching me."

"So what? The worst can happen is they fire you."

"But I don't want to get fired."

"Look. You're gettin' a fat check every week, ain't you? It's more than the printing company pays. And we got a hundred better jobs we can fix you up with if anything should happen."

"Who's *we?*"

The man laughed hoarsely, then he said, "What do you care? You gotta trust us."

"Well, gee . . ." she sighed. "I ought to know who I am working for."

"Just you bring the pages like you been doin', have your meal hour, and enjoy it."

"Okay."

"I'll have you back at work in thirty minutes."

"Maybe we better meet a little farther down the street."

"All right, honey. We'll make it in front of that filling station on the north side. By the way, how are the kids?"

"Fine. Don't forget the money."

"Don't worry, I tell you. One of these days I'll take you and the kids and we'll go out somewhere in the country and have a picnic."

"I sure don't like all this. It makes me nervous."

"You're doin' it for the kids, ain't you? You gotta do things you don't like for kids sometimes. It's part of being a mother."

"You're telling me."

"Now quit worrying. And don't be late like you was last time. We only got about fifteen minutes real workin' time as it is."

"Okay. I'll be there."

Hill heard the click of receivers and switched off the recording machine. He smiled and clasped his powerful hands together. The brain of Theo Lasher, he thought, was a marvelous contraption. It considered *almost* everything.

The border between illegal and legitimate business had become so very thin it was often only a matter of legal semantics. So why shouldn't Lasher join the cynical parade? Under the guise of the most pompous respectability, many insurance companies knowingly deceived and exploited every gullible customer they could find. Other less sophisticated enterprises were no more evil, yet because they fouled a legal technicality they could sometimes be stopped. But in all of them, trying to identify the principals was like chasing butterflies in a high wind. Lasher had expensive lawyers who knew how to outdate laws as fast as they were made. If they were clever enough they could even make a dubious enterprise seem like a public benefit. For example, this telephone numbers racket was a perfect display of the modernized criminal mind at work.

Brooding upon what he had heard on the tape, Hill understood why his city had been chosen along with several others. It was growing rapidly. Together with its environs, some three hundred new people took residence each day; which made over two thousand a week, which made eight thousand a month. A high percentage of the new arrivals ordered a telephone. Their names and addresses were held by the telephone company until they could be included in the regular book, which was published only once a year.

There was no means of knowing who all these people were

or where they had decided to live, but those who had ordered telephones could be contacted soon after arrival.

Their presence was of great interest to milk companies, furniture salesmen, laundries and appliance firms, all anxious to serve new customers.

Yet the telephone company was uncooperative, refusing to reveal the names of new subscribers no matter what the excuse. The daily list of new names and transfers was kept in a safe at the printing office where the next directory was always in preparation.

A laundry or a milk company would be willing to invest thirty dollars in a list of two hundred-odd names, knowing that out of the total they would certainly realize ten new customers.

Hill's arithmetic was so slow he had always been ashamed of it, yet he could easily calculate the impressive total in his head. If the same list could be sold to *ten* laundries in various parts of the city, the combined income was three hundred dollars a day. Ten furniture stores, another three hundred. Ten insurance men, rug salesmen, perhaps half a dozen bakeries, and at least two dairies, brought the grand total to a figure that would interest Theo Lasher. And if the enterprise could function in ten cities at the same time . . .

The only problem was to obtain the lists of new names regularly. For a resourceful man like Lasher this presented only a minor challenge. The initial approach had been made directly to a young widow who worked as a proofreader. If during her lunch hour she could remove the lists from the printing shop for only thirty minutes, she would be paid handsomely.

She was a smart girl, Hill thought, and loyal. She had told her boss of the offer. He advised her to accept and called the District Attorney's office. Though she ran the risk of a beating if her duplicity was discovered, the girl had carried out her part of the bargain. For more than a month she had been "stealing" the lists from beneath the watchful eyes of her employers. She carried the lists between the pages of a newspaper when she went to lunch, and handed them to one Toby. He rushed them to a photocopy machine which had been especially set up in a nearby apartment. Toby was working within a margin of minutes, but so far he had always managed to finish with the lists before the girl's lunch hour was over.

If Lasher was involved, why had his lawyers been so careless? They must certainly know that taking *anything* on which a value could be placed, even a business letter or a simple used postage stamp, was committing petty theft. People *could* be sent to jail for it. Lasher need only have instigated the project and he could be charged with conspiracy to commit petty theft. It was an ironic legal mouthful to throw at a man with his heavy record, but he might find it very inconvenient to swallow. Especially now, Hill believed, when his time must be so valuable.

Hill was mentally rehearsing his opening gambit with Lasher when his telephone rang. It was Deneen at the bridge and he sounded harassed.

". . . I tried climbing up part way to him . . . just to see how serious he was. I didn't accomplish much. Maybe I'm getting old."

"What's your age got to do with it?"

"Well . . . when he shot at me I turned around and came back down."

"Did you think anyone would expect you to stay there for target practice?"

"Maybe I could have. He missed me a mile."

"You used your head."

"But it seems a shame. There's something about this guy . . . I can't explain it, but none of us out here want to lose him."

"And I don't want to lose any good cops. You stay away from him and keep the other boys away. That's an order."

"There's a wind coming up. If it blows as hard as it does some afternoons, he may get blown off the bridge whether he wants to go or not. Also there's some fog with the wind, and if it gets any heavier we won't be able to see him at all."

"Have you tried talking to him with a loud hailer?"

"Yes. It didn't work, but I must say it was an interesting conversation."

Hill was puzzled. And impatient. He wanted to think only of Lasher.

"What's the matter with you out there? Are you going crazy, too?"

"I'm just not certain this guy is really nuts. Every once in a while he makes good sense."

"We all do," Hill said sourly, "every once in a while."

"He may be completely out of sight before long. How about letting me get his family out here?"

Hill hesitated. He tried to envision the scene at the bridge, but again all he could see was the horrified faces, freckled—like the faces of his own family—looking up.

"No," he said finally. "It's too risky. It may be just what he's waiting for. I'll be damned if we're going to leave them with that memory."

"Supposing they show up? The radio boys are going to put it on the air and we'll have TV trucks any minute. It's a regular field day."

"Does anybody out there know his name besides you?"

"I don't think so."

"Ask the radio men to do us a favor for a change and keep quiet. Rope off both ends of the bridge if you have to, and keep all TV trucks at least a mile away. And keep me posted."

"Whatever you say, Chief. I hope you're right."

As he hung up the phone, Hill heard the rasp of Barnegat's voice. "What's on your mind, Chief?" It was typical of Barnegat not to inquire after anyone's well-being or stoop to orthodox remarks about the weather. "What's on your mind" was thrown out as a challenge. Barnegat could grumble in greater contentment if whatever was on Hill's mind was not important. Hill wondered if his snappishness might be a sign that he too was lonely. He instantly dismissed the idea. Barnegat was all steel.

"Theo Lasher is in town," Hill said casually.

"I know that."

Of course he did. Probably before I did, Hill decided.

"He had a rap against him for suspicion of murder in 1958?"

"Harry Bandaneria. Only it wasn't Harry who got the treatment. He's still alive and lives in Pine Woods, New Jersey. Where his friends can watch him."

"There was a corpse. If it wasn't Bandaneria, who was it?"

"Nobody knows."

"How come Lasher didn't stand for the rap? Or did he?"

"Because Bandaneria was picked up very much alive, or as alive as he could be while he was sitting on his ass by a hotel swimming pool in Phoenix. Lasher found him for us, or rather, found him to save his own neck. But it was a real rinkey-dink and Lasher was plenty nervous. He couldn't decide if he would be worse off with Bandaneria alive or taking his chances with a jury."

"You've lost me."

"It wasn't so complicated if you knew it was a put-up job all around. Lasher was getting to be a big boy and his Mafia friends didn't like it. They sent him two black hands, which he was foolish enough to ignore. So they decided they were tired of his company and chose Harry Bandaneria to do the job. But Bandaneria had just gotten married and was suddenly full of the milk of human kindness, plus he didn't want trouble on his honeymoon. So he arranged to meet Lasher in that saloon which used to be opposite the East Power Station. Bandaneria is a hood of few words. He came right out and told Lasher he had to kill him, but if Lasher would just go to Honolulu or some place far away and vegetate for a few years, he would renege on the job. Lasher knew he was in real trouble and promised to go. The only hitch was he didn't leave soon enough. This made the Mafia very unhappy with both men. All of a sudden it is Bandaneria who disappears. We found out later the only reason he was told to play dead instead of actually being shot for his neglect of duty was that the girl he married happened to be Marco Cassio's sister. It took a few more days until the Mafia had everything set up to frame Lasher, including a tip to us that he was the last man seen in Bandaneria's company."

Barnegat cleared his throat several times as if the series of *ahem*'s would also assist in clearing his memory. "I forget just how long it took between that first meeting between Bandaneria and Lasher and the time the main event went on. First they covered every hour Lasher was on the loose with one or more of their own boys who could be depended on to testify Lasher was a liar no matter what his alibi. Then they found some poor bum who even the coroner couldn't identify, gave him the turkey treatment and stuffed him in Bandaneria's car with all the trimmings. But Lasher was smarter than they were and desperate. He contacted everybody he ever knew and finally dug up Bandaneria, and you can't hang a man for a murder he didn't do. But one thing is for sure. Lasher will never be so scared again as he was of Harry Bandaneria. I think he got a complex out of it—I hear he won't even take an airplane that flies over New Jersey, much less drive through the state. He's convinced himself Bandaneria will catch up with him someday at an inconvenient time . . . and just maybe he will. If so, the mighty Lasher will be a basket case."

Well, well, Hill thought. There was another man who certainly must know what it was like to be lonely. One of his names was Theo Lasher.

"Is that all you want to know?" Barnegat asked. He took off his glasses, stuffed them in an old-fashioned case, and closed it with a loud pop. Hill decided he looked much less like a Presbyterian minister without his glasses. He looked more like a cop.

"When are you planning to make a pinch on this telephone directory deal?" Hill asked.

"Maybe next week. The girl is doing a good job, but so far we can't make the principals. We can pick up the runners any time we want, but they're nothin's. The guy on the phone is an ex-bookie named Toby who is just smart enough to use pay telephones and stay away from his bosses. Meanwhile those bosses are getting rich."

"Has it occurred to you there may be only one boss? Or that it might be Theo Lasher?"

Barnegat blinked at the light streaming through the windows and appeared to consider the possibility.

"He hasn't come to town just because he likes the climate."

"Maybe you won't have to make your pinch," Hill said. "Maybe the whole thing will be folded today."

"How are you going to arrange that?"

"I'm going to have a meeting with him this afternoon. If I can tie him up with this telephone deal maybe I can scare him out

of town. The trouble is none of his runners would dare squeal.
How am I going to know Lasher has ever heard of the idea?"

"You'll have to stop thinking in a straight line because you can
be sure Lasher isn't."

Barnegat paused and blinked his eyes owlishly, and for an instant Hill resented his patronizing air. Who did the old flatfoot
think he was talking to?

"Go along with him," Barnegat said. "Allow him the pleasure
of confirming his belief that there is no such thing as a completely
honest cop. Don't disillusion him. Tell him you want a cut or
you'll close his operation down. If he's in it, he'll oblige. If he
isn't, he can't."

"Where does that leave us?"

"Nowhere if he's clean. But if you can get him on tape, he's
hung."

"Thanks very much," Hill said sourly. "I'll just ask the individual to step up to the microphone."

"You're the Chief."

"And you're a wily old bastard. Do you want my job?"

"Thanks. I know when I'm well off."

It had been years since anyone in the department had seen
Barnegat smile and Hill was not entirely convinced that he had
done so now. But the impression lingered even after he left the
office. For sure, Barnegat had been laughing inside. For sure, he
was laughing, Hill thought, because he could not weep and he had
to do something. Maybe he was laughing because in one bitter
instant and in the face of a very petty crime, his basic helplessness
had been revealed.

It was hardly progress and certainly not satisfying to realize
that if Theo Lasher resolved not to leave the city, there were so
few legal tools to force him away. Barnegat knew the law in its
clumsiness could often protect the guilty. It could easily be Lasher
who would be doing the laughing.

Unless . . . Hill thought, unless . . .

Hill reached for the switch on his intercom and spoke to
Sergeant Boyd. He told him to go at once to the Bureau of Identi-

fication and take out all the photos he could find on Harry Bandaneria.

"Inspector Hardy is waiting to see you," Boyd said.

Hill hesitated. Couldn't Tim Hardy pick another time? Then he
remembered the look in Hardy's eyes as he stood on the steps of
the cathedral and he told Boyd to send him in.

The look of defeat was still in Hardy's eyes when he came
through the doorway. He does not even move the same way, Hill
thought. My friend is suddenly an old man.

"I guess you're pretty busy, Colin. I could come back later in
the day."

"Never too busy to see you," Hill said, hating the glib phrase
which he seemed to have spoken all too easily. If it had been the
old days he would have said, "Yes. I'm up to my neck. Now get
out of here and come back some other time." But he knew every
hour was like a long day for Timothy Hardy now, and the sagging
face, the drooping shoulders, were not a part of his old friend.
Something had to be done—right now.

"Well . . . ?" Hardy said, looking at his beefy hands as if he
were ashamed of them. "I guess whatever you wanted to see me
about must be pretty serious."

"It is, and maybe it isn't. I'm sure our trouble is only temporary."

"Our trouble?"

"I have to lay it on the line, Tim. It's one of those things. It
just looks like you need a rest."

"Like what do you mean by that?"

"You've been working too hard . . . or something," Hill said
lamely. Then suddenly Hardy raised his eyes and challenged him.
And Hill thought, If there is a man who's in danger of losing his
nerve in this room, it's me.

Hardy said, "Colin, are you trying to find a way to tell me I
haven't got what it takes any more? I'll be all right in a few days.
I'll admit the last couple of go arounds made me a little nervous,
but I'll come out of it all right. I—"

"Sure you will. But for the time being it just seems like you're in the wrong detail. I don't want to see you hurt or anybody else hurt. . . ."

"But I've been in Armed Robbery for six years . . . it's sort of my baby. You know that."

"Maybe that's just it. Maybe you're in sort of a rut and need a little change of atmosphere. Now I understand they need a good man in Auto detail. It happens to be a desk job, but at least you can keep dry and sleep nights."

Hardy seemed stunned. He rubbed at his mottled nose and shook his head uncertainly. "But I'm not that kind of a cop," he said finally. "You can't do this to me."

"Now come on, Tim. It would be just as much a cop's job as anything else. It's as important as letting some hooligan shoot at you . . . more so these days."

"I'm not interested."

"Then how about taking a leave . . . or we could call it a vacation. I think we can probably do something about a sick leave so you won't lose too much pay—"

"But I'm not sick."

"I know, I know. You look fine to me, but—"

"Colin. Why don't you level with me? You think I have the willies."

A silence fell between them. Hill looked at his friend's ugly face and knew that he must stop talking in circles. And for an instant he hated his job.

"You know better than I do that a man in your detail can't be jumpy. It's the nature of the beast. How are you going to feel if you should happen to be a little slow at just the wrong moment and something happens to your partner?"

"Are you basing your opinion on rumors?"

"Of course not!" Hill snapped out the words in spite of his determination to remain calm. The last thing in the world Tim Hardy needed just now was someone yelling at him. "It's just a sort of thing that can happen to any of us."

Hill went quickly to his desk and took a large envelope from the center drawer. He opened the envelope and pulled out four pistol targets. They were perforated with numerous holes, but not one of the bullets had struck within the black circles. He laid the targets before Hardy. "These are yours, Tim. From last week at the range. What kind of performance is that from a man who usually wins every match he's in?"

"That was a bad day."

"Sure it was. But in your present job you can't afford a bad day. That's when somebody gets hurt. But it isn't just because of these targets, Tim . . . and you know it. . . ."

Again a silence came between them. Hill could hear Hardy's heavy breathing, and he saw him reach for the back of his neck and prod thoughtfully at a wen. Somehow his heavy frame appeared to shrink, and when he reached for one of the targets his hand shook. He withdrew his hand at once and shoved it in his pocket where his fingers found some coins. He clinked the coins rhythmically.

"I'll take the leave, Colin. I don't know what I'll do with it. Maybe take a trip somewhere . . . although I never cared much about traveling. Maybe I'll go off my rocker and get married or something. You know, a bachelor, especially if he's not so young, shouldn't be let outdoors without an armed escort . . . and maybe there's some dame who's half blind. . . . You know what I mean?"

At the door Hardy put his hat on the back of his head and stood for a moment rattling the change in his pocket. Hill saw that he was trying very hard to smile. "Well," Hardy said, "I guess I'll see you . . . around."

Then he was gone and Hill stood like a weary lion in the desolation of his cage. It was some time before he could force his thoughts away from Timothy Hardy. He had somehow left behind him an impression that he was still in the room.

Hill prowled the perimeter of his cage and finally stopped by one of the windows. Looking out, he saw that the men who operated the bulldozers and the pile driver across the street from the old building were sitting in little clusters of five and six while they ate their lunches. They took great bites at their sandwiches, which always seemed to get stuffed in one side of their faces so that their cheeks were puffed out and the mound of food moved up and down like a slowly bouncing ball. The men were laughing and gesturing in the air with their sandwiches. Hill saw one man fill another's cup from his Thermos and it suddenly occurred to him that not one of the men was sitting alone. He counted the men. There were thirty-three. Thirty-three men who were comfortable inside and out. Thirty-three men who didn't have to give a damn about Timothy Hardy, a man on a bridge, Theo Lasher, or any of the cruelties people were going to inflict on each other before this day was finished. They had no need to concern themselves with the fact that a red-haired, rather mangy and uncertain lion was looking at them from his cage and envying them. I'll have to watch it, Hill thought. It's getting worse all the time. Wasn't there some way a chief could do his job without being so lonely?

He continued to watch the men across the street, although his mind returned to the bridge. Maybe the man was not insane. Maybe he took to the bridge because he was trying to ease another pain. Maybe he had been just too long alone.

IN THE AFTERNOON

✧✧✧ 26 ✦✦✦

It was a quiet noon hour all through the city. Near the end of
the hour a car from Southern Station and two solo bikemen tried
to keep traffic moving after a smashup on the East Freeway. It
was not easy. Other drivers insisted on slowing, even stopping, to
behold the ragout of blood, glass, and torn flesh hanging from
the windshield of one car, and the scorched white leg of a woman
protruding from beneath the smoking chassis of the other car.
There were three people in the mess and they were all dead.
The policemen were doing their best to prevent the staring drivers
and their gape-mouthed passengers from adding to the total. It
was dangerous work because the drivers were not looking where
they were going. They were anxious not to miss any detail of
the mixture.

Before the hour was done there were seven other traffic accidents in various parts of the city. But they were minor and without
gore, so not worth the attention of passing traffic. At each accident
the police refereed while the participants explained how the other
driver had been outrageously at fault.

During the hour thirty-seven tickets were written for parking
violations, five for speeding, one for reckless driving, and the balloon test was administered to one driver who claimed he had
not had a drop to drink although he had chosen a busy sidewalk as
a freeway.

There was only one fight, which occurred at Ginger's Bar, where
a day was not complete without some kind of a squabble. The
foot patrolman who quieted matters received a cut over his left
eye for his trouble, which displeased him because it would cost a
dollar and a half to have his blue uniform coat cleansed of his
own blood. No one was arrested. The participants, including the
officer, were all of Irish descent and so understood these things.

There were two small children who became lost on their way
home from school, were found, and finally delivered in tears to
their mothers, who were also in tears.

A lily-waver proudly exposed his private parts while he stood on a box opposite the plate-glass window of a restaurant. The working-girl patronage found it very difficult to concentrate on their food until the patrol wagon arrived. On the way to the city prison, the lily-waver threw an epileptic fit in the back of the patrol wagon. Officer Melrose of the Wagon detail managed to keep him from swallowing his tongue until they could reach the hospital.

A family fight occurred at the Spinoza residence on Fourteenth and Grand. There was considerable damage to the furniture, and the television set which had occasioned the fight was thrown out the window. But there were no serious physical injuries to either Mr. Spinoza, who objected to the television set being turned on during his after-lunch nap, or to his mustachioed wife, who wept at her inability to receive her favorite afternoon program, or to her sister-in-law Rosa Spinoza, who conceived the idea of throwing the receiver out the window in the first place. So after the usual admonitions to quiet down, which as usual went unheard, the police left.

A purse-snatching occurred at the busy corner of Webster and Ninth, and another on Harrison Street, which was almost deserted. Both purse-snatchers were long gone by the time the police were aware of the incidents.

When Theo Lasher finished his lunch, he belched volcanically and found that he was still discontented. So he ordered a second parfait, which was half melted by the time it arrived in his suite. He left it nearly untouched. The omission aroused a new hunger. So he telephoned to the hotel barber shop and asked for a manicurist. It always soothed him to watch a manicurist work on his nails. Somehow their white uniforms made him at first vastly content, and then slowly and invariably aroused him. There had even been lucky times when the girls had been understanding. For an extra fee they would, without his so much as leaving his chair, allow him to enjoy additional pleasant sensations.

❖❖❖ ✦✦✦

In the crime lab, which was a cramped and makeshift affair on the roof of the old building, Matthews, the criminologist,

worked right through his normal lunch hour because Inspector
Moore wanted to know about the Perez boys' pants as soon as
possible. And though Matthews was a specialist with eyes trained
to detect the most minute signs through his microscope, he could
not discover any evidence of semen or blood on the Perez' pants.
Matthews knew it would not necessarily prove anything if he did.

✧✧✧ ✦✦✦

In the press room Spearing chewed on a cheese sandwich which
his wife had slapped together for him in a rare moment of early
morning tenderness. But her solicitude for his welfare was limited
and the sandwich was utterly tasteless. The pickle she had
tossed in with the sandwich as a condiment had been squashed
while Spearing was en route to the old building, and its juice made
most of the sandwich soggy. This pleased Spearing. It proved that
his wife's head was full of nothing but pin-curlers, which was
exactly what he had told her just before he departed. Anyone who
would put a wet pickle in anything without wrapping it separately
was a slovenly slob in pin-curlers, and cold cream, and cigarette
ash deposits all over the front of her bathrobe, bottomed off with
pink slippers with red pompons, which was sure one hell of a
clash to look at every morning, all of which was also exactly what
he had told her. But he would be damned if he would go out to
any restaurant for his lunch. Not when they were all operated by
cunning thieves who got rich poisoning the public with last week's
leftovers. Spearing had often bared his prominent teeth, which
were so big for the rest of his head, and declared that he was
not a human garbage pail willing to balance out the restaurateurs'
mistakes in overordering. The villains could all go bankrupt as far
as he was concerned.

✧✧✧ ✦✦✦

In the apartment which was so cozy, it was well past noon before she remembered two very personal things about Thelma. The
personal things offered such possibilities she was compelled to pace
around and around her apartment in ever tightening circles.
Thelma, you silly bitch! You talk too much. So you better kiss
Otto goodbye forever!

When we were all still just friends, before you really got your fangs in Otto, you told me a little secret. You said you knew I would know you dyed your hair . . . but did I know the best way to keep your whole body youthful and your skin like cream was to take a very hot bath every evening? You must make it a ritual. You must steam in a tub for at least thirty minutes without fail . . . every day. Which was why you went right home from the office so faithfully and took a long hot bath with salts and all that junk and then claimed the wrinkles and sagging flesh just melted away. And so did the cares of the world.

There was indeed a perfect place for a heart-to-heart, she thought. Timed just right, it could be in Thelma's bathroom.

✧✧✧ ✦✦✦

Beneath the marble steps in the old building, the man slept all through the noon period. He wiped a clean place on the floor with his frayed coat sleeve and put his head exactly in the center of the spot. He hooked one foot around the pedestal that supported the gumball machine, squirmed as if he were nesting in a bed of down instead of on a marble floor, and closed his eyes.

Tommie the blind newsdealer was the only person in the entire old building who was aware of the man's arrival or his subsequent activities. He heard the muted shuffle of his approaching footsteps through all the other sounds in the hallway. And he heard him wipe the marble and sigh and settle down.

He even heard him close his eyes.

✧✧✧ 27 ✦✦✦

Lowry stood in the entranceway of Miller's Department Store and watched the final moments of the noon hour. From his vantage point he could observe the four corners of the busiest intersection in the city. He watched Casovskie, the traffic cop, who had handled the intersection for years, and he wondered how many million times Casovskie had waved his arms and tooted his whistle and snorted in exasperation. Lowry was sorry for Casovskie. He thought that his lungs must be thoroughly corroded by carbon monoxide and his sense of accomplishment withered beyond hope of repair. The center of this city, like the center of every other city in the world, was the center of a village with delusions of grandeur. It had gorged too much and now nothing would pass. Its constipation was stupefying.

Lowry estimated that during the time he had been watching the intersection, which was less than an hour, some five thousand faces had floated across his line of vision. He supposed that he recognized a thousand or more, for they were the familiar habitués of his favorite hunting grounds. They were the pigeons of the surrounding area, as true to their stations, pace, group loyalties, and private sense of importance, as the other swarms of pigeons milling and strutting about the cornices and window ledges of the towering buildings.

Lowry sensed rather than saw the office workers, shoppers, and store employees. Their faces drifted past like the accents on an endless rippling carpet, and it was only when a face or figure violated the harmony of the basic design that Lowry became instantly alert.

The violation marked the passage through the throngs of a "cronkie" person.

No one knew precisely where or how the word "cronkie" had become the most important single word in police language. Some insisted it had been derived from an old Yiddish term describing one who is indisposed—*cronk*. Some believed it had been picked up long ago by the New York police when the East Side had an earthier character. Gradually the word had spread across the country, until policemen in every community found it the ideal solution to an age-old verbal problem. "Cronkie" served to specify an otherwise vexing collection of visual facts, ulterior hunches, and pure instinct. A cronkie person was one who, for a variety of reasons, was in trouble, had made trouble, or was about to make trouble. A cronkie did not fit into the surroundings or the environment either by action or apparel. Usually the signs were obvious and created a cronkie situation. There was reason to wonder what a man who wore a leather cap and a dirty shirt was doing in an expensive jewelry store. Likewise, a man in tails or dinner jacket who chose to linger about a pool hall was creating a cronkie situation—although the man himself might not qualify as a cronkie. One Negro talking to a white man on a lonely corner at night would not necessarily establish a cronkie situation. Two or more Negroes talking to a single white man in similar surroundings certainly would. There was always a why. A woman running in terror was not establishing a cronkie situation, although her action probably originated in one. But an older woman strolling arm in arm with a much younger man was not always escorting her son or her nephew to the symphony. A teenage youth in a jalopy was normal, but if he was driving a Cadillac sedan he created a cronkie situation no matter how carefully he respected the traffic laws. There was always a why.

The specifications for a cronkie person were not always so obvious. Sometimes the signals were mixed, or so subtle it took both talent and experience to be reasonably certain that something about the individual was not as it should be. In time every inspector of any worth developed a special sensory apparatus which enabled him to fix upon a cronkie person.

Now Lowry, whose devotion to the fraudulent amounted to a passion, watched the crowd as he did every working day, and all of his faculties were aimed at the separation of cronkies from the mass.

The bus stop across the street was sometimes productive of "bumpers." A man and a woman working as a team would board the crowded bus at opposite ends. They would work their way along the aisle toward each other, bumping fellow passengers and apologizing profusely. They would meet in the middle, pass at least one wallet which the man had collected, and leave the bus at opposite ends. Even if the theft was discovered, all attention went the wrong way.

Team bumpers were more difficult to spot than the lonely sex-bumpers who gratified their urges by bumping against or merely rubbing past as many women as they could contact.

Lowry also watched for street-bumpers, the majority of whom worked alone. A street-bumper carried a half-pint of whiskey and rinsed his mouth with it at regular intervals. Most were said to be strict teetotalers, which Lowry thought was doubtless a result of their constant occupational hazard. The perfectionist sprinkled whiskey over his coat lapels, shaved rarely, stained his fingers with iodine, and his coat with morsels of food. Thus equipped, he waited for a likely prospect, staggered into him and began a maudlin and affectionate pawing. Before the disgusted victim had made his escape, he would be relieved of his wallet. Most street-bumpers were accomplished actors.

Lowry watched for elements of the "Jamaica switch," although he knew it was unlikely that he would witness the full performance in this area. The scheme belonged on the waterfront, for which it was originally designed.

Lowry watched for a less naïve version of the "Jamaica switch" known as the "pigeon drop." It was a system practiced most often by women, and Lowry could not imagine why it was that the women involved were invariably fat. Lowry knew of one woman who had lost over four thousand dollars in a "pigeon drop"—her life's savings. He had heard her wails of anguish with but slight compassion because her cupidity had as much to do with her loss as her stupidity.

And Lowry watched for both women and men who might be carrying a coat over their arms on such a fine day. The innocent garment was a common tool of the professional shoplifter. When carelessly laid on a counter in any store, it provided a versatile instrument for removing all manner of things. The knack lay in knowing a potential shoplifter from a person who was simply carrying a coat over his arm.

The key was in sensing a cronkie. Lowry brooded for days afterward when he discovered he had been successfully deceived. On the occasion of such obvious failures he felt as he thought Casovskie must feel all the time. He was just waving his arms and tooting his whistle while smart cronkies passed him by.

✧✧✧ 28 ✦✦✦

The luncheon menu at the city prison was always limited. When Harry Welsh finished the spaghetti and coffee, he tossed his metal plate and cup in the slop wagon which was propelled along the row of cells by a trusty. He decided he would seek out the Perez brothers. If they had heard his record during the morning lineup, maybe they would now give him a cigarette without so much advice. He found them at the end of the cell block near the latrine. They were sitting side by side on the cement floor picking at their teeth with their fingernails. Welsh saw at once how their attitude had changed since their previous meeting.

Julio said to him, "Hey man, a course you can have a cigarette. Whyn't you tell us this morning you was a safe man?"

As befitted the recognition of his status, Welsh allowed Julio to light his cigarette and favored him with a tolerant smile.

"You never know," he replied, "who they put in here with you. Nosy guys annoy me. But now I see that you and your brother are all right." He paused and blew smoke straight upward. Then he said, "You had quite an evening."

"It didn't work out like we figured," Antonio said, staring morosely at his shoe. "And they're tryin' to hang the girl on us and it ain't so."

"Of course. Like I said, you never know who they put in here with you, so why should you tell me any different?"

Julio looked up and down the passage between the cell blocks at the other prisoners. Most of them were still slurping up their spaghetti. Then he looked at Welsh and studied him for a moment.

"How long do you figure to be away?" he asked in such a respectful tone that Welsh found no cause to consider him nosy. In fact the question mellowed him, as if a man of importance should warm to an inferior.

"It depends," he said, following the course of his smoke upward. "It depends if I can stay out of the jute mill. Last time it was easy because I am a good plumber. I kept the joint's whole system going and done over part of it. You meet people all through the joint when you got a job like that and they can see how you are rehabilitated."

"I see," said Julio respectfully.

"Maybe two years . . . maybe five this time. It depends. . . ."

"Sure, it all depends. . . ." Julio agreed. "I guess you thought I was way out callin' you a cherry this morning. . . ."

"Oh, that's okay."

"I would like to be a safe man, but I dunno," Julio said. "For one thing, I dunno how to go about it. And Jesus . . . you got to know."

Welsh laughed easily. He was finding the conversation very satisfying. At least it was better than sitting and waiting for some jerk cop to start all over again with his line of dumb questions. So now he jammed his fists down hard in his pockets, rocked back and forth on his feet, and all the while looked up quizzically at the rising smoke. His audience waited for the great man to speak again. Finally he tipped his head far back, screwed up the corners of his eyes and spoke to the rising smoke instead of the Perez brothers. His body was poised for a soliloquy, forbidding interruption. The cigarette pressed hard between his lips bobbed up and down in exact cadence with his speech.

"You got to be good with your hands," he began, "and there are many tricks which you got to know . . . one of which is using your head. Time on the job is what counts . . . seconds. Some guys don't know no better and hang around . . . fool with takin' along some food or beer, loadin' theirselves up with a lot of junk just because it's free. They don't last long. You gotta move in this trade. Why, I got a notebook to show I made three boxes in one week all wearing better than two grand each. That was a good week, I'll admit, but I never had no bad weeks . . . never less than a grand or two depending on how much I felt like workin' . . . yeah, it depends. . . ."

There was a short yet impressive silence, then Julio ventured a comment.

"Yeah. . . . I guess it sure depends. . . ."

"Now if you're plannin' on gettin' into the game," Welsh continued, "then you have to begin easy. You have to decide which box in the whole town is the easiest to begin with, because you're sure as hell goin' to find yourself rushed before the job is done . . . if you ever get it done."

"One thing I don't understand," said Julio. "You got yourself a safe here now." He traced a box in the air with his hands. "Okay, you got it. Now how the Jesus do you get in it?"

Welsh had not looked down upon the Perez brothers since the discussion began. Nor did he now while he pressed the cigarette even more tightly between his lips, then inhaled and blew. He seemed to be searching for something in the stale air above them. His stance, his total ease, suggested he would speak only of what he wished and in his own good time. Then at last, when the cigarette glowed brightly, he snorted smoke from his nostrils again and managed to achieve an almost professorial air.

"First, like I say, you gotta get *to* the box a course. Which is not always easy. I have in mind an easy box, but a difficult approach, like the one I made at Capital Van and Storage a few years back. The only way to the box was over the roof . . . which was high up. But in studying it out, I seen it is a flat roof. So I go to a surplus store and buy some parachute cord . . . it's light and easy to handle. Then I buy some kid's blocks . . . you know, like they play with . . . the wooden kind makes the alphabet? I lash the blocks at easy spacin' along the cord . . . they make good solid hand-grips. Then I get myself a big cargo hook from a pal and make it fast to one end of the cord. I'm set, understand? I don't drink none when I'm workin' so I always go to the movies to pass the time before a job. I like movies. They calm me. Afterwards I go to this van and storage outfit, heave my hook up to the roof, give it a few yanks to make sure it's set good, and up I go hand over hand on the blocks. It's a nothin'. . . ."

"But you still don't say how you get in a box," Julio protested.

"I'm coming to that, my friend. You keep your mouth shut and you'll learn. If the job is alarmed you a course got to carry insulated pliers in your kit an' be extra careful. I give up blow jobs years ago. They give you ten to forty on it now. If you can work in peace with no windows around, then a torch job is the best way . . . but be sure you drill some holes first and pour water inside because burned money is hard to pass anywheres. And a torch means hauling in a lot of equipment. Normally I like to work with a three-eighths drill or maybe a half inch, depending . . . and I drill through to where the lock bars hold the lid. Then I take a punch—I had a dandy Swedish make that would hold up real good—and I drive the locking bar back into the lid by putting the punch in the holes I already got drilled. Sometimes you got to fiddle around a little and be careful not to jam the lock bars on the inside, but like I say, it takes time and practice. If worst comes to worst you can always take a bar and a sledge and make a complete peel, but you got to be sure the noise don't make no difference. I stay away from E-type boxes entirely. When they set a box in cement you got yourself a whole new set of problems. . . ."

Welsh's reverie was complete. He ended it by removing the stub of cigarette from his lips and looking down at the Perez brothers for the first time.

"One thing I can tell you for sure," he said. "Guys who try workin' with partners always fall. Workin' alone is the only way."

"I can see that," Julio said, and then nodded his head toward Antonio. "But with Tony and me it's different, see? Because we're brothers."

"Even so. . . ." Welsh said, seeming to have lost all interest in the subject. Then he sighed. "I wish I'd got myself a little piece before I fell. It's going to be a long wait. . . . A little piece like you did."

"That's what hurts. We didn't," Antonio insisted.

"Haw. . . ." Welsh said and strolled away.

As they watched his easy, nonchalant pace, and admired the way he passed along the narrow cell alley as if it were a broad avenue, the Perez brothers heard their names called on the loud-speaker system.

"Now what the hell?" Julio asked of the air about him.

They pushed themselves slowly to their feet and, because everyone else in the felony block was watching them, they both took a casual hitch at their pants. Then in the manner of men who could take their own time, hands jammed down hard in their jackets in imitation of Welsh's manner, they walked slowly toward the gate at the far end of the alley. They placed their feet carefully, rolling slightly forward with each step as if the bottoms of their shoes were round, and each advancing movement of their legs was complemented by a quick, condescending, sidewise nod of their heads. It was not a true walk, but a saunter, the self-conscious progress of men who wanted their audience to realize how little afraid they were of anything. The success of their pose was confirmed by the sudden silence which came to the entire length of the alley.

On the other side of the gate a turnkey and Rafferty awaited them. The turnkey opened the gate and allowed them to pass out, which they did with an even more pronounced roll to their step and sidewise nods of their heads.

"What's doin'?" Julio asked Rafferty.

"You're going to be part of a showup. You know the drill?"

"Sort of. . . ."

"It's for your own good, if you're clean as you claim to be. There will be six of you standing in line. I found three fellows in the misdemeanor block who look pretty much like you two, anyhow they're about the same age and build, and I found a fourth who happens to be a Filipino cop who is here doing some studying. He volunteered. You'll all stand in line and be numbered from one to six. The guy who saw you drive away from the gas station will be in the auditorium. So will the girl. It's up to them to identify you by number, because that's all they know."

"How do we know that's all they know?" Julio asked.

"Cut it out. You think we want to make monkeys out of ourselves when this whole thing goes to court? One word from us to the victims and the whole thing would be thrown out. All we do is see they get to the auditorium and have a chance to look at six men that maybe they never saw before. In this case, out of the six they have to pick two. All we tell them is to be sure they're positive when they write the numbers down."

"Then what?"

"Then they either identify you or they don't. Since it's your show you can pick whatever numbers you want to be."

"I'll take number one," Julio said.

"Two is okay by me," Antonio said.

"Give yourselves a break and don't stand side by side. It's bad enough as it is. You're too obvious as a pair."

"Okay, Antonio here can be two. I'll be six."

"Suit yourselves. Now follow me."

In the darkened auditorium Moore handed blank cards and pencils to Harriet Rankin and a nervous little man named Leon Booth who had arrived at the filling station just in time to see the Perez brothers driving away. He had said that he'd caught only a glimpse of their faces, but he thought it had been a good glimpse.

"The men will be standing under the numbers one to six," Moore explained and indicated the still empty stage. "Write down two numbers if you can . . . but be sure. If you're *not* sure, please do not write anything. Is that clear?"

Leon Booth nodded his head affirmatively. Harriet breathed a soft and shy "yes," which Moore found strangely embarrassing. He attributed his discomfort to the still lingering shock of his first meeting with Harriet Rankin. If this girl was only thirteen years old, then he certainly didn't know what the world was coming to. Almost mischievously, he could hardly wait until Rafferty met her. He wanted to watch his face.

"I think it will be fairer all around if you sit farther apart. Then you can make your decisions completely independently. Would you please take a place about four rows back, Miss Rankin?"

She breathed the same curious "yes," which Moore was certain she had copied from some movie star, and moved farther back in the auditorium. He wondered what happened when this little girl was called to the blackboard in a schoolroom, if indeed the teacher ever had the nerve. And then, very suddenly, just as Rafferty came through the auditorium doorway, he had a hunch. It was utterly without foundation. It was preposterous, of course, but then so was little Harriet Rankin.

"The suspects are all set," Rafferty told him.

"Go introduce yourself to Harriet Rankin," Moore said.

"What for?"

"You'll see. I'll line the boys up."

Moore went to the door by the stage, knocked on it, and waited while the turnkey opened the locks. Julio Perez was second in the line of six men. He glanced defiantly at Moore, who deliberately ignored him.

"Just step up on the stage, fellows, and face out. No talking among yourselves, please."

Moore studied the assembly of men and decided that Rafferty had done a good job. They were all enough alike in size and age. The Filipino cop could easily have been of Mexican descent.

There was a long silence, then Rafferty joined him in front of the stage. He made a little whistling sound with his lips.

"How do you like our young lady?" Moore whispered.

"Um-huh."

Moore nodded his head, then he turned his back to the stage and looked into the darkened auditorium. "Is there anything you want these men to say?" There was no reply so Moore walked up the aisle and stopped by Leon Booth. He leaned down to him. "There's no sense having them walk up and down since you didn't see them move."

"I'm sure of one, but I'm having trouble with the other. Can you ask them to turn sidewise? I kind of saw them from a different angle and, of course, the light was different."

Moore turned to the stage and ordered the men to make a right turn. When he looked down at Leon Booth again he had already written two numbers on his card—2 and 6. The Perez brothers.

"You're certain, Mr. Booth?"

"Absolutely."

"Thank you." Moore took his card and moved up the aisle to Harriet Rankin.

"Well, Harriet?" He saw that she had already written down two numbers and her full lips were caressing the end of her pencil. She was completely at ease as she handed the card to Moore. He was so certain of what she had written he barely glanced at it. Of course, 2 and 6. Moore thought how often in the past he would have been grateful to achieve such quick and positive identification of suspects. Visual identification even by the direct victims did not automatically mean a conviction, but the courts had to recognize that the suspects were selected out of an anonymous group. Yet now, looking down at this young girl, Moore was strangely dissatisfied.

"You're sure now, Harriet? You couldn't have made a mistake?"

"Why . . . yes," she whispered. "Of course I'm sure."

"Those were the men who beat and raped you? Numbers two and six?"

"Yes."

Moore hesitated. He was about to go down the aisle and call in the photographer who would officially record the grouping, and then again the lack of satisfaction struck him.

"Harriet," he said, searching for words, "I hardly have to tell you that this is a very serious matter. . . ."

"No, you don't hardly have to tell me that this is a very serious matter," she said flatly.

She is resenting me, Moore thought. Why? And what am I so unhappy about? The whole thing is locked up tight . . . and in one day. "Harriet, I'm sure you realize that in the event you *had* made a mistake . . . then you would be doing two men a great injustice. They could well spend the best part of their lives in prison."

"I know them. One is Julio and the other is Antonio. They told me their names."

"Was that before or after they raped you?"

"Before. . . ."

Moore pushed his great nose from side to side with his thumb as if the gesture might ease his doubt. Then he sought desperately for a match to relight his cigar. Had there been a moment's hesitation before Harriet answered, a darting uncertainty in those childlike eyes, which were so innocent and yet were not?

"Harriet . . .?" he began again, and then could not think what he was going to say.

"Yes?"

"Never mind."

He turned and walked down the aisle. He paused to thank Leon Booth for his assistance, then he told Rafferty to take Harriet to the nearest drugstore and buy her an ice-cream soda. "Then bring her back to the office and we'll get a full statement. Take your time. I want to think."

"Supposing somebody I know sees me with that bomb?" Rafferty asked unhappily.

"Better go somewhere they won't."

When the turnkey had taken the six men back through the stage door, Rafferty escorted Harriet Rankin down the long hallway which led to the elevators. Then, to his distress, she insisted on stopping to watch Appollo Petropoulos at work on his murals. She paraded up and down before Appollo until his hungry eyes seemed begging her to leave. She refined the cruelty by suggesting Appollo might use her as a model. Rafferty found it impossible to match her composure with a little girl who was supposed to be recovering from a terrifying experience. Finally, lest Appollo lose control of himself entirely, he took her hand firmly and pulled her away.

Except for the attendant, the elevator was empty. Rafferty had begun to hope he might make his escape from the old building unnoticed. As the elevator descended, he stood solemnly beside Harriet Rankin, carefully staring straight ahead. Then the elevator stopped. Spearing entered and Rafferty suddenly wished he could become invisible, for Spearing leered until his mouth became all teeth and gums. He examined Harriet Rankin as if she were quite naked. Then he pointed to the discolored flesh about her eye.

"Did he do that to you?"

"Well . . . no," Harriet purred. And there was something about her tone that caused Rafferty to cringe inwardly. There was almost a suggestion in her voice that he *had* hit her.

"He is a cad anyway," Spearing said and contorted his puttylike face into what he obviously thought was a rakish smile. "All cops are beasts, young lady."

He continued his inspection of Harriet, opening and closing his lips over his yellow teeth, and softly grunting his appreciation, until the elevator stopped at the street level. And Rafferty was dismayed to see that Harriet not only enjoyed Spearing's attention —she understood it.

As he took her arm and half pushed her from the elevator, Spearing said, "I suppose he's going to take you out and buy you an ice-cream soda?"

"As a matter of fact, he is."

"Watch it, little Red Riding Hood. That's how they always begin."

When Moore left the auditorium, he went directly to his office. It was next to the abandoned safe in General Works, and of about the same size. The furnishings were Spartan: an elderly oaken desk with a continuous frieze of cigarette and cigar burns around its perimeter, three oaken chairs along the glass partition which separated the office from the main room, a coat stand with one foot broken so that it leaned against the wall, and a water-cooler which had not been used since anyone in General Works could remember. Yet occasionally when he was deep in thought or vexed, Moore would walk to the water-cooler and press the button two or three times, just as if he expected liquid to be forthcoming.

He pressed the water-cooler button now, while he thought about Harriet Rankin and the Perez brothers. And as always he regretted the fact that it was impossible for an inspector charged with the solution of a case to have actually been the first on the scene. All he had was a rather badly typed report composed by one Officer Slattery, badge number 6095, of Western Station. It described how he had responded to an anonymous telephone call reporting a young girl crying in the street near the corner of Lisbon and Twelfth Streets. Proceeding to the intersection, he had found Harriet Rankin, in tears and incoherent. The time was 9:12 P.M. Officer Slattery had delivered her to General Hospital at 9:20. The doctor on duty attempted to give her a sedative which she refused. For over an hour she also refused to give her name or say where she lived. Finally she told the doctor a confused story of how she had been beaten and then raped. Officer Slattery was not present during this recital and the doctor was unable to confirm her condition other than hysteria and obvious visible bruises. At 11:00 o'clock she stated her home address. Officers Slattery and Mac-Millan were detailed to escort her to said address, and if possible obtain permission for a full medical examination.

At 11:20 she was delivered to the stated address. Her uncle, who said he was her guardian, took her to her room and shortly thereafter said that Harriet had given him the complete story. He described how two youths of apparently Mexican descent had taken his niece for a ride, and later dragged her to a vacant lot where they had beaten and raped her. He gave a rough physical description of the youths and identified the car as an old Plymouth sedan. He refused permission for the officers to question Harriet further, claiming the sight of their uniforms would only make her more hysterical. Officers Slattery and MacMillan had then left the premises.

That was all. And it wasn't very much, Moore thought. Ordinarily it would have been just another rape case and he could hardly have asked for more cooperation from the victim than he had received. But he would have liked to see a vaginal examination report just for the record. Apparently the uncle had refused permission, which was not unusual in the case of a girl Harriet's age, but lack of such a report made things more difficult. Fortunately the stupid Perez brothers had decided to round off their evening by knocking over a filling station and thus conveniently landing themselves in the can. It was perfectly routine for them to lie their tongues dry from then on.

Yet somehow it wasn't all fitting together so nicely. Too many small things were *not* routine. Conceding the uncle was employed, couldn't he have at least taken the afternoon off to bring his niece down for the showup instead of just letting her come alone? Or what about the aunt? Couldn't *she* have come? And Harriet? The vision of the Perez brothers' offering to take her for a ride was easy to re-create. And who could blame them? One look at dear little Harriet and any judge or jury would throw the kidnaping rap right out the window. And who the hell said she was only thirteen years old in the first place?

Moore picked up his telephone, called Slattery's station, and found he was off duty. When he finally reached him at his home, Slattery's voice was sleepy, and he yawned continually through their conversation. Moore became rapidly convinced that he was talking to a young and not very smart cop.

"Who told you she was only thirteen?"

"She did."

"Did anyone confirm it?"

"No."

"How old did you think she was?"

"I never gave it much thought, she was bawling so."

Moore suddenly remembered his talk with the blond girl in women's prison. He asked Slattery if the uncle had appeared sober.

"Yeah. He acted so to me. Of course he was pretty upset."

"What about the aunt?"

"I dunno. We didn't talk to her."

"Did you see her?"

"No. I guess she was in the other room or something."

". . . or something? Your report says the uncle took her to her own room and then came out and told you about the pickup. Was that all?"

"Yeah. He told us what we couldn't get out of the girl."

"How long were they in the room together?"

"I dunno . . . maybe five minutes."

"Did you see the girl again before you left?"

"No."

"How old was the uncle?"

"Maybe about fifty."

Moore thanked Slattery without enthusiasm and hung up. Almost at once his phone rang. It was Matthews in the crime lab. He said that he had completed his work on the apparel of the Perez brothers and had found no traces of semen or blood on either of their pants. However, on Antonio's coat he had found blond hairs. Microscopic examination had revealed no unnatural features, but the character of the core and distribution of pigment in the cortex would indicate the hairs came from a young blond female. If Moore could supply him with hair from the victim it might help toward a more positive identification, but he should remember there were wide variations in the hair characteristics to be found in a single head.

"Never mind all that," Moore said, trying to stem his impatience. "The Perez boys have already admitted they played around with the girl."

"If she put up a fight there might be something under her nails . . . some flesh tissue or the like. We could take some blood grouping and see how they matched with any marks on the suspects—"

"Right now I'm more interested in another angle," Moore interrupted. "Can you give their shoes a good going-over and see if there's any mud or dust, or grass even . . . that might have come from a vacant lot?"

"I already did that. There was nothing remarkable."

"Let me ask you something. If two men were supposedly struggling around on a vacant lot, not to mention a few other activities, wouldn't it be perfectly reasonable that there would be something left on their shoes the next morning?"

Moore thought he heard Matthews chuckle, and he thought that no matter how many scholastic degrees a criminologist had, pinning one down to a firm statement was like pressing the button on his water-cooler.

"True. It would be perfectly reasonable . . . but not necessarily inevitable. Besides, are you sure they were wearing their shoes at the time?"

"You have me there," Moore admitted.

"Let me know if I can be of any more help."

"That I'll do," Moore said with a weary smile. He put his feet up on his desk and sat chewing on his cigar for a long time. He thought of the Perez brothers and reviewed all they had said, and he thought of Harriet Rankin sitting so confidently in the dark auditorium, choosing suspects as if it was something she did every day in her life, and he thought about the guarded way the girl in women's prison had spoken of her neighbor, and he thought about the uncle who the girl had said was so fond of his bottle. And he thought of Slattery, who must be the dumbest cop ever to join the force in recent years, and finally he wondered if he should bother going any further with the whole thing, because the Perez brothers were going to the joint anyway.

He left his desk and went to the water-cooler and punched the tap button several times without realizing what he was doing. He detested the confusion in his mind which was normally so orderly, the scramble of thoughts created by the sudden switch in his purpose. There was that foundationless yet insistent hunch again, and it made him wonder on which side he should really be.

✧✧ 29 ✦✦✦

When Celia Krank left the old building and emerged into the sunlight, she saw for the first time that her fingertips were still slightly tinged with black from the fingerprint pad. Looking at her fingers, she saw them tremble and found she was powerless to keep them still. Suddenly she clutched her hands about her waist and bent her head, because she was positive everyone on the street was looking at her. She walked very slowly away from the old building. Only occasionally did she dare to raise her eyes and look for Maurice.

How she yearned for Maurice! She could think of nothing except the stain on her fingers and the cocoon of filth which seemed to enwrap her entire body. And Maurice. He would be, he *must* be waiting for her at the fourth bench in the park—the place they always met.

Celia took a bus straight home and explained to her mother that she had spent the night with a girl friend who worked in the same office. It had happened several times before and so her mother only asked what she was doing home in the middle of the afternoon. And Celia told her they were making some repairs to the office, so the boss had given all three girls half a day off. Celia was surprised how easily she elaborated on the lie, even describing

how the boss had ho-ho'd all the morning and said he had a surprise for his little slaves, and finally when he broke the news,
ho-ho'd some more and said, well they would all have to make
it up somehow.

Later, after she had taken a shower and removed every evidence
of her stay in the old building, she told her mother she was going
to thoroughly enjoy her unexpected holiday and go for a long
walk. She strolled casually until she reached the corner, then,
turning it, she increased her pace until she was half running. By
the time she arrived at the fourth bench from the entrance to the
park, she was breathless. And a diminutive cry tortured her throat
when she saw the bench was empty. She stopped to ease the pain,
then, moving in wretchedness toward it, she forced herself to be
reasonable. Of course, he had come and gone because he was an
impatient man—but he would come again if she waited. And for
Maurice, the first true love of her life, she would wait forever.

Now she had waited for two hours, almost content because it
was something she was doing for Maurice. While she caressed the
exact spot on the bench where Maurice would be sitting, she
watched the sun drown in the tops of the eucalyptus trees fringing
the border of the park. She tried not to think of the Chinese girl
in the jade-green dress who would not be watching anything, and
she tried to forget what the awful women had threatened to do
to her.

She had almost suceeded in forgetting all that had happened in
the old building when a young man came up the path. He was
whistling softly. To her surprise he did not trouble to glance at
her, but continued on his way. Then suddenly she realized why
his face seemed so familiar. It was the same young man whose case
had preceded her own in the courtroom. She remembered the
judge had spoken to him very softly and said something about a
society of some kind and then something about finding a nice
girl or leaving the city—she really hadn't been listening very
carefully.

She looked after the young man until he reached the turning
of the path and passed out of sight. Then she instantly forgot

him. Ah, Maurice! Come soon. Don't make me prove I will wait forever.

✧✧✧ ✦✦✦

When Lawrence Potter left the old building he went directly to his apartment and fed his canary. Then he washed thoroughly and put on his best gray flannel slacks and a finely ribbed green corduroy sports jacket. He blew several kisses at his canary and then set off for the park, which was a good place to be when you felt so tremendous, so soaring, so sure at last of how the future would be. There was other loving to be done, and with discipline it could suffice! And the park was without suggestive memories. It was for loving the sound of Brahms even when whistled, it was light and shadow which now one would render on canvas as one had always yearned to do. Mother would understand. Mother would send enough money, and a whole new career would begin, and there would be no more fussing about whether the decoration of a store window was arresting, or too esoteric, or too obvious, or heaven knows what. I will become a real painter, he murmured, and then went on with his whistling. I will become a painter and grow a stunning beard. I will live in a garret and whistle Brahms while I experiment with the uniting of ocher and burnt umber rather than lonely human beings. I shall revel in my loneliness. I shall speak only when spoken to, and then only to norms—the butcher, the baker, and the candlestick maker. I shall forswear now, this instant, anyone who is even slightly gay. I shall write a formal resignation to the Mattachine Society—perhaps even a long tone poem which will reveal how I have come into a new existence, which is not dull as supposed, but swirling with creative excitations. And I shall be lamented. It will be like a resurrection.

He continued along the path until he came to an open place where the grass sloped gradually up to a fountain. The water flowed from the pipes of a small bronze statue representing Pan, and he thought it a particularly appropriate place to consider his glowing future. So he lay down on the grass and stretched his full length. He stared at the sky, glorying in the mental images of the skies he would paint, and of himself garbed in a paint-stained smock, striking out furiously with his brush at the canvas. He would be famous for his cerulean blues, famous for his rose madders, famous for his misanthropy, famous particularly for his ability to survive without the love of either man or woman. He would, of course, be tolerant of old gay friends, but he would never again associate with them. Why, indeed, when he would be so famous and self-sufficient?

He dreamed on, closing his eyes the better to see the inner visions and opening them to see the changing light in the sky, and soon he was so far removed from all the things he had endured in the horrid old building and so far into his new existence that he only heard the vibration of a voice which insinuated itself into his dreams.

"Hello there. I wish I could sleep like that."

Lawrence Potter pushed himself up on his elbows and found a well-dressed man sitting on the grass beside him.

"I envy you," the man said. "This is such a beautiful place to awaken. I was wondering if you ever would, because the loveliness here is something which should be shared. Or don't you agree?"

"Yes, I suppose I do." Lawrence Potter looked at the man carefully and saw that he was smiling in a certain way that caused a quick warmth to pass between them. Then he saw a ring on the little finger of the man's left hand, and instantly the warmth was drowned in an inner terror which passed the length of his body. He looked up into the man's eyes again and found them waiting for him. And once more the man smiled, very slowly.

"If you really want to go back to sleep, I will guard you," the man said. "You can't tell who may be in the park these days."

"No. . . ."

Lawrence Potter felt the breath leaving him and he knew that his cheeks were flushing. He caught his breath frantically, trying to appear calm and to conceal the sudden quick beating of his heart. But even as he turned away for a moment he knew the man was watching him, seeing straight through him as if he were transparent—and worse, understanding.

The man extended the fingers of his two hands, pressing them together to form a steeple. Then he said softly, "You belong in such a beautiful place as this. If I may say so, you and this quiet spot in the park almost complete each other."

"No!" Lawrence Potter shook his head vigorously. He told himself that he must fight back now, this instant—or he could not survive. For he knew that all he saw in the man's eyes was a reflection of what must be in his own.

He glanced at his watch, then said hurriedly, "I must go. I'm late for an appointment."

"Don't be silly. You're not a child. . . ."

But he turned away quickly and walked to the path. He heard the man call to him. "Au revoir. I hope we meet again."

Lawrence Potter did not look back. Instead, shivering in near-terror, he broke into a full run.

❖❖❖ 30 ❖❖❖

All through Judge Brownell's luncheon at the Commerce Club, which he took at a huge round table occupied by contemporaries, he had remained unusually quiet. And after the standard ho-ho's of parting he left the club in moody silence, and instead of striking out briskly on his regular route toward the old building, he meandered in the crisp sunlight so deep in thought that he was astounded when he eventually found himself in Chinatown. He realized that he would be late for the opening of his court at two o'clock, but the idea did not displease him. This is one of my maverick days, he decided. Brownell's court could not go into session without Brownell anyway, and he wanted a few extra minutes to think about the young blond girl whose name was Celia Something-or-other and who had regarded him as God. Or at least *a* god, he thought. Yet he knew it was not really the blond girl who had put him in such an analytic mood; it was self-generating, a process which in recent months had achieved a strange domination over his ego and which he was not at all sure he liked.

Maybe I am going through a sort of legal menopause, he

thought. I am changing inwardly. I am like a wine that is slowly going sour, becoming unstable and cloudy. And the reason for this could be that I am becoming ever less content with the back-face of the law. It is something I feel rather than know, and hence it becomes constantly more nagging and powerful until my little head buzzes with national ailments that are better left to Supreme Justices, who are not always right but can't afford to admit it, or left to God, who is so often busy elsewhere. There is something very wrong. We commit a man to death, but it does not stop killing. We imprison a thief, but thievery increases. We are always between cup and lip, mixing temporal sin with social evil and handing down punishments keyed to the nearest, handiest, recognizable crime. This is hypocrisy triumphant. It has taken us five thousand years to mix such a pure and clear distillation of insincerity.

We have a set of rules and regulations which are available to every citizen. Thou shalt not kill, steal, lie, commit adultery, et cetera—at least when they enter the game, the majority of the participants are familiar with the ground rules. When these are broken or ignored, we insist on penalties, the severity and duration of which are rarely based on the *reasons* behind the violations.

Indeed, Brownell mused, it is a rare day when reason is allowed to raise its beautiful head in a courtroom. While the original participants become spectators, we who were not present during the action determine the score by a sort of legal hocus-pocus which often compels us to ignore common sense.

Brownell crossed a busy intersection heedless of the traffic lights, for his concentration was now screwed tightly on the Fifth Dynasty, and why it was that every age looked down from a self-erected rostrum, bonged arbitrarily on great gongs of authority, and declared itself infinitely more wise and moral than the age before. But had this always been so? The Pharaohs maintained a well-organized society that endured longer than any other in history. The rules of the game were not so entirely different then —although penalties were. They tortured until a convenient confession was forthcoming, and punished in kind. Babylonia began with no concessions to mercy. If a house collapsed and killed the

purchaser, the architect or builder must die. If a man struck a
girl and killed her, not he but his daughter must be put to death.
Later, for certain offenses, financial punishments replaced the
physical. Which was the crude beginning of common sense. The
eye of a commoner could be knocked out for sixty shekels of silver, and the eye of a slave for thirty. Capital punishment was not
reserved for people who happened to kill someone else in the
wrong geographical location, or chose the wrong lawyer. There
were no lawyers, which, Brownell thought wryly, must have eliminated a great deal of the hocus-pocus. The dealth penalty did not
apply to murder, unless the slaying was done by a wife who dis-
posed of her husband to marry another man. It did apply to the
entering of a wine shop by a priestess, malfeasance in office, careless, uneconomical housewifery, or malpractice in the selling of
beer.

Well then, Brownell thought, there had been some improvement,
if one could ignore the existence of electric chairs, gas chambers,
and scaffolds, with which people still enjoyed revenge. Thank God
I am a little magistrate, Brownell whispered to himself, and so
the maximum revenge I can pronounce is a year in the county jail.
I need never trouble with twelve other minds vacillating between
mercy and retaliation. It would terrify me if twelve totally inex-
perienced minds, subjected to salesmanship and complication for
days on end, could by a process of mass ventriloquism compel me
to say—You there! Die!

Brownell was so enwrapped in his thoughts that he was not
fully aware of his entry into Chinatown until he collided with an
Oriental of approximately his own size and age. After quick little
bows they were once more on their way. But the collision jolted
Brownell's recapture of the Fifth Dynasty so severely he could not
find it again. He shifted the gears of his concentration quickly to
the Mosaic Code and was ready to make some scathing mental
comparisons when Inspector Crane hailed him from the doorway
of a souvenir store.

"Hi, Judge! What's the big rush?"

Brownell halted, peered into the doorway, and after the moment
required to steer his mind back to reality, recognized Crane.

"Oh—hello. I'm late. I don't know why I chose going back to court this way. I seldom do."

"You ought to try it more often. It's the best part of town." Crane had been reading a newspaper which he now held out to Brownell. "Did you read about the guy on the bridge?" he asked.

"No. I never seem to get around to the noon papers."

"He's a real nut, this one. Probably he's jumped by now. Why, he'll hit the water at a hundred miles an hour."

"I suppose he will . . . and I always wonder why." Brownell tugged at his ear and looked down the street. "The strongest law we're supposed to have is self-preservation. Yet so many people never seem to have heard of it."

"If I could think like that, I'd be a judge instead of just a cop."

"God spare you."

Brownell was astonished at his own answer. What in the world was the matter with him? He was sounding like an itinerant preacher, and the whole subject of God seemed to be continuously on the lip of his mind. Maybe this was indeed the menopause!

"I guess a judge must get pretty tired listening to so many lies," Crane said.

"Not if the liars are insincere, clever enough, and imaginative. Nothing puts me to sleep faster than a parade of half-honest citizens claiming to be entirely honest. They never seem to realize they are claiming something which does not exist."

Brownell tipped his hat without being aware that he had done so and once more set off at a pace which was twice that of any other pedestrian. Lies, indeed! In his own court a witness was asked to tell the truth so help him God. Which was the last vestige of religion as a prop to the law. In ancient Israel, where the Mosaic Code prevailed, the taking of an oath was a religious ceremony. A man placed his hand on the genitals of the person to whom he swore and took God himself, not only as his witness, but as his judge. And so the ninth commandment spiked almighty fear into the witness and kept him at least close to the paths of truth. Who dared otherwise when a thunderbolt was in the offing? Ahoy! thought Brownell. On *that* one we have certainly lost! He could not remember when he had last seen anyone in his court actually *look* at the Bible when he swore to tell nothing but the truth. It seemed as if their oath was a heavenward directed plea to help them tell the truth in spite of an overpowering urge to do otherwise, or a promise to be more careful after they twisted the truth so things would look better, or even a beseeching of mercy when the truth might accidentally be discovered. The oath takers— police, suspect, or witness—looked not upon the Bible but at the floor, the vacant face of the court clerk, or occasionally, if they were bold enough, at Brownell himself.

He had sighted the old building and he had said "ahoy" again, because even his nimble mind needed a momentary bridge between his reflections and the notion of being a voyaging sailor with familiar land at last upon the horizon.

In less than fifteen minutes he had donned his black robe, swooped from his chambers to his courtroom, and soared up to his bench. Soon afterward he found himself fascinated by a spectacle which was so unique in his courtroom that he tugged violently at both ears as if to reassure his hearing. For suddenly he realized that he was in danger of believing all that now transpired before him. He found it a delicious experience, something, he thought, like ascending in a free balloon. There was certainly the same suspense about just where one might land. Now, right in his own courtroom, he listened as the mouths of three vitally concerned human beings poured forth what he considered glittering jewels of pure truth.

Here was a plain case of bigamy, yet Brownell could not discover a trace of deceit, calumny, or vindictiveness. The attitude of the husband and his two wives was so refreshing, Brownell breathed deeply of their testimony because he suddenly, unashamedly, loved his fellow man.

The husband was a balding, stout little man who was a butcher. And a good one, both wives said with no attempt to conceal their pride. His name was Brodney and his first wife called him Wayne, whereas his second elaborated the name slightly to Wayn*o*.

His first wife had said, "Well, gee, I never had anything to kick about. Before Wayne married me I was working as a comptometer operator for the World Insurance Company and they paid us buttons. I lived with another girl in a lousy three-flight walkup with a bath down the hall which was all we could afford. Then Wayne came along and pretty soon I was living like a queen. He asked me if I wanted to quit my job and just look after him. That I did, and it was a breeze compared to that insurance company. Wayne never denied me a thing that was reasonable and I tried to be a good wife to him. . . ."

"How long were you married to the defendant?" the Assistant District Attorney asked quietly.

"It seems like I'm still married to him. That's the trouble."

"This is your signature on the license?"

"Yes, it is."

"Your Honor, I would like to put this wedding license in evidence."

"You may do so," Brownell replied and leaned forward for a better look at Wayne's number one wife. She was rather plump, he observed, but there was a jolly beauty about her face which he secretly saluted.

"When did you start action for a divorce?" the Assistant District Attorney asked.

"Well actually . . . we sort of did it together after we had been married about a year. That's a good trial period, I think. You ought to know by then if you just got together for sex, or because of economics, or because you were trying to escape another sort of life, or if it is the real thing. Both Wayne and I knew before the year was up it wasn't taking for us. We *liked* each other, mind you, and Wayne still never let me want for anything, but we knew we just weren't made for each other. We decided it would be a shame to have any children under the circumstances, you know . . . just to try holding our marriage together, you know . . .?"

"Have you lived together as man and wife since that decision?"

"No."

"You remained friendly?"

"Why not? Once in a while if Wayne was lonely he would take me bowling. Once in a while if I had a problem, like the water heater in the apartment broke or something, I'd phone Wayne and he'd come to fix it."

"But that's as far as your relations went?"

"Absolutely. Can't people be *friends?*"

"Until very recently you were under the impression that your divorce was final?"

"Yes. That's what the lawyer said. He said he would be sending us some papers."

"Did you ever receive any papers?"

"No. Both of us tried to find the lawyer, but he went off to Mexico or someplace . . . and with the money Wayne paid him too."

"When did you learn of your husband's second marriage?"

"About a month before it happened. He came to talk it over with me."

"Did you object?"

"No. I'm very fond of Wayne and I wanted him to be happy. It seemed to me he had made a very good choice."

"Since the time of your supposed divorce has your husband been paying you alimony?"

"Only until I went back to work. Why should he pay me the rest of his life for a mistake we both made?"

"Does he own his butcher shop?"

"Yes."

"What about community property? Is half the butcher shop now yours?"

"Of course not. I'm not a . . . prostitute. I didn't expect to be paid for sharing Wayne's bed. He worked hard to get the shop before he married me and afterward to support me. I never worked a minute in the shop. I never did a thing to contribute to it. Why should half of it be mine?"

Completely intrigued, almost frightened by his sudden admiration for this plump woman, Brownell leaned far outward from his bench so that he could see her even better and asked, "Supposing you *had* worked in the shop, would you consider a part of it rightfully yours? Mind you I say *rightfully* not legally."

"Yes. I think that might be different. I would expect what I had put into it."

By the time Brownell was quite in love with wife number one, number two was called to testify. She was considerably thinner and taller than her predecessor, but Brownell thought he saw the same mellow quality in her eyes.

"Did you realize the defendant was still married at the time you signed this license?" the Assistant District Attorney asked.

"No. Of course not. Neither did Wayno."

"Please speak for yourself only. Did you ever see any kind of paper which would have confirmed your belief Mr. Brodney was legally divorced?"

"I didn't ask. Wayno is a real level guy. If he thought he was divorced, he was."

"The fact of the matter is that he was not."

"In his heart and mind he was. That was enough for me."

"Well, it's hardly enough for the laws of this state," Brownell interrupted from aloft. He forced a sourness into his voice because he was so deeply disturbed. Wife number two was so completely forthright in manner he had also developed a shocking fondness for her. I am become a judicial bigamist, he thought. Again he tugged at his ear lobes. Certainly the husband would prove to be a scamp. Among other laws there was the one of averages.

"Before your marriage had you met the former . . . I mean the other Mrs. Brodney?" the Assistant District Attorney asked.

"Oh, yes. Wayno took me around to meet her one evening. He said I should know all the bad things about him and Esther was an authority."

"And did she describe his faults?"

"Yes. But those were faults for her, we decided, not for me. We spent most of the time talking about his qualities."

"And where was *Mr.* Brodney during this interview?"

"Out in the kitchen making up smorgasbord."

"For the three of you?"

"Of course. We had a jolly time. Sometimes poor Wayno was embarrassed, though, the way we kidded him."

"Is there no antagonism between you and Mrs. Esther Brodney?"

"Heavens, no! I'm grateful to her for the way she treated the man I love, and besides I like her."

"Were you aware of the financial arrangements in their assumed divorce?"

"Yes. I told Wayno he should pay her more alimony, that we'd get along all right. Wayno tried to talk her into it, but she wouldn't accept anything after she went back to work."

Brownell told himself that he was dreaming. Perhaps as he had passed through Chinatown he had unknowingly inhaled some special opium. He shook his head vigorously to dispel the notion.

"When you discovered Mr. Brodney was not legally divorced, did you continue to live together as man and wife?"

"Well . . ."

She hesitated, and looked at Brodney. They exchanged weak smiles.

And now, thought Brownell, she is going to lie and spoil the whole show.

"Yes," she said proudly.

Ah! thought Brownell, sighing with relief.

When Brodney placed his hand on the Bible and took his oath, Brownell prepared himself for the worst. He examined Brodney carefully. What kind of a man could be so lucky as to find two such women? But the only distinguishing feature about Brodney was an elk's tooth which hung from a watch chain stretched across his vest. Brownell wondered if perhaps the tooth had some magic powers, since its owner on first impression appeared to be something less than the accepted version of Casanova. He was pink-cheeked, pink-handed, and pink-nosed, all of which combined with his delft-blue eyes to make him look like a mature kewpie. Where indeed, Brownell wondered, does he keep his special quiver of arrows?

After the Assistant District Attorney had confirmed Wayne Brodney's signature on two wedding licenses, he asked, "At the time you signed this second license were you aware that you were still married to Mrs. *Esther* Brodney?"

"No. I thought we were divorced."

"You *thought* you were divorced? Or realizing you were committing bigamy, you just found it convenient to forget you were still married to Esther Brodney?"

"I object, Your Honor," the Public Defender said. "Mr. Brodney was clearly under the impression he had a perfect right to remarry."

"Overruled," Brownell said unhappily. "Mr. Brodney had no reason to hold such an impression except the spoken word of a lawyer." Perhaps that was the reason, he thought, why Brodney had not now hired a private lawyer but had willingly accepted the Public Defender. Or was he just a tightwad?

The Assistant District Attorney smiled and said, "Among your other vaguely based impressions, did you entertain the idea of having two wives at the same time?"

"Well, if I did have two wives I certainly would want those two," Brodney said flatly and without the slightest change of expression in his blue eyes.

Aha! thought Brownell after he had banged his gavel to subdue the tittering in his domain. Ordinary as he may seem, this man knows the power of sweet words.

"I will rephrase my question, and please remember you're under oath. Did you believe you could get away with having two wives as long as no one found out about it?"

"Objection!" the Public Defender cried with an enthusiasm Brownell had never seen him demonstrate before. "Your Honor, I object to the words 'get away with.' Mr. Brodney was not trying to get away with anything or his relationship with these two ladies could not possibly have been as it was and still is!"

"Strike the question from the record," Brownell instructed the court stenographer. In all his experience, Brownell had never seen anything like the mass sympathy which was now sweeping his courtroom. The Assistant District Attorney was doing his best at normal prosecution, but his heart was obviously not in his work this curious afternoon. Brownell thought he forced the next question from his lips.

"Mr. Brodney, who determined the amount of so-called alimony you would pay your first wife?"

"The lawyer. He said it should be about that much and I asked

Esther if it was enough for her to get along comfortably on, and she said sure it was more than enough and not to strain any cylinders about it . . . and, well . . ."

"That was that?"

"Yes."

"You and a lawyer who has conveniently disappeared arranged to deprive this lady of her legal rights without any recourse to the courts whatsoever?"

"I'm a butcher. I don't know much about this sort of thing. Everybody was satisfied all around. Nobody was mad. I tried the best I could to make sure Esther would be okay and she tried the best she could to make sure I was okay, and Grace tried the best she could to make sure we were both okay."

"Grace is the second Mrs. Brodney? Are there any additional Mrs. Brodneys we should know about?"

"Additional to what?"

"To these two. Your marriage to Esther Brodney and to Grace Brodney?"

"Oh no. Lightning may strike twice in the same place but never three times."

As Brodney beamed at his wives Brownell let the tittering in his courtroom die naturally. His mind was very busy. How was he going to uphold the law which was his trust and avoid breaking three uniquely wonderful hearts? Solomon, he thought, if you would care to fire a lightning bolt charged with wisdom in my direction, I am ready to receive it. In a few minutes that heartless monster from the D.A.'s office is going to be forced to point out this is a pure case of bigamy and I shall be forced to render judgment.

The Public Defender's cross-examination was less than inspired, Brownell thought, yet there was really so little he could do. He merely proved that Brodney was a respectable citizen who paid his taxes, an early-rising hard worker, and an occasional church-goer. He had apparently been as generous as wife number one would permit him to be.

"She refused any attempt you made to pay her money after she went back to work?"

"Yessir. But I managed to slip in a few things. Like the best turkey I had in the shop to feed her relatives on Thanksgiving, and the round-trip ticket to New York I won bowling I sent to her— things like that."

"Did you do these things because you had a guilty conscience?"

"No. I *like* her. Sometimes I wish I was two people."

"You have tried to be," Brownell snapped, more tartly than he intended.

Finally, as Brownell had known he would, the Assistant District Attorney confidently rested his case on a straight charge of bigamy. But the vision of the pink Mr. Brodney growing paler and thinner in prison was more than Brownell could bear. He called a ten-minute recess while he glided down from his bench and fled into his chambers. There he puffed angrily on a cigarette while he examined all the cowardly escape routes he could think of.

It was no help to his troubled thoughts when, after a perfunctory rap on the door, Spearing entered his chambers and said he had heard about a bigamy case which was always good for a story, but he had to know the answers right now so he could phone his paper before it was too late. What was Brownell going to do to this romantic fiend who lured innocent girls to their downfall with faked wedding licenses? How did Brownell know there were not many more victims to his lust now chopped up and hidden in his love-nest butcher shop?

"Give me a story, Judge. This has been a lousy day. Nothin' but nothin', and just remember it won't hurt to keep the old Brownell name on page one. There's an election coming and people are *so* damned forgetful—"

"Mine is a public courtroom. If you want a story, sit in it and listen." How I hate this man, Brownell thought. He whinnies when he talks.

"Now, Judge, you know I don't have that kind of time to waste. What I need is sort of a résumé is all, and what kind of a sentence you're going to throw at this Bluebeard."

"I wish we were in Babylonia," Brownell said, eying Spearing with open distaste.

"What's this about Babylonia? Did this butcher throw some real orgies?"

"In Babylonian law, if a man accused another man of a capital crime and could not prove it, the accuser was put to death."

"Very funny, Judge, but I'm too tired with this day to laugh. Now this conniving Bluebeard was sharpening his knives—"

"He is *not* a Bluebeard! And I do not as yet know what my decision will be."

"All right. So we'll call him the marrying butcher. That has a nice ring to it. Calls his wives his little lamb chops—"

"He has only been married twice. He made an unfortunate technical mistake and that's all."

"But I can't make a story out of that."

"I know you can't. Now get out of here."

Spearing sighed and his abused eyes became more sardonic than ever. "You're going to let that character get away with it? Why, bigamy will sweep the country! A thousand other guys will try the same thing in the next week. You'll make headlines all right—the wrong kind. You'll be known as the judge who condones polygamy. The church, every organization in the land, will be on your neck. You may even hear from the Pope in Rome. You can't set a precedent like that!"

"I am well aware of it. Now go out that door and stay out. You are souring my balloon ride."

"I don't understand you. What balloon?"

"The one that is going up now!" Brownell crunched out his cigarette, turned quickly so that the skirt of his robe became a black swirl, and flew to the door of his courtroom. He took a deep breath and the smile on his face became fixed as he left Spearing five thousand feet below.

When Wayne Brodney stood before him, Brownell looked into his unflinching blue eyes for a long time. Finally he said, "I find you guilty of the crime of bigamy. While I am impressed with your sincerity I am much less so with your thought processes. Strangely enough, you must be intelligent or you would not have had the good sense to twice select such charming ladies. Therefore there is no excuse for your befuddled impression that a single lawyer could assume what is properly the jurisdiction of the courts."

Brownell paused and wiped at his brow. He surveyed the landscape below him with mischievous delight and smiled inwardly.

"However, in view of the mitigating circumstances, I am going to sentence you to one year in the county jail . . . but I will suspend this sentence for a period of two years during which time you will be on probation. I order you to take immediate steps to obtain a legal divorce and to notify this court by appearing in person with Mrs. Grace Brodney and Mrs. Esther Brodney that such an agreement is final. Do you understand what my sentence means, Mr. Brodney?"

Brodney turned to smile at his wives, then he looked directly back at Brownell. "Yessir," he said quietly. "It means you are a great man."

Brownell assumed his most disapproving frown. He did not want Brodney to know that his sentence contained a certain side effect. He would see this pink butcher again and, more importantly, his two wives. And Brownell considered such a meeting might well occur just about the time his well of love for those who appeared before him was running very dry.

❖❖❖ 31 ❖❖❖

Exactly at three o'clock she telephoned Thelma at her office. She turned the radio up high so that it would provide a busy undertone, and kept her voice in that special rilling contralto which she had always reserved for the telephone. It was quite unlike her normal voice, which was pleasant enough. On the telephone she habitually used broad *a*'s and the softest of *r*'s which was a marked departure from her natural Midwestern accent. Otto had frequently chided her on this remarkable affectation, saying she sounded like Lady Astor ordering a ham sandwich. His ridicule was lost on her for she was actually unaware of any change: the hope in talking to an unseen person was to impress, and for a woman so lacking in confidence it was always a nervous business.

"Hello, Thelma!" she exclaimed the instant she heard her voice. "My dear, how *are* you?" The shouted emphasis was doubly necessary because of the radio.

"Now *really*," she continued, "I *have* been so terribly busy and I know you have been too! It's dreadful, isn't it? I don't know what happens to the time . . . and here we are not getting any younger either. But really, Thelma dear, it *has* been a long, long, *long* time since we had a chance to talk . . . and well, frankly, I *do* have something rather important I'd like to discuss with you. I shouldn't think it would take very long and we both *are so* busy, but I think we should have a little chat as soon as possible. Fortunately, I'm free between six and seven. I'll be on my way to dinner with some friends, but I wonder if it would be too inconvenient if I stopped by about then? By all means, don't make the slightest adjustment in your schedule just for me . . . but perhaps we might have a glass of sherry together even if it is your bath time, which I know is—well, a rather sacred occasion to you . . . but I *do* so hope—"

She waited, twisting the phone up and down, gasping for air impatiently, because in the urgency and consequent vocal gymnastics of every phone conversation she found it immediately necessary to restore air to her lungs. She waited, looking at the photo of Otto in its silver frame which graced the far corner of her small desk. There was a long silence which frightened her, and for an instant she wondered if Thelma could possibly have any idea what she had been planning and, if so, was arranging for another person to listen. But there were no suspicious electrical clicks in the receiver, and when she heard Thelma's voice again it sounded as coldly polite as ever.

"Oh, really, Thelma, I *do* wish you could make it *today!* It will only take a *few* minutes, honestly! I assure you I'll be gone long before your guest arrives. . . ."

Her guest, of course, would be Otto. It was now very easy to visualize her sitting in the office next to his, as if she owned the whole world—with her hair done in ringlets just so, and very likely the blue cashmere suit which she claimed to have bought herself, and the brooch of small rubies and six diamonds forming a trident which she also claimed she had bought herself, and which she apparently didn't know was a complete giveaway. Otto's favorite design of all designs was a trident because as a boy he had gone to sea. It hadn't been very clever of him—or her.

"Oh, you *are* so kind, Thelma! You may depend on me. I will be there at *exactly* six-fifteen and by six-thirty I'll be on my way! Of course, dear. It will be wonderful to *see* you!"

When she replaced the telephone she sat motionless for a long time, staring dumbly at Otto's photograph. Dear precious Otto! She was not in the least angry with him—only a little annoyed because a man of his age should not let himself be played for a fool.

She shivered though she was quite warm. Every time she thought of Thelma and what she had done, she shivered. Now a small cry of anguish like the trilling of a terrified bird escaped her. She clutched at her sagging breasts in near-panic, offering them to the photograph. "My dearest! You *must* come back! You must— must—*must!* My dearest. I need you and you need me and . . . and, oh dear God, how I love you. . . ." Her voice trailed away into a whimper which became a continuous, uncontrollable sobbing. She was unable to calm herself until she was exhausted. Then she lay face down on the couch and tried to sleep. But she could think of nothing but Thelma. I am dying, Thelma. You are killing me. I must fight. I will try once more to reason with you. Then if you won't listen, I must do it. And I *will*.

✦✦✦ 32 ✦✦✦

Lasher watched the girl with growing disapproval as she manicured his nails automatically, buffed them automatically, and finally placed the twenty dollars he gave her into the pocket of her white uniform automatically. As she packed her equipment into a small case, he reached to pinch her thigh, but she spun away and made for the door. He caught her before she had opened the door and seized her chin in his hand. He tipped her face up for a kiss, saw her disgust, and withdrew his hand as if to slap her. He wanted to break her sullen face and he asked since when was a straight manicure worth twenty dollars. She made no reply, but her lower lip curled down and in her eyes there was only contempt. He lowered his arm and propelled her stumbling into the hallway. He slammed the door, wiped at the droplets of saliva which had collected in the fatty corners of his mouth, and wondered how much money a man had to give a tramp nowadays before she smiled. He was disappointed, so much so that he moaned peevishly and then bellowed at the walls of his empty suite.

"I'll run these slave girls with their clinical airs right out of business." Then, because Theo Lasher was more than a brute, because his greatness was partly due to his remarkable ability to laugh at disappointment, he muttered, "Some women have no natural talent to be whores. And a good thing they don't try because they would only give the whole business a bad name."

He glanced at his watch and estimated the girl had spent no more than fifteen minutes on the job, including the time she had consumed in a dull review of the weather. If I want a weather summary, I'll call the airport, he thought.

And now there was nothing to do but wait for some dumb Boy Scout police chief who might cost him a lot more money.

He took a bonbon from the open box on the coffee table, nibbled at it until he was certain there was a cherry inside, and then stuffed it in his mouth. He lumbered to the window and stood for some time masticating the bonbon, hauling at his suspenders and looking down upon the streets and building tops far below. And gradually as he forgot about the manicurist his thoughts slid smoothly to matters of more immediate interest. For here was a city begging for the attention of an expert organizer. The more he thought about it the more he was inclined to give its prospects that attention.

Following his usual policy, he would avoid race tracks or any kind of sporting events. They were too seasonal. They lacked solidity and, worse yet, were terribly vulnerable to taxation. Maybe it would be worth while to examine the trucking situation? His own union could serve as wedge, and maybe some kind of an amalgamation could be arranged. There was very good money in amalgamations provided you stayed clear of the AFL and CIO. They paid people salaries which taxwise and every other wise was pure cockamania.

Doubtless some clown took care of the junk situation here, but the hell with hypes and pushers and all the gummy people you had to deal with on top. It was too nervous a business in spite of the sensational profits. Every sonofabitch and his brother fastened himself on your tail twenty-four hours a day. If you counted in the ordinary flatfoot city cops, then the state bureau, plus the Federal Bureau of Narcotics, plus the FBI, plus Customs, plus Coast Guard, plus all the rigmarole of supply—it just wasn't worth it. No other business suffered such oppression. And worse than all the fuzz, there was still the goddam Mafia—watered down sure, but New York, Tampa, New Orleans, Kansas City, and St. Louis were places to be avoided. *So* what was left? Plenty. And maybe a lot of it could be set up right here.

Lasher turned the lens of his mind to the subject of houses. It had been a long time since he had anything to do with houses and now he found it satisfying to review their arithmetic. Five girls in a house could turn at least ten tricks each every night. At ten dollars a trick, which was bargain prices, the gross was five hundred dollars a night. Of course, you had to allow for the moon spells, and some girls hit the sauce so hard they were no good for anything, and some cheated the house if they weren't watched, and good pimps were hard to find, and there was always the risk some idiot cop would forget who was who and knock the place over.

Even so . . .?

Say a chain of twenty houses located in the right places around the country, and a good rotation system. Say a man could gross ten thousand a night, give or take a few thousand with holidays and the weather. Be a big Sam and count the girls' share for five thousand. Roughly, even with overhead, that left you with twenty-eight grand per week, which was worth thinking about.

A small yet very dependable warning signal went off in Lasher's brain. He reminded himself that times had changed and he murmured aloud, "Forget it!" Everyone was too independent now. Even hookers could add and subtract. And the customer situation was not at all the same as it was only a few years back. There was such a multitude of amateurs, a certain customer potential had been wiped out forever. Today men didn't seem to realize it was costing them more to take some broad out to dinner and buy her a few drinks than it would to visit a good house. And what could you do about call girls, escort services, and some social clubs that also cut into the market? No. There was just too much competition and too many headaches when there were so many other sweet things.

He left the inspiring view and ambled back to the bonbon box. His fat fingers prodded all through the contents until he found a candy which instinct told him must be all chocolate inside. He bit into it and frowned. His instincts about houses had been right, but he had been wrong about this bonbon. The interior was coconut. Why, he thought, accurately pitching the remaining half of the bonbon at his open mouth, why the hell didn't they mark bonbons on the outside so a person would know what was inside?

Lasher had noticed many changes in the city since his last visit, which now seemed so long ago. For one thing, he was already convinced something must be done about more recreation for its citizens. As he swallowed the last of the candy, he reached down into his vocabulary and plucked out the word *paucity*. There was a paucity of jukeboxes and game machines all through the city and its suburbs. Every bar and certain selected restaurants should have such machines whether they wanted them or not. He would telephone his office in Toledo and get things going. For openers, fifty of the latest machines must be shipped right away. Six of his best salesmen should arrive at the same time. They must all be experienced men who were not in the habit of taking "no" for an answer. For the first shake around he didn't want any salesman who was hot or even on parole. And customers who failed to cooperate were not to be pushed around unless it was absolutely necessary. The same procedure must be followed that was successful everywhere else. If the customer is stubborn, the salesmen find out where he lives. They call on his wife and be nice and polite and they point out how important it is for his health to be more progressive. I want to start in here quietly, Lasher thought, until I get the feel of the place.

Again he returned to the window. Where is that damn cop? It was twenty past three. To relieve his impatience he channeled his thoughts back toward the opportunities which surrounded him. There were so many. Who, for example, was protecting the parking lots in this city? He could not make himself believe that the full fees were going straight to the proprietors, yet apparently it was so. The situation should be changed. Of course it would not be a *big* project, but the insurance business was always steady. He had only to hire a squad of smart kid punks for a few nights, let one of his salesmen interview the attendant while the kids went to work, and every open lot in the city would soon be begging for protection. There never were enough cops to go around if you created a few diversions nearby. And when the insurance business was firmly established, everything quieted down nicely.

How about the movie houses? If they hadn't been stink-bombed lately or the seats slit with knives, it was because they were already paying off to some insurance organization, or this city was *really* a hick town. If the kids on the parking lots were any good they could be used later in the movie houses. There were so many things to do, he thought, and here I am wasting valuable time waiting for a door shaker.

He heard the sharp knock, but he was actually en route to the entranceway before it sounded. A special, animal-like intuition, developed over a lifetime of wariness, signaled the approach of any intruder—invited guest or not. To such information Lasher responded without thinking, and his huge body became activated as if by the tripping of an electrical relay.

He went first to the desk, picked up a pair of heavy tortoise-shell-rimmed glasses, tucked the *Wall Street Journal* under his arm, and marched to the door. The brooding frown left his face and became a preoccupied smile as he opened the door. He raised his heavy eyebrows in surprise and peered over the glasses at Hill.

"Oh. Yeah . . . I almost forgot. Come in! Come in!"

Hill glanced at the newspaper under Lasher's arm, then moved past him. As he continued into the room he did not look back at Lasher but, in passing, he said, "Since when did you start wearing glasses?"

"I always did wear glasses for reading."

"That's the first lie for today," Hill said easily. "You can do better." He made a half-circle of the living room, slowly, moving with his lion's grace, still not looking at Lasher, but seeming to focus his entire attention on a suitable place to lie down and curl his body.

Lasher watched him warily. And he quickly reached a conclusion. This Hill was no ordinary door rattler. He had an inconvenient memory, or did he just guess the glasses were a decoration? He could be had, of course, but certain adjustments might be necessary before he would behave himself. Nothing was the same any more except the power of money. Even the cops were changing. They were no longer to be trusted.

He placed the glasses on the desk and said to Hill, "Well, time passes. I guess we're all getting older."

He waited until Hill finally selected a chair, pulled it away from the window, and sat down. Their eyes met at last and Lasher knew a vague moment of uncertainty. Imitating Hill's pattern, he also made a wary half-circle of the room, which he terminated near the couch. He eased his bulk down and sighed patiently.

"You want a drink?" he asked.

"No."

"How about some candy?" He pointed his foot at the box on the coffee table. Hill shook his head and Lasher suddenly realized that Hill's eyes had never left him.

"That's a good-lookin' suit you got on. They must be paying cops well these days."

"Enough."

"Balls. There's never enough. You got any kids, Chief?"

"Two."

"You wouldn't believe it, but I always wanted some kids."

"No, I don't believe it."

Lasher ignored his flat statement. "But my wife," he went on, "has never been in good health. Just one thing after another. We just didn't dare take the chance. Of course, there was no use us trying to adopt a kid or so. If you have a record, they won't even listen to you."

"Is that so?"

"I suppose you're planning on sending your kids to college?"

"I'll try."

"That's the trouble. It's so damn expensive these days. But they got to go. A kid don't stand a chance nowadays unless he does."

"What time does your plane leave, Lasher?"

"What plane?"

"The one you're taking out of town today!"

"Now just a damn minute. What kind of talk is this?" Lasher allowed a mixture of surprise and hurt to cross the dumplings of his face. "I come here on a little vacation and right away the Chief of Police himself tells me to beat it. Now the Chamber of Commerce wouldn't consider that exactly the way to attract tourists." Lasher was careful to subdue the color range of his magnificent voice, for his instincts were bristling with messages. He wanted time to size up this determined-looking Irishman, to toy with him awhile before he melted into just another underpaid cop. Something about Hill's face pleased him and was so suggestive of a difficult conquest that he searched the reservoir of his vocabulary again for an exact word to describe what he would do to him. After an instant of elimination, he chose *devour*. He patted his great belly in anticipation. Yeah. When this cop left the room he would be mainly garbage.

Lasher smiled forlornly, played a brief tattoo across his belly with his enormous fingers, then cleared his throat in preparation for the voice which had never failed him. Finally, his finest basso profundo, sweetened by a dolorous quality, came forth exactly as he desired.

"I just don't know," he began. "I just really don't know how a man can tolerate as much as I have. It's taken me a lot of sweat to do just what you people recommended. Sure there was a time when I associated with boys who was too smart for theirselves, but all that was a long time ago. Most of them have gone now, one way or another. . . . I really don't know or care. You notice how I'm alone these days? I don't have a flock of guys hanging around. Times have changed, Hill. I lost interest in things which are not strictly legitimate. During the past five years I worked my ass off getting a fresh start all around. It isn't easy when everybody knows you're an ex-con, when you know the whole world is whisperin' behind your back. And it's even harder when guys like you never leave off pestering or inferring that I'm not clean . . . or taking any account whatsoever of the fact I'm now a respectable businessman with responsibility toward a lot of people. . . ."

Lasher paused and watched for signs of appreciation in his listener's eyes. He could detect no change, yet he was not disappointed. He had only begun. He injected a tone of warmth and optimism into his voice when he spoke again.

"But I don't hold hard feelings toward anybody. What the hell? It isn't worth the ulcers. And I get a kick out of being clean. You'd be surprised. Why I haven't even had a parking tag in the last five years! I give a thousand bucks to the Red Cross last campaign . . . you can check the records. I put through programs for the boys in my union nobody ever dared think of before . . . like they can take a vacation anywheres they want at reduced prices, like they can buy life insurance or any other kind of insurance at a much lower rate than they could on the outside, like they can buy a car, build a house . . . almost any little thing their hearts desires they can do because Theo Lasher has the way all paved for them."

"You bet you have," Hill said coldly. "The agency which handles the insurance is run by your half-brother. The vacation tickets and reservations are handled by the Paradise Travel Service which happens to have your feeble-minded uncle as treasurer. I don't know how you're going to play it when the Internal Revenue Department catches up with your credit union, but someday they're going to find it very interesting why you'll only loan at a reduced rate if they buy a car from Hagarty and Son, Incorporated . . . especially when Hagarty has been dead for years and his son is in the woolen business, and the Ohio Corporation books list Theo Lasher as president."

Lasher took a moment to reconsider Hill. Okay, so he did know too much for his own good. Throw him a bone and for sure he'd have a sudden change of attitude. "That's easily explained," he said. "We want to make sure our boys don't throw their borrowed money away on some heap, that's all. We don't want to see them taken by some lousy used-car dealer. It's protection for both our credit union and the party involved."

"Especially you. I didn't have time to dig through your housing loans, but I do know you're listed as vice-president of Enterprise Development Company, which has a strange way of winning the contract on every house your borrowers want to build. And it must have been a great surprise to you that out of nine contractors bidding on your new union building, which you need like nothing at all, the winner happened to be the same Enterprise Development Company."

"We got inflation. It's all in the air. The best place for a union's money is in solid real estate."

"You thought of a better place. In your pocket."

There was a long silence between them. Lasher rose ponderously and approached his guest. He stood over him in the heavy silence, looking down upon him as if he were chewing and digesting his animosity, and his great thyroid eyes bulged with resentment. Finally he blew out his breath and he said, "You think you are a very smart cop. If you had any goddamned sense you would not be one."

He shook his jowls emphatically and then diluted the bile in his voice with a hint of invitation.

"Now you listen to me. I pay my taxes, so I got rights like anybody else. You can search this whole joint and you won't find rods or nothin' else. I'm on a vacation which I got a right to take anywheres I please and you're wasting your time nosing around for something that just isn't here."

He paused and licked his full lips. Then he said, "No, what surprises me is a man like you, with a family and all, gets himself so wrapped up in a tin badge he can't see what the hell he's missing. You get all patriotic and waste a lot of time and energy worrying about the welfare of your city when any city is nothin' but a collection of jerks who live close to each other because they don't trust each other or got no place else to go, and the only way they make their bread is scratchin' each other's backs. Look around with a clear eye for a change and see how much screw-you-brother-I-got-mine is right here in your city. So what happens to the poor dumb cop in all this? They let him buy a uniform to make him feel important and forget he's just another city employee workin' for buttons which he can't wear on his uniform. He's just like the guy runs the streetcar, or hauls the garbage, or sweeps the streets, and when he gets all worn out and no good to himself or nobody else, if he lives that long . . . they give him the same generous reward they give the sewer inspector and the guy who picks up papers in the park. You get a pension nobody can live on without saving from the salary you can barely live on now. Does that make sense to you? Why, I got slobs in my union make as much as you and they don't have to worry about what some politician is going to do next and there ain't nobody going to tell them what to do."

"Except you," Hill said in such a subdued manner Lasher wondered if he need bother with any further bait.

"Except me. Right now you're gettin' real smart. And why is this the situation? Because I took time to think out what is good for Theo Lasher! Nobody never *gave* me *anything*, Hill! And they won't give anything to you. Why are you the Chief? Because somebody liked the color of your hair? Because you got a relative in City Hall? Not from what I hear. You worked up from flatfoot only because part of the time you must have been thinkin' about what was good for Hill. But you didn't go far enough. You haven't realized that you're finally sitting somewheres where you can do yourself some real good. Don't tell me you get any satisfaction out of throwing a bunch of poor hopheads and drunks in the can and once in a while pinching a few punk thieves who are just a little dumber than your cops. This is a career? You want to spend the rest of your life eating porridge and kale while the rest of the world gobbles caviar—?"

There was a clicking sound from the doorway entrance, then the door slammed. Lasher turned his head slightly and smiled, but the rest of his body remained still as if he had been expecting an interruption. After a moment a plain, middle-aged woman walked into the room. She was laden with packages and somewhat breathless.

"Well! Looks like you had a ball for yourself," Lasher said heartily. As Hill started to rise Lasher chuckled easily and waved his hand toward the woman. "That's the trouble when you take the wife on a vacation. They get the idea your bank account's on a vacation too!"

The woman smiled at Lasher and placed her packages on the writing desk. She was small, with fragile fluttering hands, and her cheeks seemed abnormally flushed. She was far from beautiful in any way and a suggestion of a mustache faintly marred her upper lip. Her hat and coat were black and without particular style. Her shoes were low-heeled and her stockings also black. Only her eyes were notably bright as she looked inquisitively at Hill.

"Dear, this is the Chief of Police, dropped by to say welcome. Chief Hill, meet my wife, Arlene."

"Pleased to meet you." She nodded.

"We sort of knew each other when," Lasher said, waving his hand at Hill. Then he roared with laughter. "Now what is all that junk you're carting up here?"

"Only a few things for Paula and Louise. They wouldn't forgive us if we came all the way here on a vacation and forgot to bring them anything."

"Paula and Louise are her nieces," Lasher explained. "You'd think they were her own kids. Why the hell don't you once in a while buy something for yourself?"

"I'll just leave you two alone to visit," she said. "Theo's always got so many things to talk about with men . . . and I'm sure tired. Shopping wears me out. I guess we're all getting a bit older."

"That's exactly what I was telling the Chief. All right, Arlene. You run along and take the load off your feet for a while."

She smiled at Hill and turned toward the bedroom.

"Any place special you'd like to go tonight?" Lasher called after her.

"Yes," she said with a little laugh. "To bed."

She glanced back at Hill, smiled again, and then disappeared into the bedroom.

"There's a great woman," Lasher announced as he looked after her. "She's put up with me good times and bad times for almost twenty-two years. *Sure* I like broads! But there's only one Arlene. And different from most wives, she never sticks her nose in my business. Which brings me back to you. . . ."

"Sit down, sit down and relax," Lasher said expansively. "Sure you don't want a drink? What kind of an Irishman are you who won't go for a bracer?"

"Not now," Hill said, watching the bedroom door swing to a closed position.

"You want to keep a clear head? Good. That's intelligent. Now apply some of your intelligence to what I was telling you before Arlene came back. I wasn't suggesting you should quit your job or anything like that. It's like what you might call a base salary. The same as what I get from the union. You pay your taxes right down the line on money like that, and you and I know how much is left after that. No! What I'm pointing out to you is how you got side-line opportunities which are a natural benefit of your job and which I believe you have neglected. For example, I have in mind one little possibility which all by itself could put those two kids of yours through college and have something left over to buy your wife a new set of silverware, which incidentally I can get you a reduction on, or a new fur coat which can also be arranged, or any little item like that which you might need. We take care of our people in a lot of ways."

Hill tipped his chair partly on one side and looked under it. Then he went to the window drapes and looked behind each one. He opened the drawers of the desk, glanced inside, then carefully examined the molding along the border of the walls and the chandelier that hung from the center of the ceiling. Finally he lifted the heavy-framed oil painting away from the wall and looked behind it.

Lasher chuckled happily. "You don't have to look for bugs here, my friend. I already did all that before you came. What I have to say is just between us and I'm just as anxious as you are to keep it that way."

"Just what did you have in mind?"

Lasher maintained his smile, but his eyes became fixed in a cold and empty stare. "I wouldn't want you to misunderstand me," he said, looking beyond Hill. "Since I don't have nothing going for me here, I couldn't even suggest a small percentage. Anyway my lawyers would never approve even presenting such an idea to a man in your position. However, I have a friend—"

"You also have some enemies. . . ."

"Every man has. I wouldn't want you to be one if I can help it. Now if you're really interested—?"

"Why do you think I came up here alone?"

Lasher's eyes widened. He had enjoyed playing Hill, letting him run away and hauling him back like a fish. Now the fun was almost over. He wished Hill had been a little more difficult. But he should have read the signals the moment he appeared at the door. A police chief who really intended to keep his nose clean would have brought along at least one witness. So here was a real pig. He wanted to get his shanty-Irish fingers in the pie and lick them all by himself.

"You are beginning to see the light," Lasher said. "You were already thinking right when you came here alone."

"About this friend of yours who might help me," Hill said carelessly. "Would it be something in the nature of an advisory capacity? I have to think of appearances. We have a rule about outside employment."

"You would be called upon from time to time for consultation with my friend. We—he would not expect you to be too active— in fact, just the opposite."

"I see."

"You would be on a retainer fee which would not amount to a great deal at first."

"I thought you said it would be at least enough to put two kids through college."

"Oh, it would be, I'm sure. It would naturally depend on how much your services were required."

"I don't like that arrangement."

"Why not?"

"Because you would be the one who determined how much my services were worth."

"Not me. My *friend*." Lasher smiled.

"All right. Your friend."

"He's generous when he gets the right kind of cooperation, and later on I'm sure he will want to expand. Then naturally everybody concerned benefits."

"Would the payments be made in cash?"

"My friend does most of his business on a cash basis."

"How much?"

"You want numbers? All right. Let's say a grand a month for openers . . . something like that."

"It would have to be that, not something like that. What business is your friend in?"

Lasher twisted his lips into a tight rosette. He hesitated momentarily, then said, "The amusement business and a few other things."

"The amusement business? Could he also be in the telephone business?"

"He might be. But your services wouldn't be required on that."

"Too bad. I know quite a bit about the telephone business."

Lasher raised his eyebrows in quick surprise. Hello? This Hill might be some fun after all. How the hell did he find out about the telephone business? It was barely started. Okay. So his price would just have to be a little higher. Okay, okay. So now for a little bargaining. There was no rush.

"How long," he asked, "do you think you'll be holding your present position?"

"A long time if I don't do anything foolish."

"When is the next city election?"

"November . . . next year."

"That's not very long. We have to take into consideration that with a new city administration you might be out on your ass."

"It's always possible."

"If that happened, your usefulness to my friend's organization could be very limited. But I will try to talk him into a grand and a half a month until we see how things go."

"That sounds more like it. Especially since my services are badly needed right now in this telephone matter. I can't understand how your friend could be so careless."

A film of doubt clouded Lasher's eyes and left them dry white balls with small colored targets in the centers.

"How do you mean?" he said, making no attempt to conceal his suspicion.

Hill rose and started for the entrance foyer at a funereal pace. He looked at the floor instead of at Lasher and he moved exactly like a lion slowly pacing his cage. After a few steps he reversed his direction and said, "It's just too damn bad we couldn't get together."

"All right," Lasher said. "Make it two grand a month until we see how things go."

"You didn't ask my advice soon enough . . . or anyone else's, it seems. That little telephone racket of yours has a hitch to it because you're stealing the lists. I'll admit that conspiracy to commit petty theft isn't much of a rap, but I just have a hunch you wouldn't care to spend six months in our county jail right now. For one thing they tell me the food is lousy—"

"You can't hang a thing on me," Lasher said. He was surprised at the note of apprehension in his voice. It was an ugly sound and he stifled it immediately. "Nobody can prove I ever heard of it."

"Your friend might meet the wrong people unless he's protected and he might be persuaded to talk. But that's not what's worrying me. I came up here alone because I have to think of the future. If I go into a thing like this it's got to last long enough to make it worth the risk. The way things look right now your whole proposition could be over any minute."

Lasher's deep laugh rumbled across the room. "For Christ's sake, what's more solid than AT&T? We're part of an institution."

"We? How about you? How long are *you* going to last? All I have to worry about is who is the next mayor."

"I got no worries at all. The doctors say I'm in great shape. A little overweight maybe, but great."

Hill reached into his pocket and took out a photograph. He held it before Lasher's face so he could see it plainly.

"How about this individual? Do your doctors know about him?"

Lasher glanced at the photograph, which was of a man standing in front of the hotel. He was about to look away when he suddenly reached out and seized the photograph. He studied it very closely and his lower lip began to quiver. He could not take his eyes from the photograph. He said almost inaudibly, "Where did you get this?"

"It was taken by one of my men about an hour ago which is why I was a little late. If you don't recognize the front of this hotel, you certainly should recognize Harry Bandaneria. He's changed a little, put on some weight maybe, but I doubt if his disposition has improved."

A cold chill swept all through Lasher's fat body. I'm seeing things, he thought. But it *was* Bandaneria . . . or was it?

"Do you want those spectacles you need so much?" Hill asked. "Now what do you suppose Harry Bandaneria is doing in our fair city, let alone staying in this hotel?"

"He's staying *here?*" Lasher dropped the photo on the coffee table before him and stared at it. Suddenly his forehead became speckled with droplets of perspiration. He squirmed around, pulled a handkerchief from his rear pocket, and wiped at his face and neck.

"He's in room 429 if you want to give him a ring for old time's sake. I'm sure Bandaneria has some plans for your health . . . like a .38-caliber enema. It's too bad I can't put Bandaneria in the can but we haven't got a thing on him. Only you and I know he's not here just to see the sights."

Lasher pushed himself quickly to his feet. He crossed the room until he stood very close to Hill, and for a long time he stared at him in silence. His eyes were uncertain, but his great body was poised in a rigid position of barely controlled anger. "What are you trying to do to me?" he asked. "Harry Bandaneria is retired . . . in New Jersey."

"You're sure of that? Go ahead. Make it easy for him. Room 429. Harry probably wants company. Why don't you give him a ring?"

Lasher snorted. Still looking at Hill, he moved cautiously to the telephone. "You're bluffing." He reached for the telephone and picked it up.

Watching him, Hill said, "I was in Homicide for quite a while.

But this is the first time I ever had a chance to talk to the corpse."

Lasher hesitated, then very slowly replaced the telephone. "I think you're lying."

"Why take a chance? Bandaneria's been sweating you out for five years. This time he can't afford to foul up the job and you know it. He'll get you sure as you're standing there if something isn't done right now. Now, in my new advisory capacity I happen to have a couple of suggestions."

"Like what?" Lasher asked hoarsely. "I haven't even got a rod."

Then Lasher kicked the coffee table aside, doubled his fists and again moved toward Hill. The color returned to his face and his thick lips set in a firm line, "Why, you cheap Irish fink! You think you can take over my idea? I'll make you eat dung!"

"Keep your hands where they are. Remember you're getting older. Of course we could put you in the can, but Harry would only be waiting for you until we let you out."

"You're lying! You're trying to pressure the wrong man, Hill! I'll—"

"You won't be able to do anything if you don't take my advice. But you need more than advice. You need help and quick. You want to make a deal? I'll give it to you. Two of my men will meet you down in the lobby in twenty minutes. They'll take you to the airport. Special car, no extra charge. Take the next plane out no matter where it's going."

"If Bandaneria's got a rod you can pick him up for that. Pick him up for anything. I'll give you plenty of leads."

"We're not working for you."

Lasher pushed his massive head forward until his face was very close to Hill's. He stared into his eyes, examining him as if he were searching for some minute flaw.

"So . . .?" he said finally. "You forget all about your poor kids going to college. Because you're so ambitious you want to be a *real* Boy Scout. Well, it don't work. You don't scare me and I don't believe Bandaneria's within two thousand miles of here."

Hill shrugged his shoulders. "Suit yourself. You know the man better than I do." He walked deliberately to the entryway. Near the door he hesitated. "Just in case you get some sense and change your mind, I'll tell my men to wait thirty minutes for you. If you don't show up then . . . tell your wife to call me personally if anything should happen to you. Oh, don't worry about between here and the lobby. The two bellboys who will come for your bags will take good care of you. Be generous. Give them a big tip. They're also cops and, like you say, they probably can use the money."

"And what's the kickback, *Chief?*" Lasher snarled. "When do you get *your* tip?"

"When you get in the escort car, give the two men in it a list of everybody who has anything to do with your telephone business. I want names, addresses, phone numbers . . . everything. Be sure it's accurate because they'll radio-check it while you're en route to the airport. If you don't give them the list they won't let you in the car. So long, Lasher. Aren't you lucky Bandaneria's afraid to fly?"

Hill closed the door quietly behind him and stood listening. From within the suite he heard an agonized groan and he knew it was a sound that could only come from Theo Lasher. Hill crossed his fingers. It had been like putting a temperamental baby to bed. Maybe he would stay put, and maybe . . .?

He thought of the last look in Lasher's eyes and it reassured him. The mere mention of the name Bandaneria had thrown such a fright into Lasher even his vision must have suffered. Otherwise, he might have discovered the man in the photograph was not really Harry Bandaneria. He was a retired cop named Spanker who had been selected out of more than a hundred possible candidates as most nearly resembling the photos in Bandaneria's file. So Spanker was brought from his home by a special police car and taken to Hill's office. The facial resemblance was remarkable, but he was considerably taller than the real Bandaneria. So it had been necessary to photograph Spanker from above, and he had been instructed to bend his knees slightly. A hat helped—Spanker was quite bald and Bandaneria had a head of hair any man would envy. All of this had taken time and Spanker was even now installed in Room 429 as Bandaneria of Pine Woods, New Jersey. He would stay there until Lasher was out of town.

As he rode down in the elevator, Hill wondered how long it had been since the two men had actually seen each other. He decided it was unimportant. Individuals like Bandaneria and Lasher, any of the ungratefuls who ever had anything to do with the Mafia, slept uneasily for the rest of their lives. They knew what it was to play for keeps.

❖❖❖ 33 ✛✛✛

When Hill left the hotel he went directly to the bridge. Deneen was waiting for him. He held a pair of binoculars which he waved futilely at a gray overcast now sweeping in from the sea. The stratus clouds obscured the upper two-thirds of the towers.

"I could see him up until just a few minutes ago," Deneen explained unhappily. "But he's gone now. I've been waiting for a break in the clouds, but so far no luck. It's a strange thing . . . I can't explain it . . . maybe I'm wacky too . . . or I've been here too long. But I really *want* to save that guy. He's sort of a special 800."

"I thought he tried to kill you."

"Not me. He was aiming at an idea, I think."

"You *have* been here too long."

The cloud deck was rapidly becoming more solid. There were small, very occasional breaks through which the last of the sun glare could be seen, but Deneen explained these never seemed to coincide with the position of the support cable which curved upward to the tower. It was very possible, he added, that Barbee could have jumped, and unless someone had been looking at just the right place at just the right moment, no one would know of it.

There was one compensation. The sea wind was so chill and damp it had caused a great many of the spectator crowd to abandon their vigil. There was no longer a brazen holiday mood about the relatively few who huddled behind rocks, trees, autos, and the further escarpments of the bridge. They were simply waiting now, grimly determined not to be cheated of what they had come to see. The mothers had all left, if only because their impatient offspring were squawling with boredom and cold. The older people had left to warm their bones. There remained only a scattered herd of teenagers who seemed interested mainly in their transistor radios, and a few groups of commuters who lived on either side of the bridge. There was also a busload of tourists who preferred craning their necks and looking at nothing to whatever it was they had originally been scheduled to see. Hill was astounded to observe several of them aim their cameras at the flannel clouds and carefully photograph the nothing.

"When did you last talk to him?" Hill asked.

"Not since I tried to go up after him. He'd been doing a lot of talking, but he hasn't made a sound since the clouds came in. Actually these idiot crowds have given us more trouble than anything."

"If we can't see him, he can't see us. Maybe without an audience he'll calm down and get some sense."

Deneen said, "With these clouds maybe we could get a lot closer to him. With your permission, I'd like to try going up again. I don't think he could see me coming until the very last moment. It's a lot different than it was before."

"You stay right here and that's that. But what about trying a helicopter?"

"I called the Army. They said sure and sent a chopper with a ladder. You know what our friend Barbee did? Luckily, the angle of the cable into the tower makes it impossible to get very close to him. He fired twice at the chopper and put a fine hole in the plastic bubble behind the pilot's ear. The pilot left immediately. I talked to him later on the telephone and he said this was not a combat operation and he already had a Purple Heart."

"It's nice to be able to make a choice."

"I had the Coast Guard shoot up some rockets with a breeches-buoy rig, figuring the novelty of the thing might lure him into it. After three tries they finally hit a place about three hundred feet below him. It's just all the poop their rockets had."

"Did he show any interest in it?"

"Barbee laughed his head off and then yelled down that when he was twelve years old he made a chemical rocket that could go twice as high."

"What about getting a priest out here?"

A thoughtful smile passed across Deneen's face.

"One thing is for sure. He's sour on all churches. He had some uncomplimentary things to say about the Pope, then he took off on clergy in general. He said things hadn't changed much since the priests ate every ox that was brought for sacrifice. And he keeps asking us to tell him where they hid the simplicity of Christ. . . ."

"He sounds like a Communist."

"No, he can't be a Commie either. He raved for ten minutes about how the Commies were the new-style priests with Lenin being their Messiah . . . and how all of us were going to be living in catacombs if they won, which they were about to do."

"Maybe he's one of those warmed-over fascists?"

"I don't think he's an *ist* anything. And he certainly isn't an atheist. When he calms down, which is happening more and more often, he looks up at the sky and prays. Not for himself. For us. He talks to God like they were pals. It's hard to explain, but after a while it kind of gets to you."

"How about getting a psychiatrist out here and let him talk through the loud hailer?"

"I could be wrong, but I think it would be the worst thing we could do. Nut though he may be, he's a very fundamental guy." Deneen paused and looked up hopefully at a minute break in the overcast. It vanished almost immediately and he said, "I wish you'd let me get his wife out here."

"All right. We'll have to risk it. But not the kids."

"I'll go get her."

"No. Stay here. You know the situation better than I do. What's her address?"

Deneen gave it to him. As he did so a long tear appeared in the cloud deck as if it had been ripped open by the tower. The sky was a deep blue beyond the gash and the slanting sun transformed the tower's red paint into a glowing bronze. Deneen quickly raised the binoculars to his eyes. "He's still there," he sighed. He was silent a moment as he made a slight adjustment to the binoculars. "You know what it looks like he's doing? I think . . . he's crying again."

"Crying?"

"Yes. He did it once before. It was when he was raving on about the bridge. He said for all of us pitiful fools to take a good look at this beautiful bridge while we could. He said it was a masterpiece of man's work and the men who died building it were lucky. He was getting pretty hoarse by then and the wind was coming up, but I heard him say he was weeping for us who would soon destroy the bridge . . . all of us, he kept repeating. He said the ultimate had been reached in good and evil. This bridge and the bomb. . . ."

Hill tipped his lion's head to one side and carefully regarded his deputy. Outwardly he appeared to be the same Deneen—as always the ultra-efficient cop who usually managed to avoid mixing sentiment with duty. But something had happened to Deneen on this bridge. Although the cloud cover had closed in again and only the very lowest section of the cable was still visible, Deneen stood staring up at the murk, forlornly holding his binoculars at the ready. He seemed to be begging the clouds to part.

"Are you sure you're all right?" Hill asked.

"Yes. But that guy gets to me somehow. He's no ordinary 800. And we're . . . we're so damned *helpless!*"

"It won't help anything if you catch pneumonia. Better get something on your bald noggin."

Hill left him still staring upward. He went directly to his car and radioed Communications for a progress report on Lasher. After a moment he was able to smile. Lasher and his wife had already placed themselves in the custody of Inspectors West and Oliver. They had just driven away from the hotel, bound for the airport. Hill restrained an urge to flick imaginary dust from his hands. He warned himself not to be overly optimistic. Lasher was still not actually on a plane.

As he leaned across the width of the front seat to replace the microphone in the glove compartment, a fire truck parked on the opposite side of the bridge came into his line of vision. Several firemen were gathered behind the truck, looking up at the tower. Near them a man stood apart and alone—his back toward Hill's car. He was not looking up. There was something very familiar about his stance, so solid he seemed defiantly rooted to the ground.

Hill slammed the compartment shut and sat upright again. Why had that man seemed so familiar?

He started the car. Why had that man made him think of Timothy Hardy? He leaned back across the seat for a second look and was relieved. No. He was certain the man was a fire commissioner he knew very slightly.

As he started the car and negotiated the barriers set across the area, Hill tried to remember the commissioner's name. But he could not. All he could think of was the name Tim Hardy and he wished it were not so. There were so many other things on his mind.

❖❖❖ 34 ✦✦✦

Moore had a pad of yellow lined paper on the desk before him. On it he carefully wrote the answers Harriet Rankin gave to each of his questions. He doubted if he would ever refer to what he had written on the pad thus far, but the time required for each inscription gave him a chance to shape succeeding questions exactly as he desired. He also knew that the long pauses, during which only the sound of his pen broke the stillness, were difficult for anyone giving testimony. The intervals were too long for easy concentration on a single theme, and particularly on the various nuances of a basic lie. He planned each question so that it came slightly out of sequence, waiting until the memory of the previous answer was slightly clouded. There was a hinge point to every lie and the system had always served him well. If the truth was being told then there was no need for a suspect or a witness to suddenly remember manufactured angles. True facts were easily remembered, even though they might be out of continuity and somewhat colored by time.

Throughout interviews held in his own office, Moore deliberately kept his voice low and gentle. As the testifier strained to hear him, his entire manner suggested that what he wrote on the yellow paper was merely of routine importance—"for the record." Thus he always began with facts which had little bearing on what he believed must be swirling through an opposing mind—when was the suspect born and where . . . occupation . . . address . . . telephone number . . . things he already knew.

Unless he was trying to anger a suspect or witness or intimidate them, he rarely accused them of lying. It was usually unnecessary and might block the possibility of an early confession, which would come eventually if one by one he set down the answers and then backtracked in a feigned attempt at interrelating the things he had been told. He would appear unhappy as well as bewildered, even ask his guest for assistance so that some logical conclusions could be drawn from what had been said in a variety of ways. It was an art at which Moore was such a master that a large majority of the most skillful liars finally surrendered and told the truth. It was then that Moore crumpled the first pages of what he had written and started all over again, quietly and methodically, lest his guest reconsider and start on a new pattern of lies.

Harriet Rankin sat opposite his desk, her hands clasped behind her head, her feet crossed, but her knees spread wide. She had pushed her back away from the chair, slumping in the manner of teenagers. Her full breasts, exactly outlined beneath the tight sweater, rose and fell as she breathed in a fashion which was obviously intended to convey great emotion. She squirmed occasionally, but not like any young girl Moore had ever seen. She kept her eyes on the ceiling most of the time, although she would frequently glance sidewise through the crook of her elbow at Rafferty who sat near the door. A new huskiness had come to her voice, and most of her answers were given in an invitational whisper which Moore was certain she had adopted from the last bedroom movie she had seen.

She had several times displayed a personal affectation which both Moore and Rafferty found distressing. Before she answered a question she would push out her tongue, wiggle it a few times as if tasting the air, and then slowly wet her lips.

Moore thought, If she does it again I'll reach out and slap her, knowing that he would not.

"Now, Harriet, where do you go to school?"

"I'm changing."

"Oh? From where to where?"

"I've been in Public 49. But I'm transferring."

"To where?" he asked again. The way she smiled and the sudden excitement in her eyes heartened Moore. At least little Harriet Rankin was displaying a normal emotion.

"To Larkin's."

"That's a private school."

"Of course."

"When did you make the change?"

"I haven't yet. I'll start in a couple of days. As soon as my eye gets better."

"Congratulations. You have to be a pretty smart girl to get into Larkin's."

"I always get straight A's."

"When did you decide to make this change?"

"Oh, ages and ages ago."

"Any special reason?"

"Who wants to sit in that concentration camp they call a school, especially when you're a drillion times smarter than anyone in your class except Roland Kupper, who is a way out genius as anyone knows. A real astronaut, *he's* so far out. None of the other kids at 49 have anything. Slope-heads! You should see them, except you wouldn't believe your eyes. They eat candy and smoke at the same time . . . you know, things like that. Real raunch! Imagine such a lack of sophistication. . . ."

"It sounds pretty awful," Moore said solemnly. "Larkin's is rather expensive, isn't it?"

"I suppose so."

"Is your uncle paying for it?"

"*Certainement.*" Now where the hell, Moore wondered, did this kid learn French?

"It seems he wants the best for his niece."

"*Certainement.*" She slid a little further down in the chair so that her buttocks were poised almost on the edge of the seat. And she wiggled her tongue and wet her lips once more.

"I'm sure you'll do very well at Larkin's."

"Certainement."

"Now this vacant lot where you say the Perez brothers took you. . . . Where is it from your home?"

"Just down the street."

"Which way? East or west?"

"Oh, I wouldn't know that."

"If you were to leave your home and go to the vacant lot, would you turn to your right or left?"

"To my right. May I inquire what this has to do with my social position? I'm disgraced forever. You realize *that,* don't you?"

"Now, it's not quite as bad as all that, Harriet. It was unfortunate, but the best thing for you to do is forget it as soon as you can."

"I'm a marked woman."

"Nonsense. Someday you'll grow up and marry a fine young man."

"If you don't tell anybody."

"I'm not going to tell anyone anything. I'm just trying to get the whole picture so the Perez boys don't tell me a lot of lies."

"Let's get on to something more interesting, or take me home!" How firm she could be, Moore thought. God help the young man who finally does marry her!

Moore looked at the scribbling he had done on his yellow paper. Finally he said, "Now a while ago you told us that after you were raped, you picked yourself up and saw the Perez brothers just driving away. Do I have that correctly?"

"Yes."

"And then you told us that you ran to the corner of Lisbon and Twelfth. Right?"

"Yes."

"I'm puzzled. Maybe you can help me get this thing straightened out. The vacant lot is to the right of your home if a person starts from there. But if you started out for the corner of Lisbon and Twelfth then you'd have to turn left. Right?"

"*Certainement.*"

"Which means that when you ran from the vacant lot you would have to pass directly in front of your home before you could arrive at the corner."

Harriet said nothing. She squirmed a little way back up on the chair, recrossed her feet, but did not close her knees.

"Now it strikes me as rather strange that you went right past your house, apparently preferring a deserted street corner to a place where I assume you would have found comfort and assistance."

"What's so strange about it?"

Moore hesitated. "Well, isn't it more natural for a girl in trouble to run to those who love her?"

"Who said they loved me?"

"You did."

"*I did not!*" She suddenly sat up very straight in her chair. Finally, thought Moore. I have at last managed to make Miss Harriet Rankin sit up and pay attention.

"I should think it a very strong demonstration of affection if your uncle has offered to send you to an expensive girls' school."

"He did *not* offer!"

"How was the agreement reached then?"

"What agreement?"

"That you should change from Public 49 to Larkin's?"

"I *told* you. I just wanted to go. That's all."

"A lot of young ladies would like to go to Larkin's. Their families either can't afford it, or apparently don't love them enough."

"Well . . ." Harriet paused and licked her lips. "You really want to know the truth?"

Moore nodded his head and tried to free his mind of the certainty that what he was about to hear might not be what he wanted to hear. Those bums, the Perez brothers. They weren't worth all this, no matter who was doing the lying. He sat looking at Harriet, waiting, while she seemed to be winding up for a drama class recitation or a bedroom confidence—he was not sure

which—waiting and deliberately reminding himself that the reputation of the Perez brothers for lying far exceeded anything a
teenage girl could achieve. "Yes, Harriet. Of course I would like
to know the truth."

"It was my aunt's idea."

"I see. Do I gather your uncle might not have been so enthusi-
astic?"

"Well . . . no . . . not exactly."

"What do you mean, not exactly?"

"Well . . . he hasn't any imagination. He has to be made to
see things."

"And you, together with your aunt, did so?"

"Yes." She hesitated, then caught her breath. "But for heaven's
sake, don't tell *her!*"

"Why not?"

"It would ruin their marriage."

"Why? They had to finally get together on the idea if they
were going to make it come true."

"Yes, but you just don't understand."

"I guess I don't . . . unless perhaps your uncle gets pretty
mad when he drinks?"

"Yes," she said quickly. *"That's* it!"

"Had your uncle been drinking last night?"

"When . . .?"

"Last night?"

"No."

"You're sure?"

"Certainement."

Moore was relieved. Apparently she only knew one word of
French instead of, as he had half feared, speaking it fluently.

"Why are you so sure your uncle hadn't been drinking? You
told us the Perez brothers picked you up about four o'clock. You
went for a ride, and then they brought you back to the vacant lot
about . . . what time was that?"

"Was what?"

"The time they took you to the vacant lot."

"I . . . I can't think just now."

"I'll refresh your memory." He flipped back through his yellow pages. "When you first came in here you said you thought it was about eight o'clock. Is that right?"

"Yes. If I said so. . . ."

"Well, you did. Now how long would you say you were in the vacant lot?"

"Oh, I don't know . . . everything was happening. It was terrible."

"Did you leave their car and go to the vacant lot of your own free will?"

"Oh, no."

"How did they get you there then?"

"They . . . they dragged me. . . ." Harriet bent her head until Moore could see only the top of it.

"How?"

"How do you drag anyone?"

"I'm interested in how they dragged you. Was there one on each side or one in front and one behind you . . . or just how was it done?"

"I don't like to think of these things. Please don't make me think. . . ."

"It has to be done, Harriet." A trembling passed through her shoulders. She shook her head slowly back and forth but did not raise it.

"Would you say you were in the vacant lot half an hour?"

"Maybe."

"Then what were you doing between, let us say, eight-thirty and the time Officer Slattery found you on the corner of Lisbon and Twelfth at twelve minutes past nine? It only takes a few minutes to go from the vacant lot to the corner."

"I was hysterical. I don't remember."

"Did you go to your home before you went to the corner?"

"No."

"Were you with the Perez brothers all the time until you were dragged to the vacant lot?"

"Yes."

"Then you did not go to your home at *any* time between approximately four o'clock when the Perez boys picked you up and the time Officer Slattery found you?"

"No."

"Then please tell me how you could be so sure your uncle hadn't been drinking?"

There was a silence and Moore resolved to let it last as long as possible. It was the little things. The oddments of fact, so often half buried beneath a jungle of fiction, that eventually reflected an instant of light. The little things lying like a broken piece of glass on the side of a mountain. At just the right moment, and only then, it would catch the sun and shine with importance.

Moore's original and annoying hunch would not alone have been enough. It lacked any point of focus. If he had not learned from a girl who had nothing to do with Harriet's misfortune that her uncle drank, then he might have been a much longer time discovering how he had been led away from the framework of truth. And the strange thing was it made no difference if what a girl who was herself in trouble had said about the uncle was true, or merely gossip. It had served to betray Harriet Rankin.

He glanced at Rafferty, and saw he understood. He slowly tore off all the sheets of yellow paper on which he had written so many useless answers. He crumpled the paper in his fist and dropped it in the wastebasket. He adjusted the pad before him and smoothed it with the palm of his hand. He looked finally at Harriet as if newly aware of her presence. Her head was still bent and he heard her sigh.

"There is something you don't know, Harriet. The Perez brothers drove their car into a filling station and held it up. It happened at seven o'clock. You were not with them."

Now she looked up and Moore saw the fear in her eyes. And anger. Then suddenly and quite magically her face cleared. Once more she appeared entirely in command of herself.

"There is something you don't know. I *was* with them."

"Oh? How was it you weren't seen?"

"I was in the back."

"The back of what?"

"The car. I was hiding in the back seat."

"I see." Moore made a brief scribble with his pen as if he had seriously resumed writing.

"Where was the filling station, Harriet?"

"How should I know? I was hiding."

"That's hardly the proper place for a young lady who is about to attend Larkin's. Were you also hiding when they went on to the drugstore and held it up?"

"Yes."

"Hiding in the same place?"

"Yes."

"All right, Harriet. You can start telling us the truth now. The Perez brothers didn't hold up a drugstore."

He relit the stub of his cigar and his great nose rose slightly with each quick puff to avoid cremation. When the conflagration was sufficiently intense, he picked up his pen again.

"Now. Exactly when was it that your uncle agreed you could go to Larkin's?"

✧✧✧ 35 ✦✦✦

She smoothed her jade-green dress and twisted around on the bunk so she could count the overhead bars from another angle.

Little Sally counted things this way. Rememberin' when things was good and not so good. There was the house near the state line, well practically on it, and a girl had her regulars so you could average maybe four tricks a night . . . counting Saturdays for six. And Li'l Sally got keep which was so-so and two bucks a trick for herself. An' Li'l Sally or nobody else kept no more even if was a tip, else you find yourself with a mouthful of gums instead of teeth. You keep out one dime more and Big Louise say she call for Eddie and every girl ever worked there knew about Eddie. He liked girls' teeth—all over the floor. He liked to make gummers. Li'l Sally who was twenty-one knew better than the others . . . counted and got the hell out. You keep all the trick money for yourself.

Comes now the trouble because you had to make your own connects and buy your own bindles and Jesus you couldn't turn enough tricks to ever stay stoned. It didn't make no difference how good you could count or who rammed you in the piggy-bank.

Clear now. Everything . . . all things clear. All the time, kid, you get a paper here and a paper there and a balloon here maybe and it's anywhere from five bucks for a little no-good pop to fifty bucks from a cutter who thought he was in the sugar business.

And now you got a concrete head, that's what it's like, concrete. Like a mixer with stones banging around inside every time you try to think, like the snow cold jiggin' through your belly, like . . .

She swung quickly off the bunk and went to hang on the vertical bars which formed one wall of the cell. Slowly she lifted herself off her feet. And in doing so she turned slightly so that she saw the marks on her arm. She kissed at the marks impulsively again and again, sucking at them with all her starved intensity.

Then, dropping, she began to scream. She screamed without sound until she had slithered down the bars and become a small green thing trembling in her wilderness.

✦✦✦ 36 ✦✦✦

Spearing was almost happy he had lost twenty-two dollars on the sixth race at Santa Anita because he could direct his thoughts to lamentation rather than to the secret which so needed outside appreciation. It was a confidence which he knew he would be incapable of holding much longer. So to Oscar Munson who covered the police beat for the *Herald* and who was his only available audience, he said, "The donkey fell down!"

In Spearing's estimation Oscar Munson had always been a hoity-toity, take-on-airs, superconscientious bastard, who thought he was Horace Greeley, Hemingway, Ernie Pyle and Proust all rolled into one guy, when the only real genius he had was for making things tough for everybody in the newsroom—especially he knew who. He was, Spearing thought, a disgrace to his profession. Other people saw Munson pretend to work and read the drivel he wrote and it gave them very dangerous ideas about what Spearing should be doing. Munson spent far too much valuable time chasing all over the city trying to dig up facts, instead of sitting here in the newsroom of the old building like anybody with good sense and letting the facts come to him. It looked bad. For scale, which was also what Munson received for his labors, it simply wasn't worth going to all that effort when no one at any city desk, much less the idiots who read the stories, cared what the facts were. Spearing had told Munson a thousand times that sex and blood, the two elements combined if possible, were the only things worth reporting, because they were the only things the idiots would read. Yet Munson had many times betrayed him, proving that you could not trust a newspaperman any more than you could trust a cop. Or anyone else. Munson had on several occasions been so naïve and devious as to file a story favorable to the police. Those excretions had been the end-all and be-all of treachery.

Spearing had belabored Munson endlessly on the subject, explaining, at first patiently and finally in desperation, that the heads of all cops regardless of rank were stuffed with a fatty tissue of remarkable absorbent power. It was the reason they were cops. The most veiled compliment, the merest suggestion that cops were anything other than parasites living remarkably well on the public dole, thieving hypocrites, fascist bullies in uniform, profound liars, and career sadists, upset the whole scheme of things. Spearing had warned Munson that every time he revealed a cop in a heroic light he was planting another tangling vine in the ever-growing garden of a police state. Who knew what the bastards were really up to? Did they tell anything to anyone except their equally Irish priests who would of course be in on the ultimate spoils? Munson should realize these things which he still did not, any more than the three other police reporters who were at least neutral enough to lambaste Hill and his whistle blowers with acceptable regularity.

But the others were not in the newsroom now and the only target for Spearing's financial grief and suppressed excitement was this eggheaded Munson whose reactions were, as ever, detached. He sat on the opposite side of the newsroom reading a book on criminology. He was always reading some such nonsense and looking more like a professor in his study rather than a proper newsman. The fool had even gone through the full course at the Police Academy, claiming the experience gave him a better understanding of his job. There, in Spearing's opinion, he had been hopelessly brain-washed.

Although Munson had always avoided a direct answer, Spearing suspected him of the most heinous crime of all. It was said that Munson had graduated from a school of journalism. Only such a background could account for his disgusting industry and complete naïveté.

"The goddamned donkey *fell down* and he was twenty to one!" Spearing's oatmeal complexion became a mobile canvas for his anguish. His lips fell away from his yellow teeth until his mouth was like an open wound. For a moment no sound came from his throat though his tongue moved experimentally as if molding the stunning information he was about to deliver. "Not only did the goddamned donkey fall down, but he was three lengths ahead of Nutmeg when he did it, which is as good as putting the race in my pocket. It was exactly what Sam said would happen, only Sam did not tell me the donkey was going to fall down." Spearing shook his head in despair. "I hope the stumblebum broke his leg and the jockey's neck. I hope, I pray four hundred and forty times, which is exactly how many dollars I would have won if the donkey did not fall down, that they had to shoot them both. If Sam hadn't told me of something equally valuable I would join that nut on the bridge."

"Have you filed anything yet today?" Munson asked without looking up from his book.

"I have not. There's a rape case down in General Works, but I have to lay off rapes for a while because my dear editor's wife is tired of reading about same. I saw the girl, incidentally, and when she's ready for another rape, I'm her man. Brownell had a bigamy case which the sonofabitch deliberately whitewashed so I couldn't get a story out of it. . . ."

Spearing paused and his lugubrious eyes took on a new look of cunning. "But," he said casually, "I'm not interested in petty affairs like Brownell's bigamist, or girls with ruptured hymens, or nuts on bridges who can't make up their silly minds."

There were rollers on Spearing's chair. Suddenly he shoved against the floor with his feet and propelled himself across the room. He dragged one foot, causing the chair to make a gentle turn and come to a precise stop alongside Munson.

"What interests me," Spearing began in his most confidential manner, "is not the events of this dull day, but what gives tomorrow. For the first time in eleven years, which is exactly how long I've been sitting in this room, old honest Abe Spearing has himself a real break. In fact, it can be so big, the miserable, miserly bastards who run my sheet don't deserve it."

Spearing lowered his voice almost to a whisper and moved as close to Munson as the arms of their chairs would permit. "You probably won't be seeing much of me around here any more because I just may have my own television page which is coming up for grabs very soon."

"Congratulations," Munson said. He made an attempt to concentrate on his book, but Spearing pushed it aside.

"How would you like to know that our Chief of Police, Mr. Colin Galahad Hill, is not quite the white knight he would have us and the public believe? There is rust on his armor and the white bangtail upon which he rides so piously has fistula of the withers, pole evil, and probably the heaves."

Munson looked steadily at Spearing, but he kept a finger on the page where his reading had been interrupted. "Sometimes I think you sit up nights deliberately trying to think up ways of saying things so no one can possibly know what you are talking about. I have about ten more seconds to spare, then please let me get on with my reading. And besides, Hill's middle name is not Galahad."

"How would you also like to know that our virtuous Police Chief has been meeting privately with Mr. Harry Bandaneria of Pine Woods, New Jersey?" Spearing bared his yellow fangs in triumph. *"Now,"* he said in his most patronizing manner, "have you got more than ten seconds?"

"Where did you ever dream up a cock-and-bull story like that?" Munson recoiled as Spearing made a rapier of his tobacco-stained forefinger. He aimed his thrust directly between Munson's eyes. "You are making progress at last! You are beginning not to believe people and that is something very encouraging for me to see. When you don't believe *anything* that *anyone* says at *any time,* then you have achieved a proper monastic state. The human race abandoned the truth with the original expulsion from Eden. That apple Eve was alleged to have given her paramour was actually a persimmon which puckered up his mouth so that the whole truth could never again be uttered. But you *can* believe what I am now about to tell you."

"The ten seconds is over," Munson said, looking down at his book.

"Listen to me carefully and you will understand why I am not long for this melancholy room. The name of my wretched bookie is Sam and he is a man of wide acquaintance. Among his associates is a Ralph, who is not only a bellboy in a certain hotel in this city, but happens to have an inquiring mind. Now this afternoon Colin Galahad Hill was seen in private conference with one Harry Bandaneria at that certain hotel. I also doubted the truth of such a story. So I checked. Harry Bandaneria, who you will admit is not exactly fit company for a police chief, is registered in room 429. Hill was not in his office at the time described and left no word of his intended movements, which you also know just never happens. He merely said he would radio in later from the bridge . . . which is not where he went."

"What's the name of this certain hotel?"

"I tell you this thing is so big it scares me."

"I asked you a question."

"For the first time since I've been working for the sonofabitch, my boss thanked me for being on the ball. He said it might mean the opening guns of a full campaign . . . throw everything we have into it . . . corruption in the Police Department . . . civic rottenness exposed. He was so fired up he said he wanted to do this first big break himself. I told the ambitious sonofabitch to go ahead and win the Pulitzer Prize."

"What is the name of the hotel?" Munson asked evenly.

Spearing glanced at his watch. "In ten minutes I'll tell you."

"Why wait ten minutes?"

"Because that's about how long it would take you to phone around and find out which hotel Bandaneria is registered in. And just about now, my boss, our editor in chief and a photographer are knocking on Bandaneria's door. They're going all out and would not appreciate your people barging in on an exclusive like this."

"You are a real pal."

"At the worst I'll get a bonus. At the best I'll get that spot reviewing television. Imagine just sitting on your butt all day and watching the box. . . ."

"You deserve each other," Munson said.

Suddenly a great weariness came to Spearing's eyes. He was silent for a moment, then spoke almost wistfully. "They *wouldn't*. The sonsofbitches wouldn't dare sidetrack me after I dug up a story like this. Not after waiting all these years. . . ."

✦✦✦ 37 ✦✦✦

Celia Krank's hopes sank with the sun. She no longer caught her breath every time there was an interruption in the stillness of the park. She knew now that the crunching of gravel on the path would not announce the approach of Maurice as it had so many times before. It would never be Maurice again, she admitted; and yet she could not force herself to leave the special atmosphere of their special bench.

Just near, she could see the glade which led to the magic place where they had first made love. It was there, at just this time of day, with the last of the afternoon sun leaking through the hedges, that she had felt a joyous instant of quick pain and then melted her sighs with his. Maurice! Was there ever again to be such an instant? And the delicious time afterwards when you became still and yet remained a part of me, and you whispered of our love. And finally, when it was nearly dark, there was your soft and mischievous laughter as you brushed the bits of grass from my skirt.

There was nothing wrong in the world then. We were just two young people in love, and there was nothing wrong even when you told of your time in prison. You were so certain you would find work. Remember, Maurice? You told me it would take time though, and you'd need help. You took help, my dear one, and never said thanks. Who cared? Was thirty dollars a week too much for Maurice? It left your Celia with thirty also, which was enough because she walked to work instead of taking the bus, and had only a bowl of soup for lunch. . . . As you said, it was only a loan anyway.

Ah, Maurice! As soon as you were settled there would be time and money for other things. At least you never had to ask for money. It was always waiting for you. Hello, my love! Here! Was there anything like giving, like caring, and worrying and anticipating your arrival at this bench? Was there any pain in knowing after a while that you were not looking for work and had no interest in doing so? Any pain? Never! Better one hour a week with you, Maurice, than a hundred years with some man less exciting.

I would have died for you, Maurice.

I will die for you now, if you will come down the path, smile in your way, and take me in your arms.

There is no hell with you, my love, not even last night in a cage of witches. There is only hell without you.

It was almost dark before she rose from the bench. She folded her arms across her breasts, hugging the thought of Maurice. She walked slowly away from the bench and did not look back. For she knew as certainly as if a message had been carved on the seat of the bench that she would never see Maurice again. I have loved, she whispered to the evening. I have loved. . . .

✦✦✦ 38 ✦✦✦

Theo Lasher slumped in the back seat of the unmarked police car. His wife sat beside him. Since leaving the hotel she had expressed her disappointment only by dabbing at an occasional tear, an action which so distressed Lasher he begged her to desist.

"I got trouble enough," he said. "You don't understand the situation."

"No, I don't. I thought you were—"

"This is something out of the past. Just forget it ever happened. Next month I'll take you to Miami. How's that for something to look forward to?"

His wife made no reply and Lasher knew that she would not until she was able to rationalize the way they were being given the bum's rush out of town. Women were so goddamned touchy! Of course it might have been easier for Arlene to take if the two inspectors in the front seat were a little less smug. They knew how valuable their free escort service was. Who would be crazy enough to pick a beef with them when Bandaneria was in the same town? Or was he really?

Lasher brooded upon the peculiar series of events that had led to his temporary defeat. He had hastily bought a box of candy in the hotel lobby and was now indulging in a chilling bath of humiliation and self-criticism. As if to match his worm-eating mood, he found the candies of such inferior quality that he tossed the box out the window. He tried to smile when he thought that the next thing to happen would be his arrest as a litterbug. But his smile was only a very slight stretching of his lips.

Wallowing in frustration, he dug at the chocolate slush around his teeth with his long fingernail while he planned a series of telephone calls to be made as soon as the plane landed in another city. Wherever the hell that was going to be, he thought, didn't make too much difference so long as Harry Bandaneria wasn't in it. And he would make some telephone calls to find out where Bandaneria really was. From a safe place. From a fort.

All of this cockamania was just the preliminaries, of course. And you couldn't judge the main event by what happened now. But it was irritating, especially if you had sense enough to admit it was your own fault, which was how Theo Lasher got to be Theo Lasher instead of still being a bum like the ones he had been careless enough to hire. How could you expect first-class performance from cheap people? You had to pay through the nose for good, intelligent assistants, but it was better than a snarl like this. Any *smart* person would have known and reported that Hill was not for easy sale.

Now, Lasher thought, it would be necessary to start all over again. And he was getting too old for such setbacks. It was bad for his heart, his liver, and his digestion. Squirming in his seat and hoisting at his private parts, he decided that it might even be bad for his prostate.

There was only one satisfaction in this pot of manure stew. Hill himself, of all people, would be the one to change the personnel in the telephone business, thereby saving Theo Lasher the trouble. It had been almost a pleasure to furnish Hill with that list of names and addresses. The dumb clucks could now all rot in the can.

Lasher glanced at his wife. She had stopped crying. A remarkable woman, he thought, with a special ability to cancel out losses after a few tears and then right away start looking on the bright side.

"Arlene, you are good for me," he said suddenly.

"I'm glad," she answered.

All right. What was down the drain was down the drain. Start off new like Arlene always did. To begin with, if you were going to operate in this city, Hill must be placed on the defensive in a number of ways. This was not a chintzy operation. A quarter, perhaps a half million a year could be realized without any risk—*if* things were properly set up. Next year there would be a new mayor in office. Find out more about the candidates from some responsible party. Maybe at least one would be open-city-minded and might accept campaign contributions from people of similar good business sense. A properly educated and cooperative mayor was important, because he could send Hill patrolling the boondocks and put a man in his place who was a realist.

"All right," he said, loud enough so that his wife turned to ask if he was all right.

"I was just remembering you get what you pay for."

A wide-open city was not difficult to achieve if the actual opening could be accomplished without too much noise. Police commissioners were a nuisance because they influenced policy, but sometimes they could be reached through whatever commercial attachments they had. Now there, Lasher thought with renewed satisfaction, was another benefit of strong union connections. A sufficiently harassed commissioner might very well tip the situation to a convenient angle and persuade his police chief that a more relaxed attitude would be beneficial to all. No one was going to make Theo Lasher believe that the so-called commissioners served without pay just because they liked free rides in police cars. Hell, they had their own cars. They were rich men, and so it could be taken for granted they must know the value of a buck.

He decided that one of his first calls would be to a private detective agency specializing in divorce matters. He would make an investment. For, say, two thousand dollars the agency should be pleased to supply full background material on the three commissioners. Every man who had ever had an extra buck to spend concealed at least one thing he did not want known. If Theo Lasher knew about it, and was willing to keep it to himself, then something had to give. Like a little cooperation.

Next? Do not neglect the ordinary citizens. They were all jerks, of course, but they could be helpful. To begin with, they had to be shown what bums were living off their taxes. Finding the best way to start would be complicated and maybe expensive, but once things were rolling, human nature would take care of the rest. The dual theme must be ridicule accompanied by fear. In this city there were almost two thousand cops. At least a third of them were bound to be dissatisfied about something. Find out what the something was and see their beefs in the papers. Next, it should be easy to find a cop who was convinced he was a leader. Steer clear of men like the jerks in the front seat. They must have something special or they wouldn't be doing what they were. Find some dumb patrolman whose wife thought he should be chief of police and who couldn't understand why he was still shaking doors. Point out to such a man that one way to win leadership might be as president of a policemen's union. It didn't make any difference whether the flatfoot succeeded in starting one or not. Just make sure he shot off his mouth enough to start the others thinking they had a bad deal. Next, out of two thousand cops somebody had to be stealing, somebody was taking payoffs no matter how small, somebody drank too much, or slept on the job. The thing to do was *help* Hill. Find out who those bums were and let Hill know—right after you let the papers know. And create incidents. One a week at least. A little garbage here—a little garbage there. Little human interest incidents wherein the cops would be the clowns. What the hell. Didn't everybody like to laugh at a cop?

The second phases would be more difficult and delicate, but it had been done before and most certainly could be done again. There were ready-made organizations equipped and willing to promote the fear angle. The Muslims were becoming very promising. Find a real hot Muslim and put him on a retainer so he could devote all his time to organizing meetings. There were some fine cop haters there. They had a small newspaper. Take some big ads in it—"From a friend." Try the same approach with the Civil Liberties Union—their sanctimonious air could be useful. And again find a member with a genuine hatred for all cops—not just a do-gooder. Lasher found he had developed a sudden fondness for the word "sanctimonious." How about including any available Communists in the campaign? Un-unnh. What little their clumsy propaganda might accomplish was not worth the pain of listening to *their* sanctimoniousness. Fear and ridicule. Ridicule and fear. *Nothing* else was necessary.

Lasher realized his rough plan needed a considerable amount of polishing, but what concerned him now, as the car approached the airport, was an administrator. He quickly reviewed the inadequacies of his lawyers, his active assistants, and the multitude of partially active hangers-on who supposedly looked after his interests in various matters. In addition to those concerned with the union, real estate, insurance and construction, there were the protectors of his coin machine enterprise—those who promoted his mail order system, whereby magic charms, hair straightener, pimple pills, photo-art books, lonely hearts club memberships, and guaranteed aphrodisiacs could all be bought through the same box number in Ohio. And he considered all the energy and intelligence he had put into establishing these things, and the great loneliness possessed him as it had not done for a long time. As the car sped on, he became so disgusted with all those surrounding him, he swallowed fountains of self-pity.

When the car approached the airport, Lasher turned his massive head to glance out the rear window. He regarded the retreating city as if it were a living thing. He scowled with displeasure and buried the tip of one finger in the fat of his chops. A cunning Irishman, that Hill. He should really be working for Theo Lasher because he knew how to find and exploit weakness in other men. Oh, I could use you, Irishman! I got a hunch you scared me with only a name. And you are smart enough to know that a scared man is going to ask himself a thousand dumb questions before he begins to question exactly why or if he really should be afraid. I'm just beginning to do that, and so I'm willing to bet a thousand dollars against every mile Harry Bandaneria is away from here. Oh, I could use you, Irishman! You know I'm too smart to take a risk. But if I find out you've been smarter than me, you're going to suffer.

Lasher cleared the caverns of his throat with a sound like the ruffle of snare drums. He turned again to look back at the city. "I'll be back," he murmured.

❖❖❖ 39 ❖❖❖

Rosenburg slammed the door of his locker and turned the key with a gesture of finality. There, in a steel case, was enclosed the paraphernalia of his daily life as a cop—his uniform, cap, club, notebook, black shoes, flashlight, and pocket edition of *The Decline and Fall* which should not have been a part of his daily life, but was. He had also placed his handcuffs on the shelf beside his cap. It was bad enough to lug a gun around when off duty, but a cop in civilian clothes was asking for trouble without one. It was coincidence, of course, but cops off duty seemed to have a remarkable affinity for encountering unexpected trouble on the very day they decided to defy regulations and leave the gun behind.

Their subsequent embarrassment was everlasting, and to be discovered unarmed by a superior cut off any chance of promotion. A helpless cop was a pitiful victim of his own stupidity.

Rosenburg reveled in the comfort of his sweater, loose slacks, and moccasins. Damn all uniforms anyway, he thought. They not only concealed the individual but strapped a man in permanent discomfort. As he left the station-house locker room, Rosenburg wondered if it was the idea of uniforms which had made him a mediocre football player, a less than distinguished soldier, and, he feared, a cop of dubious promise. Or was it that he liked to dream too much of things long past? Perhaps he should have been a history professor.

He passed quickly through the station house proper, waved a good night to the elderly, purple-faced sergeant who had just come on watch, and let himself out the side door. He turned behind the patrol wagon parked in the alley, took a deep breath of the evening air, and sprinted until he came to the vacant lot where his car was parked. It was a third-hand Chevrolet, but Rosenburg had persuaded his wife they should squander his pay on such things as food, shelter, heat and light, rather than on fancy transportation. Because of its age they had named the car Abraham. If treated tenderly, it moseyed along with appropriate dignity. As soon as he started the car he turned into the main street and joined his fellow citizens in their daily fight for survival.

He drove conservatively because he had once served six months with the Accident detail, and the experience had left him forever impressed with the lethal multiplication of speed. After ten minutes of the heavier traffic he turned into a smaller street as was his custom, and he knew that in some eight minutes, provided he was not held up at the railroad crossing that intersected the street, he would arrive at his house. Then, while his wife fixed dinner, he would have a can of beer and listen to his four-year-old daughter's eloquent recital of her day's adventures, which were certain to be more thrilling than anything in his own day. There was no lodge meeting or anything else scheduled for this night, so he would have a chance to work on the bookcases which had so frustrated him. His wife had proclaimed the corner of the living room where he had pounded, shoved, and twisted in an attempt to make the bookshelves behave, a disaster area. Rosenburg was almost willing to admit complete defeat. He was not a good carpenter, a good cop, or a particularly good anything. He whistled tunelessly and decided that he was not even a good whistler.

He slowed for the railroad crossing, looked in both directions along the track, and proceeded. Once across the tracks he descended a gentle grade which led him into the shadow of two distant hills. Immediately the twilight deepened and he switched on his lights. He thought that at this season of the year the city should turn on the street lights at an earlier hour.

He was still thinking about lights as he passed a large warehouse and then a liquor store just beyond it. He drove on for almost half a block before it struck him that the liquor store had been in darkness. He knew the owner, Milt Plummer, a fine little Austrian who stood all of five feet high and who had such a peculiar guilt complex about running a liquor store that he gave the receipts of every sixth day's business to charity. But Milt was a good businessman and believed in advertising. The usual bright lights of his store were a neighborhood landmark. Rosenburg thought they should certainly be on now, unless Milt was sick or had blown a fuse.

He reached the corner before he decided to pull over to the curb and stop. He might as well pick up some beer, since the last time he had looked there were only three cans left in the refrigerator.

Instead of backing up against the traffic, Rosenburg decided to walk. He turned on Abraham's parking lights, stood looking at its weariness for a moment, and then, hands in pockets, striding easily in his moccasins, he set off for the liquor store. His intermittent whistling suited the owner of Abraham, he thought. Both were content with imperfection.

He was so blinded by the lights of an approaching car that he passed the liquor store window without even trying to look inside. He went directly to the door and opened it. He heard the familiar tinkle of the bell Milt had installed over the door to advise him of customers when he was engaged in the back room.

He glanced at the bottle displays, then at the counter behind which Milt normally stood smiling.

"Hey, Milt! You blow a fuse or something?"

He started toward the counter, moving carefully in the semi-darkness lest he collide with the displays. He reached the counter and rapped smartly on its surface. He could dimly see the outline of the curtained doorway that led into the back room.

"Hey, Milt! If you want your customers to help themselves, I'll take a case of champagne!"

He listened and thought he heard something banging in the back room. He started toward the end of the counter, intending to pass around it. As he felt his way he wondered if Milt's sense of humor had taken a turn for the worse. He was usually more subtle. "Hey, Milt . . .!"

He hesitated at the end of the counter, then started for the doorway. Immediately he felt something hard against his back and a voice commanded, "Stand still."

The hard object was jabbed at his spine again for emphasis. Before fright locked him almost senseless Rosenburg had an instant to think that this was exactly like training in police school. Only this time the gun in his back was probably loaded and it was not conveniently held in place by a fellow student. According to the endless practice sessions, Rosenburg should now spin away quickly, at the same time flying one arm behind him to knock the gun from his enemy's hand. Then—

"Put all your money on the counter, mister. And I mean all of it." The voice was quiet and professional. There was no malice or tension. *Now,* Rosenburg told himself. *Now*—when there is a reason for movement. But he could not trigger the action. He could only remember all the times he had failed to knock the gun away in school, and how many times he had theoretically been dead.

His eyes were now better adjusted to the gloom and he became suddenly aware of an upturned foot protruding from under the curtain that hung across the door to the back room. The foot was quite still. It was a small foot, so small Rosenburg was sure it could only belong to Milt Plummer.

"Hurry up, mister."

Rosenburg reached into his pocket and withdrew some dollar bills. If he remembered correctly the total was about eight dollars—a five and three ones. Yet it seemed he could not remember anything clearly except the number of times he and the other student cops had failed to knock guns away. Red Clark, the instructor, could do it, but Red was an expert in self-defense and had a black belt in judo besides. Red could knock away a gun, spin, seize his opponent's hand and arm, and send him flying through the air in two seconds flat. Finally his students could perform a reasonable approximation of the same trick. But it had been ten years since Rosenburg had even tried. And now here it was. And he was ten years slower in every reaction and ten years wiser about what a gun fired at close range could really do.

"I said all of it. Put your change down too."

Rosenburg reached into his pocket again. He was dizzy with shame and yet he could not make himself do anything other than search obediently in his pocket and bring out two quarters and a dime. At least the man hadn't frisked him—so far. He obviously didn't know that Rosenburg was also armed. And why should he? Or why should he care, when only a docile lump of flesh stood numbly waiting for his next command. If he reaches for my gun, I'll do it, Rosenburg promised himself. I'll do it—I'll spin. I'll risk it.

And yet his dry mouth told him he would not. He would just stand and do as he was told. He would just stand watching himself make one more failure at his job.

He saw a thin hand, half the size of his own, reach around and take the money from the counter. And again the gun prodded at his spine.

"Now drop your pants."

"What?" Rosenburg's voice was a stranger's. His throat seemed to be full of his tongue.

"Drop your pants, I said. All the way down around your ankles. And be quick about it."

Rosenburg found himself reaching for his belt. His hand passed within inches of the gun and yet it did not pause. He must move!

He *must!* But the pressure against his back killed his resolve. He unfastened his belt, pulled down the zipper, and allowed his pants to slip slowly to the floor. He heard the faint thump of his gun as it glanced off his shoe. Oh you are a hero, Rosenburg!

"Now be smart and stay right where you are for five minutes. Don't go for the phone. Count to five hundred, then go to your friend. He's all right, but he wasn't as smart as you. So he got whipped around a little. . . ."

Oh, God, Rosenburg thought, little Milt Plummer had the guts to resist and I am six feet two inches of jelly.

"You come here at the wrong time, mister. But maybe when your friend gets over his headache, he'll buy you a drink. Now just stay here. Take it easy. And don't even look around."

Suddenly the pressure on Rosenburg's back was gone. He heard a quick step behind him, and a pile of bottles fell over with a tumbling crash. He turned just in time to see a small, thin man reach the street door. The man yanked it open and the bell was still tingling as Rosenburg reached down for his gun.

The man started past the street window at a run. Rosenburg fired without the slightest hope of hitting such a dimly outlined and moving target. A cobweb of splintered glass instantly formed around a hole in the window. Rosenburg caught up his pants and ran as fast as he could to the door.

He looked down the street and saw the man running toward the railroad embankment. For a moment he was fully illuminated by the lights of an oncoming car.

The man was holding one hand against his hip and limping. Rosenburg took careful aim and fired. He saw the man hesitate, turn uncertainly toward the street, and then stop. He stood for a minute looking at Rosenburg. After a moment he reached into his coat pocket.

Rosenburg called to him: "Stand still and put your hands behind your head!"

Rosenburg's tongue was so thick with fear, the words labored from him. His voice was high and unrecognizable. There was almost no light on the sights of his gun, but he tried to line up one of the man's legs. But Rosenburg could not hold the barrel steady.

He saw the man start for the corner of the warehouse and he squeezed the trigger again. Instantly he saw the man's head snap back as if he were beckoning. He was propelled backward several steps and his arm flew out, clutching at the air. Then his legs buckled and he fell flat on his back.

Just as Rosenburg started cautiously toward the man the street lights came on. There was a motionless pile of clothes in the pool of the nearest light. As Rosenburg moved closer he tried to persuade himself that it was not a human being but a thing. Then he was horrified to see the thing jerk. Kneeling, he begged it to stop. A spasm followed and the clutching hands fanned open. A trickle of blood leaked from the sagging mouth. The spasms subsided. The thing was still.

Rosenburg could not force himself to look away. The last bullet from David Jacob Rosenburg's gun had struck this thing in the nose. In a hundredth of a second it had made the nose an almost unrecognizable feature. There was only a dark hole where most of the nose should have been. In the hole Rosenburg could see what appeared to be a mixture of crushed red stone. And the bullet had obviously penetrated through the thing's head because there was a slowly widening pool of thick blood behind its neck. The thing's eyes were wide-open and fixed on something very far away. Rosenburg thought he saw the eyelids flutter once, but he could not be sure. The eyes were strangely dry. The thing's mouth was so distorted that it seemed to be commencing a yawn.

"Will you please don't jerk again," Rosenburg whispered. There was almost no blood on the face except for the rivulet at one corner of the mouth and a poxlike splatter near the hole. But now Rosenburg saw a second pool of blood forming near the thing's middle. The light from the overhead street lamp made it look like black oil. Rosenburg was terribly certain that he understood the source of this pool of blood. His first bullet had passed through Milt's window and made that cobweb design, and then it hit this thing that was so alive only a few minutes ago. This thing which had been alive for twenty-eight? Twenty-nine? Thirty years?

The thing was now absolutely still, but Rosenburg's own trembling would not cease. He was amazed to see that he still held a gun in his hand. He made two fumbling attempts to return it to his holster before he succeeded.

A car stopped near the street curbing and three men in overalls entered the pool of light. They moved quietly toward the kneeling Rosenburg and one of them said, "Hey, what's goin' on here?" Then another car stopped, but Rosenburg was unaware of it. He was trying to make himself do what he knew he was supposed to do, though his brain had turned to mud and his muscles to rubber. He clasped his hands tightly to ease their trembling.

"You shoot this guy, mister?"

If I was an Irish cop I could cross myself, Rosenburg thought, and go to confession tonight or tomorrow morning, and things would be easier. But where else can a Jew go . . . except direct to God?

Rosenburg spoke without looking up at the men who had formed a half-circle around him. "I'm a cop," he said, trying to keep his voice steadier than his hands. "Go to the nearest phone and call the police. Tell them to send an ambulance."

"He's dead," one of the men said casually. "What you want an ambulance for?"

"Yes . . . he's dead. Do like I told you. Quick."

Rosenburg heard one man shuffle away and a car motor start. He wanted to run back and make sure Milt was all right, but he could not persuade himself to leave this thing on the sidewalk. The awful face held him spellbound. This awful face with the awful hole in it was something he would see for the rest of his life.

"I *was* a cop," he whispered to the face, "but I'm not going to be any more."

He took a deep breath and reached into the thing's coat pocket. He pulled out a .38 automatic and wrapped it in his handkerchief. He searched further and pulled out a folded bundle of paper dollars—probably Milt's. And a few of his own.

He rose slowly to his feet and was astounded to find that he stood in a circle of people. They stared at the thing and then at Rosenburg, their eyes roving hungrily, their jaws working in fascination. They scratched nervously at their faces and one man ripped the silence with a fit of violent coughing. A pair of teenagers squatted down for a closer look at the thing.

Rosenburg recoiled in anger. He was suddenly and fiercely determined to protect the dignity of the thing on the sidewalk. This driveling, idiot-eyed crowd of ghouls were not going to indulge themselves in a free show because something was dead on the sidewalk. The thing was not a beast killed in hunt. It did not belong to them or to Rosenburg as victor, or to any power but itself. It was still retreating.

"Get back!" Rosenburg yelled.

In a few minutes it would be different, but now there was about the thing a lingering impression of the life still escaping. Let it go easily, Rosenburg thought. I, of all people, must let it go quickly and easily from these evil faces.

For once Rosenburg wished he was in uniform as he attempted to shove the crowd away. "Get a move on. Get the hell out of here!"

"Hey, you can't talk to me like that!"

"I ain't done nothin' to you—"

"Hey, look! The guy's cryin'! For Christ's sake, he says he's a cop and he's bawlin'!"

"He's maybe a *crybaby* cop!"

"Somebody throw the big dumb bastard a cryin' towel!"

"Get outa here, I'm tellin' you—!" Rosenburg's voice broke in torment, and a mocking ripple of laughter passed through the crowd. They began to press in on him instead of moving away.

"He *better* be a cop when the real cops come!"

"Blow your nose, big shot!"

The space about his thing, and now Rosenburg could only think of it as *his* thing, was becoming smaller and smaller.

"Go home . . . go home!" But Rosenburg could not seem to inject true authority into his voice. Instead there came from his lips only a choking sound, and it was no more than a plea.

A voice mocked him. "Git movin' wherever you are. Git your ass somewhere else! He's a cop all right."

Rosenburg straddled the thing, firmly planting his feet on each side. He spread out his arms as if the gesture alone might hold the surging crowd away. Their numbers had multiplied. They would soon trample on his thing.

Horns blew as a traffic jam formed in the street. And at last Rosenburg heard the expiring moan of a siren. Almost immediately, he saw the caps of two patrolmen pushing through the crowd toward him. He recognized their faces, but he could not remember their names.

"Ili. . . ."

"He was knocking over the liquor store."

The crowd fell silent as the policemen stood looking down at the thing between Rosenburg's moccasins.

"You sure nailed him."

"Yeah. . . ." Rosenburg sighed and wiped at his eyes.

"You all right?"

"In a way."

Rosenburg heard the sound of a second siren, and in a moment a solo bikeman shouldered his way through the crowd. The faces withdrew a little and Rosenburg was able to breathe normally for what seemed like the first time in hours. And suddenly he remembered Milt Plummer. He had thought only of the thing between his feet and forgotten his friend. He borrowed a flashlight from the solo bikeman and ran to the liquor store.

Milt was sitting upright on the floor of the back room. He looked up, blinking at the flashlight, and rubbed the side of his head. He managed to smile when Rosenburg helped him to his feet. "I got hit by a railroad train," he said.

"You aren't bleeding, Milt. You'll be all right." Just as the thing had said, Rosenburg thought—only a few minutes ago. The thing had told the truth.

"Cripes! What a headache!"

Rosenburg led him to a chair before the desk in the back room, found the lights, and switched them on. And he saw that Milt Plummer was like a small and puny child who had tumbled down a stairway. So small, he thought. So very small. He held out a glass of water to Milt and wondered if there was any similar container to measure courage in a man.

"Why didn't you just let him walk off with the joint?" he asked gently.

"I didn't fancy his looks. Where is he?"

"Dead."

"Ah . . . that needn't have been."

They were silent as Milt sipped at the water. Rosenburg called the Homicide detail and told them that he hoped a cop didn't have to be dead to be right. He asked them to call the coroner and hung up. Then he called his wife and told her he would not be home for several hours. He said he had been assigned to a special duty and he was grateful that she did not ask what special duty it might be.

"Do you want to go to the hospital, Milt?"

"Hell, no. I'm all right." He hesitated and looked thoughtfully at Rosenburg. "It's you I'm worried about."

"Why?"

"You look sick."

"I am."

"Because you killed a man?"

Rosenburg nodded his head. "It was my first . . . and my last."

One of the men from the patrol car came into the back room. He placed the .38 automatic on Milt's desk. It was still wrapped in Rosenburg's handerchief. Beside it he placed the money, a key chain, a cigarette lighter, two pawn tickets, a comb, a small tin box of condoms, and a cheap wrist watch.

"That's all he had on him except this bail receipt. I radio-checked with CIB and they gave me a quick rundown. He was a five-time loser and only got out of the bucket this morning. Picked up last night on a parole violation. He was with some woman in a parking lot. Here's his name—Maurice Stiller. I guess that's all you'll need when the inspectors get here."

"I guess so," Rosenburg said.

"They're putting him in the meat wagon now and we'll take care of everything else. So you might as well stay here and take it easy. For a guy off duty you got enough troubles."

Rosenburg knew what he meant. The formalities, including a full coroner's investigation, would be the same as if he were an ordinary citizen charged with murder. He would not even have the excuse of attack and self-defense because Maurice Stiller had never actually attacked.

The telephone rang. Milt picked it up and then held it out to Rosenburg. "Some guy named Spearing from the *Journal* wants to talk with Officer Rosenburg."

He took the phone reluctantly and listened to Spearing's flat, dry voice.

"I understand we have a hero cop on our hands. Tell me all about it, chum."

"I'm not a hero by any manner of means," Rosenburg said.

"Come on now, Rosenburg. That pebble-kicking modesty doesn't sell. You shot it out with a famous gunman, didn't you?"

Rosenburg thought of the crumpled heap on the sidewalk and he saw the face again with the hole in it.

"No. He never fired a shot. I made a mistake. I didn't mean to kill him. I always was a lousy shot."

"You were off duty, weren't you? You could have looked the other way."

"I wish I had."

"Did you get him with your first shot?"

"No."

"Would you call it a running gun battle?"

"Certainly not."

"Well, it's going to be. And you're going to be a hero whether you want to be or not."

"I'm resigning from the department."

"Yeah? So much the better. Grief-stricken hero cop resigns over death of killer victim. Thanks very much, pal. You just saved my job."

"I don't think he was a killer. I was."

"What kind of likker were you drinkin'?"

"I don't know what you're talking about."

"I heard you had yourself a good cryin' jag after you dropped him."

"That's . . . go to hell."

"Don't be that way, chum. I had enough misunderstandings today. Read your tomorrow's *Journal* and find out what a hero you are."

Rosenburg heard a click in the phone and Spearing's flat voice was gone. After a moment he carefully placed the phone back on its stand. Then he stared at it for a long time as if waiting for it to ring again.

Milt gently massaged the side of his head and watched him with increasing concern. "Don't brood about it, Rosie. That won't do any good."

Rosenburg picked up the bail bond receipt and seemed to read its simple contents without comprehending. Finally he said, "I'm trying to figure out why a miserable little punk like this Stiller gets shot so dead when a guy like that reporter goes on forever."

IN THE EVENING

✧✧✧ 40 ✦✦✦

The population of the old building dwindled rapidly although not in the determined fashion of a business establishment. There were too many variables. The men in Fraud simply put on their hats and with barely a word of farewell to each other disappeared quietly from their desks. The Auto detail, the Crime and Photographic Laboratories, the Records and Planning sections, the Burglary detail, and the Safe detail turned out their lights and descended quietly to the main entrance, using either the elevator or the marble stairs. Very little had been accomplished by any of these details during the past hour. It was a time for appearing to be busy while really waiting for the minute hand of the clock to decently pass five. A few of the more independent inhabitants, like Dinwiddie in Missing Persons, whose cold was so troublesome, left before the appointed time. Three of the men in Intelligence had been assigned to observe the clientele at a prize fight, so they had also left very early.

Barnegat abandoned his office precisely on the hour, as he always did. There were a multitude of reasons why he might have stayed longer, but on every day there were many such reasons. Barnegat's uncompromising character forbade his giving the city more than its due—nor would he give it any less. He marched directly from his office to the main exit of the old building. Only his professional air distinguished him from the clerks, statisticians, inspectors and technicians moving in the same direction. Because of his rank and seniority, way was given him at the door, but his natural austerity discouraged any farewells.

The courtrooms were dark and silent, having long since been deserted by those whose arguments and agonies would be renewed on the following day. Judge Brownell had remained late in his chambers because a friend of an influential friend had called and begged him to hear privately the special circumstances surrounding the case of a wife-beater. Brownell had soon discovered that one special circumstance was the financial status of the husband. He was a rich wife-beater and, therefore, explained his friend, it would be extraordinarily embarrassing for all concerned if he spent any extended time in durance vile.

Brownell listened patiently to the friend's one-sided history of the affair and discovered a second special circumstance. It became obvious from the wife's own weeping confession that she liked being physically punished. Unsophisticated neighbors had mistaken her ecstatic yelps for screams of pain and called the police. Although the subsequent report read like a composition written by the Marquis de Sade, no great physical harm had actually come to the woman. So Brownell tugged only momentarily at his ear and hinted that on the morrow he would suspend sentence, providing both parties guaranteed to visit their psychiatrists.

Shortly after the interview, Brownell clamped his hat down on his head until the tips of his great ears were bent outward. Then he descended the marble stairs at such a speed that Tommie the blind newsdealer became at once alert to the rattle of his footsteps and called, "Good night, Judge. I hope you have a good night's rest."

Tommie had expressed the same wish countless times when Brownell departed the old building, so many times it was now like a refrain. As he emerged into the fresh evening air and sucked at it hungrily, Brownell speculated once again upon the wonder of Tommie's sensory apparatus. It reached far beyond the mere physical, he concluded. It penetrated through the finely grilled screens of hypocrisy, picked up the most delicate signals of distress, and probed straight to the soul. "I hope you have a good night's rest." What a way, Brownell thought, to cover the understanding of a little man besieged by doubt.

In General Works all of the inspectors except Moore had left for the day. They had departed cheerfully, their banter echoing against the grimy ocher ceiling of the great room; and the telephones which had been ringing all day were silent. Because the inspectors in General Works were powerless to predict the physical caprices of their fellow men, and therefore worked almost always after the fact, they were able to schedule investigations through a normal day and repudiate them en masse at five o'clock. Thus they were able to leave the old building reasonably free in heart and mind. A General Works inspector had no desire to educate his wife, much less his children, in the grotesque rites of sodomy, the fey humor of exhibitionists, the screaming uproarious savagery of rape, or even the yearning of pure lust which compelled it. They wanted their own people to believe in the good of people, if only to provide a constant rescue service for their own embattled faiths. They did not want their wives to ask, "How did things go at the office today?"

And so the families of the inspectors in General Works were peculiarly naïve. They believed what they read in the newspapers was true, as did most people. And they believed that the stories which did find space in the press told only of an evil, shadowy world populated by strangers who were not at all like themselves. All of the inspectors in General Works were content to let this persuasion hold. It was much easier when they left the old building to let the heavy brass doors slam upon their disillusions.

Yet occasionally, as it was now with Moore, the unraveling of intentions from passionate commissions did not stop with the clock. The process must continue relentlessly for the same reason that fires cooled when left untended. Postponements brought ever tighter entanglements of thought, new escapes, more inventive lies, and special confusions which obscured the facts. The irrational mind had time to reflect and become rational, and grasping the truth became more difficult with each passing hour.

Thus Moore sat in his office long after his associates had departed, certain now that if he was going to discover who had raped little Harriet Rankin he would have to find out from Harriet Rankin.

He saw that she was tiring at last. She no longer wet her lips as she evaluated Moore's monotonous questions. Her provocative tongue was still. She slumped in her chair like any weary teenager, and there were long intervals when her attention drifted.

More than two hours had passed since Moore had sent Rafferty to find Harriet's uncle and talk with him. Now Moore waited impatiently for him to telephone. He had been stalling a long time, often digressing from the direct line of his probing lest Harriet become suspicious and cut what little rapport he had been able to establish.

"I don't find this place very stimulating," Harriet stated flatly. "And the whole subject is beginning to bore me." She yawned and extended her sturdy legs. She thoughtfully admired their contours. "I should be home by now. My aunt and uncle will have a fit. They'll purple when they find out where I've been."

"What do you mean, purple?"

"Flip . . . go witless . . . purple, it's all the same for getting mad."

"They didn't seem too much concerned about your whereabouts at this time yesterday."

"Oh, they were. You just have the wrong impression. But then you have the wrong impression about a lot of things." She sighed and her attention drifted from her legs to the ceiling. Then, as if she had never really considered her guardians before, she said, "They're sweet. Really, what I mean is, they are something square, oh *very* square, *certainement,* but sweet. That's why I told you some of the things I did."

"I don't follow you." The nostrils in Moore's celebrated nose quivered ever so slightly. He tilted his head until the nose was pointing at the spot on the ceiling which had apparently captured Harriet's attention. He forced himself to appear interested in the ceiling instead of in the peculiarly sensual way she had begun to writhe in her chair. God almighty, he thought. What is this infant volcano going to be like when she is eighteen? For an instant he considered calling central station and asking for a policewoman to come at once, or at least a patrolman. A meeting like this needed a chaperon, and with Rafferty gone and practically the entire building deserted, he might have a lot of explaining to do if anything went wrong. Harriet Rankin alone in an office with *any* man, regardless of his age or capacity, represented a dangerous situation. "I don't see," he said slowly, and with as little interest as he could manage, "how the fact that your guardians might appear a trifle old-fashioned to you, should necessarily call for your lying to me about the Perez brothers."

"Well, there was a reason."

"What kind of reason could there be to punish innocent men?"

"Well, after all . . . they're only Mexicans . . . or, you know, Mexican descent, I guess you might say."

"It wouldn't make any difference if they were Hindus. They did not rape you."

"You wouldn't understand because you're pretty square, too. I like you, but I guess you can't help being square."

"Thanks." This little lady is going to drive me to a triple whiskey neat after I get rid of her, Moore thought, and then he wondered if Rafferty was ever going to call. "Square as I am," he said, "maybe you can round off some of my unfortunate corners if you'll explain why you thought it necessary to put the Perez boys in such a spot."

"I refuse to discuss the whole thing any longer," she answered with sudden primness.

Moore was amazed at her almost instant shift of mood. The voluptuous languor was gone and now she sat very erect, her feet and knees pressed tightly together. She was the ideal picture of purity rising from troubled depths.

"Have you ever considered becoming an actress, Harriet?"

"No. If you graduate from Larkin's you marry a diplomat or at least a vice-president of some big company. Of course one might engage in amateur theatricals or junior league stuff . . . and like that . . . but, of course, not for *money. Certainement. . . .*"

"*Certainement,*" Moore repeated solemnly. I am willing to go along with anything, he resolved, if I can just stay one more round with this child.

"A report was filed on your alleged rape, Harriet. We can't just throw it in the wastebasket."

"What does 'alleged' mean?"

"It means that something which happened hasn't as yet been proven."

"If something happened, what more proof is needed?"

"It means something has been declared to have happened," Moore said, wishing he had never used the word.

"Who declared anything?"

"You declared you were raped."

"That makes me alleged?"

"Not quite. You are alleged to have been raped. The term is used mostly in reference to a situation rather than directly to a person." And now, Moore thought ruefully, I am conducting a class in semantics.

Harriet appeared to be considering the matter carefully. Her prim attitude remained, but new life crept into her eyes. It was as if she had suddenly thought of a great mischief and wished to anticipate it.

"This *alleged* jazz . . ." she began, and then stopped to look Moore directly in the eye. He saw at once that she was challenging him. "Don't you believe I *was* raped?"

"It is declared that you were."

"It can be *proved* that I was. I'll go to any doctor you say right now and he'll tell you it's so. I *want* to go just to show how wrong you are."

"Not without your guardians' permission, Harriet. But for the moment I'll take your word. But why did you blame the Perez brothers?"

"I told you I had my reasons."

Suddenly Moore seized his nose as if it were a mighty handle to a long-locked door. Supposing, he thought quickly, just supposing this frightening child—"

"I had my reasons," she was saying, "but you would have to know a sort of special secret to understand."

"I'm a good man to keep a secret."

"Well, you better be."

"Please go on. You can trust me. It's part of my business."

Harriet wet her lips, then looked down at her hands folded in her lap. "If I tell you, will you promise to tear up the report and forget everything? I've been thinking that if that report got into the newspapers or something like that, you know . . . well, maybe it wouldn't be so good for me at Larkin's."

"I hardly think it would help."

"Will you tear up the report . . . in front of me?"

"How do you know there wouldn't be copies?"

"You wouldn't want the report anyway if I tell you the secret."

"I'll have to reserve judgment on that."

She hesitated and appeared to be making a great decision. Finally, still looking at her hands, she said, "My uncle is in love with me."

Moore bit so deeply into his cigar that his teeth met.

"Just what do you mean by that?"

"You heard me. I didn't say he loved me. I said he was *in* love with me."

"Are you suggesting that he raped you?"

"You can think what you please."

"So you've been trying to protect him?"

"Yes. Please don't do anything to him. *Please!* It would be terrible. My aunt would simply die if she knew."

Her aunt would simply die, Moore thought, if she knew a lot of things. "And for this bit of information," he said, "you now want me to tear up the original report?"

"It's better, isn't it . . . to forgive and forget?"

"A few hours ago you were telling us your life was ruined."

"I've decided it's best if I concentrate on the welfare of other people. Incidentally, where is Mr. Rafferty? He's so nice."

The telephone rang. Moore wanted to seize it, but he managed to control his eagerness until it had rung twice. At the sound of Rafferty's voice, Moore pressed the receiver hard against his ear and tilted far back in his chair. While he listened he watched Harriet carefully.

Rafferty said he had found the uncle, but not exactly as Harriet had described. Instead of being vice-president in charge of sales he was an ordinary salesman on the used car lot. And not a very good one, Rafferty was convinced, because his name stood at the bottom of the list on the office chart.

"He's kind of a cronkie guy so I checked his record. But he's clean except for a drunk driving charge three years ago. I guess I scared him because he was plenty cold at first—then he broke down and gave me the whole story. Maybe I'm wrong but I believe every word he said, and it all checks out for time and places. Is our dream girl still with you?"

"Yes," Moore said cautiously.

"Get rid of her before she reduces you back to patrolman or connives to have you tarred and feathered."

"Don't think I haven't considered the possibility. Go on."

"You're not only with a problem child but a class A blackmail artist. Maybe she got her original idea from the Perez brothers, but she might try sinking the hook in her uncle."

"That's already been done."

"I'm not in the least surprised, because get this. . . . When she left the Perez boys she buttonholed her uncle for what he says was the thousandth time about putting her in Larkin's School. He refused, claiming he couldn't afford it, which could easily be. The kid threw a tantrum and he slapped her all right. That accounts for the eye. But this is a girl who knows what she wants. . . ."

"Anyone witness that action?"

"No. They were alone. The aunt works as cashier at the Western Hotel. When Harriet threw her tantrum she hadn't come home yet. Are you ready for the dessert?"

"I can about guess what it will be."

"After the tantrum the uncle sends her to her room and tells her to stay there. When the aunt comes home they go to Harriet's room to talk things over and dear Harriet is not where she's supposed to be. For a while they don't worry too much. They have a drink and eat. Now we come to Slattery's report. He shows up with the kid in tow and all the stuff about her being found on the corner bawling and raped, et cetera. Okay?"

"Okay, indeed."

"The kid says she wants to talk to her dear uncle privately for a minute, so they go to her room. Now she gives it to him. She shows him the bruises on her breasts and arms and admits she pinched herself. She shows him a candle with which, so help me, she deliberately broke her own hymen. And she says to her uncle that he is going to send her to Larkin's or she is going to tell the cops *he* raped her. And because she knows he isn't a very bright guy, she even gives him an out. If he agrees right then to send her to Larkin's, they can throw the whole thing at the Perez boys who will never be found anyway because they told her they were going back to Texas. The poor dumb guy is crazy with worry and agrees.

Slattery, who also won't win any intelligence contests, swallows their story and puts it all in his report. And incidentally, she's fifteen years old, not thirteen. That's it, boss. . . . Only tell me something, since I'm new on the job. Is this normal police work?"

"Yes and no. How soon can you get here?"

"Twenty minutes."

"Make it thirty and meet me with a car at the main door."

Moore hung up the phone and watched Harriet in silence. She was calmly buffing her nails on the sleeve of her sweater.

"You asked me to tear up the report, Harriet. Possibly that could be arranged if you will accompany me on a little expedition."

"You're going to keep my secret?"

"All of them."

"I'll go if you'll tell me where."

"City prison. . . ."

Harriet gasped. "But *I* didn't *do* anything!"

For a moment Moore hoped she would burst into tears. But her eyes remained dry. "Yes, you did," he said quietly.

Moore crossed the arenalike space before the city prison booking desk with the easy poise of a prophet entering a familiar temple. He towed Harriet Rankin so closely behind him, the guard at the elevator considered it unnecessary to make his customary challenge. But at the green barred gate to the cell blocks, the turnkey somehow sensed the importance of the moment and said to Moore in his deepest voice, "What have we here? Visitors to the zoo?"

Moore took the turnkey aside and spoke to him softly. The turnkey shook his head, but after clinking his keys in disapproval, he opened the gate and they passed into the prison. The turnkey left them and marched down the brightly lit hallway which paralleled the felony block.

Because the evening meal had been served at five and most of the inhabitants were dozing, the prison was now extraordinarily quiet. Yet the slightest sounds survived in surroundings of concrete and steel, so the undertone of rustling, squeaks, thumps, sighs and mass restlessness became a relative bedlam. A man could merely snap his fingers in one end of the cell block and be heard at the other. The lack of visible movement seemed to exaggerate the petty sounds of breathing and coughing and farting and groaning, so that never at any time was there silence in city prison.

Moore led Harriet to a vantage point near the turnkey's record desk. He maneuvered her into a position from which she could not avoid looking down the alleyway of the felony block.

He stood beside her in silence, allowing the acrid *potage* of stinks to be appreciated and his own anger with Harriet to subside. He knew the juvenile authorities were going to howl with rage when they learned he had brought a fifteen-year-old girl to men's city prison, but he cared little. An inner rage now possessed him, and he was determined that Harriet Rankin would not escape from her adventure with only self-inflicted wounds.

"What do you see?" he asked quietly.

She shrugged her shoulders and he saw that her eyes were more sullen than ever.

"You may convince yourself that you are looking at living men, but you would be lying to yourself for a change if you did. Those men are temporarily dead. They are neither here nor there. They wait in a sort of municipal purgatory until someone decides they must die for six months, or six years, or sixty years. There is not a man in those cages who chose to be where he is. *All* of them thought they could get away with whatever it was they attempted . . . including two young men named Perez whom you almost murdered. Do you want to see your own special animals, Harriet?"

"No. You can't talk to me like this. I want to go. You can't keep me here."

"We have an agreement. Remember? It may surprise you to know that many of the men in those cages had people who loved them, but usually that love doesn't survive the years they're away. Their memory is not honored as in true death, and it's too long a wait. Some of the men who are in those cages are young and vigorous and handsome . . . and they want very much to be alive. It's too late. They must die for a while and be buried in other cages. When they are allowed to live again, many of those same young men will be old and tired, and the older men will be even older and even more tired, and all idea of living with ordinary people may be destroyed forever. They have no real friends. They will always be strangers wherever they are. Are you listening to me, Harriet?"

"Well . . ."

"Well what?"

"Of course, it's interesting and educational, I suppose, but I don't see what all this has to do with me."

"I doubt if the Perez brothers consider being in a cage either interesting or educational. You almost put them there for the rest of their lives."

"Well, aren't all of those people sort of sick . . . mentally? You know . . . I mean—"

Moore understood why Harriet's uncle had struck her. And he thought hopelessly that unless he was very careful he would do the same and thus certainly lose his badge.

Then very suddenly his despair left him. His great nose tilted above the horizontal and appeared to take a bearing down the long alleyway of cages, and his mouth creased into a bitter smile. The turnkey had done as he had been asked. For sauntering toward them, hands jammed down in their pockets, rolling on the balls of their feet and nodding their heads to punctuate each step, were the Perez brothers.

They were taking their time as if out for an evening stroll. But they took no interest in anything to their left or right—nor did they even glance once at Moore. They looked only at Harriet Rankin with eyes as empty of desire as they were full of reproach. They continued in silence until they reached the gate at the end of the alleyway. And without once allowing their eyes to leave Harriet, they grasped the bars slowly in their hands and hung limply against them. They remained fixed like rigid silhouettes pasted against the bars, and though they were only ten feet away, they kept their silence.

"They hate me, don't they?" he heard Harriet whisper.

"Why not?"

"I don't care. The things that count are already mine. I know about that meek-will-inherit-the-earth stuff. It's silly."

God! Moore thought. I must hope for my hope.

The Perez brothers were absolutely motionless—nor were their eyes lured once to Moore.

Then, when he was certain of his failure, he heard Harriet gasp. He turned to her quickly and wanted to cheer. For he saw a little girl learning how to cry.

"All right, Harriet," he said as gently as he could. "We can go now."

❖❖❖ 41 ✦✦✦

A rustic fence surrounded the house and on the gate there was a modest sign in plastic letters, THE BARBEES.

Hill left his car and walked slowly up the gravel path that led to the front door. He halted, looked at the view for a moment, and considered turning away. He did not like what he was doing. It was not a policeman's job—particularly a chief's. Interfering with the private affairs of a citizen was a delicate business, and it smelled of a police state. Of course, Barbee had violated a law— if nothing else would do, he was obstructing traffic, trespassing, resisting arrest—there were innumerable petty prongs available upon which a policeman might hang an excuse for coming to this personal castle. But they were of no basic consequence; not even the fact that Barbee had fired at a peace officer.

Here the important thing was Barbee's own privilege of will. There was no law, as far as Hill knew, which forbade a person's taking his own life. Then what right, he wondered, do I have coming to this man's home and presuming to interfere with what must certainly be a very personal division of his life? If I come as a private citizen anxious to prevent what *I* think is evil, then I come as a total stranger, with no license to interfere. Who knows, maybe the wife begged him to kill himself and he finally agreed? Maybe he is suffering from a known cancer and wants to save himself endless agony plus a fortune in useless hospital and funeral money which he has solemnly considered would be better used to educate his children? There were many reasons, not all of them entirely crazy, why a human being might persuade himself that the time had come to stop being one. In the eyes of the church suicide was a sin, but since when were the police the secular arm of the church?

He continued up the path, and by the time he reached the doorway he had decided that at least he would not identify himself as the Chief of Police.

In the distance there was a great city of more than a million souls, the majority existing in reasonable harmony with each other. Like the inhabitants of a massive anthill they were scurrying from point A to point B upon matters which they obviously considered important. Hill knew for a certainty that they were also dying and fighting, eating and eliminating, stealing, giving, creating, fornicating, scheming, and occasionally triumphing. For the moment, as far as he knew, there was only one man who was deliberately rejecting such activities, and his name was John Barbee. He lived in this pleasant house not far from the city and with a view of it; his lawn was cared for; the joy implements of his children, consisting of a bicycle, a tricycle, and a cart made of a wooden box on roller skates, were all happily abandoned at the side of the house. Then why was he surrendering? Barbee did not live in primitive fear. It was unlikely that any storm would blow down his shelter, or famine cause him hunger. There remained only the fear of attack by hostile people, but that possibility was endured by everyone he knew and the chances of Barbee being selected for personal combat were negligible. Then—?

He pressed the door bell and heard the ringing of chimes.

The door opened very suddenly, and for a revealing instant, which closed on itself so quickly Hill never recaptured it, he thought he understood why John Barbee was on the bridge.

"Good afternoon?"

She was tall.

You only saw a person once, Hill reminded himself. And that was the very first presentation, which rarely held for more than a few seconds. After that interval a thousand influences prevailed, so that the person was never again recognizable in the original.

Confidence flowed from her as she held the door half open. Her eyes were dark and intense and judged Hill with interest but not suspicion. Her dark hair was carefully groomed and her earrings matched the rich-looking brooch on her tailored suit. Her voice was firm and overloud.

"You're not the tree surgeon, are you? You certainly don't look like one, that is, like I thought one would look. . . . We've never had one before." There was a definite huskiness about her voice as if it was much used and a bold executive quality which seemed to serve as a barricade while she deployed whatever forces she might consider necessary. She would win, Hill thought. She would win any contest because she must.

He held out his star, placing his thumb over the word *Chief* which was engraved in the center.

"I'm from the Police Department. Are you Mrs. Barbee?"

She looked at him more carefully then smiled. "Oh, I know *you!* You're Chief Hill. I've seen your pictures in the papers . . . and cartoons. You *do* look like a lion!" The recognition seemed to please her immensely and she opened the door wide. "Come in, come in! Well, this *is* an honor!" Then in mock seriousness she said, "Or have I done something dreadful?"

Beyond her Hill could see a deeply carpeted living room with a picture window looking out upon the surrounding hills. The furnishings were predominantly feminine and obviously expensive, but Hill sensed there was something wrong. It was a strangely cold room, he thought. He wondered if Barbee had ever been able to find contentment in such a room.

"Come in, come in," she insisted. "Don't just stand there. We're not afraid of policemen. I've just come from an exhausting meeting. Our Improvement Committee meetings always are."

The commanding energy in her voice almost compelled Hill to obey.

"I'm afraid this isn't the time, Mrs. Barbee. I have some rather disturbing news for you—"

"Heavens! What's happened now? One of the children—" Her face clouded, but Hill thought it more annoyance than concern.

"Your husband is in trouble."

"John? You must be mistaken . . . no. I *thought* he was up to something. He left early this morning before I was even awake really, but then he sometimes does that when he wants to make an early start at the lab—"

"Mrs. Barbee, will you listen to me for a moment?"

"Why, of course. If John is in trouble then we'll simply have to get him out of it. He's such a befuddled dear—"

"It may not be so simple. Your husband has been on top of the bridge since early this morning. He has been threatening to jump and it's the opinion of those who have been trying to talk him out of it, that he will."

"*John?* Why, whatever for? Why, I can't believe it. Are you *sure* it's John?"

"A blue Chevrolet licensed in his name was found at this end of the bridge. He was also identified by a neighbor of yours."

"Who?"

"He didn't give his name. Will you come with me?"

"I can't understand this. I simply cannot understand John doing a thing like this."

Hill found himself wondering how much she had ever understood her John.

"He's been irrational for several hours. If you talk to him maybe he'll listen."

"Just let me get my coat. Why, this is ridiculous! I'll be right with you after I put out some milk and cookies for the children. They're at dancing class and should be along any—"

"You'd better come as fast as you can, Mrs. Barbee. A few minutes could make all the difference."

While he waited, Hill turned again to look at the city which meant so much to him. Was Theo Lasher right? How could any sensible person be in love with piles of concrete and streets jammed with stinking automobiles? He tried to visualize the city without people, and at once he knew it was not the buildings, the houses or the streets or even the parks which so firmly held his affection. He could not see into the thousands of windows which honeycombed the artificial landscape of the city and which were now just coming alight. Watching the windows, Hill became content with his limitations. There would be certain things happening inside those windows which might inspire him to even greater devotion. But there would also be many things which might explain why a man like Barbee sought another world.

❖❖❖ ✦✦✦

In the heart of the city, some two miles from the doorway in which Hill waited, a woman looked down from a window which faced upon a busy street. She watched the homeward bound traffic with increasing impatience. It had seemed to take forever for Thelma to draw her bath and finally disappear.

Now, at last, Thelma was where she should have been long ago. So the woman left the window with its view of the street. She moved a chair near the bathroom door and waited for Thelma to turn the water off.

You couldn't carry on a conversation against the sound of water splashing into a bathtub. If what had been said so far could be called a conversation, she thought. Here was dear old friend Thelma acting like a stranger and an uppity stranger at that. She had announced at the very beginning how terribly busy she was and how little time she had and how she wanted to have one thing clearly understood right now—and that was she did not think anything could be accomplished by talking about Otto.

What else were they going to talk about? She stole Otto. She thought she would keep Otto.

Thelma was a snob as well as a bitch. Look at what she had done with this old-fashioned apartment, fixing it up with big French mirrors on the walls and mirrors even around the fireplace, and carpets wall to wall, deep enough to wade in. And here was Thelma taking her bath right on schedule—her royal bawth, mind you, and be damned to the visiting peasants. She acted like you were a maid or something like that—didn't really exist, just some kind of poor relation who had to be given a few scraps of valuable time so their feelings wouldn't be hurt. Certainly you were not good enough for Otto. He was being protected by that gorgeous, glamorous, devoted business partner of his who had to be fifty years old—and must have spent twenty-five of them in the bathtub. So she thought she was just going to have a little chat with the woman who really loved Otto, and say ta-ta with a flick of her little finger, and that would be the end of everything. Well. . . .

Thelma had at least left the bathroom door ajar and now steam was beginning to slip through the opening. How gracious of Thelma, she thought. How considerate!

The sight of the steam gave her a craving for a cigarette. But nothing doing. Thelma didn't smoke herself, so it was out of the question. Even just before she died, Thelma was making the rules. A cigarette left behind, even the lingering smell of one, might tell someone Thelma had entertained a visitor. Entertained? The closest thing to entertainment was Thelma's saying there was a bottle of sherry on the table and help yourself—while Her Majesty bathed. The bitch was bathing and perfuming her body for Otto who was certainly the guest she had said would arrive at seven o'clock. Time was getting very short.

The rush of water stopped and Thelma called to her, "I'm sorry, dear, if I seem rude, but you did say you only wanted to talk a few minutes. And another time would have been so much more convenient, dear."

Dear! The bitch is all the time calling me *dear!* Trot along out of my life now, poor dear, and Otto's life too. Tiptoe out the front door and don't come back, ever. *There's* a good girl!

She listened and was certain from the sound of the water that Thelma had settled down in the tub. The odor of bath salts drifted through the door opening, and she said carefully, "Does Otto like the smell of whatever junk you're using in there?"

"I don't think I understand you, dear?"

"I was just saying maybe I'd better go along now. There were a lot of things I wanted to discuss with you if you'd had the time."

"But I told you I had company coming this evening."

"So you did."

"What did you say? I can't hear you very well."

"I was wondering when we could meet again?"

"I'll call you."

"I don't think you will."

"What . . . dear?"

She listened but did not reply. She rose from the chair and stepped closer to the gap between the door and its frame. There was now no sound in the bathroom.

"Thelma?" she called softly.

"Yes? Oh, I thought you'd gone."

"There is something else . . ."

She put her hand firmly on the door knob and took a deep breath. She pushed at the door slowly and smoothly, increasing the gap until the steam rolled out toward her. Her mind returned for an instant to the thought of having a cigarette and then as quickly dismissed it. I am not a bit frightened, she thought. I am only doing what should be done.

"What are you *doing* in here?"

"I came to say goodbye, Thelma."

"Well! I must say you have a nerve. I happen to like my privacy."

"You'll have it. You've taken good care of yourself, Thelma. For a woman of your age—"

"I'll thank you to get out of my bathroom!"

"Has Otto ever seen you lying there like that? I didn't think he was the bubble-bath type."

"Get out, *if you please!"*

"I don't please quite yet."

She stood looking down at Thelma and saw how the foam on the surface of the water clustered between her breasts. She moved slowly around the end of the tub until she stood behind her.

Thelma turned her head, following her. "What's the matter with your eyes?" she asked.

"Nothing. Does it look like there's something the matter with them?"

"They stare so. . . ."

"I'm just looking at you."

"Why have you taken your shoes off?" Thelma started to rise in the tub.

"Lie still, Thelma."

"Leave this instant or I'll call the police! You must be crazy!"

"Lie still. I'd like to touch your lovely hair. . . ."

Suddenly she bent down and seized Thelma's hair. She clutched at it with all the strength of her great passion and pushed down until her elbows were buried in the water.

There was a wild thrashing of Thelma's legs and her hands reached upward, clawing at the air.

Water slopped over the side of the tub.

Foam spattered the mirror above the wash basin. Yet there was no sound except the erratic ploshing of water and her own fierce grunting. She could feel the wet hair cutting at her fingers as Thelma's head twisted wildly back and forth. But she held on, feeling the water taps cutting into her own breasts, watching the stumps of her arms lengthen and shorten as the body she held rose and fell beneath the water.

She was glad of the foam. She could see nothing but the wet foamy legs and the outstretched hands dribbling foam. And on one of the hands was Otto's ring.

She did not know how long she bent over the tub, holding, but it seemed only a moment before the hair was easy to hold and the thrashing ceased. First the arms and then the legs collapsed and disappeared. Until at last there was nothing to be seen except her own arms reaching down into the foam. Her fingers so ached from holding she found it difficult to relax her grip. She did so gradually, carefully releasing the pressure without allowing Thelma's head to break the surface of the water.

When all in the bathroom was still, she opened her fingers and a final hiss escaped her.

She tried not to look down at the tub as she picked up the towel beside it and carefully wiped at the water on the floor. When it was dry, she went to the mirror and erased the flecks of foam.

She walked to the door with the towel and wiped the knob where she had touched it. She started to throw the towel beside the tub and at once decided against it. What would a very wet, wrinkled towel be doing near a woman who presumably never had a chance to use it? Everything else had worked exactly as she had planned. She must be careful now. A last minute of neglect could be disastrous. There would be no marks on Thelma's body, but—?

She returned to the tub and tried not to look at the body that was floating in the foam. But there were hairs to be wiped from the end of the tub and there was no way to be certain they were all removed unless she kneeled and searched carefully along the fringe of the water. Before she began, her eyes were drawn to the mounds of flesh protruding above the foam. And suddenly she realized that Thelma was floating face down. She stared at her buttocks curving upward from the foam and saw what appeared to be an aggravated rash near her hip. The sight was strangely satisfying. When Otto came he would be reminded that his Thelma was not perfect.

She scraped at the sides of the tub and raked slowly across the surface of the water until she had collected half a handful of hair. She wrapped it in paper and flushed it down the toilet.

She made a final survey of the bathroom. Careful, now, she thought. She picked up the wet towel and rolled it into a tight bundle. She glanced at herself in the mirror above the wash basin and touched at her hair while she still kept one hand on the towel. It was something she *must* not forget. Careful . . . careful! You must stay calm. Finally she went into the living room, where she put on her shoes and then her gloves.

She was congratulating herself on her poise—Why, my hands are as steady as they can be, she thought—when the telephone rang. It startled her. It was wrong and the ringing seemed overly loud. It must be a call for Thelma, of course, and the idea was frightening. She waited in mounting terror for the phone to cease its ringing. But the caller was persistent. She caught herself reaching for the phone. How stupid!

She grabbed the towel and ran for the door. The telephone was still ringing as the door slammed behind her. She heard the lock click, and instantly a small cry escaped her. My handbag! She seized the handle of the heavy door and shook it, knowing it was locked. She shook at the door until her head bobbed crazily. Everything was in that bag—the keys to her car, her driver's license, even her bankbook. She shook and pounded at the door until her heart thundered.

She could not see. She could only hear the telephone still ringing beyond Thelma's door. She continued to shake and pound on the door until a man in another apartment called the police. To the officer in Communications who took his call he merely said, "It's none of my business, but maybe you'd better send someone out here. There's some dame making an awful rumpus down the hall, and I don't like to get mixed up with hysterical women. Maybe she's just drunk or something, but you'd better come and see if you can help her—"

✧✧✧ 42 ✦✦✦

Hill glanced at the woman who sat beside him in the car and reminded himself that early in his career he had resolved to avoid bitterness. The reminder was very necessary now because Mrs. Barbee's special poison seemed to envelop her like a trailing gown and threatened to smother him. She must be the chief witch of vanity and self-righteousness, Hill thought, wishing there was some section of the law to cover such subtle crimes. Ordinary ungratefuls were subject to classification and at least some control, but not the Mrs. Barbees of the world.

He had sought to excuse her behavior during the brief time of their acquaintance, yet as the minutes passed he brooded more and more on how the most violent cruelties often failed to leave visible wounds. Now she sat very erect, chin high and feet primly together, as if she were embarked on a Sunday afternoon tour. Hill watched her carefully smooth every wrinkle from her long black gloves, and in spite of his determination to avoid judgment, her action seemed a final phase of the black ritual begun earlier. She had gone to the kitchen for a few minutes, where presumably she had set out milk and cookies for her children. Then for eighteen minutes by Hill's watch, she had disappeared. When she returned from what he supposed was her bedroom, her makeup was renewed and she had obviously dressed for the occasion.

If enough people were watching, Hill decided, this woman would weep at a stranger's funeral. She had stood for another three minutes before a mirror in the hallway while she carefully tied a black scarf around her hair. Finally she had coolly announced that she was ready to leave for the bridge. At first Hill tried very hard to convince himself that she was just being brave. Then shock had been his excuse for her, and then stupidity, all of which he instinctively knew were wrong. She was a phony. He had spent a large part of his career recognizing such people and he thought he could detect one at fifty yards. Mrs. Barbee would never trip over a law. She was not only a socially acceptable phony, she was a professional lady, which was the worst of all.

Hill slowed the car so that he could take a longer look at his passenger. He found her poise had not faltered in the slightest. If anything, she seemed bound for a distasteful and annoying duty.

He could no longer keep his silence. He had now interfered in private lives; he regretted it exceedingly, but he must now speak his mind. Something Deneen had said about her husband convinced him the bridge must not become a stage for phonies, polite or otherwise. If Barbee jumped, he must go with his own dignity.

"I've changed my ideas, Mrs. Barbee. I don't think you should try talking to your husband."

"And why not?"

"Because he's a very sick man, whether you realize it or not. Otherwise he wouldn't be where he is. There must be some reason for his illness."

"I insist on talking to him. He'll do what I say."

"Will he . . . this time?" Hill studied her, hoping to find a hint of mercy in her eyes. He was disappointed. "Has he ever tried anything like this before?"

"Of course not."

"How can you be so sure? He must have at least thought about it."

"I know what John thought. I've always known. He means well but he's a weakling. For fifteen years I've been rescuing him from one minor disaster after another."

"This is hardly a minor disaster."

"He won't do anything. He hasn't the courage." Suddenly she ceased smoothing her gloves and turned to him. "That sounds callous, doesn't it? I didn't mean it that way. It's just that John was always confused and was never able to make up his mind about anything without help. I really loved him very much."

"You're speaking in the past tense, Mrs. Barbee."

"I . . . I'm naturally upset."

"You don't act like it."

"You expect me to have hysterics? What good would that do? How would that help John? And besides, I have my pride."

"Your *pride* . . .?" he muttered, trying to control his increasing anger. And he thought how right it would be if this comfortable woman could spend some time in the old building where she might learn how often so-called pride was the key to the trouble of many women—who were not so comfortable.

As he turned into the bridge approach, he heard her say, "I don't know what will happen to the children and me if John does anything foolish. There's not much insurance."

Hill pressed his lips tightly together so he would not answer.

"What are you thinking, policeman? That I have no right to tell a stranger my husband is a weakling?"

"No, Mrs. Barbee. A good cop is more than just a man with a badge and a gun. People tell us a lot of things they wouldn't tell their own doctors. A good cop tries to forget it as soon as the trouble is over. But while things are still hot he has to do what he thinks best. Sometimes it's not so easy."

"And now you think it's best I don't talk to John?"

"I do. We'll see how things develop."

Swift-moving fog enwrapped the bridge towers so that they were abruptly truncated less than a hundred feet above the roadway. Hill sensed something had gone wrong as he drove past the barricades and the assembly of police cars and fire equipment. For one thing, Deneen was nowhere to be seen. Near the end of the bridge he stopped and beckoned to a patrolman.

"I want you to escort this lady to the bridge office."

"It's full of reporters right now, sir. They're keeping warm."

"Clear them out."

"I'm not going in there," Mrs. Barbee said.

"You are, because I'm in charge here. Please don't make it any more difficult than it already is."

The patrolman opened the door and stood waiting. Mrs. Barbee folded her arms and stared straight ahead. She said, "I insist upon being taken to my husband."

"That's impossible." He looked up at the fog. "Maybe after a while we'll get a break."

She turned her head and glared at Hill. The corners of her mouth twisted down and her voice was angrily accusing. "You are taking on a terrible responsibility."

"I often have to. It's part of my job."

Hill nodded to the patrolman, closed the car door on his own side of the car, and turned quickly away. He had taken only a few steps when he heard her call to him.

"Mr. Hill!"

He stopped to look back. He was not certain if it was only the effect of the amber bridge lights, but he thought her expression had softened. And there was at least a suggestion of humility in her voice.

"I . . . understand," she said. "Good luck, policeman."

Hill found Deneen behind a fire truck parked away from the main thoroughfare. He was absorbed in a portable radio, which had been set up on the running board. The instant their eyes met, Hill knew Deneen was very worried.

"Barbee's wife is not going to do us much good," Hill began.

"It's too late anyway. We have new troubles." Deneen looked hopelessly at the racing fog, then bent to tinker with the radio's volume control. "I can't get a sound out of this rig, but I know it's working."

"Quit stalling. What's gone wrong?"

Deneen straightened and again looked up at the fog. A pair of raucous horns beneath the bridge sounded almost simultaneously and entirely covered his first words.

". . . he took a walkie-talkie with him and I was hoping we could make contact. Either he isn't listening or all the iron around here interferes with our signals—"

"Who are you talking about?"

"Tim Hardy. He went up after Barbee."

"How did *he* get out here?" Hill was furious with himself.

That damn Lasher! He had been concentrating so hard on his departure, he had failed to recognize the difference between his old friend and a fire commissioner he barely knew.

"Tim said he'd been here for hours. He felt the same way we all do about Barbee. He asked my permission to go up. I refused. Then I got busy organizing some rescue boats to stand by under the bridge in case a miracle happened and Barbee did survive a jump. The next thing I knew a fireman told me Tim Hardy had borrowed his walkie-talkie and headed for the cable. Larsen, the man I have posted over there, tried to stop him. Tim said he had your permission and I guess Larsen thought because you're so close—"

"He was lying."

"I was sure he was, but he had disappeared before I found out about it. I'm sorry, Chief."

"How long has he been gone?"

"Twenty minutes, maybe half an hour."

Hill stared at the radio while the foghorns blared again. He deliberately avoided Deneen's eyes and wondered if he could guess what he had said to Tim Hardy in his office only a few hours ago.

"I was too busy to pay much attention to him," Deneen went on, "but after thinking about it I realized Tim wasn't exactly himself. That old iron jaw was out a mile."

"You're *sure* that radio's working?"

"Everything checks. It may be that he just doesn't want to talk to us."

Hill reached for the microphone. He pursed his lips tightly as he tried to decide exactly what he wanted to say before he spoke. But for a moment all he could see in the fog above was Timothy Hardy's beefy face and his defeated eyes. Finally he brought the microphone close to his lips and seemed to pry them apart with each word. "Listen to me, and don't be so stubborn. I know why you went up there. Okay. You've made your point. Now turn around and come down before I lose a good cop. I know more about this situation than you do. You just have to believe me, Tim. It isn't worth it. So come down. That's an order."

They waited. There was no reply. Hill spoke into the microphone again and he was aware that Deneen was watching him curiously. He didn't care. He didn't care now if the whole world heard what he had to say. "Come down, Tim. Please. I need you . . . as a friend."

The radio crackled, but there was no other sound. Hill replaced the microphone and said to Deneen, "Are you sure Barbee hasn't jumped?"

"I'm not sure of anything up there since the fog got so thick."

"Stay here and listen. Call me if you hear from Tim."

"Do you want me to go after him?"

Hill hesitated. "No," he said finally. "This is something Tim will have to handle himself."

He left Deneen and walked slowly to the concrete base of the cable. He stood beside it staring upward at the fog and he saw how the two towers, one on each side of the bridge, formed a looming hell-red gate in the amber bridge lights. The fog gave the towers an eerie look of even greater strength and weight, until they seemed mighty enough to serve as pedestals for the world. Tim's world, Hill thought. Somewhere up there he was facing a far more ruthless enemy than a pitiful maniac. He would be facing Timothy Hardy.

"You fool," Hill murmured. "You wonderful fool who are not a fool. God bless you. . . . And be careful."

Then as if to vindicate his doubts, Hill quickly crossed himself.

Far above, Hardy paused for breath. It was not until moments later that he discovered how fiercely he had been gripping the guide wires. His fingers were numb and seemed permanently curved as if to match the diameter of the wire.

He stood upon the huge supporting cable which was encased in a steel pipe of such dimensions he could not see straight down. He had decided the bridge engineers had made a minor mistake. The two hand wires which allowed him to follow the main cables' ever-steepening curve were too far apart. Maybe all right for steeplejacks but definitely too high for an ordinary man, he thought. Their position made his arms ache even when he rested. But then was this any place for the Timothy Hardy who had become a very ordinary man? You're on vacation, Tim. The Chief of Police said so. You're supposed to take a rest. And you always were afraid of heights. But only that, Tim. Just heights.

Actually he had lost all sense of distance and height. The only existing things in addition to his body were the main cable and the guide wires. The fog was a womb in which he moved like a minute cell and from which he yearned to escape. When he had resolved to free himself of the radio's cumbersome weight, he had simply dropped it into a void. There was no sound of its ever landing anywhere. The radio had just instantly ceased to exist.

Now the vertigo, which had sickened his belly while he climbed beneath the fog and could still see enough to establish his position, had left him. The blossoms of light had faded as he gained altitude, and once he had become a part of the fog, all relationship with natural objects dissolved. It gave him an uncanny sense of being reborn. "I'm not really here," he said to the wind. "I have not yet arrived."

His mind repeated the notion monotonously, as if his growing fear would lose itself in it. He would never arrive anywhere unless he moved. For a long time he had remained in one place on the excuse of a pounding heart, which was really not pounding at all. Go on, Tim. Move or you will never move. Maybe you can't hit your hat with a cannon, but you can move. You must.

He looked at his hands, which remained firmly fixed on the guide wires. From the angle of his body against the wire, he judged that he must be hardly more than halfway to the tower. He could still hear the humming of traffic below, and the foghorns seemed as loud as when he had first begun his climb.

Again and again the horns bellowed as if urging him on and upward.

He begged his body to move, but neither his legs nor his arms nor his fingers would respond. His mind said clearly, Now come off it! How often does a man get to play steeplejack? No partners depending on you here. You're it.

Yet his body disregarded every message from his brain. He stared helplessly at the guide wires, then at the cable beneath his feet. He listened to the soughing of the wind through the hundreds of bridge wires, and his nose recognized the smell of the sea so far below. Every physical sense was extraordinarily alive, yet his system of locomotion was apparently dead.

He began to insult himself, hoping to break the spell. At forty-five you're an old and terrified man. You are a fake cop with a tin badge. You are chicken. The guts you once had must have been phony. Colin was easy on you. You let him down; everybody knew you were friends and what could he say? Go back down and hide behind the lion. Spend the rest of your life on your hands and knees and wait in some office for a city pension. Cut off your balls so they don't drag in the mud. Tim Hardy? Oh, him? I knew him when. Tim Hardy, the has-been.

At last, as if freeing his body from a sucking ooze, he managed one step upward, and then another, and another. His heavy, mechanical movements required so much effort, he failed to notice the gradual thinning of the fog. He climbed as in a trance, one hand forward on the guide wire followed by a leg, each foot placed firmly upon the steel piping and held until the other could be persuaded to pass it. He was so absorbed in this process that when he saw the first star he believed the vertigo had returned and he was looking down at a light instead of upward.

It was some time before he understood that he had emerged from the fog and was staring at the great cable arcing upward to the top of the tower. Below, an iridescent strip of fog marked the thoroughfare of the bridge, and far to his right the lights of the city created a vast, luminous patch. Red aircraft warning lights blinked from the top of the tower. Between his own position on the cable and the tower itself, Hardy saw the figure of a man. He stood isolated in the starlight, motionless until he raised his hand. Hardy could not be sure if the hand held a gun.

"What are you doing on my bridge?" the man called.

"I came to take you down, Barbee. Be sensible."

"Go back!"

"I can't."

"Then I'll kill you."

"I am dead. Can't you see?"

Hardy could not understand why he had said such a thing. Certainly the words had not been uttered with forethought. It was a ridiculous thing to say, and the words had tumbled from his mouth as if phrased in a foreign language. *I am dead. Can't you see?* His mind echoed the thought and was astonished. Standing in this eerie world aloft, attached to the guide wires by hands which had become claws, it was as if only his body remained in position. His mind had taken up its own perch in the air a few feet away, and from its independence looked down at two total strangers clinging to an enormous cable. It was this new and separate mind which had caused his body to say "I am dead." It sounded like a blasphemy. I'll make repairs next Mass, he decided.

Barbee moved toward him in silence. Hardy saw him lower his arm. Does he know that I *can't* move—that my mind is several feet away looking at us with only a slight sense of attachment?

"What do you mean, you're dead?" Barbee asked calmly. Then he said with sudden hostility, "Are you a priest?"

"No. I was a cop." Again his severed mind had spoken. It was suddenly a maverick mind, he decided. Crazier than Barbee's.

"And now—?"

"I told you. I'm dead. I guess I died about noon today."

"Then what are you doing up here?"

"I came up for you. But nothing works. I can't move. I'm afraid. It's a disease I caught somewhere. I can't seem to lick it."

"Afraid of me?"

"More of falling."

"Falling never hurt anyone. Not when there's so far to go. Not even when you hit. And if you're dead, what difference will it make?"

"A big difference. I want to live."

"I don't understand you. If you're dead it's too late to worry about living."

"You've been worrying about it, or you would have jumped a long time ago. I think you died just like I did. We both lost faith. We can still get back . . . if you'll help me." He could not see Barbee's face clearly enough to be sure of his reaction, but his voice became newly suspicious.

"You're pretty smart. I'm going to give you ten seconds to

turn around and get down off my bridge. Your fancy double-talk won't make me change my mind. Can you see this gun in my hand?"

"Yes, now I can. But I *can't* turn around. You'll just have to believe I can't move a muscle. I don't give a damn about you any more. I'm interested in myself. I didn't really come up here for you. I came up for myself. It was a foolish idea but now I'm stuck with it. You're the only person in the world who can help me. I'm begging you for my life."

A foghorn groaned far below.

"I'll be damned," Barbee said quietly.

"What?"

"I said, I will be damned. Why do you want to live so much? What's so good about it?"

"I don't know. But I know less about the other. Sooner or later we'll both find out. I'm in no hurry and I can't understand why you should be."

"I'm sick."

"So am I. And I still want to live."

"For over a year I've felt my brain slipping," Barbee said. "Then I began to see things clearly and I knew I had to go."

"For over a year I've known my nerve was slipping. Look up. Can't you see the stars?"

"Of course."

"Then you can see. Listen. Can you hear the wind?"

"Yes."

"Then you can hear. You climbed up here and you can still raise your arms . . . so you can move. How the hell can anyone who can see and hear and move want to die?"

"You don't know despair."

"I do now."

A stillness fell between them. There was only the wind and the hushed whirring of the traffic far below. Even the rhythmic bleating of the foghorns sounded subdued, and Hardy's mind, which still refused any return to his body, clearly appreciated how all other sounds were lost with altitude. Without the wind they could have conversed in whispers, yet the soft drumming engines of a distant airplane seemed strangely close.

"Well?" Hardy said at last, and even as he spoke the bizarre sensation that his mind was not a part of him became stronger. "Are you going to help me?"

"No. I've been thinking about it. Up here things are final. That's why I like it. It's every man for himself."

"I can't help myself. It's a physical thing. I'm paralyzed. If you'll only get me started maybe I can keep going."

Another silence, then Barbee said, "Will you promise to leave me alone?"

"Yes."

"If you try anything. . . One wrong move and I'll push you off. I mean it. Remember, I want to die."

"All right. Please. Come to me."

"Only if you understand why I just might help you. It's not so bad an idea to spend the last of my love endowment on a stranger. Listen. My wife bore our children by what she seemed to consider an immaculate conception. She found sainthood in the delivery room and doctors became her high priests. There is nothing unusual about the way she behaved. Oh, no! She was originally a fine woman who saw me as a man. It was only after my love endowment had been nearly emptied that I became invisible. Have you ever become invisible, mister?"

"Please. Right now I feel more like I'm turning into a stone."

"You aren't listening to me. I won't help until you do."

Hardy tried in vain to move his feet. While he attempted to will movement he thought angrily, To hell with this nut. I'll get back down alone. But his mind remained suspended by itself and neither his feet nor his hands would move.

When his will was exhausted, he heard himself say wearily, "I'm listening."

"That's all I ask. I don't care if you agree with me. Just understand. Understand that every person has his own endowment of love. It varies only in amount and rate of expenditure. And even after the supply is emptied, the process continues. It has become habit. If I had thought my wife was different I would have tried to find another, because from every side of my daily life I was propagandized, bullied, persuaded, and ordered to continue loving. But I was sure that if I married again I would be in a worse mess. With my endowment nearly gone, I would soon become invisible to my new wife. Except on paydays, of course. When I got the gist of that idea, despair began. But the love habit demands you keep giving. Now where was I going to find a female creature interested in true giving to her husband, when modern custom and the law keep telling any wife she doesn't have to? If she pleases, and many do, she can expend her endowment solely on her children."

"Can't you tell me your troubles down below? I'm freezing."

"You told me you were dead."

"I was. But I didn't mean to say it just that way. I started to live again as soon as I made it up here."

"I'm not going to help you turn around until you thoroughly understand why I'm doing it. You can't understand unless you listen."

"All right. I'm trying."

"A man is just not capable of preserving his identity when he is totally cut off from the receiving end of a love endowment. His mother provides it when he's young, then various females take care of it until the fateful day when his own endowment tricks him."

Hardy's mind protested although his lips did not move. "I'm clinging to a wire five hundred feet in the air and I have to listen to this 800's babbling! This is a nightmare. I must wake up!"

Barbee said, "Everything and everybody is at work to convince a male that one remarkable female will maintain her interest in him for the rest of his life. Even the radio is telling him about it while he shaves in the morning. He goes off to work and even those of his own sex who are not ordinarily hypocritical will be downright sentimental in this matter. They will not, they *cannot* admit their love habit has become their master. So our young man becomes ripe, and when the tree is shaken even slightly, he falls into the wilderness. Today, on this bridge, I wept for all young men and a lot of other things. I didn't have many tears left to spare for myself. . . ."

Barbee fell silent and looked up at the stars. When he spoke again, the passion had left his voice and he examined Hardy curiously as if he had just discovered his presence.

"I made the mistake of expecting truth on earth, and when I saw how hard it was to find and how few people even understood what it was, something exploded in my head. So I came to this marvelous bridge. I knew I couldn't exist any longer without the encouragement of truth, any more than a plant can grow without water. The love habit, which had kept me sort of docile and vaguely content for years, had finally been revealed for what it was. I tell you it was a shock."

Barbee paused and rubbed his eyes wearily. "I've tried so hard to find the truth, but I can't. I only know now that without love and without truth, a man automatically becomes a neuter. Do you understand what I am trying to tell you?"

"No. I'm not really listening. I'm still thinking of myself."

"What is your name?"

"Timothy Hardy."

"You must have some truth in you or you wouldn't be here. Or say what you just said. Maybe it's because you're a policeman and so you can't entirely hide behind a wall of pretended innocence . . . or find it so easy to hide from yourself."

"I was hiding from myself."

"But you still hope?"

"Yes."

"All right. You've got two things working for you. You didn't lie to me and try to claim you understood what I was trying to say. And you still have hope. I envy you hope. It is something else I lost down there . . . somewhere."

Hardy saw that Barbee was moving toward him, and in a moment felt his cold hand descend upon his own. Finally they stood face to face on the cable and he was certain Barbee was smiling.

"Now turn around," Barbee said.

"I just can't manage it."

Barbee lifted Hardy's left hand from the wire and held it firmly.

"Turn. I won't let you fall."

Hardy's mind, still a spectator, said, "Watch it! You are trusting

your life to an 800 and they are full of tricks. If you turn your back
to him you're asking for it!"

Yet, slowly, while the stars reeled above him, he allowed Barbee
to lift his right hand from the guide wire, and he faced down the
cable.

Behind him Barbee said gently, "Now take a step. You can.
You can because you will have hope."

Hardy felt Barbee's hand fall heavily on his shoulder. He knew
an instant of near-panic when he realized how vulnerable he had
become. But Barbee's hand was steady, neither pushing nor re-
straining. And suddenly, Hardy's mind rejoined him. He became in
an instant more of a whole than he had been for a year. A great
warmth seemed to flow from Barbee's hand. It rushed through
Hardy's blood, tingling his senses, awakening him as though from
a long sleep.

"Go on, Hardy. You are a brave man."

Very slowly, deliberately, inching each downward step, Hardy
began descending toward the fog. When he hesitated, Barbee simply said, "Keep going . . . you're all right." His hand remained
firmly on Hardy's shoulder.

At last they reached the frothing surface of the fog where the
cable stabbed into it like the root of a gigantic tree. Here there was
a heavier sound of the wind in the vertical wires, and Hardy deliberately paused to look back at his escort. For he knew something very important had occurred within him. All of his fear had
left and he was sure it would never return. This crazy man had
somehow restored the old Tim Hardy and destroyed the has-
been. What was it he had said about endowment?

Now Hardy was determined to take Barbee all the way down. It
was impossible to use force here. Then he must try to hide the
change that had come to him. And he must be careful. Barbee had
the perception of the mad.

"I'm shivering because of the cold," Hardy said.

"I know," Barbee answered. "I didn't think it was because you
are still afraid."

"But I don't think I can make it alone. Not yet anyway."

"I'm taking my hand away."

"All right. But stay with me."

"Go ahead, poor man. I'll stay until you don't need me any longer."

They passed deeper into the fog, and the noise of the horns and the traffic below gradually increased.

"I won't forget what you said, Barbee. Even if I didn't understand exactly everything. . . ."

Now the lights on the thoroughfare and the bridge made the fog opalescent. Hardy paused once more and deliberately shivered while he considered how quickly he could turn around and snap the cuffs on Barbee. He must do it soon, before they emerged from the bottom side of the fog. Or was it necessary? They were so close to the bottom. And the thought of putting manacles on Barbee was so disgusting, Hardy was not sure he could do it even if Barbee volunteered. Maybe he could be persuaded to talk just a little longer—he must feel needed.

Hardy affected near-panic as he resumed his descent.

"There are a lot of my friends would like to hear what you have to say, Barbee. You're an interesting talker."

There was no reply, and Hardy wondered if the wind had carried his invitation away. He raised his voice. "Did you hear what I just said?"

There was only the sound of the wind.

Hardy halted suddenly. And once again his body froze into a rigid position. He did not want to look behind him.

"Are you there, Barbee?"

A horn from below was his only immediate answer. When its echo subsided, he heard the shifting gears and blatting exhaust of a heavy truck directly beneath him.

"*Answer* me, Barbee!"

Slowly he turned his head. There was the fog, the great cable stretching up into it, and nothing more.

"Barbee! Barbee!"

Hardy started to retrace his steps, then halted. For he saw how short a way they had come since Barbee had last spoken. Even in the fog he could be seen at such a short distance, and it was impossible for him to have climbed far enough upward to become invisible. *Invisible!* "Until you don't need me any longer. . . ."

He must have known! His lunacy had not been so blinding that he missed the return of Tim Hardy to himself. Ah, Barbee. . . . He had only wanted one last chance to give. Ah, Barbee. . . . Thank you for more than my life.

At the end of the cable, where it joined the concrete mooring, Hardy saw Hill waiting for him. He stopped and stood motionless, watching Hill's face. And he saw, with relief, that he was smiling.

"I'm sure glad to see you, Tim."

Hardy quickly descended the remaining few yards of the cable. He jumped down from the base and landed directly in front of Hill. They regarded each other in silence for a moment.

"I failed. I couldn't get him all the way down. I'm sorrier than I can ever explain . . . even to you. He was a very special guy."

The smile left Hill's face and he said, "So are you." He reached out, seized the lapels of Hardy's suit coat, and shook him gently.

"You faker! You liar! You no-good, scheming, loafing bum! What a lousy act. Going around for weeks pretending to have the willies, missing targets . . . any damn thing just to get a vacation with pay—"

"Colin!"

"Well, that vacation is hereby canceled and you better be back where you belong tomorrow morning or I'll haul you before the Commission!"

"Colin. . . ." Hardy knew it would anger his friend if he said thanks, so he let his eyes do it for him.

❖❖❖ 43 ❖❖❖

As always in Communications, the rhythmic flicking of incoming call lights increased with the arrival of night. Though the number of crank calls diminished, the real appeals, attacks and discoveries quickly multiplied until the call boards were jammed and the officers on duty shifted immediately from one call to another. Even this pace would quicken as the night became older, and it would continue to build until sometime after midnight. Then, as if the city was exhausted, the flow of calls would very suddenly collapse into occasional hot prowls, holdups, ordinary bar beefs, and disagreements between man and wife which became boisterous enough to alarm other citizens.

The men who worked in Communications were constantly reminded that these inhabitants of the city who were bent on deliberate crime or spontaneous acts of passion had inherited certain instincts from times when darkness brought constant peril to all human beings. In darkness the ordinary man sought the warmth and protection of his cave and stayed there. He had friends, so if he ventured forth at all, he ventured to friends. Yet with the coming of darkness, the troubled and lonely became ever more restless and desperate.

So every night as darkness came, the friendless emerged from their caves, seeking each other in a neon world, taking a measure of comfort from the activity of passing traffic which they were not part of, and from the voices of pedestrians whom they would never know. These were the people who simply wandered without real purpose or direction.

Others were hotel sitters. They sat in the lobbies of small hotels identified by street signs which were in such poor repair they rarely illuminated more than half the name. They sat in the Shawmut Hotel, the Balzar Hotel, the Funk Hotel, the Victoria, the Swanson, the Elite, the Luxor, the Atherton, the Commerical, the Video, and they stared past each other at the walls. They rarely conversed.

There were the people who sat in small, brightly lit cafés drinking cup after lonely cup of coffee. They stirred their coffee in a special way, very slowly, and always with a rhythmic tinkling of spoon against cup. Like the hotel sitters, they rarely spoke, but they knew how to nurse a single cup of coffee for an hour or even more, and so they contrived to sit . . . and sit.

There were the people who preferred their local bars which they used as clubs, and where total strangers were regarded with hostility or at least chilling indifference. The bar people never stopped talking to each other, because they had nothing to say and found any conversational void unbearable. Many of the women in this specialized society were determined alcoholics and were therefore noticeably dead of hair and mincing in gait. The more they drank, the more they spoke in stylized formalities, such as "to whom are you referring . . . I wish to ascertain . . . in view of the present situation . . . it behooves me to do something about . . ." It was sometimes difficult to translate and grasp the intended meaning of their verbal passages, even for the knowing, but the effort occupied the long and dreadful hours of darkness. At least it was better than sitting in an empty room, for even with the radio and television and all the lights left full on, there was not any true association with the outside world.

So the people of the darkness waited all day long for their darkness, anticipating the moment when they could pretend they were mixing with their fellow men. Hence they were uncommonly ripe for the exploitation which was dutifully accomplished by pimps, whores, and bunco artists, perverts, bullies, junk peddlers, liars, and simple thieves, who often posed as newly won friends.

These were the people whose day began with the ending of day. They were prone to be involved with one of the call board lights in Police Communications.

❖❖❖ ✦✦✦

When Hill and Deneen returned to the old building, their actions were exactly similar although they went straight to their separate offices. They glanced at the accumulation of paper work on their desks, frowned, and refused to examine it. They called their wives and asked for something to be left in the icebox against their eventual homecoming. They explained they had just not found time to eat, and since it was past eight o'clock, they were already late to the Commissioners' meeting. Immediately after the calls, they changed into their uniforms—Hill's bearing two gold sleeve stripes and Deneen's one. It was custom to be in uniform for the occasion now at hand.

They met outside Hill's door as if by prearranged signal and proceeded, out of step and in self-conscious silence, to the Commissioners' room. It was a large room, mahogany paneled, like

Hill's office. The three civilian Police Commissioners were seated on a dais facing an audience of ten police captains.

There were murmured greetings, and as Hill took his place on the dais, he apologized for being ten minutes late.

Commissioner Stanton opened the meeting with a brief address he knew everyone present could repeat by heart. Hence he spoke quietly and without forced solemnity, merely stating that they were gathered to vote on various applications for meritorious awards. He then asked Deneen to read the first report.

Deneen stood up and pulled down the blouse of his uniform. As he read, he found it impossible to avoid thinking of Timothy Hardy.

"At seven-thirty o'clock on the morning of November twentieth, Police Officer Charles E. Petro was assigned to three-wheel motorcycle duty when he responded to a police radio broadcast of a man with a gun. As he entered the building he observed a man armed with a shotgun. The man pointed the gun at him and pulled the trigger . . ."

Outside the Commissioners' room the fifteen candidates for meritorious awards stood on one foot and then the other, waiting for their turn to be called. They were all trying very hard to behave as if the results of voting on their individual actions were of no real consequence to them. They claimed that the fifty or one hundred dollars, which was determined by the class of award, was the important thing. Thus in mutual lying they covered their mutual nervous embarrassment.

On the other side of the old building, Spearing waited for Marvin Fat to finish shining the shoes of the sergeant in Communications. He had feared that Marvin Fat might have ceased his labors for the day, but in Communications there was still profitable action and there Marvin Fat would certainly be—at least until all the customers were satisfied.

When Marvin picked up his box, Spearing crooked his finger at him. Marvin came to him unsmiling.

"How," Spearing asked with such warmth as he could manage, "is the richest young man in the United States?"

"You want a shine?" Marvin asked.

"No. Wisdom, my half-pint Confucius." He took Marvin's arm and escorted him out the door of Communications. He looked up and down the hall, saw it was deserted, and then squatted so that he was eye-to-eye with Marvin Fat.

"How much money did you take in today, Marvin?"

Marvin shrugged his shoulders. His black eyes avoided Spearing's and became focused on his shoe box.

"Come on, Marvin. I'm not the income-tax man. But I am in trouble. I may even lose my job if I can't get something straightened out."

Marvin remained silent. He transferred his attention from his shoe box to Spearing's left ear.

"I'll make a deal with you, Marvin. I'll match what you made today if you'll tell me what happened in Hill's office early this afternoon. You were there. I know that. Was a man named Bandaneria also there? Or was just some man told he was supposed to be a Mr. Bandaneria?"

Marvin remained silent.

"This is easy money for you, Marvin. Think of the things you can buy. Don't force me to be mean, Marvin. If you *don't* tell me what happened in the Chief's office, I am going to inform the juvenile authorities that here in the Hall of Justice, of all places, we happen to have a small Chinese boy who should be in school instead of making money all day. You will not like that, Marvin, because as you know, going to school is not profitable. . . ."

In the long silence which followed, Spearing saw that Marvin's lower lip was beginning to tremble. But he could not catch his eye.

He squeezed Marvin's arm hard enough to make him wince. "You will go bankrupt, Marvin. You will have to throw away that key you have to the National Bank. *Tell me what happened.* This is your last chance. . . ."

At last Marvin looked directly into Spearing's eyes. He pressed his lips tightly together and the whole of his small body became rigid.

"Phooey!" he said suddenly.

With one quick movement he twisted away from Spearing's grip, seized his shoe box and ran down the hallway. Rounding the corner at the end of the hall, he skidded on the marble floor and then vanished.

Spearing rose slowly to an erect position and massaged the crick which had come to his back. And he knew that he would not tell any authority whatsoever about anything. As something to believe in, he very much needed Marvin Fat.

◇◇◇ ✦✦✦

In the Commissioners' room, Officer Petro had related how his crazed antagonist pulled the trigger of the shotgun a second time, and again the weapon had misfired. Petro explained how he had disarmed and handcuffed the man who was taken to General Hospital, where he was pronounced dangerously insane. An examination of the shotgun revealed the shell in the chamber had two indentations from the firing pin. There was no explanation of why it had failed to explode.

Petro was excused with thanks and congratulations on his luck. When he left, the voting began. The method of voting had been established so long ago not even the most elderly captain in the room could remember its origin. A small wooden box was passed from captain to captain and then to each Commissioner. The box was divided into two compartments, one of which was open and filled with black, green, white and red marbles. The second compartment was closed, but there was a round hole in its hinged top. The voters selected a marble according to their opinion of Petro's just reward, and dropped it into the hole. The box was then passed to the dais and the marbles counted by color.

Officer Petro received enough white marbles to qualify for a Meritorious Second Class, although he had been recommended for First. There were those who thought Petro should not have given the man a chance to shoot at him twice.

◇◇◇ ✦✦✦

In a bar known only as Daisy's, which was a few short blocks from the old building, the jukebox played classical music exclusively. The customers were equally special and most of them were dues-paying members of the Daughters of Lebidus. They were of all ages and yet were divided into two distinct categories. The "Butches" were easily recognized by their commanding manner. They wore their hair very short and eschewed makeup and jewelry. They smoked incessantly, were mostly inclined to fat, and drank with firm and determined gestures. Their combination of gray skirt and sweater was so common it was almost a uniform. They occasionally bought drinks for each other and always for their "femmes."

The femmes were less drab and sometimes of naturally stunning beauty. They dressed simply and, except for lipstick, were sparing with cosmetics. The discontent lurking in their eyes disappeared after they had consumed sufficient alcohol, and it was then that they most freely permitted their Butches to fondle them.

There was rarely any trouble in Daisy's until someone started a jealous argument. These most commonly occurred just as the place was closing, and the screeching profanity was sometimes raucous enough to interest the police. On this night, as on every night, business was brisk in Daisy's. And as on every night, men were not welcome in Daisy's.

❖❖❖ ✦✦✦

On the other side of the city, in a small furnished room, a man of thirty sat staring at the walls. He waited for the right time and for all the necessary preliminaries to stimulate his desire.

He was now no longer lonely, and past experience had taught him he would soon enjoy himself beyond measure. He had studied his small collection of pornographic photos carefully, then closed his eyes and thought of the four girls he had entered during the past year. The memory of their stifled protests and little cryings further aroused him.

Everything was ready and laid out on the table before him—the bayonet which he had bought at a surplus store, the black silk stocking which he pulled over his face until he had the girl alone, the adhesive tape and the sash cord which he had found to be so strong.

He would use the same method he had the last time and the time before. It was something like fishing, he thought, and if he had no luck, then he would simply return to his room, look at his photos, and masturbate.

It was now nine o'clock. In thirty minutes he would start the long walk to the beach. He would buy a Coke at the beach, stand and talk to the man and say his watch was wrong and ask for the time. He would double back from the beach until he came to the narrow road on the other side of the highway. He wondered how many teenagers knew about the dirt road that twisted around the hill. Not too many, he decided, because he had been there several nights when the road had been deserted. But usually on Friday night, fishing was good. His tennis shoes were perfect for the first approach. He could stand by the window and watch a boy and girl wrapping themselves around each other—thinking they were all alone. No lights. No sound except the sea in the distance. Then open the car door quick before they had a chance to untangle. Push the bayonet in the boy's side hard enough so he'd stay quiet no matter how big he was. Tell the girl you'd kill him if she moved an inch or made a sound. Make the boy lie down beside the car, face down, and tie him up with the sash cord. Put the adhesive tape over his mouth good and hard. Then take the girl up to the top of the hill where the trees were. If she made any trouble, prick her with the bayonet. Don't talk to her. Just yank off her skirt and jump on her. It was even better when she cried all the way through.

Getting back to the room was easy. Tape her ankles together tight so she'd stay put for a while. Then go down the hill on the opposite side from the car and circle back toward the beach. No hurry.

It was Friday night. No school tomorrow. It should be a good night for things on the little road.

❖❖❖ ✦✦✦

In the Commissioners' room Deneen read the eighth report of the evening, which concerned an Officer Logan.

"In response to a holdup alarm, Officer Logan entered the front door of the bank and saw the employees standing together behind counter in the rear. The bank guard motioned with his head to-

ward the right side of the bank. Officer Logan saw two men coming from behind the counter. They were both armed and one carried
a white sack. They ignored Officer Logan's command to stop, and
one man, Richard Lane, fired at Logan twice. The first bullet
passed close to his head and was later found embedded in the
wall. The second bullet struck Officer Logan in the right knee.
An instant after, he fired his own gun and fatally wounded Lane,
who had a long criminal record. Lane's companion surrendered
and was placed under arrest by Officer Logan. Amount found in
the sack, $25,024, identified and counted by . . ."

❖❖❖ ✦✦✦

While his superiors were voting Logan a Meritorious First
for his courageous support of the bank's insurance company,
some four miles from the old building a solo bikeman named
Emerson was in hot pursuit of a stolen car. It was a fast car, and
just before it entered an underpass near the city limits, Emerson
saw his own speedometer standing at ninety-two miles per hour.
Like so many solo bikemen, Emerson was always tempted to ex-
ceed the limitations of his vehicle. The pursuit had immediately
become a race, and Emerson was now determined the car would
not get away even if he had to follow it out of the city. He knew
it would be far safer to call the Highway Patrol and hope they
could make an interception, but something about the driver compelled Emerson to stay with him. He could not explain exactly
why he was being so stubborn any more than he could explain what
happened in the five seconds after the underpass appeared. Just
past the entrance there was a wet spot on the pavement. The car
hit it, then spun out of control. It caromed off the side of the
underpass, bounced backward, and slewed to a stop directly across
the thoroughfare. Emerson had also entered the underpass, and
even before he could physically react, he knew his position was
hopeless. He was still going fifty miles an hour when he piled
into the car.

Two men in a patrol car found Emerson a few minutes later.
He had landed eighty feet from his point of impact. In the nearby
hospital, when the attendants removed the torn and scorched

remnants of Emerson's uniform and dubiously examined his multitude of bruises and abrasions, they were at first professionally discouraged. Yet Emerson soon regained full consciousness, and further examination indicated that his most serious injury seemed to be a broken thumb.

The discovery saved the attendants considerable bitterness when they turned their attention to the driver who sat waiting in the next room. He was handcuffed and humming tunelessly. Except for a scratch on his chin and a split lip, he was unhurt. Thus the attendants were free to observe other things about the driver, including the obvious fact that he was totally without remorse. He was unimpressed when told that if he had continued his joy ride through the next busy intersection, he would undoubtedly have killed several people.

A sense of great futility came to all the attendants when they learned the driver was fifteen years old and had been in the custody of the juvenile authorities three times in the past year. No one, including his parents, knew what to do with him, since his mental development was that of a ten-year-old. This was the driver of a ninety-two-mile-an-hour torpedo. It did not make sense to anyone in the hospital's emergency room that a man like Emerson should be obliged to risk his life so that a retarded child would not commit mass murder.

❖❖❖ ✦✦✦

While Officer Emerson was still trying to persuade the hospital attendants that he was well enough to go home, Lawrence Potter sat late over his dinner and finished off the wine he had ordered in celebration of his new life. When he left the restaurant he considered going to a foreign film, the only kind worth seeing in his opinion, and besides it gave him the impression that he could understand whatever language was spoken. Yet he was restless, and his recent experience in a movie theater was the last thing he wanted to think about—on this night especially.

He strolled aimlessly at first, his thoughts tender with the wine, and he created great paintings and saw them adjudged not only in ordinary art pamphlets, but in the national news magazines.

". . . Lawrence Potter's complex play of shadow and form can be taken as an indication of the esoteric and yet universal soul which allows him to paint anything from the innocence of a child's puppet to the thunder of an ancient god . . . he is sad, joyous on occasion, violent and tender . . . he most certainly ranks among . . ."

As he envisioned himself besieged by patrons, his pace quickened to match his excitement. Not until he reached the same gravel path he had crossed during the afternoon did he realize that ever since finishing his wine he had been drawn toward the park.

He hesitated and looked into the semidarkness ahead. But you are not a child, the man had said. And only a child could be afraid of the dark. Suddenly a delicious sense of power surged through his thoughts. I will go along this path and come to the same place by the fountain. If the man is there I will merely greet him and say that I must return to my studio and finish a painting. I will then move on even though it tortures me. I will sweeten love with torment. I will deliberately tempt myself by lingering near the fountain. I will resist. I will see how long I can resist.

✦✦✦ ✦✦✦

As Lawrence Potter put his hands in the pockets of his jacket and hurried up the path, Moore and Rafferty swallowed their fourth straight whiskey. They leaned heavily against the bar of the North Star restaurant, finding great comfort in its masculine solidity. They had not spoken since their original demand for refreshment, merely holding out their empty glasses when they required refilling. They had no desire to violate the unwritten rule of the North Star by discussing business, but they did so in spite of themselves. They talked eloquently for the better part of an hour about the wonder of little Harriet Rankin. And yet not a sound passed between them. They merely sipped at their drinks, then looked into the bar mirror and eventually caught each other's eye. They would then shake their heads and sometimes accompany the gesture by shrugging their shoulders. After more visual exchanges of understanding they would raise their glasses and drain off the contents. As a conversational pause, they would look all around the North Star and try to concentrate on either Walter or Ernie, the proprietors, or the other customers. They were unsuccessful. As soon as their glasses were refilled they resumed their conversation in the mirror.

At last Moore said aloud, "I wonder what Harriet's going to—" Then he stopped deliberately. He pointed his great nose at the kitchen, which was at the end of the bar, and said, "I guess my belly can stand a little nourishment now."

❖❖❖ ✛✛✛

In the Commissioners' room Deneen read out the last application to be considered. Like the majority of the others, it was for a First Class Meritorious and involved Officer Patrick of the Mounted Patrol.

". . . Officer Patrick could see that two of the swimmers had managed to make the safety of the beach, but one boy was in the heavy surf seventy-five yards from shore. He was obviously unable to make any headway. Without regard to his own danger Officer Patrick immediately spurred his horse into the surf, which constantly broke over both officer and his mount . . ."

After Officer Patrick confirmed the facts of the report and was excused, the captains and Commissioners held a brief discussion. A First Class Meritorious was rarely awarded in spite of the original application, and the rules specified the recipient must have been in physical contact with a deadly enemy or exposed to his gunfire. How could the sea be classified as a deadly enemy, one captain wanted to know. And another, who considered the Mounted Patrol an anachronism anyway, argued that Officer Patrick was only doing what he and his horse were supposed to do, and that at best he deserved a commendation.

While the debate continued, another of a more boisterous nature occurred five floors above the Commissioners' room. Three common drunks, two of whom had stood before Judge Brownell twelve hours previously, were booked in city prison. As they were led stumbling through the green gates on their way to the tank, they passed the felony block. They waved and shouted obscene greetings at three men who stood watching them. The drunks could not comprehend what was happening to them any more than they could understand why their greetings were ignored. It was impossible for them to appreciate how men like Harry Welsh and the Perez brothers could look down from their status pinnacles and consider them scum.

After considerable Irish opinion upon the sea and its perils had been aired by various captains, Officer Patrick was awarded a Meritorious Third. Since he was the last on the list, the meeting was immediately adjourned. At the same time a noisy company of fierce individualists began their nightly descent through the old building's more visible areas. These were the cleaners who swept, swabbed, brushed, picked up and gathered everything their discouraged spirits told them could not be left the way it was. Their banging pails echoed through the empty marble halls and their shouts of gossip, complaint and dismay were attempted at such great distances that no actual continuity could be maintained. They were like people shouting in a vast and complex cave, attempting to pass intelligence over cascades of flushing toilets, swishing of underground rivers, and tympanic crashes of waste buckets, pails and spittoons.

Eventually this band of noisemakers reached the main floor of the old building, which they swabbed at with more diligence than the other floors because it was the first to be seen every morning and they instinctively wanted to make a good impression.

Their activities were viewed with impatience by a man who shivered and waited just outside the revolving doors of the main entrance. When the cleaners were done and the last pail had been banged, when the echoes of their final triumphant shouting died against the marble, the man pushed his way through the revolving door. He passed the closed newsstand without looking at it, knowing Tommie would not be there. He stopped beneath the curve of the marble staircase, yawned, and laid himself carefully down on the still wet floor. He waggled his head until it was comfortable on his outstretched arm, curled his legs about the gumball machine, and slept.